FERAL KING

Sparrow Beckett

Belfry Publishing

Cover art by Rebel Book Designs

Edited by Nerine Dorman

Chapter One

Minnow was pretty sure her ears were bleeding. Henry's Coffee Emporium was a cacophony of sound, making it necessary for her to answer Ms. Sutton's interview questions at a volume that was neither polite nor pleasant. Why had Minnow suggested Ms. Sutton meet her here on a Saturday?

Stupid.

It was better than doing the interview at her rundown apartment, though, and it was too cold to go to the park. Meeting at a restaurant would have required money, which Minnow didn't have. She smoothed the front of her coffee-stained uniform, wishing she'd at least had time to change. Ms. Sutton's expensive clothing put Minnow at a psychological disadvantage.

"So you're used to dealing with difficult clients?"

"Yes, my most recent client was very difficult – at least initially. Her family and the caregivers before I was hired weren't able to convince her to cooperate with basic activities of daily living. After only a few weeks we became friends, and she let her guard down. I can be convincing, or even firm when it's important."

Ninety-six-year-old Sophia had resisted eating, bathing, sleeping, or anything else she was supposed to do. Minnow had found ways to motivate her to accept help, and eventually Sophia had loved and trusted her more than her own children. It had been a hard loss for Minnow when the older woman passed away.

Ms. Sutton nodded.

"Have you ever had a client who used foul language or berated you?"

"Yes. It doesn't bother me." Maybe it bothered her a little, but with the amount of money they were offering for this position, handling a bit of verbal abuse wouldn't be the end of the world. Not always having rent money at the end of the month and often not having enough food – now that bothered her. It was all a matter of perspective.

"What is your five-year plan?"

World domination? That was always the worst interview question.

Minnow smiled pleasantly. "I'm very motivated to find employment that's both challenging and fulfilling. I would enjoy finding a position that's long term."

The elderly woman readjusted her navy cardigan then pushed her glasses higher on her nose. She peered at Minnow, brown eyes magnified and owlish through the substantial lenses.

"Cut the professional bullshit answers, if you please, Miss Korsgaard," the woman said, her tone bland. Minnow managed not to laugh. "Are you planning to start a family or move out of town any time in the near future?"

The woman's bluntness took her aback, and she caught herself before she laughed. "No. I'm unattached and have no plans to relocate."

Ms Sutton nodded gravely. "So you're good at establishing rapport?"

"Yes, that won't be an issue."

The look of abject skepticism in Ms. Sutton's eyes was unnerving. "Mr. Leduc has a habit of doing his utmost to scare away every caregiver I hire. He's brilliant, so naturally he's quite impossible."

Minnow nodded. "What physical limitations does he have at this point? What's his diagnosis?"

"Diagnosis?" Ms. Sutton snorted. "Severin is an impossible, self-important ass who was born rich, ignored by his family, and spends most of his time alone. He doesn't need a support worker for medical issues. It's more that he needs a handler. He has no people skills and no desire to learn any. His patience with people is abysmal, and he comes off as brash and arrogant...because he's brash and arrogant."

"So my role would be?"

"You would basically be his companion – you'd encourage him to see to his grooming, and help keep him organized. Pick up after him. Make sure he eats."

This sounded ridiculous. "So I'd be babysitting a grown man whose only issue is that he's a jerk?" she asked sardonically.

"Oh, I like you." Ms. Sutton's eyes gleamed. "A difficult man. A passionate man. But yes, you'd be a glorified babysitter."

The money was too good to pass up.

She nodded slowly. "I could do that. Are there...other expectations attached to this job?"

Ms. Sutton glanced at her sharply. "No, but smart of you to ask. Severin doesn't seem to be interested in that sort of thing from anyone. I've never known him to date or even to..." She waved her hand, letting Minnow fill in the blanks. "He's intensely focused."

"Always best to ask up front." The last thing Minnow wanted was to quit her coffee shop job and let go of her apartment only to find out this old man expected a 'full service' employee.

"There may be occasions where you're required to go on outings with him, both to keep him organized, and to try to curb his temper. Oh – and you can't be too overt when you direct him, or he'll fire your ass on the spot."

"So, like any other service industry job."

"Yes. I'm the only other employee who lives at the house. I've been there for years." She grinned, her dentures very big and white in her small, wizened face. "I'd like to say affectionate things about him, but the man is insufferable. I love him like a son, but he needs a smack in the head sometimes."

"Got it."

She shook her head. "I'm hiring you instead of a man, so don't be surprised if he brings it up. He always thinks he wants a male handler, but he fires them as fast as I can hire them. Time to try something new. Female, young, pretty. He won't know what to do."

That didn't bode well, but she had student loans that wouldn't be ignored. Ms. Sutton gathered her purse and coat.

Shit. She wasn't sure if she'd managed to charm the woman yet. She couldn't leave.

"When will you be deciding?" she asked, walking the woman to the door in the hopes of winning her over before she made it back to her red Mustang GT. Definitely not the type of car she expected a sweet little old lady to drive, but Minnow seriously approved.

"Oh, I'll send Churchill around for you tomorrow. Pack for a week, to start, and if you last that long we'll send someone for the rest of your things."

Wow. Okay.

"Is there a uniform? A dress code?"

"Just pack whatever you're comfortable in. The house is out in the middle of nowhere, and we rarely leave."

*

A day wasn't enough time to organize her affairs, but luckily Leduc's estate wasn't far from town – only an hour by car. A lot of things would need to wait anyway, at least until it didn't seem like he'd fire her. For all she knew, she'd be back at her apartment later today.

Her front door buzzer went off promptly at eight AM, and she descended the stairs with her small second-hand suitcase, trying to look organized and composed.

Churchill, or Church, the driver of the SUV, was a tall African American man, with wide shoulders, a wide smile, and an easy manner – he was hot, charming, expensively dressed, and she guessed about thirty. Unfortunately, the sneeze guard between the front and back seats kept her from making conversation. She wouldn't have been at her best anyway, worrying about all the things she'd left undone at home.

The dishes were all clean, the garbage taken out, and she'd quit her job at the Coffee Emporium, although she still felt bad about leaving Henry, the owner, scrambling to cover her shifts. As Churchill pulled onto the highway, she realized she'd forgotten a pair of pants she'd meant to bring. And... Had she unplugged the iron?

The city became the countryside. Trees flashed past, a blur of verdant serenity after the bustle and crowding she was used to. No more coffee shop. No more aching feet. Maybe she'd have time to read more. Maybe, after a few months and after paying off some bills, she'd finally be able to afford an e-reader.

When she'd gone back to school, she'd thought personal support worker training would land her a decent job – something above minimum wage – but with the economy the way it was, no one was hiring. She'd been lucky to get the job at the coffee shop.

Minnow pulled out the paperback she'd been reading, but couldn't concentrate long, and soon she was staring out the window again, the trees a wall between her and the hungry life she hoped to leave behind.

After what seemed like eternity, Church turned off the highway onto a private road, then onto another, stopping when they reached a walled estate with a breathtaking wrought iron gate.

The gate opened for them, and they moved up the tree-lined drive to a sprawling house. The place looked like someone had stolen a museum from Europe and dumped it in the middle of Nowheresville, New York.

It was...intimidating.

Surrounded by the type of landscaping she'd only ever seen on television, the house was massive and elegant. Yeah, the jeans she packed weren't going to cut it, no matter what Sutton had said. This was definitely, at least, a pretty day dress sort of position.

A grand stone stairway led up to the arched set of doors, but the driveway curved around the back of the house. They didn't have to go through the front? Excellent.

In the back, Church stopped and came around to open her door for her. As soon as she stepped out, the strange sound that had reached her in the SUV became much louder.

"What is that?" she asked, scanning the grounds. The noise must be coming from a large garage that stood, door wide, far removed from the house. The building was across the extensive lawn, past a huge pool, and a tennis court. Lights flickered in the open doorway of the garage, and smoke came from the chimney. The noise stopped.

"That?" Church blinked, then shrugged. "That's the forge. You'll get used to it." He said the latter in a way that implied he didn't even notice the banging anymore. It was hard to imagine getting used to that kind of racket.

"So the help goes in through this door?" Best to get questions like this out of the way early.

"There aren't any fancy divisions like that here. We all use this door." He grinned. "The whole house is at your disposal. Feel free to use the pool, library, entertainment equipment – whatever you want. There aren't any servant stairwells or anything, and we all eat dinner together."

"Who the fuck is this?" a gravelly voice asked, so low that Minnow was pretty sure her toes kept vibrating after the words stopped coming.

She turned and saw a man stalking toward them. Man wasn't really the right term. He was more like a...she didn't even know what. Dirty, sweat-slicked, shirtless, wearing old ratty jeans and a pair of steel-toed boots, the man could star in his own blue-collar calendar and be every damned month.

His shoulders and arms were almost shockingly huge, tapering to a narrow waist and hips, but even with the baggy, low-slung jeans, his legs didn't look scrawny either. His face, when she could draw her gaze away from the rest of him, was so strong it was almost ugly. He had a prominent bottom jaw with a slight underbite that made him look mean, although maybe that impression wasn't from the underbite at all. He was more beast than man. His long dark hair was pulled back in a braid that was coming loose, and his ice blue eyes were narrowed and appraising, with thick black lashes that almost made him look like he was wearing eyeliner. And there were tattoos. So many tattoos. All together, he was very...startling.

"Hello, I'm Minnow," she said before Church could stop grumbling to respond.

He stopped slightly too close, staring down at her with a rude intensity. Rather than back up to a more comfortable distance, she raised her chin and smiled at him. She didn't bother to make it a nice smile.

The man snorted and turned to Church. "Sutton inside?"

"I think so. Just got here."

"Well, you can put that back wherever you found it." He flicked a finger at her. "I don't need some little cunt to babysit me."

"Sutton said to get her, so she's here." Church shrugged, as though to say he wasn't about to challenge the natural order of the household. "If Sutton ain't happy..."

The man turned his head and spat as though that was his opinion, then strode into the house, ignoring Minnow completely.

She stared after him, stunned.

"You okay?" Church asked, patting her shoulder kindly. "Severin can be a little rough around the edges, but he's a nice guy if he lets you get to know him."

"That was Severin?" she stared after him, aghast. "I thought Severin was a little old man." Although she supposed she hadn't asked, just assumed. "I don't usually work with people who are..." She waved a hand in lieu of finishing her statement.

"I know. The other stuff we've tried hasn't worked, though." He crouched and picked up a stray pinecone, then tossed it into the tree line. "He needs people in his life. When he's alone too much he gets weird."

"Weirder than this?"

"You have no idea." Church sighed. "I love my brother, but I'm married now. I've got kids. I can't stay here with him all the time. At least Sutton lives here, and she cooks and manages things. Rodrigo is around sometimes. He takes care of the finances, and is our best friend, but he doesn't live here. There's no one else."

He led her into the opulent house, their steps echoing in the cavernous back foyer. In the distance she could hear Ms Sutton shouting, and Minnow looked at Church with concern.

"Don't mind Sutton. Sometimes volume is the only thing that will make Sev hear you."

Great. Minnow could be stern, but she wasn't much of a yeller – not to mention the fact that yelling at a man that huge seemed like a bad idea.

"So is he developmentally delayed?"

"No. He's just a dick." He walked her through the main floor of the house. The main foyer was elegant, with carvings and white stone and gold detailing. It matched the outside of the house.

"The original owners were in love with Versailles, so the entire place is Rococo."

"It's so beautiful. It reminds me of those old movies, like *Dangerous Liaisons*. Hard to imagine *him* living here."

Church nodded. "Hard to imagine anyone living here, really. The first time my mother brought me to the house to introduce me to Sev, I remember asking why a kid would live in a museum. After you're here for a few weeks, though, you forget to stare at the architecture. Living here is easier if you don't notice the cherubs staring you down with their beady little eyes." He poked wiggling fingers out on either side of his head, and grimaced like he was used to entertaining children.

She snorted.

He grinned at her. "I'm serious. Don't make eye contact with them. They're creepy."

They moved on. "Through there is the ballroom." He indicated a set of double doors. "It doesn't get used for much. I think all of the furniture is covered at the moment. There's a piano in there, though, if you play." He pointed out the library next, then Severin's study.

Next was the elegant dining room, the breakfast room, the kitchen – which was now empty. The kitchen was the only room with hints of modernity. The rest of the house seemed as if it had been frozen in time.

"Upstairs things are a little more updated."

They climbed the stairs, and he showed her a screening room, with state-of-the-art equipment, and a long corridor of suites. "There are more rooms that way in the servant's wing. Sutton's room is down there, but she wants you in the blue room so you're closer to Severin in case he needs you."

She wondered what a man like that would need her for in the middle of the night, but was too chicken to ask.

He stopped and gestured her into a room. "This one is yours."

Minnow entered the lavishly appointed room then shook her head and almost backed into Church. "I can't stay in here." She'd be afraid to touch anything.

"They're all like this, even in the supposed servant's quarters, and this is where Sutton wants you," he replied, putting her ratty old suitcase down on the five billion thread count duvet that was folded along the foot of the king-sized, four-poster, bed. "You can unpack, relax, wander. Do whatever you want until dinner. It's at eight sharp every night. If you want some lunch there are always several plates of ready-to-eat food in the fridge."

"Shouldn't I be...doing something?"

Church winced, then continued in a low voice. "For today I'd keep my head down – give him time to get used to you being in his space before you try to approach him. Think stray dog."

"More wolf than dog, from the looks of him," she whispered back.

He grinned. "Yeah, maybe. Might have rabies too. Maybe mange. And, by the way, his bite is worse than his bark." With those reassuring words, he grimaced and left.

She eyed the ornate dresser with trepidation. It seemed too nice to keep things in, to the point where just touching it without museum inspection gloves felt as if it might be sacrilege. The wardrobe was just as bad, but her suitcase was too much of an eyesore to leave out. Without other alternatives, she unzipped her case and put things away. She really hadn't brought much that seemed classy enough for this place. Not that she owned much that was classy. Both Church and Ms Sutton had that understated, clean-lined and casual way of dressing that screamed money. So they weren't servants? They were, more or less, his family? Church had called Severin his brother.

So, poor little damaged rich boy had been adopted by the people who were supposedly just the help. It would have made for an awesome Hallmark feel-good movie if he were a sweet child rather than a fully grown asshat.

A scuff sounded nearby, and she turned. Severin was standing in the hallway outside her door, his dark brows drawn low over his cold blue eyes. Her heart kicked into overtime, and she had to push away the fight or flight instinct. Every instinct she had screamed that she was in danger.

He was clean now, dressed in a loose T-shirt and torn jeans, his feet bare. How the man managed to find a T-shirt that was loose on him was a mystery. Fuck, he was huge. Now that his arms were clean, the tattoos were more eye-catching. And how had she missed the septum piercing? The man looked heart-stoppingly evil.

"Hi?" she said, watching him. She didn't fake a smile. He didn't seem the type to respond well to fake.

"You shouldn't be here." That voice again. So low, she was pretty sure it shook the floor or maybe it was her shaking.

She swallowed, trying to compose herself. "No? Ms. Sutton hired me."

"I don't need a fucking nanny."

It was almost impossible not to imagine him with dripping fangs and raised hackles. The tattoos snaked up his neck in places, and they were hard not to stare at. His face was much more menacing than his artwork, and his eyes commanded her attention even as they made her want to avert her gaze.

"Of course you don't need a nanny," she replied. The man looked like he could explode in a fit of rage at any given second and snap her neck without a second thought. "Ms. Sutton was hoping I could help out around here, and that maybe you'd find me tolerable."

He stared at her for a long moment, the coldness of his gaze making her want to shiver. "What kind of parents name their kid Minnow?"

She snorted, knowing he'd meant to insult her, but not giving him the satisfaction. Did he really think a woman her age would get flustered about her name? This wasn't grade school.

"Religious people. Quasi-hippies. Think *Godspell*." She leaned a shoulder on the bedpost and crossed her arms, trying to look nonchalant instead of slightly terrified. "I'm lucky they decided against Sunnybrook. Sounds like a retirement village."

He arched a brow and walked away.

"Oookay. Bye," she called out rudely after him, wondering why she was trying to bait him rather than cowering. Some sort of death wish, maybe.

Chapter Two

There was a stranger in his space.

He paced his room like a trapped animal, hating the waiting time until dinner even more today than he usually did. Fucking Church had gone to his wife and family for the rest of the day, and Sutton had already made it clear the girl was staying for at least a week. He wasn't that messy. There was no reason why Sutton needed backup. She kept saying she was getting old, but she was exactly the same as she had been when she came to live with him and Church after their other mother died.

Yeah, Mom was dead, and eventually Sutton would be too. They all left. Even Church had moved out, even though there was plenty of room in the house for him and Ilse and the kids. Maybe if he hadn't been such a dick to Ilse they would have tried it, but that was water under the bridge now. No way to fix it, even though she'd long since forgiven him. Probably.

He'd told Sutton, though, that if she had to bring in someone, it needed to be a man. Women were weird and flighty and got all prissy about things. This one was afraid of him, he could tell. Surprising she hadn't run for the door yet. The thought of the way she'd watched him, as if he was a mugger in a dark alley, annoyed him. He hadn't even done anything yet.

Finally the bell rang, and he headed downstairs, deliberately not looking into the girl's room when he passed.

"What was that bell for?" she asked as he strode by.

"Dinner," he muttered.

Great. She was stupid.

"I think I'm overdressed." From the tap of her shoes on the marble, she was following directly behind him.

His back straightened. She was too close.

He stepped into an alcove, and gestured for her to go first. It was good manners, but it was also easier to keep distance between them.

Although she moved past him, she glanced uneasily at him over her shoulder, her eyes wide and nervous. Her long dark hair was pretty, and he couldn't help but let his gaze drift down to the lush curves of her figure in the blue wrap dress. Her ass was...

He jerked up his gaze, but the damage had been done.

She needed to leave.

When she passed the breakfast room and headed for the dining room he didn't correct her.

"Did you see Minnow on your way down?" Sutton asked, placing a serving bowl on the table as he entered the room.

"She went to the dining room."

"You could have told her we eat in here."

"If she's too stupid to figure it out, she can starve."

"Quit being a jackass and go get her."

"Fine."

He was about to step out of the room when the girl collided with his chest and bounced off. He didn't bother trying to catch her, and she ended up on the floor, which would have been funny if the sight of her blinking up at him hadn't come with a gratuitous flash of thigh. She looked shocked, her face pink and her lips parted. The top of her dress gaped slightly, giving him a healthy view of cleavage.

"Severin!" Sutton barked.

He held out a hand, but Minnow rose without touching him, which he approved of.

"Apologize," Sutton prompted.

Why was she so damned determined this one needed to work out? He didn't want this one. "I'm sorry you're so off balance. I figured that with your build you'd be harder to tip."

Sutton *tsked* at him, but the girl's eyes narrowed.

"Running into a brick wall will make even the curviest of women tip over, Mister Leduc," she replied smoothly. "And if you want to insult me, you're going to have to try harder than making fun of my name and my figure." She smoothed her dress, and he had to force himself not to follow the enticing path of her hands.

He ignored her and waited by his chair until Sutton and the girl had taken their seats before he sat too.

They filled their plates and ate in silence for a few minutes while he surreptitiously watched the girl.

"At least she has decent table manners," he eventually conceded to Sutton.

Sutton glowered at him. There was no making the woman happy some days.

"What?"

"You'd do well to watch her manners and try to emulate them."

He finished his last bite and belched. "Why?"

"So I could have a pleasant meal for once before I die?"

They glared at each other. "You're not allowed to die, remember?"

"Yes, I know. Too hard to train new help."

He frowned at his empty plate, hating when she talked like this.

"The chicken was really good," he said, waiting.

Sutton sighed then nodded at him. He was on his feet and out the door before he had to make more conversation.

*

Church lingered in the doorway of the forge. Severin could feel him watching, but he didn't acknowledge him at first. It had been a long night lying in bed with her two doors down, trying not to imagine what she slept in. Women were too damned distracting, and this morning the handlebars he worked on weren't cooperating.

"Is this one going to be ready on time?"

He glanced up at Church and his brother's half smile as he looked over the Frankenbike was enough approval to let him know he was on the right track. Church had always been his biggest fan as well as his biggest critic.

"Does it matter? If it's not ready, they'll wait."

"Rodrigo would give you hell for saying that."

"Rodrigo is in France," Severin reminded him. "What he doesn't know won't hurt him. Besides, you can't rush this shit."

'This shit' being his art.

"It's cold without the forge going in here."

"You're getting soft in your old age," Severin said, grinning to himself. Church threw a punch, and Severin deflected it with one hand while he put the metal he was working on down on one of his workbenches. "See? Soft."

They tussled, and eventually he got Church down on the ground, but then they fought to see who could pin whom. Church was leaner, and almost a head shorter, but he knew all of Severin's tricks and weaknesses, and he was still well muscled, especially for an old married guy.

"Good thing I didn't wear anything nice out here. Ilse will kill me if I rip another shirt."

"How are the kids?" he asked, kneeing Church in the groin – not hard, just firmly enough to make him squawk.

"Fuck off!" Church shoved him off and he rolled onto his back next to him. "We want more than two, so watch the jewels."

"So that's how you end up so dirty," a female voice came. "I should have guessed."

Severin cut his gaze to Church, but rather than tell her they were having a private conversation, his brother got up and brushed himself off.

"Hey, Minnow. Settling in okay?" He smiled, the white of his teeth dazzling against his dark skin.

The girl smiled back at Church. "Yes, thank you. I don't think I've ever slept in a bed that comfortable before."

Severin rolled up onto his feet and headed back into the garage, leaving them to their conversation. He slid his welding gear back on, grabbed his tig torch and filler rod then finished a few welds. By the time he pushed his mask up, Church was alone, standing just inside the door.

"For fuck's sakes, Sev, you're not even trying," Church grumbled, moving closer.

Severin stepped back from his project and pulled his mask off to get a better look at what he'd just done. "Is it that bad?"

"Not the handlebars, fuckwad."

"What? That little cunt Sutton hired? I've barely said a word to her."

Church scowled at him. "Minnow is a nice girl. She needs this job. You know Sutton won't keep her on if you don't make nice with her."

Anger and discomfort made Severin hunch his shoulders. "I am being nice."

"No. You're being marginally less of a dick than you were to Todd."

"You couldn't stand that prick either, so don't even go there."

Church grabbed two beers out of the fridge and handed one to Severin.

"Beer? It's not even noon." Severin arched a brow.

"Am I insulting your delicate sensibilities, your majesty?"

Severin cracked open his beer and took a swig. There was only one reason why Church would be feeding him beer this early in the day. "So what is it this time? You sign me up for another therapy group?"

"No, no. Not that."

He relaxed a fraction. As long as it wasn't that, he didn't give a shit.

"Then quit being a pussy and spill it."

"You need to give Minnow a chance. We're running out of options."

"Options for what?"

"You have to make your world bigger, Sev."

"It's big enough," he growled. How many times did he have to veto this damned conversation before they understood he was serious? "Leave if you want to leave. You can't buy me a fucking family to replace you. I'm fine with quiet."

"Ha." Church chugged his beer and banged it down on the workbench. "Do you remember what happened when Ilse and I went away on our honeymoon? We were gone a month, and you ended up in jail again."

Severin shuddered and swallowed more beer. "That won't happen anymore." Sharing a cell had been worse than solitary. He'd learned his lesson – not that he had to stop beating people because it was wrong, but he had to stop beating people because they'd force him to live in a small space with people he couldn't get away from.

"Will you try, for me?" Church asked. "Just have a few conversations with her where you honestly try to be nice."

"So what – I'm nice to her and then what happens next? We become BFFs and do each other's nails? I don't know anything about women. What do they even talk about?"

Church rolled his eyes. "What do you talk to Sutton about?"

He shrugged. "Welding? What we should have for dinner? Her misguided desire for more hellion grandchildren from you?"

"You never talk to her about music or TV or anything?"

"Sometimes. Maybe we host big fucking block party barbecues when you're not here and invite all the fucking neighbors. You'd know if you still lived here."

"Kids grow up and move out. It's just how things work."

"I know that." He also knew he didn't have to like it. "I'm not an idiot."

"I've accepted a job offer in Virginia."

His heart stuttered to a halt. "Virginia."

"Vox Vogel. It's my dream job, Sev. I wouldn't have said yes if it wasn't. I went to school for a million years to become an architect, and I can't make all of my life decisions around keeping you in your comfort zone."

Severin nodded. He wanted to ask how often he'd come back, but knew better. Once Church was gone he wouldn't be back. It was funny how the knowledge that Church would eventually leave hadn't kept him safe. He'd let him in. Loved him. Panic tried to surface, but he stuffed it down.

Stop.

The feelings got iced.

It wasn't love. It was just habit.

Severin was used to having him around, but he'd get over it.

"Your entire world has shrunk down to just Sutton, Rodrigo, and me. It's not healthy." They'd had this conversation so many times that it had its own script. "You should have gone to high school with me in town. Home schooling yourself out here was a mistake. You shouldn't have been alone so much."

Severin wanted him to leave for Virginia now – to get it over with – but somehow he kept up his end of the conversation. Weakness was never rewarded. "There's nothing wrong with home schooling."

"No, but you were alone too much, man. You're fucking weird. You haven't been socialized."

Socialized? That made him want to laugh, but he didn't trust himself not to sound crazy. "I'm not a dog. I rarely bite unless provoked."

"Oh, you're a dog. You're just not a *pet* dog. You're like the stray at the pound that no one is comfortable sending home with a family."

"So they sent me to a farm to live out my days chained to the garage. Someone feeds me and makes sure I don't freeze to death. Yeah, I get the analogy. It's pretty much my life. Someone should have put me down by now." It would hurt him if he had feelings, but he'd outgrown that shit a long time ago. Everyone knew he'd been thrown away. Years of other people's obnoxious pity had thickened his skin.

"It always comes back to this. What they did to you was wrong. It was fucked up. You act like this to get back at them, but they don't fucking care – they don't even know. So in the end the only person you're punishing is yourself and the people who love you here and now." Church's dark eyes were full of rage. "Even when I was a little kid I knew this whole situation was a shitshow.

Now that I'm a father, I can't even wrap my head around it. You never deserved any of this, Sev. Don't let them fucking win." He got up and moved toward Severin, but one look from Sev stalled him in his tracks.

He watched Church, wary he'd come closer, but his brother knew not to touch him without permission, even now. Part of him wanted the affection, but he couldn't handle it today.

"They always win," Severin finally said, putting his beer bottle on its side on the workbench and spinning it. Easier to occupy himself rather than see the raw emotion in Church's eyes. Not when he was having so much trouble keeping himself in check.

"Only because you let them."

*

Footsteps.

He was sitting up in bed, heart pounding, before he realized he was awake.

Nightmare?

Listening hard, he closed his eyes, willing the feeling that came with the sound to go away. Yes, footsteps, but quiet ones. No one wandered the house at night, so it had to be the girl.

He rose from bed and followed the sound of her footfalls. Someone needed to inform the girl of the house rules.

Blue light spilled into the hall from the screening room, but the sound was muted.

"Why are you in here?" he asked as he stepped into the room.

Her eyes went wide. "I..." She seemed to be at a loss for words as her gaze darted shyly from his face, then dipped to his torso – naked above his jeans – the jerked away to the plasma screen.

"You..." he prompted. Despite the coolness of the house, she wore a tank top and short shorts. The press of her cold-hardened nipples against the thin fabric of her shirt made it difficult for him to stay focused on her face.

She gripped the television remote as though it was a lifeline.

"I couldn't sleep, so I thought I'd watch something for a few minutes." She moistened her lips, and he narrowly avoided looking at them.

He needed to get rid of the light in the room before his gaze slipped down to her body. He was already trying not to consider what it would feel like to touch her.

"There's a TV in your room." He took the remote and glanced at the screen. Before bed he'd been watching the movie channel, so of course, at this time of night, there was porn playing. The woman on the screen was giving an enthusiastic blowjob. He raised a brow at Minnow, as though she'd turned porn on deliberately, and her cheeks turned pink. He hit last on the remote, and it switched to Discovery before he shut it off.

In the dark, Minnow whispered, "They say watching TV in your sleeping space can cause insomnia."

"Miss Korsgaard, no one is to be out of their room when everyone else is asleep, unless there's an emergency."

She moved into the moonlit hallway. "Oh...I had no idea." When she turned back to face him, she was a fragile outline of shadow.

He was trying not to think of the way the woman on the movie had been looking up adoringly at the man she was sucking off because his mind was trying to superimpose Minnow's anxious expression into the scenario. The fact that he made her nervous turned him on.

"But why? I mean, no one leaves to go to work and there doesn't seem to be set hours here, other than for dinner."

He gritted his teeth. "The rule is because that's how I like things, and I'm fucking paying you to deal with my bullshit."

She backed a step, and the small show of deference satisfied him.

"So you don't like people walking around at night."

"No."

"I'm sorry," she said, sounding sincere. "I didn't mean to upset you."

"I'm not upset. There's just a certain way things are done here, and although I expect you to follow the rules, I understand it may take some time for you to adjust."

Her chin rose slightly. "I've always been the kind of person who finds rules easier to remember if I know them. Even better if I know the reason for them."

"Miss Korsgaard, I'm the master of this house. I don't explain myself. You will be obedient in all things, or you will leave." He'd done his best to be polite and interact, but now he was reaching the end of his patience.

She drew a shaking breath and the sound went straight to his hardening cock. Why was this turning him on? Why was she reacting to him like this?

Sutton never should have brought a woman here.

"Yes, *Mister* Leduc." The girl inclined her head, and he wished he could see her face rather than only its outline. Her inflection on Mister when she said his name always sounded slightly like master. It was a whole word, all on its own, and not the vaguely polite short form of Mr. she used with other men. It turned him on. She turned him on. "Again, I apologize. Goodnight."

She moved away, the clean scent of her hair reaching him just as he thought it was safe to let his guard down. The girl smelled warm and slightly afraid. For a long time he sat in the darkness of the screening room, trying to block the memory of other footsteps outside his room, trying not imagine how beautiful it would be to hear Minnow cry.

*

They were taking too damned long in the kitchen. After a lifetime with people whispering behind his back, Severin's first guess was they were discussing him, and his surliness since Church, Ilse, and the girls had moved. It was stupid for it to still upset him.

Church had stood by him since the day he'd moved in when they were six.

Church was the one who'd shared his mother with an unwanted child, and who'd pulled Severin, scratching and snarling, out of his shell of nonverbal, animalistic behaviors.

Church had taught Severin to read, and gave him the play by play of the social parts of school in such detail Severin had felt as if he was there. He'd insisted Severin help with his homework and projects where no tutor who'd ever been hired for him could get him to speak, let alone learn. They'd played together, fought, got into scrapes, gone on adventures. Together they'd buried their mother. It wasn't that Church was family. It's that he was Severin's only family. Sutton was now too, but Sutton had missed the early years. She hadn't even known Mom.

His brother had proven himself loyal beyond any shadow of doubt. This had been a chance of a lifetime – he'd had to go. However, that didn't mean it wasn't a blow to lose him.

Ilse had been a threat to Severin's relationship with Church, then each child, but it was the job that had finally stolen his brother.

He hadn't realized how lonely his life would be with Church gone.

Aside from his usual interactions with Sutton, the only thing keeping him from complete boredom and despair were the projects he was working on, and tormenting Miss Korsgaard.

As if on cue, the girl entered the room with a platter of meat and put it on the table. She smiled, but there was a hint of guilt behind it, as though they had, indeed, been discussing him.

"Sutton will be here in a minute. She's just putting the potatoes in a bigger bowl."

She sat in her customary chair directly across from him, even though there was no reason why she shouldn't take Church's closer seat now that he was gone. She was careful. She seemed to always be trying to read him.

As soon as her gaze met his, he put his fingers on his fork and slowly slid it off the table. It hit the floor with a clatter. Such a stupid game. It reminded him of when Church's daughters had started testing gravity by throwing things off their high chairs. He, too, was testing his new toy.

She stared at him for a long moment, her cheeks flushing pink and hot. She was so easy to fuck with, and her reactions made him hungry for more.

"A fork."

"Yes, Mister Leduc," she said, voice quiet. "I'll get you a clean one." She swallowed hard, then stood, walked slowly to where his fork had landed. Her gaze stayed fastened to his the entire way over, but once she got to the fork, she looked down and didn't look back up. She retrieved it far more slowly than necessary, her rapid pulse fluttering visibly in her graceful throat.

By the time she rose, his cock was hard as hell and he had no fucking idea why. He kept doing things like this to her, and she kept letting him. She seemed to like it the same way he did. As though in a daze, she passed Sutton who was coming out with a bowl of mashed potatoes.

"Severin, quit being a dickhead," Sutton admonished. "You haven't dropped your fork once in all the years I've known you, and for the past week it's been every night."

"She likes being useful." He shrugged innocently. "I'm just being friendly."

"Careful now," she said, putting the bowl down by his elbow and handing him the spoon for the potatoes. "You don't mind this one, but if you push her too hard with your peculiarities, she's going to leave."

"The girl won't leave," he said, his lip curling in amusement. "I pay her too much."

Chapter Three

"Do you have to be in here?" he growled.

"Sutton wants me with you today."

Severin's top lip curled but he didn't order Minnow out. It was the first time she'd trespassed into his lair, and she and Sutton had both agreed he'd probably toss her out on her ass. This was progress. It was hard to work with a man who seemed determined to ignore her. Church had been gone a week, and Severin had barely said a word to anyone.

Sometimes she caught him looking at her, his expression inscrutable. Usually his attention seemed to be distrust or irritation, but there were times she caught flickers of something else. Interest? Or maybe the fact that they were alone together so much made her see things that weren't there.

It was so wrong, but between his gruff commands and his imperious aloofness, the man triggered every submissive reaction she owned. Normally she had no problem resisting dominant men when she wanted to, but Severin Leduc was ugly and mean and dangerous, and had a beautifully muscled and tattooed body that she wanted to lick. The power that emanated from him was lethal in a way her brain translated as sexual, and she kept fighting not to think about how big he was and what he might do to her.

Not that he would do anything. They'd been alone often enough and he didn't so much as flirt. Forget flirting, he even flinched from accidental contact. She didn't miss the way he kept meticulous space between them.

And the rules. There were so many. Every time Minnow thought she had a handle on them, they changed slightly. Some of the rules applied to everyone. Many were only for her. Sometimes it felt as if he was grooming her to be what he wanted in a companion, but sometimes his random demands felt like deliberate punishment for being in his space.

"Sit in that chair," he said, pointing.

If she sat in the chair to the left or right of the one he indicated, he'd get pissy and make her move. There were times she did it on purpose, but she cut him some slack, considering he'd let her stay in the workshop.

"Don't touch anything."

"Yes, S – Mister Leduc." Damn. That was close. There'd been so many times she'd almost called him sir without intending to. A hazard of her past two relationships being D/s. Hopefully if she ever slipped, he'd think she was just being extra deferential.

He turned away and drew a glowing piece of metal out of the forge with a pair of tongs. The dirty canvas apron he wore over his chest did nothing to obscure his bare back. It was impossible to look away from the play of muscle under the collection of monochromatic demons tattooed over the wide expanse of his back and shoulders, blending into the ones on his arms. The demons fought, fucked, and ate each other, their faces twisted in agony and ecstasy, but it was the man who wore them that drew the eye.

For ages she watched him heat the metal, bludgeon it with a hammer. As the reddish orange heat faded, he would slide the piece back into the forge. No small talk. If she didn't know better, she would have thought he'd forgotten she was there. When he went back to working the metal, he switched the hammer to his left hand without any hesitation, completely ambidextrous in his work.

The flex of his arms as he worked, beautiful and mesmerizing, had her fantasizing again before she realized she was doing it. Slowly, the piece took shape, the serpentine body and rearing head of a cobra rising gradually out of the hot metal.

His big hands on the tools, with his scarred knuckles and thick fingers, had her squirming unintentionally in her seat as she imagined him holding her down, spanking her. She couldn't imagine taking two of his fingers would be comfortable, and the rough calluses would hurt. One finger would be doable, but two? He'd have to be patient. She could almost feel the stretch of her pussy as he coaxed a second finger into her body, his cruel gaze focused on her as he forced her to take it –

"If it's too warm in here, Miss Korsgaard, go outside." His voice startled her. "Are you prone to fainting?"

"I'm fine."

"Your cheeks say otherwise."

Her hands flew to her face, and the heat emanating from her cheeks was extreme. "Maybe I'll take off my sweater."

He grunted and went back to work. She unzipped her hoody and drew it off then realized he was watching her even though he was still hammering the metal. When she looked up, she briefly met his enigmatic gaze before he refocused his attention on his work.

"What?"

"Your clothing is inappropriate."

She glanced down at her top and jeans, wondering what he was talking about. "You don't like what I'm wearing?"

"This isn't a fashion show."

She laughed. "It doesn't get much more casual than this – unless you have some rags I can borrow? Maybe a slave collar? Do I get to wear shoes or do you want me to suffer?"

His hammer hesitated and he glanced up at her, the molten lust in his gaze nothing compared to the forge. He jerked his gaze back to his work and resumed hammering.

Had she imagined his reaction?

When he didn't say anything, she wondered if she'd stepped over the line. With her kink friends what she'd said would have been considered a bit flirtatious, but unless Severin was kinky he should have rolled his eyes, at most.

"I'd buy something more casual to wear, but with Church gone I don't have a ride into town."

"Call a cab."

"They won't come out here. I've tried."

"Where were you trying to go?" he asked, his tone blasé, but his expression alert.

"Just to go see a movie."

He grunted. "You can borrow a car."

"I wouldn't be comfortable with that."

"I'll talk to Sutton. Maybe she'll have a solution."

He worked for about another hour, and when he was finished, he tossed the snake on the table between them.

"That look okay?" He pulled off his apron and went to the fridge in the corner and took out two beers, then put one down in front of her.

She caught herself staring at his nipple rings just as he tugged on his T-shirt.

"It's beautiful," she replied honestly, meaning the snake, but guiltily thinking about his chest too. Around the house, Sutton had pointed out his work – the support for a table, several statues, smaller sculptures. His work was primitive and fierce – too aggressive for the flow of the house, and yet the contrast was somehow attractive.

He opened his beer and chugged it, then took the snake back from her and put it on a worktable along the far wall.

"No beer for you?" he asked, pointing at her unopened bottle.

"Well, I'm working. You're my boss. It seems inappropriate."

He snorted and got himself a second beer. "I think if the boss hands it to you, you're safe to drink it."

When she opened her beer, he nodded in approval. Her cheeks went hot, and she took a long pull from the bottle, the bitter aftertaste doing wonders to distract her from her perverse, subby crush. She downed it quickly, and gave Severin a look of apprehension as he put a second one in front of her before retreating to a seat on the other side of the room. The last thing she needed to be doing was lowering her inhibitions, considering how attracted she was to him. This job paid too well to take a chance of fucking things up, and it was so much better than schlepping coffee.

He watched the way she put the bottle to her lips, but she pretended not to notice. She may have rubbed her bottom lip along the lip of the bottle, just to see if she was delusional, but from the way his eyelids drooped, he hadn't missed it.

Hot boss was checking her out, and the beer was making her giddy. Her thighs were numb.

Why did she already have a buzz? Oh damn. No lunch.

"So Church used to hang out in here with you a lot?"

"Yeah."

"Did he help out or just keep you company?"

"Mostly company."

"Well, next time tell me if you want me to do anything."

"Anything?" He quirked a brow. "Careful now or I may have you doing things you'll find unpleasant."

"Like what?" She arched her brow.

Rather than answer, he picked at the label on his beer bottle, carefully not meeting her gaze.

She drank the rest of her beer, then the third he *thunked* down in front of her, with awkward bouts of conversation interspersed. It was the most pleasant interaction she'd had with him since they'd met. Progress had seemed impossible only this morning.

"Come with me," he said suddenly. He rose and walked out of the garage. Confused, she followed, wondering if she should have grabbed her hoody.

Without explanation, he walked through the grounds to the back of the property. She hadn't realized how far the holdings extended. Even though it was a cold day, the treed garden and lawns were serene and lovely. On the way to wherever he was taking her, they passed a huge fountain with spouting dolphins and stone benches – all of it a complete surprise, hidden from the house as they were by the canopy of trees.

When they reached the end of the manicured lawn, he kept going, taking an overgrown path through the woods. She hesitated then followed him in, the buzz she'd gotten from the beer making her reckless. If the man was dangerous, they would have told her, right? Or she'd already know?

She followed him down the path, hopping over deadfall and puddles, jogging to keep up with his long strides.

"Where are we going?"

He didn't answer, but stripped off his shirt. She slowed to a walk, trying not to stare.

Why was he getting naked?

Moments later she heard the quiet lap of water in the distance. They reached a gap in the trees and descended a gentle slope to a secluded beach. No road or other path led to where they stood. Across the expanse of water there was only trees and rocks, with no hint of civilization to mar the view. Birds wheeled overhead. The whisper of wind through the long grasses that flanked the few dunes made her decide she never wanted to leave.

"Is this a lake?" The beer was affecting her mental processing times.

"Yes."

"What's it called?"

"Mine." He was watching her, and his lazy smile stopped her heart and sent all her blood straight to her pussy.

Oh...the lake. Duh. Earth to Minnow.

He toed off his boots, and stripped out of his filthy jeans, standing naked in front of her in all of his tattooed, pierced glory. Hell, the man had nothing to be shy about. She'd tried not to sneak a peek at his equipment, but hey, it was impressive and fucking pierced. And she wasn't exactly a saint.

"Every go skinny dipping, Miss Korsgaard?"

"I...no."

He strode into the water, not flinching from the cold. They'd had unseasonably early frost overnight for the past few nights. There was no way she was going in there.

Fuck. Naked Severin was bad news on the controlling herself front, especially when he turned to look at her over his shoulder and smirked before diving in. The man had an impossibly wide back that tapered down to a narrow waist, and a muscular ass that made her feel faint. And the tattoos? So many more than she'd anticipated. He came up with handfuls of sand and scrubbed the grit over his arms and hands, then smoothed his hands over his beautiful bare chest, then rinsed off.

"Korsgaard," he called, his husky voice making her self-control waver. "Let me get this straight. When I want you to leave, you stay because it's good for rapport. Then when it's something I ask you to do, you refuse?" He ducked under the water again and resurfaced moments later, much farther out.

"It's too cold for that!"

"I'm unhinged in here," he mocked. "Don't you want to fix me?"

"I don't need to go skinny dipping with you to be an effective companion."

"If you come in, I'll answer three questions."

"Any questions?"

"A few subjects are off limits. I'll let you know if you stumble across one of those."

Fuck. She was drunk. She knew she was drunk. But he was so hot and naked and bossy, and he wanted her in the water. Rather than strip naked, she kicked off her boots and peeled off her top and jeans, but left on her bra and panties.

A low rumble of sound that turned out to be Severin chuckling filled the clearing and tripped along the glass-smooth surface of the lake. Tentatively, she touched her toe to the water, and his eyes took on a wicked gleam as she shuddered.

"It's too cold," she complained.

"Get in the fucking water, Minnow."

Crap. He *never* said her given name, and in her slightly hazed state it was the most erotic thing he could have said.

She waded in partway then dove, ready to run back out again, but as the water closed over her head, it was warm. Not pleasant, but also not forming a thin crust of ice over her bare skin, as she'd half expected.

"See? If I wore underwear, I could have been polite like you," he said, looking amused as she bobbed to the surface. "You know, I've only ever come here with my brother."

"Your brother?"

"Is that your first question?"

A cold breeze caught her and she sank lower in the water to get away from it.

"No. You mean Church," she said. "I know that much." She was hyperaware of the fact that he was naked, and she was only in her underwear, but he didn't come anywhere near her, even though she felt him watching her whenever she looked away. "Okay, question one."

He ducked under the water, then came back up slightly closer, water sheeting off his impossibly long, dark hair and making him looking like some sort of evil merman...mob enforcer...Viking. It was hard not to stare at the runnels of water as they skimmed over his muscle. Drops of water clung to his tattoos and dripped from the silver rings in his nipples. The things she thought about doing to those rings...

Damn he was fine.

"You had a question?" he asked.

She could tell he'd noticed her perusal. "About a million."

"You only get three." His cold eyes were narrowed. He was acting so different today. Was it the alcohol or something else? Maybe he was tired of being alone.

"I know, I know." What to start with? "How long have you lived here?"

"Since I was about five. You ask boring questions."

Five? She had trouble imagining this rough man had ever been a little boy.

"Did you ever have a normal life – with a family and school and friends?"

"No. My biological family lives in France – mother, two younger sisters. I've never gone to school. I've never really known anyone other than Church, his wife and kids, Sutton, and my financial manager, Rodrigo. There was my nanny too – Church's mother – but she's dead."

"Why on earth don't you get to know more people?"

"Most people aren't worth knowing."

Sometimes she felt that way too, but this was extreme.

"We're going to fix that," she said decisively.

"You think?" He moved closer, and she was reminded again that this wasn't some timid and lonely little boy. He was a hulking, rude brute – who was now just inside her personal space.

Instinctively, she splashed him, moving back from the magnetic pull she'd started feeling around him. The water she'd doused him with dripped down his face, but he made no move to wipe it away. He only stared at her with an intensity that made her shudder.

"Cold?"

"Yes! And we don't even have towels." She laughed. He responded with a half-smile that seemed rehearsed, as though he had a guidebook to humans that said if one laughed, respond like this. "You're a lot more friendly when you've been drinking."

"Oh, I'm perfectly sober. I just find your sexual attraction to me fascinating."

She stilled then glared at him. "You're imagining things."

"Lying isn't a very good way to establish rapport, Miss Korsgaard."

"I'm not lying," she lied.

"You are, but not to mislead, only because you're embarrassed and uncomfortable. It's fine, you know. I see the way women look at me when I go into town. I'm not an idiot."

Okay, time to cut the bullshit, as Sutton would say. "Yeah, I'm sure you rarely have an itch you can't get scratched."

He seemed closer now, but she wasn't sure whose fault it was. Maybe she'd moved closer to him without noticing.

"I don't engage in casual sex."

"Saving yourself for marriage, are you?"

He snorted, but she caught his gaze lingering on the swell of her breasts. Thank God she'd worn a nice bra today. She never could have anticipated this scenario.

God. What the hell was she doing? The little buzz she'd had from the beer was fading fast, and now this all seemed like a big mistake. She needed to end this interaction before she did something stupid.

Ignoring his perusal, she waded toward shore, squeezing water from her hair as she headed for her clothes. She could feel his gaze on her, and although she tried to act like she had no idea he was watching, she couldn't help but put a sway in her hips.

She heard the slosh of water as he followed her out, and tried to focus on how cold she was rather than on how she was hoping he'd move up behind her and warm her up.

Inappropriate!

He was her employer, not some guy she wanted to pick up.

She slid on her top then her jeans, fighting to tug them back up her wet legs. From her peripheral vision, she could tell his gaze was fastened to the wiggle of her ass as she tried to get the pants back on. She unhooked her sopping wet bra and pulled it off through the armholes of her top, hoping her puckered nipples wouldn't be too visible through the pale yellow fabric.

When she was relatively sure it was safe to look at him again, she did. His mask of disinterest was back in place, but his eyes did flick over her nipples, as though he couldn't resist looking.

She shoved her feet back into her shoes, annoyed at the grit of sand between her toes, but in too much of a hurry to stop.

"I'd better get back to the house. I'm freezing." She headed for the gap in the trees where the path began, but he was behind her before she got far.

"Are you running away from me because you're having trouble controlling yourself?"

The nerve of this guy.

She whirled on him, glaring. "I have no problem controlling myself."

"No?" he asked, his tone mocking. He leaned against a tree trunk bordering the path. "I think you'd let me do whatever I wanted to, even though you find me distasteful."

"You're pretty full of yourself, you know that?"

"So I'm imagining the way your lips part and your face turns pink when I give you orders?"

She'd always prided herself on being unreadable, but this hermit had her pegged.

"You're always bossing me around – even more than you do with Sutton and Church. Why?"

"It's hard to resist when you like it so much."

"I don't!"

"Then why don't you storm off or tell me to go to hell when I get overbearing? Instead you move closer. You obey. You look away, but your body trembles."

"No! You're wrong."

"When I tell you to crawl under the table to fetch the forks I drop, you do it. Every fucking time. No complaints."

"You're my boss."

"I may be your boss, but I'm not paying you to like being treated like a slave. That's all you."

She shivered, wrapping her arms more tightly around herself as her nipples tightened at the remembered arousal. Shit. He had her number, and now he fucking knew it.

"I don't sleep with my employers."

"Oh, I'm not offering you sex, Miss Korsgaard. I don't sleep with anyone. Not even silly girls who like power games."

"No one?"

"No one."

"How long has it been?"

"You asked question three a long time ago, so I'm not answering that." He chuckled, and it actually sounded like sincere amusement. "What a curious kitten you've turned out to be."

She shook her head, confused.

"So we're just going to keep playing your little game?"

"I like this game." His voice was a low growl that made her want so much more than he was offering.

"You don't like me, but you like the game?"

"You I barely know. The game intrigues me. You intrigue me."

He wasn't even shivering, meanwhile she was shaking hard. Some of it was even from the cold.

"Come on," he said. "You need to keep moving or you're going to freeze."

They started walking again. This time he was so close she could feel where his body blocked the breeze from hitting her. When they reached the grounds, he moved up alongside her and brought her to the house.

As soon as they were safe inside, she started to relax. He wouldn't do anything with Sutton wandering around.

"Go take a warm shower and change into dry clothes," he ordered.

"I was planning to."

"Meet me in my study after that." His gaze was commanding, imperious.

She could say no. Should say no. If she got involved with him, things would inevitably go south, and she'd lose her job and her income. For a moment she pretended she had the willpower to refuse this. Refusing him might be just as detrimental to her position here, but she doubted it. The interactions with her that he liked so much were all voluntary.

She wished she was still tipsy so she'd have an excuse to back out, but she was already stone cold sober.

"Drop a lot of forks in your study, do you?" she finally asked, her tone sardonic.

"No. Things will be different in there."

"But Sutton's around." Such a lame excuse, but a valid concern for her. She didn't want the older woman knowing she was so weak.

"She went into town. She won't be back until late tonight."

They stared at each other for a long moment.

Fuck.

She swallowed, knowing there was no point in being coy anymore. "Is there something specific you want me to wear?"

"Surprise me."

She bowed her head and withdrew.

Chapter Four

Severin showered and changed, ignoring the ache of his cock while he wondered what the hell he was doing with this girl. He wanted her, but then there was the rest of it. After he dressed and dragged a comb through his hair, he glanced at his phone. Still nothing from Church. If there had been, he would have been tempted to ask him what to do.

He caught his reflection in the mirror, and for the first time in years he realized how deranged he looked. His clothing was tattered – ripped jeans stained with motor oil, T-shirt threadbare. For all he'd teased the girl about looking too fancy, it had been years since he'd bought himself clothes. His hair had grown far longer than he would have let it grow if he'd taken the time to notice. Unbound, it fell to the small of his back. His beard needed trimming too. With the tattoos and the nose ring he looked like the kind of man people crossed the street to avoid, which was the whole point, but maybe his appearance had gone a few steps too far into creepy.

Why the hell did women look at him the way they did? Weren't they only supposed to want men like Rodrigo, with his tailored suits and good manners? His financial manager looked like money, talked like money. He was handsome, well educated, and articulate, and women drooled over him, not knowing that under the pretty façade he was a much different man.

The halls were empty as he headed to his study. As he walked, he listened for her, forcing down the tight anticipation in his chest. When he reached his study he lit a fire in the fireplace, and within a few minutes the room had warmed. He picked up the manual he'd been reading the day before and sat at his desk, leafing through it to find where he'd left off, but he couldn't focus on the words.

Would she join him or change her mind?

He was alone in the house with a beautiful woman, and there was no one around to hear them, or stop him from doing anything he wanted. No one around to judge him, except her.

Considering how worried she'd seemed about Sutton being home, she wasn't about to gossip about what happened between them. She hadn't told Sutton about their little game up until now either, although she'd noticed some of it.

A soft knock sounded at the open door. The girl stood in the shadows just outside the doorway, looking tiny and apprehensive. He could almost taste her hesitation. It was fucking perfect.

"Come in, Miss Korsgaard."

She stepped into the room. The tight black T-shirt she wore showed off the swell of her breasts and trim waist, the same way the yoga pants complemented the shapely curve of her ass and legs. Like naked, but with a cloth skim coat. No bra. No panties. If she was wearing any, there'd be lines in the thin fabric.

"I wasn't sure what to wear," she admitted.

"That will do. Stand there." He pointed at the spot directly across the desk from him. There were two chairs he could have offered her, but he chose to keep her standing.

He went back to reading his manual, pretending to be engrossed in it even though he wasn't processing a word. Instead he was listening to the shaking breaths the girl drew, and surreptitiously watching the way she fidgeted and tried not to.

"Miss Korsgaard," he snapped. "This is important. You'll have to wait."

She made a strange, strangled sound, but stilled.

For about ten minutes he left her standing there, pretending to ignore her while he worked on trying to both curb his erection and feign reading. When he couldn't wait any longer, he closed the book and slid it aside.

"This isn't the first time you've had this type of...interaction with someone?"

"No, Mister Leduc." She shifted where she stood, then stopped when he gave her a look of censure.

Good. He wouldn't have to tiptoe around the situation.

"Are there things you won't let me do?"

"I've been a submissive before, but there are a lot of things I've never done."

"Is that what I asked you?"

"No, Mister Leduc."

He waited.

"I don't like hardcore humiliation." She sighed. "If you give me a safeword we can figure out my limits as we go along."

"A safeword?"

She blinked at him in surprise. "A word that lets you know I need you to stop."

"Why not just stop?" Safewords had never made much sense to him, but then he'd never had a reason to find out more even though he could have looked it up or asked Rodrigo why people used them.

Her teeth caught at her lip. "Some dominants like hearing a submissive beg for mercy without having to stop, and some submissives like that too. A random word the submissive wouldn't normally say in that situation lets the dominant know when there's a problem."

A reddish tinge had crept up her neck to her lovely face, even though her tone was nonchalant. Was she remembering things she'd done with other men? Part of him was pleased she knew what she was doing, but at the same time the knowledge she'd done all of this before made him want to stamp his mark on her.

"You trust me to stop?"

"Shouldn't I?"

"I suppose you'll find out."

There was a hum of energy across the connection of their gazes. Was she as aroused as he was? He felt barely in control of himself.

"I'll use the word..." She paused in thought.

"Tattoo."

"I'm supposed to choose it!" She grinned at him, and it was the prettiest smile he could remember seeing. How had he never noticed her dimples? Fucking adorable.

"With me you don't get to choose anything."

"No?" She shrugged. "You don't scare me."

He stood and walked around to her side of the desk, standing behind her. She didn't turn to look at him.

"Listen to me carefully. You are never to touch me without asking. Not only do I hate being touched, I can't guarantee your safety if you do so without warning me."

She stared down at the desk, but her forehead creased. "Yes, Mister Leduc."

"I'm not fucking kidding about this, girl. Understood?"

"Understood."

"You will do as you're told when we're alone together. I won't tolerate balking or attitude. As much as I referred to this as a game earlier, it's not a game. There's no start and end – it just is. Your employment is not dependent on us doing this. If we decide to stop for whatever reason, your job is safe."

"Thank you," she whispered. "It sounds like you've given this a lot of thought."

"For the past few days."

"Do you know much about BDSM, Mister Leduc?"

"A bit." Why lie? She'd have him figured out soon enough. "I've watched but don't understand everything about the interactions. I've never let myself research it."

"No? Why not? The internet is your friend."

"I've had thoughts like these since I was young. I've always done my best to keep them in check – mostly by ignoring them. If it wasn't for a friend of mine, I wouldn't know anyone else even felt this way."

She did look back at him then, her gaze full of compassion. "You aren't alone. We're everywhere."

He aware of that from an academic perspective, but it was different hearing it from someone he knew, other than Rodrigo.

"You don't know what I think about," he warned.

"You don't know what I think about either."

True.

"Put your palms flat on the desk."

She complied, arching her back to make her bottom stick out more. Such a luscious ass. His dick had almost gone off just seeing her in her underwear at the lake.

"As long as you don't harm me, we can explore what you're interested in."

"Harm?"

"Hurting me is okay. Permanent damage is not."

Maiming people wasn't what he was into anyway. "You like pain?"

"I like being controlled."

"So if you disobey me, how am I supposed to punish you?" he asked, his mind trying to process this idea that she might actually like almost everything he wanted to do to her.

She gave him an enigmatic smile. "That's something you'll have to figure out for yourself. I'm a submissive, not an idiot, Mister Leduc."

He barked a laugh, surprising himself as much as Minnow.

"You're a ballsy little thing."

"Nope. No balls, Mister Leduc. Not even in a jar on my nightstand."

The feeling – the need to control this girl and bend her to his will – fought its way to the surface.

This was the thing he was never supposed to let himself do. The girl was daring him to set his urges free.

He reached for his belt. He shouldn't let himself, but his desire for her was tangled with his desire to control her and hurt her. Wasn't this how serial killers thought? What if he couldn't stop? How was doing this acceptable?

"It's okay. I have a safeword," she said quietly.

"It's not okay." He forced his hand away from his belt buckle. "This isn't normal."

"Normal is boring, Mister Leduc," she replied, arching her back. "You don't seem like a man who's content with his halfhearted life."

She was daring him to take her in hand, to dominate her, and damn, did he want to.

Fuck it.

He unbuckled his belt, every nerve in his body hyperaware of her, of each twitch of muscle in his hands, of the crackle of the fire in the hearth. He tugged the buckle, and as he pulled the leather free of his belt loops, the girl sighed, closing her eyes and dropping her forehead to the desk.

"Don't fucking move," he reminded her, voice harsher than he'd intended.

"Oh, god."

His cock pulsed, and he readjusted himself.

Sick. He was a sick man, no matter what the girl thought.

The leather slid through his hands, worn, supple. He choked up on the belt until it was a length he felt he could control. He swung it experimentally, not wanting to scare her. Would she compare him to the men who'd done this to her before? The others must have known what they were doing. His lack of proficiency made him self-conscious.

Her ass swayed slightly, as though she was trying to lure him closer.

The dreamlike state stripped away, and his heart thundered in response to what he was about to do. Sharpening focus, he brought the belt down on her gorgeous ass with a sharp crack.

She squealed, her ass jiggling for an enticing moment before she clenched it and went up on her toes. He gave her a moment to calm down and did it again.

Three, four, five...

Each belt stroke made him impossibly harder for her. Her hands curled into fists on the wood of his desk and she whimpered, the sound perfect and orgasmic in his mind.

Six, seven, eight, nine, ten, eleven, twelve, thirteen, fourteen...

He gave them to her fast and hard, and she took them, eyes frantic, mouth hanging open.

"Stop, stop!" she gasped, blocking access to her ass with one of her small hands. "Fffffuck."

The arm supporting her gave out and she flopped belly down on his desk, panting. She wriggled and gasped and clutched at her abused ass, and he watched, heart pounding so hard he was sure she could hear it.

Stop wasn't her safeword. Was he allowed to ignore requests if they weren't her safeword? Maybe he should be careful or she might not let him do it again.

His breaths escaped him in harsh grunts, and his cock strained at the confines of his jeans, feeling like it might blow just from watching her process the pain he'd inflicted on her.

He paced back and forth, the adrenaline high almost unbearable, urging him to hit her again. To grab her hair. To...to... He didn't even know what he wanted to do. Everything. He wanted to hurt her with his hands – control her. Force her down and make her...

What the fuck was he thinking?

He'd known this would happen, that his control would slip. The vile urge to keep hitting her tore at him. He snarled something inarticulate and left the room before he did something evil and unforgivable. Long strides took him up to his room where he prowled around in frustration, eventually smashing a glass in the fireplace. That felt so good he threw a chair at his television, smashing the screen. As soon as he'd done it, he felt like an idiot.

"Whoa there, big boy," the girl said, reaching the doorway to his bedroom. She walked in uninvited, her hands up in front of her in a warding gesture.

What the fuck was she doing in his space? Couldn't she see he was out of control?

"Wow. I've never had a guy go full-on rock star because of me before." She bit her lip. "I'm flattered."

"This isn't okay. I'm not okay."

"Shh. You're okay. Sometimes we freak ourselves out. It's almost expected, and it even happens sometimes after we've been into it for a while." She came closer, but didn't try to touch him.

He paced, feeling caged, backing away from her to keep her safe from him.

"Did you like it too much? Did you have trouble stopping?"

He was gulping air, panic making him want to escape her and go out to the forge. Lock himself in and never come out again.

"This was the one thing I was never supposed to do," he ground out, the words the echo of a condemnation.

"And yet you're still turned on."

He flashed a glare at her, and she smiled sympathetically.

"I am too, even though you destroyed my ass."

There was no way she could understand this feeling of loss of control and the self-condemnation that went with it.

"I'm sorry."

"Don't be sorry." She smiled up at him. Not angry. Not afraid. "This is part of what some people enjoy. You liked hitting me, and I liked you doing it. You're new to this, and you don't know me very well. You just hit a little harder than I'm used to."

"You didn't safeword, but I had to stop."

"You were afraid you wouldn't be able to stop?"

He nodded, watching her warily. She was close enough for him to feel her body heat, but she still didn't touch him. Maybe he could bear it from her.

"You need to blow off some steam."

Yes. He needed to go out to the garage and work on a project. There must be something he needed to do with a sledgehammer.

He tried to go around her, but she moved to block his path.

"Where are you going, Mister Leduc?"

"To work in the garage for a while."

"Why don't you let me take the edge off for you?"

His mouth went dry. "What?"

She bit her lip. "When was the last time someone went down on you?"

"I'm not sure." His voice was hoarse.

"It's been a while?"

"More than."

"Like...never?" She wasn't laughing at him, she just looked curious. Maybe interested.

"Never."

"And sex?"

"Never."

Her mouth opened in surprise. "Wow," she said, finally.

"Like I said, I don't like being touched."

She sighed. "Do you really want to go through your life without finding out what it's like? Aren't you curious?"

Curious was a polite word for it.

"If you were in control of it, you'd be touching me, not the other way around. I could keep my hands behind my back."

Imagining her mouth wrapped around his cock was almost good enough to get him off. He wanted to, but why would she even offer this? Didn't women hate doing it unless they were faking it for porn?

"I don't know," he muttered. "Why would you want to do that?"

"Because you're hot and you've got me all worked up." Her mouth twisted into a self-deprecating grin. "There isn't much you couldn't convince me to do right now."

His mind strayed deeper into his list of perversions, but he reined himself in.

Could he really turn this down without even trying it? He'd never gotten to know a woman well enough to get this far before. He got offers when he went into town sometimes, or to the parties at Rodrigo's, but letting a stranger touch him wasn't going to happen. The girl seemed to understand his limitations. She didn't seem to judge him.

It would be so much easier to walk out of the room and not push himself so far out of his comfort zone. He'd avoided sexual contact this long – did he honestly need it?

"Do you have a rope or something to tie my hands with? Maybe that will make you feel more comfortable."

Maybe he'd tie her hands and see how that felt. He could still back out.

He went to his closet and scanned the sparse contents, settling on the necktie he'd worn for Church's wedding.

"A tie? *You* own a tie?" She was teasing again, and he had to remind himself that it was just her way, not a serious desire to mock him. "In case of formal blacksmithing emergencies?"

"Church's wedding," he forced out. He went behind her and bound her slender wrists together, trying to touch her as little as possible. The simple act of tying her made his balls ache.

"You didn't find a wedding overwhelming?" she asked, as though he wasn't tying the final knots, making her more helpless. Because of their size disparity he could control her easily without resorting to binding her, but this would remind her to keep her hands to herself.

"They held it here at the house. Other than Sutton and Rodrigo, only Ilse's parents came."

"Small wedding."

"That was for me." He shrugged, even though she wasn't looking at him. "I make everything complicated."

She sighed sadly. "Why do complicated men turn me on?"

Teasing again.

He snorted then swatted her ass, surprising the hell out of himself. She yelped and went up on her toes.

"Careful! I have bruises on my welts on my bruises!"

"I didn't hit you that hard."

"My poor ass will never be the same. Go ahead and look at what you did."

His hands hovered near the waistband of her yoga pants.

"Are you using your x-ray vision back there? You're going to have to pull my pants down to see." She glanced over her shoulder at him. "It's not like you haven't seen most of my ass before, Mister Leduc. I saw you looking when we were at the lake."

That wasn't the issue. It was undressing her that was the issue. It felt too intimate.

"Don't you want to see the marks you left?"

Yes. Yes he did.

Carefully, he tugged the back of her pants down, loving the way she gasped as he revealed inch by inch of naked, blaze-red flesh. He longed to bite her there. Why he get such perverted urges around her? Her ass was covered in red welts and a multitude of purple bruises was already forming.

"Your ass is even hotter with my marks on it." He especially liked the faint handprint on the right side.

"Hotter? I'm pretty sure you could light a candle from it right now."

Tentatively, he brushed his fingers over a particularly vicious welt and he shuddered at the same time she did.

"You like being touched, Miss Korsgaard?"

"Yes. You're the only person I know who doesn't. It's an interesting dilemma."

"Dilemma?"

"It's hard to seduce a man who doesn't want you to touch him."

"You want to seduce me?"

"I probably shouldn't have said so. Honesty isn't very seductive."

He needed honest. If she'd been coy about it, he probably wouldn't have caught on. "Why would you want to?"

She chuckled. "Because your brain turns me on. The rest of you ain't half bad either."

He swatted her ass again, right on top of a bruise, and her moan made his cock twitch. The feel of her bare bottom in the palm of his hand was too good, and he squeezed her there, now completely understanding why Church was constantly groping Ilse when the kids weren't looking. The next time he smacked her, she teetered, and he led her over to his bed and bent her over it.

"Mister Leduc! What are you doing?" she asked, feigning innocence with the believability of a porn star.

"Whatever I want, apparently." He spanked her for a few minutes, finding it easier to control himself without the belt in his hand. Her squeaks and sighs were erotic rather than panicked, but when he'd worked out a good tempo, she started making sounds of real distress. The kind that made him rock hard. It didn't help that he kept getting glimpses of her pussy, which looked slick and ready for him, not that he dared touch her so intimately.

He could fuck her facedown like this. If she wasn't touching him and wasn't looking at him, he could see himself succumbing to the temptation. Teenagers fucked all the time. It couldn't be that hard to figure out. She knew he was inexperienced and likely wouldn't expect much.

"Mister Leduc!" she finally sobbed. "I can't take anymore. Please stop!"

"What if I don't want to stop?" he asked, wondering what she'd do.

"Please," she begged. "My poor ass! Wouldn't you rather fuck my mouth than beat me?"

The girl had a point.

"Okay."

"I can't unbutton your jeans with my hands tied like this, so you'll have to help." She gazed back at him. "May I kneel on the floor, Mister Leduc?"

"You may."

She slid down into a kneeling position, then hissed and jerked slightly away from her heels as they met the bright red skin of her ass. "Your hand is evil. It's like being spanked with a paddle covered in sandpaper."

"And yet you didn't use your safeword."

"Safeword a spanking? Never."

He arched a brow.

"That wasn't meant as a challenge, Mister Leduc." She smiled wryly. "Are you sure you haven't done this before?"

Why would he lie about something so humiliating? "I'm sure."

She ducked her head. "I wouldn't usually be directive with a dominant, but do you want me to tell you what to do to start off with?"

"Yes." He put his hand out and touched her hair, needing to remind himself this was really happening. She was so beautiful, and she was being so understanding. The few times he'd let himself think about what this would be like, it had included various terrible scenarios where the woman would mock him.

She looked more aroused than amused, her half-lidded dark eyes making him wonder how long he'd be able to hold out. He was already so painfully hard.

"If you want to unbutton your jeans and sit on the edge of the bed," she said, her voice quiet and husky, "it'll be easier for me. If you stand I'd have to kneel on something just to reach you, I think."

Sitting sounded like a good idea. His knees felt like water. He unbuttoned his jeans, then sat on the bed, not sure what to do next and feeling like an idiot.

"Please pull your cock out for me, Mister Leduc?"

"Please?" he repeated, his brain scrambling at the thought that she wanted to do this enough to ask politely rather than just allowing it to happen.

Her lips curved into a sexy invitation. "Yes. Please."

Before he could panic and bolt, he complied. His hands were shaking as he drew his cock out from where it was bent uncomfortably sideways in his jeans. This had to be hilarious to her. Feigning macho indifference was difficult to do when his dick didn't know how to play it cool.

Her eyes widened. "Wow."

Wow? What did that mean? "What?"

She blinked at his shaft, then up at him. "I'll do my best but that thing's – intimidating."

"The piercings?"

"The piercings. The size. The man it's attached to." Her cheeks stained pink as though she hadn't meant to say all of that aloud. She moved closer. "If you want to grab my hair so you can control what I do, that's pretty standard for people like us."

He wanted to say something rude about the 'people like us' comment, but as soon as his hand tangled in her hair she gasped, and he lost the ability to think coherently. He shuddered and dragged her mouth down to his dick. Before she did anything, his cock twitched in anticipation, thumping against her face.

Rather than laugh, she stuck out her little pink tongue and licked his dick from the base to tip. Pleasure, hot, ticklish, twisted in his lower belly, his balls tightening so hard he felt faint. He braced his free hand against the bed. She swirled her tongue around the head of his cock and studied him as she played, tasting him, kissing him, rubbing her face along his shaft and the heaviness below. Her hair was silk in his fist, and once he remembered to breathe, he tugged experimentally, fascinated by her gasp of pleasure. He tightened his grip and she cried out in pain and dismay, but she didn't stop. If anything, it made her more eager.

She sucked his length into her hot, wet mouth, tugging, stroking, twirling, insistent. Not all of it would fit, but her eagerness was enthralling. He gritted his teeth, trying to resist the insanity her mouth threatened to unleash. She suckled him close to the brink and kept him teetering there, knowing exactly how to ease or stop when he was about to explode, and doing this freakish thing with her tongue that had him panting for control.

He snapped.

Grabbing the sides of her head, he fucked her mouth, hard and rough, stuffing his cock in farther than she managed on her own, loving the way she gagged and struggled to breathe when he let her. Drool seeped from the corners of her mouth dripping down his cock.

A strand of her long, lovely hair escaped one of his fists and hit his stomach, then slid downward over his cock, tickling maddeningly, and finally stopped to bob back and forth as he fucked her face, sensuously brushing against his aching balls. Every hair on his body stood on end, and the tension in his hips and ass and lower back had his control coiled so tight it hurt. He panted and his dick pulsed hard in her mouth, and for a long moment he was caught in an aching static moment of frozen time, back arched, thighs taut.

She gave one last long hard pull with her mouth, sucking his fucking soul out of his cock.

His come burst from him, and the staggering amount of pleasure that came with it forced him to give a ragged cry he couldn't control. But she wasn't done. She sucked, worshipping, and he watched in aroused disgust as she swallowed every drop of come she coaxed from his balls. Lightheaded pleasure brought an erotic dizziness, as though he'd forgotten to breathe ten minutes ago, and only just remembered to start again.

No wonder men obsessed over this act. Before he even let her pull away he wanted more. Angrily, he tightened his hold on her hair, but in response she moaned around his cock, making it stiffen again before it even went limp. She'd trapped him – made him want her – and now she'd expect something in return. He had no idea how to bring a woman off, and as much as he wanted to explore her body, the fact that he didn't know how to do anything with it made him feel stupid and foolish. He wasn't a boy. He should know these things. How dare she put him in a position of owing her when he had no idea how to make things even again?

He pulled her off him, and they stared at each other – him angry, and her gaze a desperate plea. Both of her cheekbones had the harsh red imprint of his thumbs from where he'd taken control of her. The marks were brands of dishonor, proving what he was capable of if he let himself get carried away.

"Mister Leduc, I –"

In the distance the front door slammed.

The girl's eyes widened, and her mouth fell open.

Damn. Sutton had said she was gone until tonight.

His heart shifted from thudding hard with his anger and release, to pounding with humiliation. He couldn't let the others find them together. Not like this. It was wrong. Undignified. He was technically her employer. He was a thirty-year-old man perving on his young assistant, and he'd crossed the fucking line. As willing as she'd been in the beginning, he'd still held her still and forced his cock down her throat. He'd forced her and he wanted nothing more than to do it again.

"Get out," he snapped.

"But –"

"Now. Before she comes looking for us."

The girl rose from the hardwood with the grace of a dancer, and he watched her flee the room, his tie trailing from her wrists like a sad, tickertape tail. Hopefully she'd figure out how to free herself. He was too fucked up to touch her again.

Chapter Five

Even though Minnow worked side by side with Sutton in the kitchen, there was a silence and peace that came with the work. They'd prepared so many meals together that they moved around the space like ballerinas in frilly floral aprons, weaving around each other as if every move was choreographed.

As Sutton seasoned the meat, Minnow peeled and rinsed potatoes.

"So when I'm gone to visit my sister, don't forget to check the leftovers," Sutton reminded her for the second time. "They're labeled, but they'll need to be thrown out when they hit the best before date I put on them, or else Severin will eat them."

"He claims to have an iron stomach."

"Yes, then he gets sick and can't figure out why. A day later he's eating spoiled food again. If you see him eating anything with mold on it just slap it right out of his hand."

Minnow laughed. "I doubt he'd take that kind of intervention from me."

"Tell him 'Sutton's orders.' Call me if he gives you a hard time." The older woman looked at Minnow sidelong. "You seem to be able to handle him just fine."

He'd gone back to mostly ignoring her, but at least he was more polite than before. Other than vague civility, he'd completely shut down. No covert glances. No tension from him. Just...nothing. He'd sworn so much when he was coming in her mouth that she never would have expected this tepid reception from him after the fact. It was like he'd panicked, but instead of being embarrassed or angry, he'd shut down his feelings. As if he'd blocked out what they'd done.

His indifference to her kind of hurt. It was a worse rejection than an outright 'it's not you, it's me,' line. Apathy was harder on her self-esteem than outright rejection.

Well, he was damaged, and she knew she wasn't exactly a catch compared to who he could attract if he chose to, but it still made her sad. It had been stupid to let herself be attracted to an emotionally stunted eccentric billionaire. Between the dominance and his loneliness, though, she'd been helpless against his awkward pseudo-advances. Why did she always fall for the broken ones?

Her sigh made Sutton's gaze drift over to her. "He's not the easiest man to get to know," she said quietly. "He's a runner. If he thinks you're getting too close, he'll put some distance between you." The older woman began peeling a carrot more viciously than the vegetable could possibly deserve.

"Has he said anything to you about me in the last few days?" Minnow asked carefully. "You seem angry."

"No. He would never talk to me about you unless it was to tell me to fire you." She laid aside her work and took a sip of her coffee. "And yes, I'm angry, but not at you. Not at him." Absently, she straightened her apron and picked up the next carrot. "I just worry. Church and Severin have basically been my sons since they were fourteen. Sev acts like an ass, but he...had it rough in the beginning. Church's mother, Mrs. Davis, did her best, but she couldn't fix everything. When she got him at six he was feral. At least he can sit at a table now, and talk to people without automatically flying into a rage." She pressed her mouth into a thin line. "I'll always love Davis for loving my boys before I knew them."

Minnow's heart broke a little for the boy who had become the man. "You didn't know Mrs. Davis?"

"No, no. I just know what Church has told me. He knows things from a child's perspective. He remembers the rages and the destructiveness and the violence. Sev was a very angry little boy by the time the Davis family came."

"What happened to Severin's family?"

"Nothing. They're alive and well in France, last we heard. Two daughters younger than Severin. The mother sends him a gift at Christmas and his birthday. Money transferred into his account, usually, because they don't know him."

"But...why?"

Sutton viciously sliced the carrots into a pot of water. "No one knows for sure. Well, maybe Sev knows, but he doesn't speak of it."

"But five? What made them give up on him so soon?"

Sutton passed behind her to the stove and put the pot on the element, then squeezed Minnow's arm. "Who knows? He won't see a counselor or a psychiatrist for a diagnosis. Maybe PTSD. Maybe he's got ADHD that made him hard to handle. Maybe Asperger's. Attachment disorder. Fetal alcohol. Bipolar. There are so many possibilities with symptoms that overlap, so your guess is as good as mine. Possibly as good as his. Whatever the reason, they dumped him here and more or less forgot about him. He's provided for, but ignored." She gave Minnow a pat before gathering ingredients for the piecrust for dessert.

"It's good you're here now, anyway. My sister needs me in Illinois while she goes through moving Joe to the nursing home. Joe's been a hoarder for a few years, and the closets at the nursing home are so small she has no idea what to send." She shook her head. "Hopefully she'll let me throw out some of the shit he leaves behind at the fucking house."

Minnow snorted. It was still shocking to her when Sutton swore.

"I made a list of what needs to be done around here. Groceries are delivered Wednesdays, as you know. The meal plan is posted in the pantry. You can deviate from it, but don't get too crazy. He doesn't like things that are unfamiliar."

"Why does it feel like you're leaving me with your cranky toddler?"

"Because I am." Sutton mixed ingredients in a bowl. "Except he's six foot six, and when he gets cranky it's hard to put him down for a nap."

Minnow shook with laughter.

"I don't share my toys, either." Severin's low rumble came from the doorway, making her jump. How had she not noticed him standing there? He moved through life like a ghost. His quiet gaze riveted Minnow where she stood, and warmth traveled from her cheeks, to her breasts, then crept lower.

Was he implying she was his toy? If so, she damn well felt like one. Or was he just trying to join in their joking?

"Toys?" Sutton asked.

"Like Miss Korsgaard."

Oh god. In front of Sutton? Really?

"People are not toys, Severin," Sutton admonished lightly as she rolled out her dough.

"Some are," he countered, his eyes never leaving Minnow's face.

Now Sutton did look up at him, frowning. "Severin Leduc! For once in your life will you try to be a fucking gentleman?" She grabbed an apple and threw it at his face, so fast she put some pro pitchers to shame. Severin easily caught the fruit out of the air and bit into it.

"A beast with good manners is still a beast, Mother," he grumbled sardonically. "There's no sense in pretending I'm something pretty." He wandered away, every bite of his apple sounding farther away.

Sutton sighed.

"He calls you Mother?" Minnow finally asked.

"Only when he's being a sarcastic prick." The older woman's mouth pulled into a sad smile, her creped skin folding comfortably around her eyes. "The hardest people to love are the ones who need it most."

*

Somehow the damned necktie still smelled like him. Sexy.

Curled up in bed, Minnow inspected the way the tie looked wrapped around her wrists in the pale half-light, wishing that masturbating brought her any relief.

Sutton had inadvertently ruined everything that day by coming home too early, leaving Minnow more turned on and helpless than she'd felt in her entire life. The feel of Severin grabbing her head and fucking her face still had her waking from erotic dreams and having to constantly shake herself out of lurid memories about the sound he'd made as he came in her mouth, the hot spurt of him on her tongue, his look of disgusted arousal as she'd swallowed him down.

God, he was perfect and wild and gorgeous, and he hadn't spoken to her much since, other than when he'd had to. Not knowing why was making her twitchy. Had she done something wrong? Disgusted him?

Ugh. Why did she care? Why was she still fantasizing about him fucking her?

She tried to pull her wrists apart, but the silk tie kept her deliciously trapped, just as his hands had caught at her hair as he pushed his thick shaft between her lips and dampness had pooled between her thighs. For a man who claimed to have no experience, he somehow knew exactly what she craved, and made her almost desperate enough to beg for more.

She brought her hands down between her thighs, touching herself through the thin cotton of her sleep shorts while feeling her bound wrists and thinking about his frigid, imperious gaze as he used her mouth. She wet a finger and eased her hands into her shorts. Maybe this time she could concentrate on him hard enough to end her own suffering for a few minutes.

Tentatively, she slid her damp finger down to her hot core, trying to remember the exact dream she'd been having. She stroked over her aching clit, barely touching. In her dream, he'd been forcing himself into her ass, and she was crying out in pain, trying to accommodate his girth. She could feel every vein, every piercing, as he forced his way in. He'd grunt and smack her ass, saying something ridiculously hot, like "Cooperate or this will hurt, Miss Korsgaard." Maybe he'd even swear at her. She could still hear him swearing as he'd come down her throat. So fucking sexy. She teased her clit, her ass and thigh muscles tightening, her stomach clenching...

Her door banged open so hard it rebounded off the wall.

Severin loomed in the doorway. He had a body made for looming, and in that moment his appearance was almost enough to send her over the edge into violent orgasm.

She gasped, jerking her hands out of her shorts, glad she'd pulled the sheet back up after she'd tangled the tie around her wrists.

"You can't just barge into people's bedrooms!" she said, perhaps a shade too hysterically. Under the sheet she fought to free her wrists. It had been a bitch to undo it herself when he'd been the one who'd tied her, but this time she hadn't bothered with knots.

"This is my house," he growled. "I'll do whatever I want to, at any time."

"You're an asshole."

"Why is it such a big deal?" he asked, walking in, apparently not intimidated by her glare. "What were you doing?"

"I was sleeping!"

He frowned, moving closer until he was crowding the foot of her bed. "You're wide awake."

"Well I am now! You gave me a heart attack." She sat up, drawing the sheet with her both to cover the outline of her hard nipples where they had to be obvious through her thin white camisole, and in the hope that his necktie was concealed and not dangling out somewhere. "I could have been naked or something!"

His brow arched, as though she was silly for thinking that was a problem for him. "Get dressed. We're going out." His gaze was cold and hard.

She shivered despite herself. Almost a week of ignoring her, and now he was being all intense and mysterious?

"Where are you taking me?" Had she sounded like her victim-self in one of her kidnapping fantasies? Shit. All she could smell was her own arousal, and the object of all of her latest tawdry fantasies stood far too close for comfort. He was almost in her bed, and she was a couple of tugs away from being naked. If he ripped the sheet down and crawled over her, she'd orgasm before he even put his weight on her. She shuddered.

A long look passed between them, but his expression was unreadable. Did he ever think about pinning her down and shoving his cock deep inside her? Hell, she was thinking about that enough for the both of them.

"Do I have time to shower, at least?"

"Yes. But you don't have time to finish masturbating or get fussy with your make-up. If you take too long I'm coming back in here to speed up the process. Bring a jacket."

Asshole. He'd known what she was doing and wanted to play games? Fine.

She jammed her hand back into her shorts and gave him a defiant look as she started to pleasure herself again, this time using the actual sight of him as her inspiration – daring him to say anything. His gaze caught the movement of the sheet and his massive chest heaved a few struggled breaths before he turned away.

"Fifteen minutes, Miss Korsgaard," he grumbled as he walked out of the room. He wasn't even polite enough to close the door behind him.

*

"Where are we going?" Minnow asked again as Severin led her to the parking garage. She frowned at the morning sun. Sure, it was nine in the morning, but she'd gotten used to sleeping in. Neither she nor Sutton were early risers.

"I have to get some things done in town and you're coming with me." He didn't look at her, although he'd done enough of that after he'd slammed her door open again fifteen minutes after the first time. He'd caught her about to pull a T-shirt over her head, and if he'd been going for playing it cool, he'd failed miserably. There'd been no hiding his fascination with her body even after her shirt bottom met the waistband of her jeans.

"You can't go by yourself?"

"Aren't you like my service human or something? If you're afraid they won't let you into the mall, I could always get you a little 'working human' vest. Something with a sign that says 'no touching.'"

"Will that sign work on you too?"

"You're my service human. I can pet you when I want to."

He didn't even look over his shoulder at her when he said it, but it stoked the heat between her thighs, and she cursed herself for not being able to orgasm after he'd left her room. The time constraint had weighed too heavily on her mind.

"Do you get anxious when you go shopping?" she asked more seriously.

"No. People don't try to talk to me. I just need a second opinion."

And here she thought she might actually have a chance to do her job. "A second opinion about what?"

He grunted. "You'll see when we get there. It's too much trouble to explain."

When he opened the garage door, Minnow took a long minute to peruse the selection of cars – new, classic, all expensive. All pristine. Then there were the trucks. Four pickups, all new but all dirty. And the bikes. The motherfucking bikes. About a dozen hideous creations, in every shade of black. They looked like they belonged in *Mad Max*.

"Have you been on a bike before?" he asked skeptically.

"I've had my license since I was sixteen." Against her parents' wishes, which had been the best part.

His brows drew together as though his failure to make her nervous irked him. He grabbed a helmet and threw it to her, then slid on a pair of goggles that made him look like he was going to some sort of steampunk party.

"Well, you're not driving any of mine, so get on the back." He kicked his leg over a huge, ugly Frankenbike parked near the garage door, and she got on behind him, hoping he wouldn't notice the warmth between her legs when she was snugged up against him.

"Is this one you made?" she asked, knowing it was just by looking at it. It had the same ugly, sexy arrogance as its creator.

"Yeah. All of these." He didn't seem impressed by his own work.

"Do I hang onto you or the bike?" she asked, not about to assume anything after his clear no touching rule.

"Me." His overt nonchalance was far too nonchalant-y for her to believe it. He cared that she was going to be touching him.

As he started the bike and pulled out of the garage, she wrapped her arms around his waist. He flinched under her touch yet tolerated it. From Severin Leduc, tolerance felt like a small victory. She wished she dared to slide a hand under his shirt to feel all that muscle bared to her, but she knew better than to try it.

As he drove, the cold made her glad she could use him as a human windshield. The man threw off heat like a blast furnace, but she still wished she'd brought gloves. His proximity and the low growl of the bike between her legs kept her on edge all the way into town. He parked in the mall parking lot and walked toward the building without glancing back to make sure she was following. She trotted along at his heels like a good service human, and tried to dispel the sexy mental image of being on the end of this man's leash.

He strode through the crowd milling around the entrance. People automatically melted out of his way. Handy. Maybe the next time she went to a concert she'd bring him along so she could get closer to the stage.

A shoe store had a BOGO event, and she gazed into the window just long enough to collide with Severin's chest when he unexpectedly stopped and turned to face her. She bounced off, and he had to steady her so she didn't end up on her ass.

"Ow." She rubbed her forehead. "Do I have an imprint of your nipple ring on my forehead?"

He arched a brow in mocking amusement. "You should be paying attention to me, not sales. Service humans aren't supposed to get distracted."

"I'm poorly trained."

"We'll have to fix that."

They stared at each other, and the flutter in her lower belly amplified.

Don't think about leashes, Minnow. Don't think of him training you to his own specifications.

"Why are we here?"

"Sutton thinks I need new clothes."

"Oh, do you?" she asked innocently. "I thought you dressed like this on purpose."

"How do I dress?"

"It's a hardcore shabby chic...without the chic." She gestured at the worn leather jacket and ripped denim, but refrained from including the wild hair escaping its braid and the goggles on his chest. Then there were his cold blue eyes. His uncivilized air. His height. His build. There was no way to make this man blend in.

"I detest shopping, so I brought you to do it for me. Be grateful I don't wander around naked."

"Grateful isn't the word I'd use," she murmured.

"What did you say?"

"What kind of clothes are you looking for?" she said quickly.

He shrugged. "What I have, but newer."

"Where do you normally shop?"

A couple unwittingly walked too close, and Severin straightened where he stood, then angled himself to shield Minnow, looking ready to deal with a threat. The couple glanced up then hurried off.

"I don't know. I think I got these from Church for Christmas a few years ago."

She snorted then realized he wasn't joking. "Don't rich people shop at boutiques rather than the mall?"

"How would I know? I never got lessons in how to be rich. It's surprisingly unintuitive." His tone was joking, but there was something jagged at the heart of it.

"Well, if you're looking for help spending money, I'm your girl," she said lightly. "Let's start with a jeans store. What size are you?"

"I'd have to look at the tag on these."

"Those don't fit!" Minnow laughed and led the way into the store behind him.

He looked down at himself. "They stay up fine with a belt." He tapped the buckle, and she had trouble dragging her gaze away.

"Can I help you?" a young saleswoman asked, looking directly at Minnow. From the stiff way she held herself and the way she ducked her head she was more than aware of Severin, she just knew better than to look a beast in the eye.

"There's nothing wrong with belts," Severin continued, as though he hadn't noticed the saleswoman walk over to them. "You seemed to like mine just fine the other day."

The saleswoman turned a violent shade of crimson.

Was it hot in the store? It was hot in the store. Minnow resisted the urge to fan herself, and noticed the saleswoman wouldn't meet her gaze anymore either. Great.

Minnow frowned at Severin, and the corner of his mouth twitched. The bastard.

"My friend here needs jeans, and he has no idea what size he is."

"Yes," he said, his voice low. "My service dog here probably knows better than I do."

Was that innuendo? The saleswoman sure thought it was.

"Stop it," Minnow warned under her breath. "You're embarrassing the poor woman."

"What?" he whispered back in that non-whisper men with big voices thought was quiet but really just drew more attention to what they were saying. "What did I say?"

She smacked his arm and his expression grew menacing.

Shit. No touching. She grabbed her own offending hand, feeling as if it had gotten away on her. "Sorry. I forgot."

"Don't forget again or you'll be punished."

Punished? She shivered. Hell, this man was deliberately fucking with her submissive tendencies. He had to be.

Before she could think of something to say, he stalked off after the saleswoman, who grabbed a pair of jeans off a pile and held them out to him like an offering to a wrathful deity.

"Why is this woman trying to sell me jeans that have holes in them?" he called to Minnow as she approached. "I already have jeans with holes. I'm here to get jeans without holes."

"It's the style, s-sir," the saleswoman stammered. "There may be some that aren't as distressed." She scurried off, doubtlessly to flee for her life.

The saleswoman calling Severin 'sir' made Minnow want to claw her eyes out. Like she had any right to be jealous, or reason to be from this poor woman?

"Hear that? We can go home. Tell Sutton I'm in style," he grumbled. "Distressed is in."

"Hey, that means I've been emotionally in style since I started working for you."

"Ha."

Minnow held up a T-shirt to check the size, wondering if anything in the store would even fit him.

"Not that."

She looked at the blue T-shirt. It had a paler blue logo on it. "What's wrong with this?"

"It's too...busy."

"There's one little logo on it."

"Yes. It's fussy. I don't like it, and it's too cheery."

"It's dark blue."

He grimaced. "Black or gray only. Not white. White gets stained."

"The blood of your enemies doesn't wash out well?"

"No. Then Sutton gets all pissy about it."

"You're impossible."

"Usually."

She piled her arms full of clothes he only seemed to dislike rather than loathe, then shooed him into a fitting room.

"I'm not trying this shit on."

"Yes, you are."

"I'll just buy it, and if it doesn't fit I'll give it to Sutton to get rid of."

"Quit being a weirdo and try on some clothes."

The tension in his body increased dramatically. He didn't like this idea, apparently, or he didn't like her getting bossy.

"Come on, just the jeans?" she asked, holding up three pairs. "Whichever ones fit best we'll buy a bunch of, and you won't have to come back for a while."

He glowered at her, and she was pretty sure if he'd been able to breathe fire out of his nostrils she'd have been incinerated.

"Just try on these three pairs of jeans and we can go look for the next thing."

"If I do this, you owe me." He moved closer, crowding her but not touching.

"Oh, do I? And what exactly will I owe you if you agree to try on jeans...for you?"

"You have to wear something I buy you."

She rolled her eyes. "Fine."

He grunted and walked into the fitting room, kicked off his boots, then started stripping out of his jeans. As soon as she could drag her gaze away from his taut stomach and the vee of muscle leading downward, she slammed the door closed and held it, since he apparently he had no qualms about people seeing his dick.

"Show me the pair you like best."

He didn't answer.

"Did you hear me?"

"I'm busy."

"It's okay if you don't want to try the skinny jeans. You might have too much muscle to fit in those."

A pair of jeans came sailing over the top of the fitting room door and landed at her feet.

"No skinny jeans."

"Hey, they're sexy on the right guy."

"I'll never be the right guy for skinny jeans, Miss Korsgaard."

He pushed the door and she stepped away. He was wearing the same jeans he'd had on when he went in.

"None of them fit?"

"These are fine." He handed a pair to her.

"Do they fit?"

"Close enough."

"You could try on a size smaller?"

"No."

Just no. No argument. His patience had apparently timed out.

She grabbed five other identical pairs of jeans, about twelve T-shirts he didn't say no to, and then paid after he handed her a wad of cash and stalked out of the store. When she came out with the bags, he was standing alone against the far wall of the hallway, watching her.

"You okay?" she asked.

"It's loud in here and it smells weird."

"You spend all day hammering metal and breathing in fumes from your forge and you find the mall loud and smelly?"

Then again, people didn't stare at him when he was in his garage. And people were staring – women in fascinated horror, men with distrust or aggression. She'd gotten so used to him that sometimes she forgot what other people saw. To her, he was just hot. His attention was focused only on her, even though a leggy redhead with a tight dress walked between them. It was like he hadn't even noticed the woman, even though she'd given him an appreciative once over.

"Where to now?" she asked. "What else do you need? Boots? A coat?"

"Sutton wanted me to get a haircut, but not today."

"It's fine to leave it long, but you'd have to tie it better to make it look neat." She held out the bags and he took them from her. "I could do it for you."

"You're going to be my valet?" he asked. "You're too pretty for that."

Pretty? The statement had come out so awkwardly that it meant more than some flatterer eloquently praising her. Knowing Severin, he'd probably never said the word pretty in his life except to be sarcastic. "And I'm too smart too, but hey, you're the boss."

"True. And you really seem to like it when I order you around."

So flirty today. What had gotten into the brute?

"I have to admit, being ordered around while I'm fully dressed is a new one for me," she said, without missing a beat. If he wanted to play that game, she was more than able to keep up. "Kinky, but I can handle it."

"You really think you can handle me, don't you," he said. "Hellion. You're not afraid of me anymore."

"Hellion? Is that what you think my first name is?"

"Well, Hel Korsgaard would be better than Minnow. Very Norwegian. A bit of armor and a flying horse and you could moonlight as a Valkyrie."

"If I was a Valkyrie, you wouldn't be able to boss me around. I definitely wouldn't let a man treat me like you do."

"What have I done that's so terrible?"

"Giving me the silent treatment because I gave you a blowjob wasn't very nice."

Abruptly, he veered off and walked down a service hallway. She followed, unsure. Was he looking for a restroom?

He stopped, then turned on her and dropped the bags. Using his body to corral her in, he backed her against the wall without touching her. He put his hands on the wall to either side of her head, trapping her there. His face was close – too close – and for a heart stopping moment she was sure he'd kiss her. The need for his lips on hers made her feel like her bones were melting.

"You're making me crazy on purpose."

"You were crazy long before I came along, sir."

He was breathing hard, and she wished she could reach down and grab his cock. His eyes were wild. Every time his chest rose, it brushed against hers, and she wanted to drag him even closer.

"Sir?" he finally managed to say.

Shit. She shrugged like the slip was no big deal. "You're my boss. Sir is respectful, isn't it?"

"You're doing this on purpose."

"What am I doing on purpose?"

He smacked his hand against the wall. "Why do you smell like that?"

"Like what?"

He leaned closer, inhaling near her hair. She froze, pressing her hands flat against the wall behind her, afraid she'd forget herself and touch him. The sight of his bared stomach in the fitting room had made this no touching thing even harder. The man had so many ridges of hard muscle hiding under his baggy T-shirt it boggled her mind. She needed to explore them, count them maybe. His face was in her neck, and she was desperate for something – any kind of contact from him.

He breathed her in and shuddered, then dragged his tongue up the side of her neck, tasting her.

It felt like he was barely in control of himself, and, like an idiot, that excited her. She probably shouldn't be sticking her hand in the wolf's cage, but he was a magnificent beast. And it was her job, right? Yes. This was about work. Totally.

"If you didn't like having your cock sucked, Mister Leduc, you could have just said so. There's no need to be nasty about it."

"You let me come in your pretty mouth and you fucking swallowed it," he said harshly. Slowly, his body crushed hers against the wall. His erection dug into her belly, and she gasped.

"Was I supposed to spit?" she asked, her voice low and suggestive. "Sorry. I didn't think you'd mind."

"It was disgusting." His mouth closed over the spot where he'd licked, and his teeth sank into her skin – sharp, punitive. She whimpered, hot chills running through her, making it so hard not to touch him. This no touching thing was fucking hellish. If it was just because he wasn't used to being touched, she was going to make it her mission to fix it. Wait. Did no touching mean she also couldn't push him away?

"Uh huh. And how many times have you jacked off thinking about it?"

His teeth let go of her neck. "Too many." He grabbed her hair, yanking her head back. Slowly, as though waiting for her to object, he lowered his mouth to hers. The first brush of their lips sent a spark through her, and his breath hissed in as though he'd felt it too. He brushed his lips back and forth over hers, testing, then deepened the kiss.

Unable to resist, she kissed him back, flicking her tongue over the seam of his lips when he didn't automatically open his mouth. His lips parted, and she sought out his tongue with her own. Tentatively, he kissed her back, gradually getting bolder until he'd completely taken charge and her spine was in danger of melting completely. The commanding dart of his tongue in her mouth, and the movement of his mouth made her imagine what it would be like to have him go down on her, but she doubted he ever would if he thought that her swallowing was disgusting.

His leg nudged between hers, and she whimpered as his thigh pressed against her heated core. The heat and pressure of his thigh against her pussy forced a moan from her, which he caught in his demanding mouth. She clutched at her shirt hem, trying to keep her hands to herself while also trying to keep her clothing decent while he investigated the boundaries of her bra with curious fingers.

An indignant, unfamiliar giggle reminded Minnow of where they were, with his tongue down her throat and his hand slowly and possessively roaming her body.

"Oh my god, get a room," a teenage girl admonished as she and her tittering friend strolled past into the back. They thought they were funny until they glanced back and got a better look at Severin, whose wrathful gaze was enough to make them duck meekly into their break room.

When his gaze swung back to Minnow, she shrank back against the wall and shook her head.

"Don't even think about it. We need to stop."

The combination of pissed and horny in his expression didn't bode well.

"I forgot where we were," he admitted.

No subterfuge with this man. It was an interesting change after the type of men she normally dated – self-possessed, controlled, smooth. Severin's reactions to her made her want to push him into losing his composure. Not a safe thing to do with a man who weighed at least a hundred and sixty pounds more than her, who was well over a foot taller.

He leaned in again, and for a moment she thought he was going to keep making out with her, but he only licked her bottom lip and backed off. It was as if he hadn't been able to stop himself from taking one more taste. His gaze had gone hazy and sensual again, and she bit her lip where he'd licked her. Visions of him putting her to her hands and knees and taking her roughly from behind intruded into her thoughts. If there was a sign up list for that, she wanted her name at the top.

Regretfully, they had to stop this before they got arrested.

"Taking you to the mall was a mistake," he grumbled as he grabbed the shopping bags and led her from the hallway. Thank goodness his hands were full. It might keep his hands occupied with something other than her for a while.

"I'm not a good service human?"

"Not if you're leaving me painfully hard in a public place, no."

"Who dragged who off into a secluded hallway for nefarious reasons?"

"Nefarious? An eighth-grade makeout session at the mall is hardly nefarious." He smirked.

"Well...it was more like ninth grade for me. I was a late bloomer."

He smacked her ass, shocking the hell out of her. She felt heat staining her cheeks, and she glared at him.

"Hands to yourself, Mister Leduc."

"You going to report me for sexual harassment?"

"Well, I'd have to report myself first, and that would be all kinds of awkward."

He led her out front and hailed a cab, then gave the driver his address and another roll of cash, along with his purchases. Apparently cabbies delivered things to the middle of nowhere if you paid them enough upfront. Who knew? They always refused to come to the house for her, but money in hand seemed to be enough incentive.

"Where to now?"

"I need to see my financial planner, right after I do one more thing."

"Sounds exciting."

"He's also my best friend."

She frowned at him. "So you have a housekeeper who's your mother, a former paid companion who's now your brother, and a best friend who's your financial planner. Are you married to your hairdresser?"

"When you only know a few people, they have to pull double and triple duty, but no when it comes to the hairdresser."

"I'm the only person in your life who's just an employee."

His gaze slid to hers, but he said nothing.

"That's what you told the saleswoman at the jeans store when I said I was your friend, then you dragged me into that side hallway and groped me. What's a girl to think?"

"Come on." He brought her back into the mall and up the elevator to the ritzy section she never went to.

"Now we're talking, rich boy. Tell me what we're shopping for."

"I'll know when I see it."

He prowled through the stores, drawing a mixture of glares and interest. Following Severin around a mall could essentially be a social experiment if anyone bothered to record and interpret the data.

In a small jewelry store he bought a simple stainless bracelet made of sturdy chain links, and with a price tag that would have made her faint a few weeks before. It was more than her monthly rent.

"Is it Sutton's birthday soon?" If so, she should pick something up for the woman too. They'd become close.

"No."

They walked back outside and he motioned for her to get on the bike. She picked up the helmet and threw her leg over the seat. He grabbed her arm as though to steady her, and something cold touched her wrist. The bracelet. He latched it in place then looked off across the parking lot as though he was assessing traffic.

"What are you doing?" she asked, staring at her wrist, then back up at him.

He shrugged one shoulder in a detached masculine way, as though it wasn't fucking weird. "You said you'd wear something for me if I tried jeans on."

"I thought it was going to be something perverted. Jewelry is...a little strange. Do you often given bracelets to your service humans?"

"Shut up, Miss Korsgaard."

She raised her brows at him, and his face set in a scowl. He pulled his goggles up from his chest and secured them over his eyes, and she rushed to put her helmet on. There was never any predicting what he was going to do, but at least he wasn't boring.

Chapter Six

Bringing her to see Rodrigo was stupid, and yet they were already through the security gate and pulling up in front of the house before Severin had really thought it through. Sure, Severin, introduce the attractive young woman you're getting infatuated with to fucking Rodrigo – smooth, worldly Ro, who didn't have any of Severin's issues.

Stupid idea, but it was too late now.

He got off the bike and shoved his goggles back down, surly where he'd been excited only moments before. Without waiting for the girl, he strode off to the front door, the tall glass-and-concrete structure making Severin's house seem silly and old fashioned by comparison. Everything about Rodrigo and his life spoke of money and power and ability. Normally that didn't bother him, but he liked the way Minnow looked at him, and he didn't want her looking at Rodrigo the same way – or with even more interest. Damn. Well, if she was going to be around for a while, she'd end up meeting Ro sooner or later.

The girl appeared in his peripheral vision just as the door swung open. Rodrigo's valet, John, held the door for them, his work-casual attire probably not giving Minnow a hint as to who this man was. With the white hair and deeply creased face, John could be Rodrigo's father or grandfather.

"Mr. Leduc, welcome. Mr. Solis wasn't expecting you," John said much more formally than he normally would if it had just been Severin at the door.

"You can't expect someone who never calls ahead, John," Severin countered, patting the man's shoulder.

"I see you've brought a guest?"

"Yes, this is Miss Korsgaard," he said. "She's my new handler."

John gave a shallow bow. "Pleased to make your acquaintance, Miss Korsgaard."

"Please, call me Minnow," she offered.

"Minnow?" His brow rose.

"Yes, that's my first name."

"Oh no, I couldn't possibly," he protested with a friendly but remote smile.

"Is he in the basement?" Severin asked.

John's gaze drifted to Minnow then back to Severin, a frown of disapproval creasing his brow.

"It's fine, John. She's open-minded."

John inclined his head but still seemed reluctant to say much. "The master is entertaining."

"Upstairs or down?"

Rodrigo strolled into the foyer then, buttoning the cuff of the tailored dress shirt that hid a wealth of tattoos, his usually smooth hair rumpled in a dashing way. The bastard. When he saw Severin, his face broke into a wide, warm grin.

"You really need to learn how to call ahead, jackass."

Severin felt his mouth twitch in an attempt at a smile. Rodrigo was the only person on earth who was always happy to see him. "Who's here?"

"No one now. Jenny and Antje just left."

"You don't even look tired."

Rodrigo laughed. "You know those two. No work for me. I'm just their voyeur."

Minnow made a small sound of amusement, and Rodrigo swung his head around looking for the source. He hadn't seen her standing off to the side.

"Well hello there." His usual smile of amusement turned up several watts, and he took a few steps toward her with that smooth grace of his.

Why couldn't Severin have a best friend who was a bit unfortunate looking? Maybe someone who wasn't almost as tall as Severin, who didn't have the polite kind of muscle that looked dashing under a dress shirt, and who didn't have a wicked smile and mischievous eyes. Women always wanted to know what he was amused about. Rodrigo's ex always bemoaned the fact that he had that mix of danger and fun that made him irresistible to other women, even though he wasn't one to stray if he was in a relationship.

"Hello."

"Rodrigo, this is my new handler, Minnow."

"You know my first name, Mister Leduc?"

"A handler?" Rodrigo laughed, the sound booming through the foyer. "Does she keep you on a tight leash, you big bastard?" He slapped Severin's shoulder companionably. Severin gritted his teeth, but he'd grown used to Rodrigo's manhandling over the years. "No one envies you your job, *preciosa*. How long have you been working for Sev?"

"Awhile, although he just started tolerating me a few days ago."

His smile quirked up further at one corner. "Did you bribe him with food? Food doesn't always work, but it's more likely to get his attention than anything else."

"I let him boss me around. He likes me more when he gets to tell me what to do."

Ro snorted, but his sharp eyes were assessing her, assessing Severin, reading body language and making calculations.

Severin didn't like the way Rodrigo was carefully not checking her out now, as though he'd figured out Severin liked her.

"Come on up. You wouldn't have brought her here if she was squeamish. Then again, knowing you, maybe you would."

Rodrigo led them up the staircase, with Severin insisting Minnow go first so he could watch her ass. Instead, his gaze fastened on the bracelet she hadn't taken off. A heavy wave of satisfaction rolled over him. Stupid. Crazy. If he thought he could get away with it, he'd weld a metal collar around her neck even though she wasn't actually his.

Today a basic array of equipment and implements stood around the sun-drenched living room. Severin had done most of the metalwork to Rodrigo's specifications, heavy, but easily folded and moved by men their size with the features Ro had asked him to include. Hinges, lockable wheels. It meant rarely walking into the same dungeon twice. It also meant things could be put into storage if necessary.

Minnow's gaze swept over every bit of the room but she didn't seem fazed.

"Nice set-up," she said to Rodrigo, who seemed to be waiting for a reaction from her.

"Thank you. I take it you're a kinkster?"

"Submissive masochist."

"You'd have to be to put up with Brutus over there."

They shared a laugh, and it felt like Severin's blood was going to boil out of his veins. Three seconds of conversation, and they were already buddies, with the girl freely offering personal information?

Rodrigo offered them drinks then the two of them got to know each other for a while, while Severin learned more about her than he had during the past month.

"I can't believe you know Malachi," Minnow said, shaking her head. "I guess the kink community in the area isn't that big."

"No, it isn't. If you hadn't gone away to school you'd know all the regulars too." He leaned back in his chair, draping his arms imperiously along the back of it. "Malachi and I did our apprenticeship at the same tattoo shop, back in the day. Back before I did my degree. We keep in touch. He and the girls have been busy, between the farm and the kids."

"Yeah, I'm sure they are." She combed her fingers through her hair, and Severin caught a flash of the bite mark he'd apparently left on her neck. "I haven't gone out much since my last break-up."

"No dominant at the moment?"

"No."

"Ah. I wondered when I saw the bracelet. It looks like someone staking a claim."

She ducked her head and fiddled with the stainless links.

"I put that on her," Severin said, breaking his silence for the first time in a half hour.

Minnow bit her lip, her cheeks blazing.

"Catch and release?" Rodrigo asked, raising a brow.

Severin bared his teeth. "No." He wasn't sure what had come over him, but he wasn't going to sit here and let Ro think she was available. Not that she was his, but she sure as hell wasn't going to be Rodrigo's.

"So you two are in a relationship you negotiated?" Ro asked.

Severin stared him down, wanting to deck him. Why was Rodrigo pushing him on this? Probably because even though he'd just met the girl, he could tell she was worth keeping. They weren't in a relationship, and he wasn't even sure if he was capable of one, but he didn't want Rodrigo to steal her already.

"It's complicated," Minnow cut in, not letting Rodrigo corner him. "It's also none of your fucking business."

"Submissive but not a doormat, I see." Rodrigo winked at her. "And loyal. I like her, Sev."

"Like her less and I may let you live."

Rodrigo roared with laughter. Asshat.

"So what did you come by for, other than to hang out and show off your new...handler?"

"I want some work done."

"Now?" Rodrigo sighed but got to his feet. "I haven't seen you since Church left and you show up looking for favors. Figures. Is that all I am to you?" His eyes held a mocking challenge that Severin sometimes had the urge to answer. It was better that they keep their friendship platonic.

Severin shrugged. "Pretty much."

"Just tell me I'm not putting another hole in your junk. You're starting to look like a tragic fishing accident."

Minnow snorted.

"Did he tell you his dick is pierced?"

"Oh, I'm well aware," she said, chuckling. "I just didn't know you were the one who did the work."

Rodrigo hid his incredulous expression with a mocking bow. "I'm a multipurpose friend."

"I think this means you win the contest of which of Severin's friends is the most multipurpose, Rodrigo."

Severin didn't like the way the girl said Ro's name – with too much familiarity. Interests in common. Friends in common. A strange discomfort ate at his stomach.

"No," Rodrigo countered, "I think you've won that one." His tone held a hint of envy, but Miss Korsgaard didn't seem to notice.

They followed Rodrigo through the impeccably decorated house to the basement.

"So what am I doing to you today?"

"A tattoo," Severin replied. "A relatively small one."

"Sure." He started moving around the tattoo studio, prepping things.

"You're also going to pierce this hellion's nipples for me."

Minnow sucked in a breath. "What?"

Rodrigo paused long enough to frown at him. "I won't do it unless she consents."

"She has a fucking safeword." The words came out as more of a growl, and he didn't miss the way the girl's eyelids fluttered. He grabbed her hair and she mewled, making his cock twitch. "Do you have any objections?"

"No, Mister Leduc."

"I didn't think so."

Rodrigo kept working on getting supplies ready, giving them a moment.

"You like him," Severin whispered in her ear.

"No, sir," she whispered back.

Mollified, he stripped out of his T-shirt and took the picture he'd sketched from his back pocket. Rodrigo took the paper and examined it before setting it aside.

"Like we talked about? On your ribs?"

"Yes."

Minnow drifted over to the table where Rodrigo had set down the paper, and glanced at it before rolling her eyes.

"A girl demon on the boy demon's leash? Having her kneeling wasn't enough?"

"Both is better."

"Beware. Your Mister Leduc has a serious leash fetish. He'll be leading you around town on one soon if you don't safeword."

"He's warned me. He tried to disguise it as a joke about me being his service human, but I wasn't fooled."

"A *full-service* human, are you?"

Minnow smirked at Severin and gave him a challenging look. "Maybe if he's a good little dominant."

"A sexy girl with a bratty mouth." Rodrigo groaned. "Be still my heart."

Severin's hand flashed out and grabbed her wrist before he realized what he was doing, and he upended her on his lap. He paused, but she didn't try to get away, so he delivered six hard smacks to her gorgeous ass before shoving her back to her feet.

"Don't fucking test me, Miss Korsgaard."

"Holy shit," Rodrigo blurted. He'd frozen in place just within Severin's peripheral vision, but it was the girl who held his attention. She was staring at him with her lips parted, her expression a mix of desire and humiliation.

"Sorry, Mister Leduc. I –"

"Didn't think I'd correct you in front of someone you don't know well? I warned you."

"You did, sir," she said meekly, her eyes wide and still surprised.

"Next time your pants are coming down first."

She blew out a shaking breath. "I understand, Mister Leduc."

The matter settled, he turned back to Rodrigo who was standing beside him with the bottle of disinfectant dangling from his fingers.

"Well?"

"I never thought I'd see the day." His friend shook his head as though to clear it but said nothing else as he finished setting things up.

Rodrigo made the demon and his little slave come to life on his ribs, filling in a spot where the demons on his back wrapped around. The burn helped calm his nerves, like it always did.

Why *had* he decided to bring the girl to Rodrigo's?

First of all, because he wanted Ro to like her. Just not too much.

Second, because he was feeling out of his depth. Letting her direct things felt strange, but the only experience he had was with watching. Not the best teacher. What the hell could Ro do to help, though?

As for piercing Minnow's nipples – that had been a flash of inspiration. Possibly the best idea he'd ever had in his life. The idea of watching Rodrigo slide a needle through the poor girl's nipple make him really fucking impatient to get his tattoo over with.

Minnow watched the process eagerly, and after her shock at the spanking had subsided, she started asking questions.

"I'm surprised you don't have any tattoos, Minnow," Rodrigo said as he worked. "Most of the masochists I know have at least one or two."

"Honestly, I was afraid."

"Of the pain? It's not that bad."

"That I wouldn't be able to stop. That I'd end up covered in tattoos. Between the fact that they're beautiful and I like pain, I don't know if I could stop myself, and I know how people with tattoos get treated – particularly women."

"True. That's why mine are all in places I can cover with clothes," Rodrigo said. "If I'm going to get people to trust me with their money, I can't risk it."

"Exactly. If I'm trying to get people to trust me with their vulnerable loved ones, I have to try to look sweet and demure."

"But you aren't."

"No. It's completely false advertising." Her gaze shifted from Rodrigo to his work, then to Severin. "I must have fooled Sutton, though. I feel bad for corrupting poor Mister Leduc."

"Watch yourself, girl," Severin grumbled. It was hard to know when to correct a playful submissive. He wasn't particularly playful, himself, but he enjoyed the quality in her.

"Done!" Rodrigo announced. "It was hard not to give you a rush job considering what you want me to do next. Unless you've chickened out?" He sluiced the tattoo with disinfectant one more time then spread cream over it and bandaged it. "Once the piercings are in you have to leave them alone for months to heal. No nipple play, and you'll have to follow the cleaning schedule I give you."

She opened her mouth, but Severin held a hand up to silence her.

"She answers to me, not you, Rodrigo. If she wants out of this she has to take it up with me."

Minnow laughed nervously. "I can follow the instructions. I always wanted to do this, but I've always worried I'd freak out and move at the last minute."

"Maybe Sev should help you stay still," Rodrigo suggested, smiling crookedly at Severin. "Sit on his lap and he'll hold you for me."

This ganging up on her feeling was fun. Leave it to Ro to have the brilliant ideas.

"Come here and I'll take your shirt off," Severin commanded, getting up from the chair.

Rodrigo took off his gloves and washed his hands, then prepped the piercing station.

"I don't need help taking off my shirt," she objected, even though she went to Severin readily enough.

"I didn't say you needed help, I said I was going to do it."

She opened her mouth, probably to protest, but he cocked a brow and she shut it again.

"Does it have to be all the way off?" she groused.

"Of course." He tugged off her shirt, and lost his train of thought as he caught sight of the creamy swell of her breasts against her lacy black bra. Bra. Shit. He'd set himself up to unhook her bra too. No sense in pretending he knew what he was doing. "Turn."

She did as she was told, and he unclasped the bra, glad he'd decided not to pretend he could do it without looking. Fumbling that much in front of Rodrigo, who could probably unhook a bra with his mind, was far too humiliating.

The lacy confection of an undergarment slowly slid down her arms, and she held the cups of it in place shyly. Between the gesture, the mottled red blush, the submissive duck of her head, and the subtle flirtation in her gaze, Severin's mouth went dry.

"Sit her on your lap, Sev. I can tell she's going to give us a hard time."

A hard time? Oh, he was already hard.

Severin sat and drew the girl into his lap. She sat cautiously, as though his dick might explode. It wasn't out of the question.

"Am I too heavy, Mister Leduc?" Her voice had gone low and husky.

"Not at all, Miss Korsgaard." He wrapped his hands around her hips and pulled her more firmly against him. The smooth warmth of her naked back against his bare chest was heady. It was difficult not to imagine them in this position with less clothing. Heat from her pussy radiated through the fabric of her jeans. Maybe she was nervous, but she was also aroused. "Let me help you with this."

He slid the bra straps further down her slender arms, then pulled the garment out of her grip, smiling as she made a small, plaintive sound. Even with her sitting on his lap, from over her shoulder he still had a perfect view of her pert, rosy-tipped breasts. Her nipples had peaked, and grew harder as he drew her hair behind her shoulders. He planted a kiss on her neck, over the bite mark she probably didn't even know was there, and she shuddered, squirming in his lap.

As she watched Rodrigo collect the supplies he needed, she continued to wriggle in his lap, until Severin held her more firmly.

Her skin was so incredibly soft, and the warmth of having her pressed against him was killing him. Part of him wanted to shove her away – to stop her body from touching his at so many points, but her skin was sensual silk against his own, and he never wanted to let her go.

Severin let his hands drift to her belly, then followed the smoothness upward to her perfect, unmarred breasts. His hands cupped her there, replacing her bra, and her taut nipples lured him into plucking them between his fingers.

She moaned then whimpered as he pinched harder, deliberately hurting before starting to tease, stroking and brushing, then hurting her again. Now she squirmed against him, needy, her breathing harsh, making him a slave to the rolling of her hips, the rubbing of her ass against his jeans-covered erection.

Rodrigo watched for a moment, his gaze hazed with arousal, then moved closer as he put on a fresh pair of gloves. "Spread her legs over yours." He smiled evilly. "I need room to work."

Severin pulled her legs apart, draping them over his own.

"I'm scared," she whispered.

"You're fucking killing me, Miss Korsgaard," Severin said in her ear. "Be a good girl now so that Rodrigo can clean the area with disinfectant." He moved his hand lower, cupping the underside of her breast and holding it for Ro. His gaze met his friend's. Ro's dark eyes were filled with lust, but Severin couldn't blame him. She was so fucking perfect for men like them – soft and sensual, craving pain just as they craved inflicting it.

Rodrigo did his best to keep the stroke of the disinfecting pad professional, but Severin felt the girl stiffen and shift from the contact.

"Hold her still."

"Her safeword is tattoo, in case it comes up," Severin informed him. "Don't move, Miss Korsgaard. This is going to hurt like a bitch."

The whimper she gave them as Rodrigo opened the sterile needle with exaggerated slowness made both men groan.

"You're really not making this easy on us," Severin complained.

"It was your idea, and you're both teasing me on purpose!" she complained.

Severin chuckled evilly in her ear, the quiver of fear arcing from her small body almost enough to make him come in his damn jeans.

"No matter how bad this hurts, don't you fucking move," Rodrigo growled.

"Oh my god, oh my god," she chanted.

Ro shook his head in disapproval. "You'd better hold her tighter, Severin. I don't know if she's going to be able to handle this. And whatever you do, woman, don't scream."

Severin wrapped his arm around her waist and took a rougher grasp of her breast. The girl cried out, melting against him. It wasn't going to hurt half as bad as she thought, but he had to admit that Rodrigo's mindfuck was making the situation even hotter than he'd expected it to be.

Ro slid the forceps over the stiff bud, pinched then pulled the skin taut.

"Are you going to close your eyes?" Severin asked her.

She shook her head. "No. The needle is so sharp! Is it supposed to be that sharp?"

"He's going to sink it deep into your pretty pink nipple, and do you know why?"

"No!"

"Because we want to hurt you."

She froze as Rodrigo paused, needle ready. Severin could feel the wet heat of her seeping through her jeans and making a damp spot on his thigh. Rodrigo menaced her soft flesh with the thick needle longer than necessary, and Severin realized he was holding his breath. Rodrigo's eyes slitted, and a muscle in his jaw ticked.

"Breathe through it," Severin coaxed.

She blew out a breath just as Rodrigo pushed the needle through.

"Oh god!" She bucked in Severin's arms, but he held her still, hoping he wasn't bruising her.

"Shh. The hard part is done," Rodrigo murmured.

She keened and shuddered, fighting his grip, then cried out, grinding against his thigh before collapsing against him. For a moment he thought she'd fainted, but then her eyelids fluttered open.

"Oh my god. I'm so sorry," she giggled, then sobbed, putting a hand over her eyes.

"Fuck." Rodrigo laughed. "You'd better trade that bracelet in for a collar fast, my friend, otherwise I'll steal her from you."

They smiled at each other, but it wasn't friendly. The girl was amping up the sexual tension in the room, but that tension was often there anyway, when the two men were alone.

"You okay?" Severin asked, loosening his grip on her rib cage temporarily. She drew a deep breath.

"After an orgasm like that she'd better be okay." Rodrigo fed the barbell through and fastened the other end of it, his hands shaking. When he was finished that side he disposed of the sharp and stripped off his gloves, then made a show of fiddling with equipment, but from the size of the bulge in his jeans he was probably just stalling until he calmed down. Damn good thing because Severin needed to calm the fuck down too.

The girl was looking down at her new piercing, and he could feel the muscles in her ass shifting as she whined under her breath. He was all too aware of the brush of her bare skin against his chest and how good it felt to have her pressed against him, but facing away so he could control the contact. Her pain was turning him on, but so were her reactions, and the feeling of dominance from holding her still while Rodrigo hurt her. The pain of each of his own piercings came back fresh, and his ribs burned where his new tattoo was.

By the time Rodrigo had composed himself, Severin still hadn't. Then again, Ro had presumably gotten off not long before they arrived.

"You ready?" Rodrigo asked them.

"Yes. For almost anything at this point." She laughed in what sounded like self-derision.

Rodrigo grinned at Severin. "You ever want to double team her, you know where to find me."

An uncomfortable feeling threatened, but he was the king of uncomfortable feelings. Jealousy. Like he had any call to be jealous? He'd marked her, but she wasn't really his. And this was Rodrigo. The man had handled him more intimately than anyone else except her. They didn't talk about what happened the last time Rodrigo had pierced him, but Severin hadn't forgotten.

Hell, double teaming her might be less intimidating than being alone with her. At least someone would know how to satisfy her. Would Rodrigo win her away from him? Yes, if he wanted her. Losing her was inevitable. Losing her to Rodrigo might be easier than losing her to some other idiot. At least Rodrigo would deserve her.

For now, though, she was sort of his. He could enjoy her while he had her.

Severin settled the girl more comfortably on his lap again as Rodrigo put on a fresh pair of gloves.

"Okay, Severin. Are you going to play with her first or are we just doing this?"

Like he'd object to touching this woman? Slowly, he slid his hand up from her slim waist to her other breast, enjoying the way she was gasping and arching into his fingers by the time he reached her nipple. He pinched it gently at first, but she squirmed and complained until he squeezed hard. The firmer pressure had her grunting and whining, rocking her ass against his cock. Good to know. When she was aroused and distracted, he cupped the underside of her breast for Rodrigo.

"Look how ready you are for this," Rodrigo hissed. He swiped the disinfectant over her nipple then tugged at it. Severin watched his friend toy with her while he sucked and bit at her neck. She was whining now, writhing in his lap again, each tug of Rodrigo's fingers making her hips jerk in response.

"Do you want it, pretty girl?" Severin murmured in her ear.

"No...no...please," she whined. "He's going to hurt me."

"If you want him to stop, beg me to make him stop." The words came out as a harsh rasp.

She made a guttural, feral sound that almost made Severin come. "Oh fuck. Just do it."

"Hold her tighter, Severin. Make sure your little toy can't get away."

This time Severin slipped his free hand between her thighs, pressing against the heat of her pussy, his other arm firm around her torso. She gasped, moving against his fingers, and he wished he'd taken the time to unzip her jeans and slide his hand into them. Too late now.

Rodrigo jerked the needle package open then held the sharp up between himself and the girl so she could take a good look at it. "I'm going to jab this through your hard little nipple, and it's going to hurt like hell." He turned the needle in his fingers, letting the steel catch the light. "You're trapped, little girl."

"No please! I'll be good! I'll be a good girl. Please don't hurt me."

Crazed lust blazed in Rodrigo's eyes, reflecting Severin's own reaction as Ro slid the forceps onto her nipple and tugged.

Severin tensed. He wanted to hear her scream, to see her bleed – to taste the copper of her blood on his tongue. His balls ached, making him desperate to pump come into her sweet little body, not even caring that he didn't know how. He could figure it the fuck out. He loved this – having her at their mercy. He and Rodrigo could do so many things to her.

"Don't you dare fucking come." Rodrigo sank the needle into her nipple as Severin's dick pulsed against her ass.

"Fuck!" she sobbed, coming apart in Severin's arms. He pressed harder between her legs and she convulsed, gasping and shuddering. "Fuck me...please. I'll be a good girl now. I'm sorry I'm a bad girl. I'm sorry..."

She went limp against his chest and he watched as Rodrigo fumbled to thread the barbell through. He cleaned the few droplets of blood off and bandaged her, but there was no calming down from this for Severin. Not on his own.

"You're not a very obedient girl. Severin is going to have his hands full with you."

"What did I do?" she asked petulantly.

"You came after we told you not to, and now we're both suffering. What are you going to do about that? I'll live, but what about him?"

She peered over her shoulder at Severin, her eyes glassy and feverish. She slid off his lap and knelt between his feet. "Do you need me, Mister Leduc?"

He unbuttoned and unzipped his jeans, then eased his aching cock out. Her tongue swiped shakily along her lips as she stared at his erection, but she didn't touch him.

Rodrigo grabbed her by the hair, holding it tight enough that her eyelids drooped, and her mouth dropped open.

"Suck his cock," Rodrigo growled.

"Why? You like to watch?" she asked, not moving to obey.

"Do it." He nudged her forward, but she held herself away.

"No offense, but I only take orders from Mister Leduc." She didn't glance his way, only watched Severin. "If he doesn't want to use my mouth, I won't beg."

Rodrigo let her go. "He doesn't know how to handle a submissive," he murmured, as though he didn't want Severin to know they were discussing him. Considering how close they all were, it wasn't like Severin could avoid overhearing.

"Mister Leduc handles me just fine. He sure as hell doesn't need you taking over."

Severin grabbed her chin, reminding her exactly who she should be paying attention to. "No, I don't need him taking over, but I also don't need you fighting my battles for me, Miss Korsgaard. If I didn't like something he was doing, I'd tell him myself."

"I only take orders from you." Her dark eyes flashed with a challenge he longed to correct, but he couldn't complain about her loyalty to him, especially since he'd done nothing to deserve it.

"You'll do what he says because I'm telling you to," Severin snapped, getting in her face. "But he won't touch you more intimately than he has, without my permission, because he knows I'll bust his pretty face if he tries it."

The girl frowned at him then averted her gaze. "Fine."

"Is that how you speak to me?" he asked mildly.

She flushed. "No, Mister Leduc. I'm sorry."

"If you pull that passive-aggressive bullshit with me again, it will be dealt with."

"Yes, sir."

Why did even this small exchange turn him on so much?

"Now Rodrigo is going to make you suck my cock."

Rodrigo seized her by the hair again, and she gasped, shuddering.

"But sir, I want to." She gazed down at his erection and edged closer. "I was just waiting for permission to touch you."

"I know, but I enjoy watching you struggle against a man twice your size. Between the two of us, there isn't much we couldn't force you to do."

She glared. Rodrigo forced her mouth toward Severin's cock, but she turned her face away and pressed it against his denim-clad thigh.

"Do you want to use your safeword, Miss Korsgaard?" Severin asked.

"No, sir."

"Then you're trying to show us that you're bigger and stronger than we are?"

She struggled, and Rodrigo gave a long, dark chuckle, wrapping a forearm around her middle to keep her from escaping.

"Open your fucking mouth."

She shook her head, lips pressed tight. Her eyes gleamed and the rapid rise and fall of her chest hypnotized him. Frightened? Excited? Probably both.

"Do you really want us to play rough?" Severin traced a finger over her lips and she jerked her face away. He'd take that as a yes.

She went wild, bucking and squirming, trying to force Rodrigo's fingers out of her hair. From her movements it was obvious she'd taken some sort of self-defense, but the little training she did have was no use against the sheer size difference between them.

"It's so cute that you think you can fight this, Minnow," Rodrigo whispered. "Unless you safeword, this is happening whether you like it or not."

Her breaths came hot and hectic.

As Rodrigo held her still, Severin dug his finger between her lips then pried her teeth open. She nipped the tip of his finger in warning, and he tapped her cheek.

"You fucking bite me, and you won't be sitting down for a month, bitch." He forced open her mouth again then stood. Awkwardly, he sank his cock into the depths of her supposedly unwilling mouth, but between he and Rodrigo they managed to hold her still long enough to make it happen.

"Suck," Rodrigo commanded.

She whimpered, the sound making her mouth vibrate. When Rodrigo shifted his grip on her hair, she finally gave in, running her tongue along the underside of his cock like a good girl. His knees gave out and he sat, but she followed him eagerly down.

How had he gone through thirty years of life not knowing how fucking amazing this felt? How did dominants manage to stay in control of sexual situations when a submissive's mouth could be so fucking enthralling?

She took over, suckling, swirling her wicked tongue, teasing with an intense expression of bliss, her gaze fixed on his face. Rodrigo forced her down on Severin's cock, from time to time, making her open wider to try to take more of him. Severin gritted his teeth, trying not to come even as he marveled at how pretty she was when she was drooling and tears leaked from her eyes.

With his hand around her throat, it felt like something between them settled, establishing itself more deeply – or maybe he was a gullible idiot with his cock wedged into a pretty girl's mouth. It was hard not to be obsessed with her every expression, every reaction.

He clenched his jaw and tried not to come, shifting with discomfort at the closeness of his orgasm as her pretty little mouth tried to steal his control.

"Ah, ah," Rodrigo admonished, pulling her back until Severin's cock popped out of her mouth. "No rushing."

Inches from her, Severin's cock pulsed, threatening to paint her lovely face.

"Please," she begged, struggling against Rodrigo's grip, choking herself on Severin's hand. The edge of Severin's boot nudged her knee, and she lowered her pussy onto it, rubbing herself against it through her jeans. The girl wept, trying to reach him with her tongue, while rocking her heat against his boot. Rodrigo's harsh breaths were a match for Severin's as they watched her debase herself. "Please, I need to make him come. Let me go!"

Severin should have taken control of the situation, but he was too lust-crazed to trust himself.

Still holding her hair, Rodrigo slowly let her closer. Using only her mouth, she took Severin's cock back, moaning in relief as she closed her lips over the head. Pleasure shot through Severin, renewed and aching. Rodrigo moved closer, lowering his face until it was next to hers, watching avidly as her mouth sucked and tugged at Severin's cock. His friend was too close, but Severin didn't care anymore.

Ro grabbed Minnow's jaw with his free hand and used his hold on her hair to shove her down on Severin again, using her mouth to fuck his cock. Her gaze locked on Severin, lustful and hazed. Rodrigo kissed Minnow's ear and murmured to her about how she was a good girl.

Minnow's mouth coaxing, sucking. Her breath hot then cold every time she gasped. Rodrigo controlling her movements, pulling her away just as Severin was about to come, then letting her go again.

Severin meant to push Rodrigo aside, to ask him what the hell he was doing, but it was too hot, too good, and he leaned back in the chair just letting it happen, watching the sensual slow motion movements of the girl's mouth along his aching cock. Pained ecstasy tightened his balls overfull.

Minnow latched onto the head of his cock, torturous, insistent. He struggled to maintain control, but holding off had started to hurt.

Her tongue performed some sort of magic trick, moving in a way he'd never anticipated. He gasped, knowing it was too late. Come exploded from him in hot, painful spurts. Minnow fought to keep up, but she lost rhythm even as she drew more aching pleasure from him. Severin watched as long as he could before his mind couldn't handle more, shutting down even as his body accepted every bit of feeling she forced on him. Through the fog, he watched her finish him off, licking him clean. He should be disgusted, but that emotion was alien to him – there was only a profound euphoria, paired with underlying confusion.

He should hit Rodrigo and storm out.

How had this even happened?

Rodrigo rose from the floor, offering a hand to Minnow and assisting her to her feet. His friend was very pointedly not meeting his gaze.

"Has anyone ever told you that you're a control freak? Just had to show me how it was done." Minnow smiled at Rodrigo, who smiled back wickedly.

"I'd hardly try to school you in something you're obviously good at, but that was fun."

Severin's anger simmered as he watched Rodrigo brush her hair back from her face. It was a tender, possessive gesture, and it made Severin want to gut the man.

Severin got to his feet, buttoned his jeans then searched for his shirt, hand over his tattoo bandage. Now Rodrigo would take her. Why had he ever brought her here? He never should have let them meet, let alone instigate their meeting. He'd thought Rodrigo was his friend but maybe he was just a naive idiot.

"Mister Leduc?"

He tugged his shirt on, not answering her.

"Severin –"

"Just leave it, Ro." His chest hurt, and he just wanted to get away from them. He needed space to breathe.

Rodrigo put a hand on his arm, but Severin shrugged him off and headed for the door, fighting down the urge to jump on him and fucking throttle him. Twice Rodrigo had touched him without asking today. Rodrigo knew the fucking rules. He'd been breaking them for the past eight years.

He thudded down the stairs and was out of the house before John even had a chance to get to the door. He threw a leg over the bike and threw her helmet in the grass. Korsgaard would have to get her own ass home.

Both her and Ro constantly with their fucking pushing. He didn't need to push himself. He needed a life he could control. Hell, Miss Korsgaard could stay with Rodrigo, for all he cared. They were a good match.

Chapter Seven

"Fuck." Rodrigo strode to the front room and Minnow followed him, pulling on her shirt. They watched from a window as Severin gunned his bike down the driveway, the gate at the end barely opening on time for him not to crash into it.

"He ran last time too," Minnow murmured. "Maybe I'm making a mistake pushing him."

Rodrigo stiffened. Had he forgotten about her? He strode to the drink cart and poured himself some whiskey.

"What the fuck was I thinking?" He tossed the drink back. "He trusted me, bringing you here like that. I never should have laid a hand on you."

"I'm sure things will be fine. He's probably just a little freaked out. He'll regret taking off like that." The lie was polite, and they both knew it for what it was.

"This never should have happened." He poured himself another drink. "Eight years of friendship, then he shows up here with you and I lose all of my self control."

He sat heavily in one of the wingback chairs, hand on his chest, as though in pain. "If he ever speaks to me again it'll be a fucking miracle. Fuck."

The word was on repeat in her head too. No other word had the versatility to express everything she was feeling.

"I'm sorry. This is my fault." Minnow pushed back her hair, running her fingers through the snarls he'd put in it. Rodrigo's hands had felt so good controlling her, and the memory of him forcing her down on Severin was still hot, even though she was upset about what happened afterward.

"It's not your fault. I got caught up in the moment. The worst part is, even knowing how things turned out, I can't say I wouldn't do it again. I'm no saint."

Minnow sat across from him. "If he didn't want you involved, he should have pushed you away. You honestly think he's too polite to say no?"

"You don't understand. He'll never trust me again. I betrayed him."

"Yeah, I can see how helping him get a blowjob is at the top of a list of reprehensible acts."

"Whether he seemed into it at the time is irrelevant."

"Maybe the orgasm will put him in a forgiving mood. I can attest to the fact that your participation didn't turn him off any. I wasn't prepared for a drink from the fire hose."

Rodrigo laughed as though in spite of himself. "I hope I didn't wreck things between the two of you. So many times I've offered to arrange women for him, but he's so fucked up he can't even accept temporary physical relief."

"I hope he doesn't stay mad at you," she said honestly. The poor man seemed just as upset as Severin was. As she was.

"Yeah." He sipped at his whiskey. "So is it the money?"

"The money for what?" she asked blankly.

"Is that why you're interested in him?"

The shock in her expression must have said everything he needed to know because he his smile turned more genuine.

"Have you met the man?" She shivered. "I tried to keep things professional, but between how he looks and how he looks at me, I was shit out of luck."

He barked a laugh. "Just try not to break him too bad when you leave him."

"Despite what happened earlier, our relationship isn't your business." She smiled when she said it, but the last thing she wanted was this man meddling in things, even if he was Severin's best friend.

"It's hard not to overstep myself where he's involved," Rodrigo admitted. "I'm overprotective."

"And I seem dangerous to you?"

"Submissives are the most dangerous creatures on the planet. You convince a dominant that you're theirs, and then when they finally trust you, you destroy them."

"Spoken like a man who's had his heart broken."

"I'm irrelevant. Severin is the one who needs protecting."

"Oh? Are you in love with him or something?"

He coughed, his brows raised in surprise. "Just friends, little girl." He shook his head in teasing disapproval. "Typical female."

"I'd watch."

"...and dirty!"

"Oh, like watching the two of you would be a hardship? Participating was even better."

He swirled the remainder of the whiskey in his glass. "I won't interfere again. I shouldn't have in the first place. I'm happy for him that he's found someone he trusts to let closer."

They lapsed into silence, but Minnow was so wrapped up in her own thoughts, replaying what had happened, she hardly noticed.

She came back to herself and pressed a tentative hand to her breast, then winced. Rodrigo shifted in his seat.

"If he wasn't so upset, I wouldn't have regretted any of this," Rodrigo admitted.

"I feel the same way." She pressed her lips together and drew a long breath. "It was fun while it lasted." Whether she meant this afternoon, or her entire relationship with Severin, even she wasn't sure.

"Fun, yeah." He snorted. "You can say that because you're not sitting here with blue balls."

Glaring, she grabbed a pillow and threw it as him. He deflected it and raised a brow.

"You doms and your dommy eyebrows." She grimaced. "It's your own fault – you and Severin. I was lured here under false pretenses."

"Poor Minnow. You got off when I pierced your nipples. There I was just trying to do my job."

"Your job is to force orgasms on unsuspecting submissives?"

"You were more than a little suspecting by the time it happened."

"If that's the usual process for piercings and tattoos around here, I'm surprised there isn't a huge lineup."

He laughed. "There is, but it's an exclusive club. Severin only. He paid for that room and everything in it." He shrugged. "After I graduated from finance I never thought I'd tattoo again, but Sev has ways of getting what he wants."

"Oh? How?"

"He asks people who like him too much to say no. I used to cut his hair too, when he used to bother cutting it. Never had a lesson."

She sighed. "He's such a broken boy, but so fucking pretty."

"Pretty?" He furrowed his brow. "Not a word I'd use for that ugly bastard."

"He makes the ugly work for him, somehow."

Rodrigo saluted her with his glass. "I like you. Anyone who can find a soft spot in their soul for a man like Severin has to be good people."

"Well, I try to be a good person. I'm not out to hurt him. If he can get past whatever spooked him just now, I might be lucky not to lose him entirely." What on earth was she supposed to do now? Call him? Follow? Look for an apartment and a new job?

"I don't see him more than about once every week or two. If you can at least try to smooth things over between him and me, I'd be eternally grateful."

"Eternally, huh? I'll have to get that in writing." She tapped her chin impishly. "Having you owe me could be a good thing. Payback might be a bitch."

He shifted in his chair again, frowning at her. "You should know better than to brat around a dominant."

"You're not *my* dominant."

The gleam of interest in his gaze held a meaning she decided to ignore. Rodrigo was hot and fun, but he wasn't the one who made her giddy and afraid.

"No, I'm not. I'm going to give you a ride home now, before I can't resist flirting with you anymore."

A feeling of foreboding made her stomach clench. Time to find out if the man she was half in love with now hated her.

*

The ponderous clang, clang, clang of Severin hammering a piece of metal influenced Minnow's gait as she walked toward the garage. Two steps for every hit. The heat of the covered plate she carried was welcome, considering the nip in the air. It hadn't been long since they'd gone swimming together at the lake, and yet the idea of swimming now seemed completely absurd. She should have worn a coat, but for the past week the garage had been almost too hot to bear.

As it was, Severin rarely came inside, and hadn't spoken to her, even though they were the only ones in the house.

He didn't look up as she entered, but the shift of the muscles in his neck made it obvious he knew she was there.

"I brought your dinner," she said, putting the plate on an unused workbench. She gathered the dirty dishes from lunch and piled them to take back to the house with her. "If you want, we could watch a movie or something tonight?"

"No." He didn't turn to look at her, but it was the first word she'd gotten out of him in days.

She smiled cheerily at his back. "Well, I'm going to start watching something after I clean the kitchen, so if you change your mind you know where to find me." She moved closer and he whipped his head around to watch her, his gaze wary.

"I said no." He frowned. "I have work to do."

"Okay." She moved closer yet, and he turned to face her.

"What do you want?"

She shrugged, wishing she could run her fingers over his beard. His eyes were bright and half-mad in the flickering light from the forge. With all of the electric lights off and him stripped naked to the waist, his skin sheened with sweat, he looked like Vulcan from the leather-bound illuminated book of Roman mythology she was reading in the library. It was easy to imagine Severin depicted in the style of the book's illustrations, burnished golds and dark shadows lit by the crimson and orange of the forge's flames.

Although she'd tried to stay and watch him several times, he'd kept rushing her out. This time he only watched her. Sexual tension thrummed through the air like an electric charge, making her blood feel like it was buzzing through her veins. Everything about the man said 'crawl to me and lick my boots.'

"So what are you working on today?"

He glowered at her. Not ready to talk, apparently.

"It's nice and warm in here. I hadn't realized how cold it had gotten." She lingered, running her fingers over his tools but not going so far as to pick anything up. Even this, she could tell, was difficult for him to accept.

"Why do you keep trying, Miss Korsgaard? Why don't you just go home?"

She frowned. "I let go of my apartment, remember? If I leave, I'm on the street." Things had seemed so pleasant and relaxed before Sutton left that she hadn't worried about becoming homeless at the time.

"Call Rodrigo and ask him to take you in for a while."

What the fuck?

"Mister Leduc, I don't even know Rodrigo. Why would I want to live with him? Why would I even have his phone number?"

"Like you didn't fuck him after I left?"

"What? No!" She stalked right up to him, her fists balled at her sides. The man was insufferable.

"Why not? You seemed to like each other well enough."

She forced her hands to relax. He didn't respond well to battles of will. Instead, she ducked her head and pushed her hair back from her shoulder. She didn't want to fight with him anyway.

This close, she could feel the heat coming from his heavily muscled torso.

"Your pleasure was the whole point. That was about you, not about him and I."

"No, that was about you and the fact that he wants you."

She rolled her eyes. "No, he doesn't – but even if he did, so what? He can't just take me. I'm a human being with free will, Mister Leduc. He can't just throw me over his shoulder and walk off with me."

"Why not? I would."

The dangerous look in his eyes made her want to lick him.

"So why haven't you then?" she asked, finding it impossible to stop the words from coming out. "Besides, if you think Rodrigo would jeopardize your long-standing friendship over a woman he'd just met, that you'd marked as yours, you don't have a very high opinion of the man."

"What about you?"

"What about me?"

"You let him touch you."

"It was your idea."

His jaw set under his scruffy beard.

"Did it make you jealous?" she asked carefully.

"No." It was obvious from the glittering anger in his eyes that it had and still did. "Maybe you should get to know him. He's a man worth knowing." He was quiet for a long moment, but she doubted he was done saying what he had to say. "Actually, once I would have said that, but now I don't know." He turned toward his forge, and she examined his strong profile. Maybe this was more distress and confusion than anger.

"Because of what happened? Because he got caught up in the moment?" She reached for his arm, then realized what she'd almost done and folded her hands together behind her back. "Rodrigo loves and respects you. He did what he thought you wanted."

"I won't be talking to him again."

"But why? He's your best friend. You seemed to be into what was happening – how was he supposed to know you wanted him to stop?"

He glowered into the flames.

"And now you don't like him because he made me give you a blowjob? That sounds like a pretty awesome friend, if you ask me."

His eyes narrowed. "It's not funny."

"Was it – do you feel like he did something you couldn't stop him from doing?"

"I didn't want to stop him at the time. It was after, but by then it was too late."

"Because it made things weird between you?"

"No."

"Then what, Mister Leduc? What's going on in that twisty mind of yours?"

His mouth opened, then closed, then opened again. "If he really liked me, how could he touch you?" he asked, his gaze stark.

"You asked him to. He thought you'd given him permission. I thought you had too." She grimaced at him. "With kink there has to be clear communication. If something is happening that you don't like, you need to let me know. If we hadn't started playing around in front of him he wouldn't have been anything but professional, I'm sure. He thought he was doing what you wanted."

He reached for her with one of his rough, grimy hands, and grabbed her hair, then pulled her to the workbench where she'd put his lunch. Arousal spiked through her, unexpected and unwelcome. She was trying to have a serious conversation with him and had been making headway, damn it. Stubbornly, she forced back her desire and tried to focus on communicating.

"Did you enjoy it?" he growled.

"I thought it was what you wanted."

"That's not what I asked you." His fist tightened, and he gave her a small shake, his body half covering hers and his face so close she could feel his breath at her ear.

"Yes, Mister Leduc. I enjoyed feeling helpless." She gasped, her healing nipples tightening and making her all too aware of the piercings he'd ordered put through that most sensitive of flesh. Every time she caught sight of them or became aware of them, she got aroused all over again.

"You liked his hand in your hair as he forced you down on my cock," he accused.

"Yes." There was no reason to deny it.

His erection dug into her hip, and she lost her determination to keep the conversation going. He let go of her hair and pinned her down with one big paw on the back of her neck. Brusquely, he kicked her feet apart and got between them, then his hardness pressed along her ass.

"I keep thinking about it, and then I get like this even though I'm angry. Does that make any sense?"

"Feelings don't have to make sense. They just are."

"I try not to have them, but you keep forcing them on me," he snarled. "I can't control myself like other people can. I get angry, and I don't know how to stop myself."

Great. A horny, angry man with a poor opinion of his own self-control now had her pinned down in a building on the grounds of a house in the middle of nowhere. They were completely alone. No one was around to stop him.

"If I didn't trust you, I wouldn't have agreed to stay alone with you when Sutton went to visit her sister." Her heart thudded hard, calling her a liar.

"You shouldn't trust me!" he bellowed. Rising panic made her struggle, but he didn't let her go. "You don't know what I think about. You don't know all the things I fantasize about doing to you. I try to stay away from you, and you push and push. Why aren't you afraid of me?"

"You haven't betrayed my trust, Mister Leduc."

"Do you have any idea how hard it is for me – having you living under my roof? Sleeping just down the hall? Having you walking around smelling like this...wearing clothes I could tear off of you?" He groaned and thrust against her ass. "You're a heartbeat away from being stripped naked and fucked anytime you're within arm's reach. I'd crush you to the ground as you fought me, but you're too small to get away. I could do whatever I wanted."

He shuddered on top of her, breathing hard. Her pussy twinged with a mini-orgasm just from the feel of him on her and knowing he was barely in control. No one had ever wanted her like he did.

"Why do you go out of your way to tempt me, Miss Korsgaard?"

She didn't. Not really. Accusing her of tempting him on purpose just by existing wasn't fair, but was she sorry he found her tempting? No. She couldn't even pretend she was sorry.

"Why do you think I'd try to stop you?"

In a rush, he brushed up her flared skirt and groaned – she assumed because he'd discovered her hose was actually a pair of stockings. Her panties came down next then he was on his knees behind her, dragging the scrap of silk all the way off. She waited, her breath harsh, wondering what the hell he was doing back there. Just...looking? Her cheeks burned and she frowned down at the table in dismay.

Sharp pain to one ass cheek made her screech in surprise. Teeth? That had definitely felt like teeth. He kissed the spot better and the feel of his lips on her bare flesh made her whimper.

"Your ass makes me crazy."

"You were crazy before my ass made an appearance, Mister Leduc."

He bit her again. Again. Again. Gentle nips interspersed with hard bites, and there was no way of anticipating which would come next, but the sound of his groans when she hissed in pain made every cruelty orgasmic. She spread her legs and angled back with impatient invitation, wishing he'd plunge his cock into her already.

He flipped her onto her back, and splayed her legs wide, held prisoner by rude, rough hands as he examined her in the low light. He spread her labia, looking as if he planned to draw a diagram from memory later.

She whimpered and thrust her hips upward, wanting more but not game to ask.

"What?"

"Nothing, Mister Leduc."

"You sound upset."

"Just..." She sighed. "Impatient for relief."

"You want to come?"

She bit her lip and nodded.

"What if I like leaving you horny? I've left you in a bad way twice now." He blew a gentle stream of air over her damp slit. "I love thinking about you frustrated and squirming in bed."

"I'm a big girl." She swallowed a groan. "I can fix it myself."

"No. Bad girl." He glared and slapped her pussy four times in quick succession, shocking her, each smack stinging and unhesitant. "If I leave you horny, you don't get to fix it yourself." The smacks had done more to turn her on than correct her behavior.

She struggled to get her breathing under control. "Okay, okay! But what about just regular masturbating, when it's not because of something you did?"

"You masturbate to thoughts of other men?" he asked, looking ominous.

"No, not lately," she admitted, shame-faced. "I think it's only been about you since I met you."

He grunted. Was that a pleased grunt or a displeased grunt? She needed a Neanderthal to English translator.

"I want this off," he growled, tugging at the fabric of her blouse.

"Of course, Mister Leduc." She reached for her top button.

He beat her to the button, and she let her hands fall away so he could do it himself. With a sharp tug, he ripped her blouse open, sending buttons pinging and skittering across the workshop. When he eyed her bra, she held up a staying hand.

"Good bras are impossible to find. Let me take it off, okay?"

"The next time you wear a bra in here, I'll destroy it."

"You don't like what they look like?"

His heated gaze traveled over the swells of her breasts. "It's in my way."

She unhooked the clasp between her breasts, being coy about it, pretending she was shy. Slowly, loving his rapt attention, she let the bra and the shreds of her blouse slide off her shoulders and fall to the floor.

He groaned when he caught sight of the piercings, and his hand came up as if he wanted to touch, but didn't.

"Fuck. That's hot."

"The piercings or the fact that they're there because of you?"

"Both." He traced a finger along her collarbone and then downward, circling her breast but not touching her nipple.

"They make me hyper-aware of everything that goes near them."

"Sore?"

She nodded. "A bit."

"I like making you hurt even when I'm nowhere near you." A faint smile curved his lips.

Sadistic prick. God, he turned her on.

"Now lose the skirt."

She sighed, as though she didn't want to obey, but hopped down off the workbench and stripped it off.

In just the stockings and business-appropriate heels, she felt a little silly. Stilettos they were not.

"You're always so fucking classy. It makes me want to mess you up."

"You like ruining things?"

"I do." He grabbed her ass. "And this skin of yours is so fucking pristine."

"My job isn't as physically demanding as yours. My new boss doesn't even need help showering."

Interest flickered. "That might be enjoyable as long as I was the one washing you."

"But then what would I do when Sutton comes home? I won't remember how to do it myself anymore."

He chuckled, and she could have happily rolled in the sound. "Are you suggesting I tell Sutton about us? Considering the phone lectures I've been getting about you, I think she's well aware."

She felt her cheeks heat. "This has all been very unprofessional of me."

"Yes. Very." He lifted her back onto the workbench and slid his rough hands up the insides of her thighs, coaxing her legs apart. Her clit ached, and if he didn't find it on his own, she was going to point out where it was, damn it.

"Show me what you do when you think about me."

She rolled her eyes.

"What?"

Sighing, she tapped the corner of her eye and then rolled her eyes again. "That's what I do when I think about you."

He leaned closer and bit the inside of her thigh, making her cry out as the pain leeched into her body and made her squirm. Ugh. And his mouth was so close to where she wanted it!

"So I'm not allowed to play with myself, but you're ordering me to play with myself. These mixed messages are going to make me a poorly trained service human."

"You can play with yourself if I give you permission to. If you want permission to, you have to ask. Nicely."

"And will you say yes?"

"Not unless I'm around to watch." He grabbed the bracelet he'd given her and used it to drag her hand down where he wanted it. "Now do as you're told."

He had that dickish dommy glower she couldn't resist.

"Yes, Mister Leduc," she said, almost wincing at the sex kittenish tone she'd been helpless to stop from using. She held her index and middle fingers up in front of his mouth. "A little help here?"

Glaring, he closed his mouth over the tips of her fingers. He sucked and nipped at them, using his tongue in ways she hadn't thought he'd figure out so fast. She gasped, and her hips bucked. Now that she'd felt what he could do with his mouth, all she wanted was his mouth on her...but orders were orders.

Regretfully, she pulled her fingers away and slid them downward. Her clit ached so bad that she couldn't even touch the hood without wincing.

"It hurts?"

"When I'm too turned on, it gets overly sensitive."

He crouched between her legs and spread her pussy with his fingers as she sucked a breath in at the contact. She propped her free hand under her head so she could see him – she had a decent view through the valley her breasts made. She touched herself, exploring, feeling strange and hot about him watching so closely. A rough finger prodded her clit and she squeaked.

"That's it there?"

"My clit? Yes." Her voice was several octaves higher than normal. Damn him and his ability to learn quickly. "But everything feels too intense right now."

"Don't stop," he commanded. "You're going to show me how to make you come."

More heat trickled through her. His orders shouldn't arouse her like they did, but he just intuitively knew how to make everything sexy to her.

"But I thought you didn't like me anymore."

His laugh was more a derisive exhalation of air than a vocalization. "You'd be better off with Rodrigo."

"I just met the man. Besides, he doesn't scare me like you do."

"I scare you, do I?"

"In the best way." She arched her back in invitation and touched herself, focusing on the threatening look in his eyes and knowing that was the last thing that should be turning her on.

"There's a good way to be scared?"

"Of course. The thrilling kind of fear – like being on a rollercoaster and being pretty sure you won't die."

"So you're pretty sure I won't kill you?"

"Depends on the day." She winked.

He trailed his fingers over hers. Ugh. So close, and yet nowhere near close enough.

"I like gentle. Not every woman does, though."

"I don't care what other women like." He leaned in and ghosted the tip of his tongue over her clit hood. She sobbed and tried to squirm away, but there was no escaping the iron grip he used on her thighs. He did it again then flicked his tongue over the sensitive skin around it. Flick, flick, flick. She held her breath and dug her heels into the wood of the workbench, arching against his grip in an effort to get closer.

"You said you like gentle," he reminded her.

Noooo.

His mouth investigated her, tasting her, far less squeamish about it than she'd expected, and far better at teasing than he had any right to be.

When she was panting hard and writhing in his grip, he still seemed to have all the patience in the world. Oh, yeah – he'd told her to masturbate. It had not so strangely slipped her mind.

She wiggled her hand between his mouth and her sex, toying with her clit harder than he'd been doing, desperate for relief. He nipped her finger, then sucked it into his mouth, released it again and attacked her clit, then moved lower. He spread her pussy open to him and he slid his tongue inside her, exploring, tasting, then moved lower still, touching his tongue to her perineum. She gasped and tried to push him away, but he ignored her protests, the stroking of his tongue there making her whimper nervously.

"What's the matter, Miss Korsgaard?"

"I don't –" It was hard to focus with his tongue moving like that, unhurried, dipping back into her pussy, but then moving lower again. He spread her legs wider then pushed them toward her chest.

"Oh fuck. Please, Mister Leduc. Don't."

"Don't what?"

"Don't go any farther. Please, Mister Leduc. I don't – I've never..."

He stopped, then moved up to torture her clit again, already knowing too damn well how to keep her on edge and not let her come. He nuzzled feathery-soft kisses all around her clit, making her cry out in desperation.

"Just because you haven't done something, doesn't mean you won't like it. Isn't that what you keep trying to tell me? Don't you want to set a good example?"

"Oh fuck. This is extortion." She'd never let anyone have her ass, not that there'd been a lack of trying. What was it with dominant men wanting every inch of a girl?

"You keep pushing all sorts of my boundaries, and you're not even willing to let me do this?"

"I –" Willing wasn't the issue. She didn't actually want him to stop, but it was something she had issues with, even though she knew ass play was pretty vanilla.

When she didn't finish her sentence, his mouth drifted lower again, his tongue flicking and feeling far too good.

"You taste like you just showered," he murmured between licks. "What's the problem?"

"I –" She gasped desperately. "...don't like it."

"I thought you said you hadn't tried it."

She whined as he got to her perineum again. Her legs shook. Anticipation knotted her belly.

"That's true."

"Then how do you know?" His mouth moved lower. Last chance to safeword.

She squeezed her eyes shut and let him press her legs wider. He dragged his tongue downward, flicking over her anus so gently it tickled.

"No...please!" She tried to close her legs, but he wouldn't allow it.

"Ah, ah. I'm not done."

"No, no. No more," she begged. It felt too weird and too personal and too damned good and she didn't want to like it – not after refusing anal again and again with every ex she'd ever had. "Oh fuck...fuck."

He paused, as though listening for the safeword she couldn't bring herself to say.

"Yeah, that's what I thought." He bit the back of her leg where it met her ass, hard enough to make her cry out in pain. "I have dreams about that little sobbing noise you make."

"Sadist!"

"Yes."

He kissed the spot better, rubbing his lips back and forth over it, so close to her pussy and yet much too far away. She shifted her hips, trying to get her clit closer to his mouth and wishing she could grab him to direct him. Between the no touching rule and the fact that he was a dominant, she doubted he'd appreciate being grabbed by the hair and yanked where she wanted him.

At least he'd cared enough to find out where it was, unlike some guys.

His tongue flicked over her anus again and she squealed so loud it mortified her. Taboo pleasure shivered through her, making her ache for more even as she tried hard to hang onto her disgust. He kissed her there, licked, sliding his rough fingers along the seam of her sex, finding her clit far too proficiently. He tapped it with the pad of his finger, rhythmically until she was so fucking close but couldn't go over the edge. She squealed and bucked, but he pulled away, his blue eyes positively glacial in the heat of the garage.

Rather than dropping his jeans and shoving into her, he mercly chuckled and turned his back. Casually, he walked to the tray she'd brought him and sorted through it, unwrapping one of the roast beef sandwiches she'd brought out and biting into it.

She sat up on the workbench, watching him in horrified disbelief – her pussy and ass tingling and needy as she watched him. He was dismissing her?

Trembling, she slid off her perch, her thigh muscles sore from being held in the same position so long. Her wetness mingled with his saliva, drenching her thighs. Even the tops of her stockings felt damp. Her clit pulsed, and her legs shook as she held onto the workbench, trying not to fall off her low heels.

"That will be all, Miss Korsgaard."

"Oh my god," she whispered.

As though he'd forgotten about her, he kept eating his sandwich, turning the piece he was working on and examining it from a different angle.

He was serious?

She was going to die, but not before she murdered him.

"Mister Leduc, sir? May I –"

"Of course not."

Bloody hell. That wasn't what she wanted anyway, but she felt like her heart was never going to slow down again if she didn't get some relief.

In a last-ditch effort to change his mind, she turned her back to him and bent from the waist to gather her clothes, hoping to give him an eyeful of what he was forgoing. When she straightened, he was in her face. Her heart beat erratically and she sucked in a breath.

"Did I say you could take these?" he asked. He walked to the forge and stuffed her skirt and blouse into the flames. The bra he tossed to her. The panties he twirled on his finger.

"Quit being distracting. I have work to do." He hung her panties on a hook above one of the workbenches he used often. "And remember, no masturbating."

Humiliated, she turned to go.

"And don't even think of putting that bra back on today."

In the ultimate walk of shame, scurrying back through the chill air, she tried to be angry. Instead, she only wanted him more.

Chapter Eight

In the darkness of his room, Severin stared at the shadows of trees swaying against the back lighting of the swollen moon. After hours of shifting and rolling in her bed, Miss Korsgaard had been still for about an hour, her soft breathing just barely audible in the chill silence of the house.

He'd laid a fire in the hearth in her room, and the quiet crackle of it pleased him. Doing things to take care of her filled him with a weird satisfaction. Clothing arrived for her in the mail almost every day now. Watching her wear the things he'd picked out to replace the things of hers he'd destroyed was...lovely.

Tension thrummed through his body remembering the glimpse he'd gotten of black lace she'd been wearing under the black silk robe when she'd come to say goodnight. The long, smooth legs. The swell of her breasts. And barefoot. He groaned, clasping his balls hard, willing his wide-awake dick to go to sleep.

He rose from bed and padded to her room, tugging his jeans up even though they only slipped down to ride his hips again. Readjusting his erection was more difficult, but having it poking above his waistband would be hard to conceal when he was shirtless. He collected a few things and stalked down the hall.

Standing at the door to her room, he watched her sleep. Why did he do this? It was so hard to resist seeing her with all of her defenses down, hair tousled, and lips parted, lit by the mysterious flickers of light from the fireplace. Nights were difficult, but days were worse. She was so impossible to ignore during the day, with her subtle submissive flirtation – the angle of her head, the openness in her gaze. Even her voice drove him crazy. She didn't touch him, but gave him every indication that if he let her, she would rub against him like an affectionate cat. More like a cat in heat for the past few days.

Teasing her and leaving her wanting had become a game. Four days of it so far. The fact that she slept so soundly when he was awake and thinking of her just wouldn't do.

"Miss Korsgaard," he barked.

She bolted upright in bed, blinking in confusion. She pushed her hair from her eyes, and the movement made the blanket slide down to her lap. The black, lace-edged tank top she wore stretched indecently over her pert breasts, and her breath shook.

"Yes, sir? What happened?" Her gaze darted around the room, scanning for an emergency.

"Nothing happened."

"But..." Her brow furrowed and she drew her blanket up over her breasts and tucking it primly under her arms. She searched his face, her dark eyes wide. "Is there something I can assist you with, Mister Leduc?" Her body squirmed hopefully. He almost felt bad.

He pulled the blanket from her, leaving her on the white bottom sheet with only the obscene tank top and a tiny pair of boy short panties to preserve her modesty. Not lingerie, and probably not meant to be seen by him, which made it all the sexier.

He tugged her tank top up, exposing her breasts and her sexy pierced nipples, then drew down her shorts and threw them on the floor. He grabbed a pillow off the wing back chair and tossed it on the bed.

"Face down with your hips on the pillow."

"Nooo..." If he had any empathy, her whimper would have made him feel guilty, but she did as she was told.

"Spread your legs."

"What are you doing, sir?"

"Whatever I want to, Miss Korsgaard."

He spread her legs wider, kneeling between them. She tilted her ass toward him, the round cheeks of it begging for his hands.

"Please," she whispered, shivering. "Please use me. Please let me come."

"So you've never had anything in your ass?"

"No!"

Whether that was an admission of being inexperienced, or a protest because she wanted to stay inexperienced, he wasn't sure.

He dropped the lube and small glass plug onto the bed beside her face.

"Please – why are you doing this?"

"Because you're letting me." He grabbed her ass, separating her cheeks and looking at her tightly puckered anus. How did men fit in their women this way?

"No, please. I'll be a good girl," she begged. "Please – I'll suck your cock so well you'll forget all about this idea. I'll give you orgasm amnesia!"

"Is that a real condition?"

"I'll do my damnedest to make it one, sir," she babbled.

"I think this is called the bargaining stage, Miss Korsgaard. You'll feel much better when you simply accept this is going to happen."

"No...oh, God. I'm so desperate right now it would take one second. Please can I touch myself?"

"Absolutely not."

Her bottom lip trembled, but she nodded. Four days of teasing, and she was completely biddable. Her muscles relaxed, and she melted into the mattress.

He ran the pad of his thumb over her anus, and her breath caught and held. Gently, he teased her there, circling, stroking, tickling. She wriggled but didn't try to get away. He opened the lube and squirted some at the top of her ass, then watched as it started its slippery descent to her back hole.

"I'm trying to teach you better self-control, Miss Korsgaard. If you can stop yourself from soaking that pillow with your needy pussy, maybe I'll choose to let you come."

She rocked her hips against the pillow and he landed a stinging smack on her ass, his print blooming bright red, making him want to add more yet not destroying the perfection just yet.

"Stop that, or I'll take a belt to your pretty pussy," he said, wishing that keeping her on edge wasn't part of the plan. Watching her do something so instinctive and uninhibited because of him was a power trip, and the motion of her hips and ass, almost made him too weak to stop her. Precome leeched into his jeans, but he ignored his own discomfort.

She stopped rubbing against the pillow, dropping her forehead to the bed.

"You are the cruelest man I've ever met. That huge plug is never going to fit. You're going to hurt me."

"Hurting you makes me hard, Miss Korsgaard, but that's not the point of this." He picked up the plug – the smallest in the set he'd ordered. "This shouldn't hurt. This is so that I don't damage you when I take you here sometime in the future."

"So you *are* planning to have sex with me eventually?" she ground out.

"Maybe," he teased. "I'm not sure I'm interested." If he were any more interested his dick would explode.

He slid the plug against her anus, watching in fascination as she clenched against it. Her fists curled into the bottom sheet and she was whispering "No, no, no."

"No?" He pulled the plug away, and she shifted backward as though her body wanted it even if her brain didn't.

"Oh, for fuck's sakes. Just do it."

He raised his hand to swat her again, but decided words might be better this one time. "Now you're in a rush? Maybe I should skip prepping you and shove my cock in there." He pressed his hips against her ass and slid his finger through the lube.

"No!" She shuddered. "I'm sorry. I'll behave. Don't stick your monster cock in my ass with no prep or you'll have to bring me to the hospital." Even though the words were vehement, her hips started to rock again, pushing against his finger with every rock backward.

Her body started to open to him, and his finger slipped slowly into her up to the first knuckle. She hissed and her ass clenched around his finger. A grunt escaped him, and his cock twitched hard.

"Please, Mister Leduc...sir...master." She was sobbing, and his cock felt as if it was going to burst. She moaned. "Oh fuck, do it if you want to. I'll take anything right now. Anything you want. Please just let me come."

Reluctantly, he withdrew his finger, and pressed the plug against her instead. She mewled, but let him fuck it into her as he watched her body accept it bit by bit. By the time it was fully seated in her body, the base holding her ass cheeks slightly apart, and they were both breathing hard.

"Master? Now why would you call me that?" he asked, his voice gruff. "If you're a slave to anything, it's to your body, not to me."

"It's you I want." She shoved back at him, nudging at his cock again, smearing lube from her ass across the front of his jeans. "You've shown me who's the master of my body, and it's not me."

He flipped her over and pulled the pillow out from where it was still half under her body. Soaked. He shoved the pillow close to her face.

"Look what you did."

She shook her head, sweat dampened strands of hair sticking to her face and curling around her neck.

"Please, master! I'm sorry. I can't control how you make me feel." Her arms fell helplessly over her head, and her breasts jiggled, the barbells in them glinting prettily in the firelight.

"I told you the rules." He crawled on top of her sweet little body, and straddled her thighs. One tug and his jeans unbuttoned with a quick series of pops. The girl panted and wriggled beneath him.

"Please, Mister Leduc, can I suck your cock?" she whispered, pleading with her eyes.

So tempting.

He wrapped his hand around his painfully erect dick and drew it from his precome dampened jeans.

The girl squirmed, trying to move lower, her gaze fastened on his cock. Her lips parted as if she was already imagining sucking him off. She was so fucking beautiful.

He ran his hand over his shaft. So desperate for her, but this was good for her – to feel who was in charge, rather than just saying the words.

Watching her hungrily, he began to slowly stroke himself. She claimed she'd never wanted a man so badly, but he'd never wanted a woman before her. Now she was all he could think about.

"Don't fucking move."

"What?" she squeaked as she clued into what he planned to do. "You wouldn't!"

Her eyes widened as he stared at her beautiful face. His own abrasive hand tight around his erection, he pleasured himself. Not using her when she was begging for him was the most extreme display of self-restraint he'd ever managed.

He loved this game of cat and mouse, with neither yet both of them winning.

"If you come on my stomach instead of in my mouth, I'll never forgive you. Maybe you don't want to have sex with me, but this is too much. I can't do this anymore." Tears welled in her eyes, spilling over even as she held very still, like he'd told her to.

"Such a good girl," he murmured, jacking off to the delicious combination of the smell of her arousal and the tears that trickled from her eyes. "You'll get this eventually, but you have to prove that you understand the order of things between us."

"But I do!"

"No, you don't." He grunted, and his hips bucked spasmodically as he tried not to come right away. It was a miracle he'd lasted this long. "If you understood, you'd ask what I want, not tell me what you want. You keep trying to get your way."

"Please, Master – don't you want me?"

"I do. But anyone can fuck a woman's body – fucking her mind is so much sweeter."

His balls were so tight it set his teeth on edge. Pressure built as he pumped his erection in a cruel fist, watching the trembling of her bottom lip and the tears streaking from her eyes to drip into her ears before hitting the mattress.

Come – hot, agonizing – boiled up from his balls, burst from his cock, spewing all the way to her chin, painting her from there to her navel in thick ribbons. She cried out as every lash of it hit her skin. Grimly satisfied, he smeared the mess he made with one hand, coating her chest and belly but avoiding her still-healing nipple piercings.

The girl hyperventilated, weeping, her distressed cries making his cock jerk back to attention.

"Look what you made me do," he admonished, holding up his hand to show her.

"Please..." she whimpered.

"Clean this." He held his hand in front of her face, and she licked the sticky mess from his palm with frantic movements of her adorable little tongue. She sucked each one of his scarred fingers, moaning with impatience. The suction of her pretty mouth on his fingertips almost swayed him to relent.

He got off of her, trying to hide the weakness in his legs. He was shaking almost as badly as she was. She crawled after him, stopping when she reached the edge of the mattress. As he tucked his still rampant hard-on back in his jeans and rebuttoned, she watched him with forlorn disbelief.

"Master, if you don't want me, may I touch myself?"

"You may," he replied, loving the relief in her eyes because it meant his next words would be all the more entertaining. "But you may not come."

She shrieked and threw a pillow at him. He deflected it easily and grabbed her hard by the hair. She screamed and screamed, crying, almost touching him, but ultimately not forgetting the rules.

"That's enough with the hysterics, Miss Korsgaard." He gave her head a little shake, and she quieted, watching him miserably.

"Now – that plug stays in until you shower in the morning. If you need to relieve yourself before then, you must ask my permission to remove it. The come I've marked you with stays on your skin until you shower in the morning."

She sobbed, but nodded.

"After your shower I'll be forcing the next size plug into you, so make sure you work though your feelings about that beforehand. Some protesting is cute, but I won't tolerate it every time."

She nodded again, turning to kiss his palm when he cupped her cheek. As much as she'd protested, it was obvious she fucking loved this.

"What do you say to me?" he prompted.

"I'm sorry, Master. Thank you, Master."

"For?"

"For plugging my ass and marking me. For being patient. And for reminding me who I belong to."

Belong to. They'd never discussed it, but she understood his feelings on the matter and accepted them. The fact that she didn't seem to need fancy words or declarations from him meant everything. She read him, and he needed that from her.

He nodded. "Good girl." He stroked her hair and she leaned into the caress. "I know the past few days have been difficult for you, but if you continue to behave, tomorrow evening you'll be rewarded."

Her eyes lit, and he smiled at her more confidently than he felt.

"Goodnight, Miss Korsgaard."

"Goodnight, Master."

He left the room and headed back to his own, knowing it would take forever before he slept again.

*

The tap, tap, tap of Miss Korsgaard's patent kitten heels on his office's flagstone floor distracted Severin from the documents he was supposed to be reviewing. Figures danced and writhed before his eyes as he struggled to make sense of the information Rodrigo had brought for him to review.

"So, as you can see, it's finally done. The property. The house. All yours."

Severin leaned back in his chair, staring at the paperwork. He'd never completed high school, let alone college. All he knew was how to manipulate metal and fire to do his bidding. He wasn't someone who could think in chess moves, three steps ahead. His life was designed to be controlled, predictable. Thoughts about certain things, like fighting and art and finding balance in a piece he created – physical things came fast. There he could be decisive.

But he wasn't a businessman. No one would ever discuss philosophy or literature with him. He'd read a lot, but couldn't analyze what he'd read the way people like Rodrigo and Miss Korsgaard could. And numbers like Rodrigo dealt with? They didn't make sense to him on the best of days.

"So the investments you suggested turned out in our favor."

"Yes." Rodrigo's expression was neutral. It was never like the man to pat himself on the back, but he'd taken Severin's stipends from his family over the years and turned them into a fortune for them both.

Severin sighed, the turmoil of his thoughts confusing him. The money meant freedom from people who'd never cared about him in the first place. Rodrigo had helped Severin put an offer on this house, and they'd accepted. No other Leduc had set foot on this land in almost twenty-five years. Sutton once claimed his mother had come when Church's mother died, but if she'd been there, Severin hadn't recognized her.

There'd been many strangers in the house that day, and he'd spent most of it locked in his room listening to loud music. He hadn't been there for Church. Couldn't be. She'd died, and Severin had tried never to speak of her again. She'd betrayed them both by leaving. She'd fucking promised. It had been a pretty lie.

As for the Leducs – he didn't know how to feel. He'd given up his stipend years ago, paying Sutton, himself. The money that transferred into Miss Korsgaard's account every two weeks came from his personal account. He monitored each transaction to make sure she was adequately compensated for her work. He'd told Rodrigo to double it because she'd taken over Sutton's work in her absence. Miss Korsgaard had objected, but her reaction had been fleeting, guarded, until he'd explained his reasoning. Their sexual dynamic wasn't what she was being paid for, even though her nipples, which poked impudently at her blouse, distracted him through the entire conversation.

But enough about Korsgaard and her perfect body and lovely face. Enough of how he caught her giving him looks of longing, and how he could hear her squirming in frustration in her bed at night.

Focus, man.

The house.

The house and the property were his last tie to his fucked-up family. Once he signed the paperwork – that was it. Done.

"As you can see, it's a fair price. More than fair."

Yes. The number they'd set was almost a gift – to finally be rid of him, he assumed. The house had been bought specifically to store him. A mansion for a child. They'd never lived there as a family. Never slept in it overnight. It was a pretty cage for the animal they hadn't wanted to keep.

Miss Korsgaard set out the coffee she'd made them then lingered on the threshold of the room. None of this had to be a secret from her. There were things he'd pieced together that he didn't want her to know, but then Rodrigo didn't know those things either. Sutton knew, and Church, but there was no reason to cheapen harsh memories with too much retelling. His childhood wasn't a sideshow.

"Join us if you'd like, Miss Korsgaard."

Gingerly, she sat.

He scanned the document in front of him. The pen in his hand bent and almost snapped as he stared at the name of the other signatory.

"Who is Loïc Leduc?"

Rodrigo cocked his head. "I'm not sure. We know Martine, Aurelie and Camille. Loïc is a new one."

His mother, Martine. His sisters, Aurelie and Camille – if he was even remembering their names right – had been born before they sent him away. Who was this Loïc? They'd tried to find out his father's name, but that man was elusive. Maybe this was an uncle or something?

"Like I've said before, Sev – if you want answers, we can hire another private investigator. They don't have much online though, and the last two investigators came up empty for some reason."

Severin nodded, but he didn't want to know. Not really. If they didn't give a shit about him, why would he go out of his way to find out more? They were strangers to him because they'd chosen to be strangers. He'd harbored a small hope that his sisters would initiate contact with him when they became adults, but the years had passed with nothing. They would be twenty-five and twenty-eight now. Did they even remember he existed?

"They don't deserve you, Severin." Rodrigo's tone was harsh.

Severin smiled automatically. Well-meaning people had been saying that to him for years, but it didn't erase the feelings that came with knowing he wasn't worth keeping. Not even worth giving to a new family. He'd been mothballed and forgotten, like the cars he kept at the back of the garage.

"Stop it," Rodrigo snapped.

Severin narrowed his eyes. "Stop what?"

"Even after all these years, you still think you were the problem. They're either idiots or monsters, Sev." Rodrigo jabbed a finger at the paperwork. "Just sign. Get them out of your life and forget about them."

"Like they forgot about me?" He sighed. "If they hadn't kept my sisters maybe I could feel differently, but if they're not here with me, I'm guessing they kept them. Maybe my issues made me difficult to parent."

"Your issues are all the direct result of what they did to you!" Rodrigo snapped, shoving his chair back and lurching to his feet, his dark eyes ablaze with fury. "For fuck's sakes, Severin, no matter what you were like as a child – even if you were the most terrible little shit on the planet – you didn't deserve this. You remember the big house and the horses and the fancy cars. The servants. They bought you a fucking mansion. There was no reason to send you away like they did, even if you were emotionally disturbed, which I don't think you ever were. They had the resources to keep you close and to get you help. To have nannies raise you nearby, if not in their house. Something happened. I wish you'd tell me. I wish you'd let me go there so I could punch every last one of them in the face."

Severin didn't know what else to do except laugh at Ro's strong feelings on the subject. "How would that help anything?"

"It would make me feel better," Rodrigo said, sitting back in his chair, as if he'd just realized he'd made a scene. It wasn't like him to lose his temper. That was more Severin's forte.

Rodrigo smoothed his hair and straightened his jacket. So debonair. He and Miss Korsgaard were a perfect match. As usual, Severin was the one who didn't fit.

"I think you're afraid to find out why," Rodrigo went on. "The truth will change the story you pieced together in your head when you were a kid. You're too comfortable playing the villain."

"You can say that again," Miss Korsgaard said with a bitterness that was probably a reflection of the second plug he'd worked into her ass before the meeting.

Rodrigo arched a brow and turned his gaze to the girl, as though her statement had been in reference to him and he planned to correct her.

"I could have opted for a larger plug, Miss Korsgaard."

Her calm façade dissolved and she groaned. "Please, Mister Leduc." She eyed Rodrigo uneasily then turned her attention back to Severin.

"Please a bigger plug?"

"No!"

"Go remove the one in now, Miss Korsgaard, then come back."

"Yes, Master." She covered her mouth with her hand and glanced from him to Rodrigo, then away, her face glowing a charming red.

Rodrigo chuckled as he watched her go. "Master? You've taken her well in hand."

"You think her submitting to me is funny, Rodrigo?" He let his words and eyes convey cold menace.

"No, I...I didn't mean to start a fight with you. She's just so prim that you'd never suspect."

"Like you," Severin pointed out.

Rodrigo gave him a sharp look.

"No one would suspect the wolf that hides so quietly in that suit," he clarified.

The other man inclined his head.

Although Rodrigo wasn't all wolf when it came to his kinks, no one but Severin knew that.

"You're attracted to her."

"I don't know a dominant that wouldn't be, but I'll never touch what's yours without your permission."

Severin turned his coffee cup with his fingertips. "I'm training her."

"For?"

"Me." He shrugged. "I'm enjoying it, but I'm not sure how far it's safe to go before I break her."

"You're in a position I've never been in, Sev, having her live under your roof and being alone together so much. If you start feeling like you've gone too far, that's probably a good indication to stop."

"Is five days of edging too much?"

"Five days?" Rodrigo asked, incredulous. "If you were only seeing her once in a while, that would be one thing, but you're together twenty-four seven."

"So should I stop waking her up in the middle of the night?"

Rodrigo whistled, sounding impressed. "Bastard."

"She fascinates me," Severin admitted. "I'm a little obsessed."

"That's how you're supposed to feel about your submissive. Minnow's a very beautiful woman. If she's managed to get you out of the self-made prison you're in, I'll love her forever."

Severin frowned.

"In a completely platonic way."

"Well..."

"What?"

"I have a favor to ask."

"Anything."

"I want you to hold her down while I fuck her."

Rodrigo slipped a finger into the collar of his shirt, tugging on it as if it was too tight, even though he wore no tie and his top two buttons were undone.

"Why?"

"Because I think it'll blow her mind, and I also think she'll hurt herself."

"Hurt herself?"

"I'm not going to let her come, and she's probably going to lose it."

Rodrigo sighed, sounding pained. "Asking me to do this isn't fair. You know how much I like to watch, but I don't want you getting angry at me again."

"Like you give that much of a damn, Ro? You have a million friends and business associates. Even if something makes me angry, it's not like I'm your only friend."

Rodrigo rubbed a hand over his face in frustration. "Do you still think I'm so attentive to your portfolio because of your money?

It was never about the money. I've never enjoyed someone's company as much as I enjoy yours – even when you're being a fucking jerk. I don't have to act civilized around you."

"So quit acting like you don't want to hold her down for me."

"You know I do. I just want to know what the rules are, and I want a guarantee that you're not going to change those rules without telling me."

The fire in the hearth made the room uncomfortably warm.

Rodrigo averted his gaze to one of his metal cuff links. "And what will Minnow think of this?"

"Does it matter? She can always safeword. I doubt she will." They assessed each other for a moment. "What did you say to each other after I left?"

Rodrigo coughed, his expression neutral. "Her feelings were hurt but she spent her time trying to calm me down."

"That's all?"

"Pretty much."

The conversation Severin had imagined taking place between them about how pathetic he was hadn't happened? He'd imagined them laughing at his flight response all the way back to the house, where he'd drunk himself into a stupor. After that, he'd sat in the same chair in which he was now sitting, and imagined them having sex on Ro's living room floor.

"You didn't fuck her?"

Rodrigo grimaced at him. "No! For fuck's sake, why would I do that to you? And why do you think she'd want me? It's you she's obsessed with. I can hardly argue with her taste in men."

"You think you'd like to trade places with her, but I don't think you're enough of a switch to handle submitting to me."

A heavy silence ensued. Rodrigo didn't bother arguing, but Severin knew what he was thinking.

"You are attracted to her?" Severin asked, shuffling papers on his desk, trying to look like he didn't care.

"I won't take her from you."

As if on cue, the click of Miss Korsgaard's shoes neared.

She paused in the doorway.

"Kneel there, Miss Korsgaard."

She knelt quickly, either out of fear or eagerness. If she wasn't more careful she'd ruin her hose and he'd need to spend hours buying her another million replacements for them on the internet. This dominance business was hard work.

He gazed at the papers from his family and pushed them aside for now. "Mr. Solis will be spending time with us this evening," he said, meaningfully.

Her brows knitted. "Oh?"

"Are you going to refuse?"

She pressed her lips together. "What are you going to do to me?"

"You have a safeword." He got to his feet and went to her, then nudged her knees wider with the toe of his boot. She couldn't spread them very wide because of the sleekness of her pencil skirt.

She gave a bemused shrug. "Okay."

"Good girl. This will be fun."

"Fun for me, Mister Leduc?"

"Hmm..." He looked over at Rodrigo. "Probably not."

Chapter Nine

Severin held out his hand, and Minnow took it, even though it was probably a bad idea. After the past few days she was ready to do anything to please him – to get relief. She'd never felt so out of control before. The edging was making her...edgy. Reckless. The unrelenting ache in her lower belly flared and dulled in a series of waves that didn't let her rest. She'd barely slept in days, between his hands and mouth on her, and the hooks he was inserting into her mind.

"First things first," Severin said as he began to unbutton her blouse. The impatient tug of his fingers as he worked rekindled her need in the span of a heartbeat.

He slid his hand into her blouse, cupping her bare breast and running a thumb absently over her nipple. "No bra. Good girl." He pinched her nipple lightly and a tight pull ran from her breast to her pussy. She gasped, wanting to rub against him like a cat, but remembering not to touch him.

She wanted his cock immediately – any way she could get it – but how much would he expect her to play with Rodrigo?

Without fanfare, he unzipped her skirt and let it fall to the floor. In only her stockings and panties, she felt far too naked and vulnerable in front of the two men. They were so damned big. And dressed. And they were both staring at her with a hunger that made her shiver.

As easily as if she was a toy, Severin lifted her to the edge of his desk, the wood surface warm under her because of the nearby fireplace. Her ass still felt achy and uncomfortable from the plug she'd taken out.

Severin took off his own shirt, baring his disconcerting muscle, then went to Rodrigo.

"Are you sure you're okay with this?" Severin asked him, voice low.

"Yes."

The two of them clasped hands, as though this were a business deal, but the heat in their gazes as they turned back to her belied the civil gesture.

Button by button, Rodrigo opened his shirt, revealing his toned chest and a surprising wealth of tattoos. He tossed his impeccable, well-tailored shirt on the couch.

"This one is new," Severin said, pointing at Rodrigo's chest.

"I got it a few months ago."

Where Severin's skin was covered in demons, Rodrigo's was covered in monsters. The two of them almost matched in tattoo styles and coverage, except that clothing could cover Rodrigo's.

The sight of them approaching her together made Minnow dig her fingernails into her palms, as she tried to calm down. What was Severin planning?

More torture? Probably.

She wanted to cry in frustration – maybe to bite him and yell and be a brat – but didn't want to break down or misbehave in front of Rodrigo and embarrass Severin. If she'd figured anything out about the man she served, it was that his mind moved in unexpected ways. Whatever he intended to do, he'd probably make her love it even as she hated it.

Severin grabbed a condom from his desk drawer and tossed it to Rodrigo.

"What's this for?" Rodrigo asked as Minnow looked from one to the other in panic. "You said I was just watching and holding her down."

"Watching in an active sense."

"Have you fucked her yet?"

"No. You're going to give me a demo."

"What?" Minnow blurted. Her outburst was covered by Rodrigo's own.

"No. You got so jealous last time you took off. I'm not going to fuck your girlfriend. You're not even a voyeur."

"Please no, Mister Leduc!" Was he serious?

"I'm sorry, Miss Korsgaard. You know how things are with me. I've been stalling for two days because I can't get past the fact that I don't know what the hell I'm doing. I need to see the real thing. Porn isn't trustworthy."

"It's intuitive, Sev. Just start and she'll help you."

"I don't want her help. When I take her for the first time, I want to know what I'm doing."

"But Mister Leduc," she said plaintively, crawling closer to him on the desk, "It's you I want, not Mr. Solis." She leaned toward him, mouth hovering over his corrugated stomach, wanting to lick her way down to his cock and coax him to change his mind.

He stroked her hair affectionately. "Oh, and don't let her come, Rodrigo."

"No, no!" Minnow cried. She grabbed Severin's hand then let go of it so fast she wasn't sure it hadn't burned her. "Please, Mister Leduc! Can't you just practice on me when I'm asleep or something? I'll sign consent forms. I don't even care!"

"Miss Korsgaard," he said coldly, "you're insulting my guest. You may choose to safeword, and I'll respect that, but at this point all I'm seeing are theatrics like the ones you had last night."

Shit.

"Sorry, Mr. Solis. I just..."

Rodrigo chuckled. "You want him. Believe me, I get it. It's no offense to me."

"Yes!" she cried, kneeling on the desk and clasping her hands in her lap. "I want him so bad I feel like I'm going to die."

"You can't die from sexual frustration," Severin grumbled. "Trust me."

She wanted to argue with him, but she had the feeling undermining his authority would be end in punishment, and not a light one. Rightly so.

"If I let you do this," she said to Severin, gazing up at him earnestly, "I'm afraid it will make you think I lust after him, which I don't. I have...feelings."

"Feelings?" Severin asked, as though not familiar with the word.

She groaned, knowing saying her next words aloud were going to be a mistake. "I have feelings for you. I don't want to jeopardize what we have by obeying your order in this."

Real smooth, Minnow. This is where he freaks out and bolts again.

He blinked at her as though she was speaking a language he didn't really understand. Maybe she was.

"I'm doing this for what we have. You deserve a dominant who knows what he's doing, not a fumbling teenage boy."

She spread her knees and pouted up at him. "You already know exactly where my clit is. That's more than what a lot of men know."

"Nice try." He lifted her down and guided her to the leather ottoman coffee table and pushed her belly down. "So will you do this for me or not, Ro?"

"You're asking me to fuck your hot girlfriend?" Rodrigo snorted. "Like I haven't done it mentally several times since I got here?"

"Asshole."

"Hey, if she was mine you'd do the same."

"Touché."

"You know, this is exactly what I was thinking of when you bought this table," Rodrigo murmured. "Miss Korsgaard is much prettier on it than the girl I'd envisioned at the time."

"This isn't at all what I was thinking when I bought it."

"No?"

"Of course it was what I was thinking, you idiot."

Rodrigo choked out a laugh that was far too lighthearted for the situation Minnow was about to be in, as far as she was concerned.

Men.

As Rodrigo's mirth calmed, Severin handed him a set of ropes. Where had he hidden those? Sneaky jerk.

A small sound of protest slipped out, when Severin spread her legs, but she cooperated. He tied her thighs to one set of ottoman legs as Rodrigo tied her wrists to the other two. With her whole belly and chest supported, she could have taken a nap if she wasn't naked and being admired by two hot guys with impressive bulges in their pants.

Rodrigo moved behind her to stand near Severin, who seemed to be admiring his handiwork.

"She keeps begging for sex instead of asking how to please me."

Rodrigo *tsked*.

"It's her selfish little cunt's fault, I'm sure," Severin continued.

"The submissive always claims it's not their fault. It's our job to teach them otherwise."

Minnow ground her teeth in frustration, but knew better than to offer a rebuttal.

They both shifted to the floor. At least the area rug under the table was plush.

Hands rubbed her back, and she relaxed into the chestnut leather, breathing it in. The bench was so well padded the upholstery tacks didn't dig into her skin.

"Sexy little pussy," Rodrigo said to Severin. "Hopefully I fit."

She rolled her eyes. Men and their dick hubris.

She tried to ignore them, but they went on discussing her as if she was as sentient as the coffee table they'd draped her over.

A hand smoothed over her ass cheek.

"Didn't you send her upstairs to take out a buttplug? Must have been a small one. She's closed right back up." A finger brushed her there, sending sparks of arousal through her. She tried to jerk away but the ropes held her in place. "Good thing you hadn't planned on using her ass tonight."

"Typical. She's disobedient if I don't keep her in line."

Minnow glared down at the ottoman. Severin accusing her of being disobedient right down to her asshole was completely unfair.

"She doesn't like being touched there but won't safeword it." Severin said with a smile in his voice. "You don't get to have her ass, though. At least, not the first time."

"She's never been fucked there?"

"No."

Rodrigo groaned. "She's going to break your dick when you take her there. Make sure you work her up to it. Even then – go slow and lots of lube."

"Yeah, I know. I looked it up. Did you see her nipple rings? They're healing well. You did a good job."

"Of course I did, even though the two of you were determined to distract me from my work. Good idea to put her facedown like this though. It would be far too tempting to play with them."

"Tell me about it. It's a constant temptation."

They talked about her hair, how pretty it was, how good a handhold it made. They talked about her clit and how a clit hood piercing would, be hot. She was manhandled, groped, smacked, tickled, teased, kissed, licked, bitten – then they both sat down and had a drink while they chatted about some upcoming movie that wanted two of Severin's motorcycles.

The tight knot of frustrated desire in her belly spread heat through her body. Her breasts and pussy ached. Her asshole tingled. She shifted in discomfort trying not to beg for Severin to ease her as she rubbed her pelvis against the leather, not quite able to get any pressure on her clit no matter how she tilted her hips.

One of them put their glass on her butt cheek, and the chill from the ice made her shiver.

"Hmm. Your coffee table is lovely, but not very functional with all of the rounded parts."

"I know. It keeps shuddering too. Maybe it's not very good for holding things."

She squirmed, clamping her mouth closed on all the words that wanted to come out. The glass on her back teetered, tipped, then ice slid out onto her skin. She gasped, and the wet, cold puddle pooled in the valley of her lower back.

"Damn. I guess I'd better clean this up," Severin rumbled. He pretended to try to grab the ice cubes, then slid them over her back instead, trailing one up the back of her neck and around to her chin, eventually pushing it into her mouth. The bite of whiskey on her tongue was welcome, and she sucked on the cube hoping it would help to distract her. She needed to cool down.

Severin put the other ice cube in his mouth then took it out again. With the help of his fingers, the ice cube started an alarming descent, leaving a shivery, dripping pattern of ice water on her ass then sliding down to her clit. He rubbed it over her there as she tried to shift away – the molten heat of her pussy responding to the ice in violently pleasurable, yet disturbing ways.

Something freezing prodded at her entrance, then broached her, easing the sensation of cold up inside her heat, freezing her and making her hotter. Was he trying to start a fucking tornado in there? She tried hard not to move, but the thickness of his finger in her pussy was too good, and she rocked against it, whimpering, and clenching her inner muscles until he groaned.

"Are you sure you want me to do this?" Rodrigo asked him as he tore the condom open. Minnow watched in desperation as he rolled it on, no longer caring who or what fucked her, as long as it happened immediately.

"Yes," Severin replied, the word ragged as it left his mouth.

"Last chance to safeword, *preciosa*," Rodrigo said.

She opened her mouth to say something – maybe to give one final protest even if she didn't safeword, but looked up at Severin's face and shut her mouth again. He was watching her with such affection, she couldn't object to giving him this, if he felt he needed it. He leaned in and brushed his lips along her cheekbone, and the tenderness of the gesture made tears well in her eyes.

"This won't change how I feel about you," he whispered in her ear. She shivered at the feel of his breath, but her chest felt full. Maybe he didn't love her, but the fact that he'd admitted he felt anything about her was a big fucking deal.

She caught his lips with her own, and he reciprocated the kiss rather than pulling reproachfully away.

Rodrigo's cock slid through the copious lubrication her body had been manufacturing for days, and Severin moved down her body to kneel beside her posterior, putting his big hand on her lower back so that her ass arched up.

"See? You know how to signal her to do what you want, even though you don't realize it." Rodrigo rubbed the tip of his cock up and down until Minnow squirmed impatiently. "With your size, don't rush this part unless you've been having a lot of sex with her. If you shove in hard and fast you'll hurt her. You don't want to break your pretty toy – well, not unless you mean to."

The thick head of his cock broached her and Minnow's eyes widened. Rodrigo shouldn't be rushing anything either, apparently. She had the urge to look back and make sure he wasn't shoving something else up there. The warmth after the ice, the fullness after the days of torment, made Minnow's eyes roll back. Goose bumps chased over her skin, and she made a small sound of distress as he fucked his length into her. He bottomed out before he was all the way in.

Rodrigo grunted. "Fuck, Sev – she feels so fucking good. This is going to be brutal for you. Take it easy with her if you want to use her regularly." He stayed still and swept his palms over her back, relaxing her and giving her time to get used to his size. "Once you're in, give her a minute to adjust, and so that you don't blow your fucking load right away." His voice was tight, but not as tight as the ball of need in her belly.

Someone needed to touch her clit. Fuck. It was so humiliating and hot having Rodrigo talk Severin through this as though he was teaching him how to fix a carburetor.

Rodrigo thrust into her, giving her more than her body could handle, and she whimpered. He pulled out until just the tip was inside her, and she whined an objection at the loss.

The slow, rolling thrust of Rodrigo's hips took Minnow's breath away.

"From here you just have to decide what you want to do. If you want her to come, play with her clit. If you don't, fuck her hard and fast, or hurt her to distract her – but either of those can backfire on you. Don't forget you have other ways to touch her. You can bite her, spank her, play with her ass –"

His breath caught and he seemed to lose his train of thought as he bucked into her hard and fast for a few strokes. She cried out in bone-melting pleasure even though her teeth rattled. God – she hadn't been used roughly for ages. Severin's hand came down on the back of her neck. Rodrigo slowed again, both he and Minnow panting. Someone started playing with her ass as someone toyed with her clit. The intimate teasing touches, and the feeling of being trapped and used, had her skating close to the edge, her pussy clutching and aching. When she finally came, she was going to cramp up like a bitch.

"You have to decide why you're fucking her? Your pleasure? Hers? Are you doing it to make a point about who's boss? If it's a reward, keeping a rhythm and making sure she gets clit stimulation is most likely to get her off."

The words washed over her while she imagined Severin doing those things to her. Close – she was so fucking close. Her body clamped down, cramping in preparation for a massive orgasm.

Rodrigo stopped, gripping her hips hard to stop her from moving. They stopped touching her.

She sobbed low, the sound not quite human. They were so fucking evil.

"Not giving her what she wants is beautiful. Look at her shake," Severin growled.

"She almost came," Rodrigo laughed in self-derision. "Ugh. She's twitching around me. It's so hard to stop. Fuck...so close."

Severin pressed his index finger between her lips, and she latched on to it, frantically sucking while he watched her with feverish eyes. "Please," she begged. "Please Severin – please just let me come. I'll do anything."

"You're interrupting the dominants talking, girl." Severin swatted her ass and Rodrigo gasped and pulled out fast, dropping his forehead to her back. The tickle of his breath was torture. Could she come just from the feel of a man's breath caressing her skin?

Rodrigo laid his cock between her ass cheeks and thrust against her, sliding against her sensitized bottom hole and pressing her pelvic bone against the leather, close and yet miles too far from her clit.

Severin grabbed hold of her hair, and as she gasped as he thrust his cock into her mouth, stretching her lips uncomfortably wide as she tried to accommodate him. Rodrigo swore and shuddered over her, the slip of the condom teasing her ass while he found his release. Severin lasted only a few thrusts before emptying into her mouth, forcing her to swallow fast if she wanted to breathe again.

She shuddered hard, on the very edge of orgasm.

"Don't you fucking come," Severin ground out, his grip on her hair tightening to the point of real pain.

Too late.

The painful tightness in her belly wound tighter, burst. Torturous pleasure boiled over her, scalding. She cried out in agony as her body clenched around nothing, the muscles in her stomach so taut and hard that it fucking hurt. For long moments she quivered and twitched, wishing the orgasm had been satisfying and brought relief, but it only made her aware of what she hadn't gotten. She lay limply in her bonds, exhausted and floaty, hating Severin and wondering when he'd pulled out of her mouth. Had she bitten him? He looked irritated.

Rodrigo was laughing and slapped Severin's arm. "Sometimes that happens, man. They get so wound up that they just spontaneously come all over themselves." Rodrigo patted her ass. "Was that a good orgasm, *preciosa*?"

"No," she whined, shifting in place, hoping someone would take pity on her.

"A ruined orgasm is almost worse than no orgasm," Rodrigo said.

Yes. Fucking yes, it was so true.

"You disobeyed me." Severin pulled his belt out of his still undone jeans, which were barely staying up. His dick was still out, and he was hard again. Still? The man was going to be the death of her.

"I'm sorry, Master. I didn't know how to stop. I tried to stop," She lied, cringing, waiting for the blow, but it never came. She'd meant to *try* to stop, but in the moment she'd forgotten.

He sat down heavily on the floor beside her, dropping the belt, and put his forehead on hers. "I can't punish you right now." Rodrigo untied her as Severin stroked her hair. "It's okay. You were a good girl, Minnow. You let me have what I wanted, and you tried your best to obey." He pulled her into his arms and carried her to the couch. Rodrigo had disappeared.

She blinked at Severin, trying to keep his face clear, but her eyes were too lazy to focus. Hearing him say her name with such approval had shot straight to her chest, starting a warm glow that had no business being there.

His mouth moved gently on hers as he whispered his approval, holding her carefully, as though she might break into a million pieces.

She was fucked.

He was so broken, but she was already his.

*

Minnow woke in bed alone the next morning, not remembering how she'd gotten there. When she realized Severin must have dressed her in his own shirt and put her to bed, her stomach fluttered. He hadn't brought her to bed with him, but the T-shirt meant something. Affection? An instinct to take care of her?

She stretched, realizing only then how sore she was. It would have been better if Severin had been the one to make her sore, but this was okay too, even if they'd ruined her orgasm on purpose. Submitting to Severin meant doing things his way, even if that meant letting his best friend screw her while he watched. If she'd come into this house vanilla or a virgin, none of this would have worked the same way. As it was, she was used to demanding dominants and was difficult to shock.

When she padded down the hall past his room, Severin wasn't in bed. He wasn't in the house at all, or at the forge, where she'd assumed he was, when she went to bring him lunch. The house was clean, so she took a long bath and read an entire eBook. Reading a romance had been a bad idea, though, because it had turned her on and Severin wasn't around to help her out. For a moment she wondered if she could get away with masturbating, but the gorgeous bastard would probably show up just in time to catch her.

It was difficult to believe Sutton would be home the next day. She'd been gone three weeks, and so much had changed between her and Severin since then. It almost felt like Sutton had been a figment of her imagination. Minnow felt herself blush at the thought of the older woman finding out how things now were between her and Severin.

Nervous, she gave the kitchen one last cleaning, hoping she hadn't left anything out of place. She also went through the house to make sure there weren't any stray undergarments or sex toys or bottles of lube lying around the common areas.

At about four the phone rang. She ran to the landline in the study, trying not to look at the coffee table she'd been tied to the night before.

"Hello?"

"Minnow? Hey – it's Church."

"Hi! Before you ask, no, he's not here. Not in the forge, not in the garage...I'm not sure where he is. He was gone when I woke up."

There was a pause at the other end. "No offense, but are you good with messages?"

She sat in Severin's big leather chair at his desk. It was ridiculous, but she felt like a rebel sitting there. In a momentary flash of brattiness, she propped her feet on his desk, then put them back down again because she'd gone far.

"Yes, I'm good with messages. I told him you called and I've been badgering him to call you back. I get the 'your king is displeased, peasant' face when I nag too much though."

Church's laugh was just how she remembered it, rumbling, warm. Too bad he'd moved away so soon after she'd joined the staff.

He must have lightened the mood around here. She could hear the kids shrieking in the background, like usual.

"It's so hard to be here when I should be at the house knocking him on his ass." He sighed, blowing a gust of air into the phone. "You know he's written me off at this point."

"No, I'm sure that's not it," she reassured him. "Maybe he's just not big on using the phone."

"He's a simple man, Min. Either you're with him or against him. It doesn't take much for him to believe you're against him."

Poor Church. "You're just trying to get established so you can make a secure life for your family. He's got to understand that."

"Yeah, but he doesn't. As far as he's concerned, we could have lived at the house, and off of him, forever. He doesn't get that I needed to do something with my life other than living there, waiting for him to need me. He keeps trying to give me half of everything, but my relationship with him has never been about the money."

"Is anyone's?"

"No. Between me, you, Sutton, and Rodrigo, no one gives a shit about the money. Even he doesn't give a shit about the money. If anything, I think having it has made it too easy to hide from the world. He doesn't trust people because he doesn't know many." He told one of his daughters to give a toy back to her sister then had to tell them to stop shrieking.

"Between his first family abandoning him, and our mom dying, he just can't get over this idea that he was meant to be alone. It's turning into a self-fulfilling prophecy. Even when we were little kids he never trusted I wouldn't leave him. He'd be such a dick trying to push me away and prove he was right. It's exactly what he's doing now." She heard a loud bang and Church grumbled something under his breath. "Do you have any idea how fucking frustrating loving someone like that is? I wasn't the one who betrayed him, but I get to reap what they sowed. Fucking asshats."

"Does anyone know why his parents abandoned him?"

"His first parents," Church corrected. "My mom was his real mom, and then Sutton. I don't know what we would have done without her. That woman – I mean, I know she's paid for her trouble, but who would agree to take over parenting two teenage boys when they're in the middle of grieving? No amount of money could have made her love us like she does. At that age we needed someone who gave a damn even more than we needed someone to take care of us." His voice was thick with emotion, and she felt her heart breaking for them all over again.

"It just makes me so mad that he's writing me off. I've been with him for twenty-four years. Why doesn't he trust me?" He snorted. "I know why, but it doesn't make it any easier. But how can I fix that? I wanted to go look for the Leducs. Rodrigo and I were going to go, but Severin threw a fit and we backed off. I think he's afraid to find out the truth."

"Yeah. That's what Rodrigo said to him the other day." She thought about the forms Rodrigo had brought over for Severin to sign. Hopefully it would give him some closure, if it didn't give him peace.

Would Church know who Loïc Leduc was? Finding out had seemed important to Severin, but if he and Rodrigo didn't know, chances were Church wouldn't either. And as much as Church was on Severin's side, she didn't want to talk loosely about Severin's legal affairs, and yet felt bad that Severin had pushed him completely out of the loop.

"Anyway, I have to go help Ilse. Thanks for letting me vent, Minnow. Kick my brother for me, okay? Just in the shin. Tell him he's an ass."

"I like you, Church, but have you seen the man? Kicking him seems like a bad idea."

"Nah. He's a pussycat."

They both laughed.

"Call anytime. If he won't talk to you, I will. This place is making me stir crazy."

"Yeah. You have to find some hobbies that send you into town regularly. If you don't, civilization will seem unnaturally loud and busy in no time. You can't help him adapt if you let yourself become a hermit too."

"Point taken."

"Make it so."

"Aye-aye, Captain."

"Oooh...I knew I liked you."

They hung up, and Minnow went looking for Severin again. No luck.

She had a quiet dinner, putting aside a plate for him. How long before she should start to worry?

With Sutton coming home tomorrow, she'd sort of expected to spend the evening together fooling around, or at least being sexily and pointedly ignored, but maybe Sutton's imminent return didn't mean much to him. As much as she was excited to have the woman back – it got lonely at the house sometimes when Severin was in a solitary mood – she was also going to miss the lack of privacy for the relationship she and Severin seemed to be starting.

At eleven she put on her flannel pajamas and walked down to the car garage. Although she'd looked for him there earlier, and none of the cars seemed to be gone, she couldn't remember if she'd counted the bikes. She flipped on the lights and counted. All accounted for, and the garage didn't even smell faintly like exhaust.

Where the hell was he? Did someone pick him up to take him out somewhere? Had he gone out walking and broken his leg? Had he gone swimming in the lake and frozen?

Alone, in an old silent mansion, in the middle of nowhere, she suddenly didn't feel so safe. She lay in bed for a few minutes. There was a loud bang somewhere in the house, and she sat bolt upright again. Severin? Or was it a serial killer?

Fearful, she tiptoed through the entire house, finding no sign of what could have made the noise, scaring herself more with each passing minute, imagining dangerous criminals lying in wait for her.

Maybe Severin was back at the forge by now. What was better? Getting killed alone in the house, or getting killed alone in the yard? At least in the yard maybe Severin would find her before she bled out.

Why didn't she have his fucking cell number? Because the man never went anywhere, that's why! She should have asked

Church for the number when he'd called, but she hadn't wanted to admit she didn't have it.

Fine. She'd go looking for him yet again. She pulled on her jacket and boots, grabbed a flashlight, and crept through the barely lit house, feeling the chill before she even got to the door. Usually Severin laid fires in the fireplaces in the rooms they were using at night because he preferred them over the electric heaters, so she had no idea where the controls were, or if she was even allowed to touch them. She was afraid to set up a fire herself in case she did it wrong and burned the house to the ground.

At the main door to the back of the grounds she hesitated. She squinted into the darkness, expecting a creepily masked man or a dead body to appear any minute. Adrenaline coursed through her, and she had the urge to run back up to her room and hide in the back of the closet until morning. The house was so big no one would think to look for her in there, right?

A light flickered in the yard, but it was off to the far right of the forge, mostly concealed by trees. Her heart leaped. But then, maybe it wasn't Severin. Maybe it was her imagination. Maybe there was a brush fire.

Maybe he was regularly abducted by UFOs.

That would explain a lot.

Fuck. She wasn't leaving the house unarmed. She went back to the kitchen and grabbed a butcher knife, half afraid she'd panic and fall on the stupid thing, but carrying the whole knife block with her was an even dumber idea. She stared at the knife for a few minutes, imagined having it grabbed out of her hand and used on her, and put it away. Besides, if she nicked the blade, Sutton would use it to skin her alive.

Holding her breath, she opened the door and slipped outside, her heart hammering so loudly in her ears she couldn't hear anything else. She paused, waiting for her eyes to adjust, and turned on the flashlight before breathing again.

The grounds were silent other than the sound of wind in the branches. The chill seeped through the fabric of her pajamas, numbing her legs as she moved toward the flickering light. She passed the pool area and kept going, dry grass crunching under the soles of her boots no matter how quietly she tried to move. Her heartbeat tripped over itself as she neared the edge of the trees and attempted to peer around their obscuring wall. Fire crackled, and the scent of wood smoke drifted to her on the breeze.

"What are you doing?" a deep voice boomed from behind her.

Minnow shrieked. Her flashlight tumbled out of her fingers and she ran like hell.

Footsteps followed, just as fast, but somehow quiet compared to the pounding of her feet. Fear made her scream again, and she cut a circle around the forge and headed back toward the house, dodging around dark shapes on the ground. Hands snatched at her clothes. So close! She was almost at the house. She wanted a locked door, a knife, something!

She stumbled, like she'd dreaded she would, and he was on her – arm wrapped around her waist. Forgetting every self-defense course she'd ever taken, she wriggled and bit and scratched, but he took her down to the ground anyway, crushing her belly down on the frigid lawn. He covered her with his body, pinning her there, catching her flailing hands and trapping them against the ground.

Hot breath in her ear. The rapid thud of his heart against her back.

She bucked and shrieked, then whimpered when she realized she was completely at his mercy. Hips ground against her ass, along with an all too apparent hard-on.

"You shouldn't spy on me, Miss Korsgaard," Severin whispered harshly in her ear.

Oh fuck.

Oh God.

She sagged in relief.

"You scared the crap out of me!" She struggled to shift him off of her, but he didn't budge.

"You scared yourself."

"You chased me!"

"You came out here wanting to be chased," he accused. "You've seen horror movies. You know how this works. Pretty girl goes snooping around where she doesn't belong. Big man with a knife chases her."

"You have a knife?"

"I live outside. I always have a fucking knife."

She shuddered, and he snorted.

"For fuck's sake, Miss Korsgaard – does anything *not* turn you on?"

She laughed as the rush of endorphins and physical contact worked their evil magic.

"With you? I don't know, and that scares me."

He groaned and thrust against her ass. She arched into it, and he shifted just enough to swat her bottom. The sting, along with the rest of it, made her wish he'd yank down her pajama pants and fuck her.

Instead, he got off of her and picked her up, throwing her over his shoulder and walking through the night. In the circle of firelight he sat, then maneuvered her belly down over his lap, as if she weighed no more than a doll.

"You know I like my privacy, Miss Korsgaard. You shouldn't have come out here." He ran a hand over the back of her pants. "You're wearing flannel pajamas? Are you a child?"

"It's cold in the house!" she complained. "Some big jerk left me alone to freeze all day."

"I figured you could use some time alone too," he grumbled. "Even if you didn't, you have no right to spy."

He yanked down the back of her pants, and she shivered as the cool air caressed her bared flesh.

"Hey! I was worried all day, then by bedtime I was scared."

"Worried? Scared?"

"Well – I didn't know if you were angry at me," she explained. He never seemed to understand other people had feelings. "Then when you were gone so long I was afraid something might have happened to you." When he said nothing, she went on. "Then tonight I heard a noise in the house and I was afraid there was a prowler."

"A prowler?" He made a sound of amusement. "I don't think I've ever heard anyone use that word in real life. If you're going to be using words like prowler you need to start sleeping with curlers in your hair."

"I was worried about you, and you don't even care!" She swatted his calf in semi-mock annoyance, and the sound of irritation that came out of him made her insides twist into a knot. Self-preservation made her try to slide off his lap, but he held her in place.

"Sometimes I need to be alone. You can't follow me around all the time."

"It's my job to follow you around."

"Yeah. Your job." His laugh was humorless. "Don't fucking spy on me, Miss Korsgaard." The first swat landed hard, stinging her ass, and rattling her teeth. The next several were just as intense. Punishment. Not a joke. Not kink.

Damn it. Why was that hot?

He held her still, his big rough hand coming down on her ass again and again – smack, smack, smack. She'd thought she was pretty tough, but after several minutes of hard, fast spanks the fire in the firepit was nothing compared to the fire in her ass cheeks. She began to yelp in protest. When she tried to block with her hands, he caught both wrists at her lower back and held them there with one hand. Reflexively, she kicked out, and the next spank was even harder, jarring.

There was no way to get away from him – not with the disparity in their strength – and there was no way she was going to safeword something as minor as a spanking. He seemed to need it, because the longer it went on the less it seemed to be about her.

She sank into it, accepting the pain even though it went past the point of being something she could physically enjoy. Fuck, he was huge, and he had a hard fucking hand. It hurt, but she took it for him, pushing her safeword down when it threatened to spill out. She stared at the ground as it blurred in her teary gaze, wondering what had triggered his mood. It was hard to comfort a man who hated being touched.

Once it had gone on far too long, he slowed, and eventually stopped, resting his hand on her burning, throbbing ass. She could hear him struggle to slow his breathing. After all the worry of the day, she was glad just to be with him. Glad to have given him what he needed. Maybe she'd needed it too, to reconnect after he'd given her to Rodrigo last night.

Sooner than she wanted to move, he set her on her feet. She was shaky, but he grabbed her hips and turned her ass toward the firelight. The warmth hurt. He inspected his handiwork, then grunted, but his expression didn't give her any clue as to what he was thinking behind those hooded eyes of his. When he brushed his mouth along the damage he'd done, the kindle of arousal he stoked in her boneless exhaustion made her knees tremble. His mouth was hot and stung, but it also tickled and felt sexy, and his tongue and teeth explored bits of her he'd left undamaged. Her nipples were so hard they throbbed in time with her ass. Her pussy ached worse than the spanking had. When he stopped, her moan of distress gave her away.

"Get to bed, Miss Korsgaard. It's late."

She turned to face him. In the firelight his expression had already grown distant.

"You're not serious. You don't want..."

"No." For a man who didn't want, his dick seemed to heartily disagree.

"You don't have to talk. I could just –"

"Do men never tell you no?"

"Never before you. I'm not in the habit of offering men blowjobs if I'm not pretty sure they're interested." She decided not to gesture at his cock which, right then, had to be composing a note to the complaints department of Severin's twisted mind.

Whatever. Far be it from her to throw herself at a man who didn't want her. Okay, well with Severin that was a complete lie, but damn he was worth fighting for. It helped that she didn't really believe he was *dis*interested. If she'd had an ego, the man would have shattered it the first day.

Gingerly, she drew up her PJ bottoms, making sure not to let the elasticized waist drag over her skin. Even so, the drape of the fabric touching her, hurt.

"Anyway...goodnight, Mister Leduc," she said, trying to appear calm even though the itch of her drying tears probably meant her makeup was tracked down her face. "What do you want me to make for dinner tomorrow?"

"Whatever you feel like making."

"Don't you want me to make something special to welcome Sutton back?"

"She's not coming."

Her brows shot upward. "But – I thought she said tomorrow."

"She did. She changed her mind. The work at her sister's is taking longer than she thought." His expression was bleak. It had to be hard with Sutton leaving so soon after Church.

"She's coming back soon though?"

"Another week, she said."

Minnow shrugged. "A week is okay. We're okay here alone another week."

He bared his teeth, but it wasn't really a smile. "Go to bed."

All of his body language said this was what had him riled. A week, though? What was wrong with one more week? Sutton had been around for the past fifteen or so years – why was he begrudging her a bit of extra vacation? Was he that much of a control freak?

Duh. Yeah. He had every reason to be, though, after what life had done to him.

"Sutton will come back, Mister Leduc."

"She said she would." His tone was skeptical.

"Why wouldn't she? She loves you. You're her family."

"I'm not. Not really." He tossed a stick into the fire pit.

"She's coming back."

He glared. "They don't come back, Minnow. They never do."

"Stop it. You're being ridiculous."

"You're being naïve."

"But –"

He got to his feet and stalked off into the night. She waited for him to come back, but the bench was too hard to sit on, tender as she was.

When the fire had burned down to embers, she doused them with the bucket of water that sat nearby. She was frozen and literally falling asleep on her feet. Giving up, she trudged back to the house, not sure if she should be angry or sad – wishing she could track down his first parents and get in line to smack them.

Chapter Ten

Curled on her side, with her legs pulled up, the girl was a tiny bump under the covers in her big bed. One hand was curled in front of her mouth. In the pale morning light her face was young and vulnerable, and it made him feel things he didn't like. She was out here alone with him for another week, and he couldn't be trusted with that kind of responsibility. Not when his feelings for her sometimes turned dark.

Trusting himself alone with her out here was too much temptation for one sadist to handle. Well – maybe Rodrigo could trust himself, but Severin was new at having to control himself around a willing woman who apparently rarely if ever used her safeword. He'd never been good at controlling himself, and he didn't know if he could pass this test.

Only a few more days until Sutton came home. Then they'd have a chaperone at least. He was still talking to her every day, but her absence made him uneasy. The second delay in her coming back had been less unexpected than the first, but he hated it all the same. Too much could go wrong with her out there by herself. And her sister wasn't getting any younger. What if she decided to stay indefinitely? Her sister was probably easier to take care of than he was, and better company. And she was Sutton's actual, real family.

Sutton had enough money stashed away to retire anytime she pleased – to buy houses and cars and a new start. He was a grown man. It wasn't like he needed a nanny anymore.

How could he expect her to choose him over her own flesh and blood?

If she didn't come back it wouldn't surprise him. Church was never coming back. Maybe Church was what had kept Sutton here all along. They'd always had a strong bond. Church had always been the easy one, so Severin had never begrudged the fact that Sutton liked him more. She'd never said so, but Church was never any trouble, and had turned into someone she could be proud of.

Severin was a disappointment. None of the things she'd ever worked on with him had sunk in. He was the same mess he'd been as a teenager, only in a bigger shell.

Minnow gave a small cry but didn't open her eyes. Were people supposed to wake someone having a nightmare? He couldn't remember. Her breathing changed. She rolled onto her stomach and squirmed against the bed, whimpering. Not a nightmare. She was such a sensual little thing with her long eyelashes, pouting lips, and with her rounded ass that begged for his attention. He groaned inwardly, sinking back onto the couch beside the window. Apparently she even thought about sex when she was asleep. She mewled, and his cock went hard immediately, more than willing to accommodate.

What was she dreaming of? Or more importantly, who?

"Please." The word came out as a breathy whimper. "Oh please. I'll be a good girl."

He palmed his erection, meaning to readjust himself in his jeans, but he'd been up half the night wondering why he hadn't taken her the night before, and the series of erections he'd had as a result were starting to wear on him.

She was probably thinking about Rodrigo, and how hard she'd come when he fucked her. It was his own fault for insisting, but now she was probably going to fantasize about Ro forever. He'd have to live with that.

Watching Rodrigo fucking her had been so fucking hot though – because he'd told them to. Both of them looking to him for direction and approval had been a heady experience.

A plaintive sound of pain split the silence of the room, and her hips rocked harder against the bed. "Please no, you're hurting me, Mister Leduc."

Fucking hell.

Her eyelids flickered, and her desperate whimpering grew louder.

Nights ago, she'd given him permission to touch her while she slept, so really there was nothing stopping him but his own stubbornness.

"Miss Korsgaard!" he barked.

She frowned in her sleep, but didn't rouse.

"Minnow!"

This time her eyes did open – warm brown, confused. She winced as though waking pained her.

She rolled back onto her side and slid her hand under the covers, focusing on him drowsily. She gasped, and her eyes fell closed for a moment. When she opened them again there was undisguised lust in her gaze.

"You just had to ruin that for me," she said, her voice husky and full of mock accusation. She bit her lip, and her hips bucked. "Be a gentleman and let me come, Mister Leduc."

"How's your ass this morning?"

"You'd have to try it and tell me." She stretched out on her stomach again. "Probably tight," she said sleepily, raising her hips as though to give him better access. "You'd have to use your fingers first."

He swallowed hard, trying to compose himself enough for a clever comeback.

"If I took you up on that, you'd probably regret it."

"Probably, but it felt so damn good in my dream, I'm willing to take the chance." She laughed to herself. "That's how you can tell you're getting to me. You've kept me on edge for so long I'm grateful to dream about getting something I don't even want." Her gaze dropped to his jeans. "Could you use some help with that, Master? You can use my mouth, if you'd like."

"I'm perfectly comfortable. Let me see the damage I did last night." He pulled back her covers, and she shivered.

"It's cold!" She burrowed into the mattress, but stuck her ass out at him in invitation.

He sat next to her on the bed even though he didn't have time for further temptation. Slower than strictly necessary, he slid down her flannel pajama pants, revealing her mouth-wateringly curved posterior. She had the kind of body they rarely put in magazines, but most men had to fantasize about. The only thing better than the way her tits jiggled when he spanked her was the way her ass jiggled.

With the tiny waist to hang onto, and that sweet face to make you believe she'd never had a perverted thought in her life – and yet the mind behind those innocent eyes was so fucking dirty.

When he finally got her pants down under her ass, the flesh there was mottled red and purple, and one large handprint was a perfect raised welt on the back of her thigh. He was simultaneously disgusted with himself and turned on all over again. She made the sexiest sounds when he spanked her, and she had an ass made specifically for spanking.

"Does it still hurt?" He prodded at a bruise and she hissed.

"Uh huh." She pouted at him reproachfully. "You broke it."

"It's not broken," he said, smiling at her bid for sympathy.

"It is! I can't even sit on it."

"That's no problem. You're supposed to kneel at my feet, not sit around on your ass all day."

"It's hard to kneel at your feet when I can't find you."

He stretched out beside her and she turned onto her side. Face to face, they were so close to each other they could almost kiss. She wriggled even closer, and her brows drew together in supplication.

"You need to shower and get dressed. We're going into town."

She groaned, and her thigh brushed against his erection.

"Please, can I suck your cock before we go, Mister Leduc?" She shifted lower and moved her fingers to just in front of the button of his jeans. "Please? I need something. I can't go out in public in this condition."

"How is sucking my cock going to help you?"

She groaned again. "If you come in my mouth I can guarantee it'll help me." She brushed her fingers over the button of his jeans and whined like a puppy that wanted a treat.

"Denial is good for the soul." He got out of bed, denying them both, and the sound of desperation she made was so sexy his cock twitched.

"You're making me crazy. I need to get you used to being touched – at least by me."

"So you can touch me whenever you want?"

"No, Master. I wouldn't take liberties. I just think you'd give in to pleasure more if you got used to me touching you."

"And how do you propose to get me used to something I don't like?"

"Let me do things for you. I could shave you, brush your hair, give you massages."

"You're just trying to get your hands on my dick."

"My hands? Sure, but that's not all I had in mind." She pulled her pajama pants the rest of the way off and his body responded immediately to the implied invitation. When she knelt up on the mattress and her fingers moved to start unbuttoning her top, he was riveted in place. The prim neckline became exposed cleavage, soft belly, bellybutton, open shirt. She slid the edges of her shirt slowly aside, lingering over her nipple, brushing back and forth over it until it was a stiff upturned peak begging for his mouth. The smoothness of her pussy beckoned to him, inviting him to explore her again.

Fuck exploring. He wanted to claim her as his...

But not yet. Especially not when she was trying to bait him into it.

He gave her an arrogant grin. "Shower and get ready."

"I couldn't be more ready," she said, begging with her eyes.

"I'm serious. We're going into town."

She swore and collapsed onto the bed, her hand sneaking down to cup between her legs. The subtle play of her fingers made him grit his teeth.

"You'd better not come without permission."

Her gaze grew hazed with lust as she watched him. Slowly, her legs parted and she began to stroke herself there, her hips shifting as she teased herself. She angled her lush body to show him what she was doing.

"I'd never come without your permission unless it was an accident, Mister Leduc." Her breath caught and her eyes fluttered closed as her cheeks bloomed pink with desire.

Watching was rewarding bad behavior, even if it was sexy bad behavior, so he went through her closet.

"What are you doing?" she asked, laughing. He heard the rustle of her sitting up in bed.

"Choosing what I want you to wear."

"To go out?" she asked, incredulous. "Is this some sort of fancy date with power dynamics thrown in?"

"No. This is me choosing what I want to see you in." He chose a red sweater that would go well with her coloring, and a pair of jeans he liked on her, and threw them onto the bed.

"Oookay."

He went to her drawer and she scrambled off the bed. "Stay on the bed," he snapped.

"But –"

"But?" He turned to face her, and she nibbled at her bottom lip. "I hope there's nothing embarrassing in here."

"You're going through my things?"

He snorted. "Yes. And I will whenever I please."

"Ugh." She pressed the palms of her hands against her eyes, as if she couldn't bear to watch.

More curious now, he went through the contents of each drawer, holding up various bra and panty sets he hadn't seen on her yet – some functional, some meant for the eyes of a lover rather than to be worn under clothing. Both aroused him for different reasons.

As he sorted through things, he took note of various personal items she had tucked away. A picture of her with an older man and woman – all three of them smiling. He assumed they were her parents, from the resemblance. Strange how there was only one picture. He held it up.

"Parents?"

"Yes."

"Do you like them?"

"Sure."

"Why don't you ask me for time to see them?"

"We were – never close. They moved to Africa to do missionary work after my sister's wedding. They're nurses." She shrugged. "They're nice people, but they don't understand where they went wrong with me." The one-shouldered shrug said it didn't matter, even though he could tell it did.

He got a handle on the unexpected rage this roused in him. How dare they think there was anything wrong with her. "There's nothing wrong with you. You're fucking perfect."

She blinked at the ferocity of his words.

"If you locked me in a tower and threw away the key, it would be years before they noticed I was missing." Her voice was quiet, but her expression was one of self-mockery, as though her pain was silly and inconsequential.

Her pretty mouth twisted mischievously, apparently done with being sad. That momentary flash of vulnerability, though, clung in his thoughts. So many fucking people were alone in this world, sometimes even the ones who supposedly had families.

"I'm too...sexual to fit into their world. They completely wrote me off at sixteen after I asked for birth control."

"Sixteen?"

"Yeah...I probably shouldn't have told them my boyfriend was in college."

"You were fucking a college boy?"

"Kind of."

"How can someone kind of be in college?"

"Well...he worked there."

"As?"

She sighed then smiled wryly. "A professor."

Protective urges surged. Some asshole had taken advantage of her when she was hardly more than a child? Had the guy been prosecuted? Had someone broken his fucking legs yet?

Her hands went up in a warding gesture, and she grimaced. "Don't blame him. I worked at the coffee shop on campus. He thought I was several years older than I was, and I never corrected him."

He snorted. Ridiculous. Like anyone would have believed a sixteen-year-old was an adult? "You seriously think he never figured it out?"

"Oh...when I ended up in his freshman class a couple of years later he was horrified. I don't think he could have faked his reaction to finding out my real age at that point. I got a great mark in that class," she mused.

He started to laugh, but was still skeptical about the guy being that obtuse. The funny part to him was that Minnow was obviously still proud of her conquest, even though in retrospect she had to know it had been completely inappropriate. "So you've always been a hellion?"

"Yeah," she sighed. "It's hard to be a good when I get a total girl boner for men in authority."

"Should I be checking your ID to make sure you're not underage, Miss Korsgaard?"

She gestured at her handbag, which was on a chair by the bedroom door. "It would be less embarrassing than what you're going to find if you keep going through my shit."

If that wasn't incentive to keep going...

"So who introduced you to kink?" he asked casually as he piled the trinkets he came across on top of her dresser. A small stuffed bunny that had obviously been well loved, a bundle of ancient-looking letters tied with ribbon, a child's jewelry box with a fairy on it. Handcuffs, nipple clamps, a vibrator.

"The professor," she replied. "Well, that's not entirely true. I was kinky even when I was a kid."

"Was he your first lover?"

"No."

He raised a brow at her and she rolled her eyes.

"But you hadn't needed birth control before that?"

"Nah. The girl I dated before him was always careful to pull out." She winked.

He would not allow his mind to drift to Minnow making out with a woman. No. Not letting himself think about it.

"Nothing?" she asked, incredulous. "Not even a flicker of interest?"

He shook his head. "I'm not saying I wouldn't watch, but you'd still need permission."

"Of course, Master. I'm an honorable slut."

He inclined his head, glad she followed those sorts of rules, at least. "Who are the letters from?"

"From my grandparents to each other, during the Vietnam War."

"Have you read them all?"

"Nooo... No, no. I can't read them. They're really fucking dirty." She giggled. "At least I know where I get it from. My mother was going to burn them."

He turned to the next drawer.

"Wait!" she said, her voice shrill. "Don't you think that's enough self-disclosure for one day?"

He gauged her reaction to his hand on the drawer pull. She looked like she might faint.

"Apparently not." He opened the drawer.

"Don't be upset. I can explain."

In the drawer with her socks and flannel pajamas was a very familiar looking shirt.

He pulled the shirt free and held it out. "And here I thought you were an honorable slut."

"There's honor among thieves?" she said hopefully.

When he crossed his arms and raised a brow, she shivered.

"Why is one of my T-shirts in your drawer, Miss Korsgaard? It's not even clean."

"If I washed it, it wouldn't smell like you." She fell back on the bed, the shirt she wore parting to reveal the bounce of her breasts as her body settled on the mattress. With her legs hanging over the end of the bed way they were, he was tempted to part those creamy thighs of hers and use his tongue to find out just how aroused she was.

"Why would you need a shirt that smelled like me?"

"I just...wanted it. I'm sorry. I didn't think you'd notice."

"Is this the one I put on you after the night in my office with Rodrigo?"

"Yes." She smiled shyly, looking up at him from her back, her expression soft and receptive. It was so difficult for him to believe she liked him more than Ro, but she was gradually convincing him.

He put the shirt back in her drawer and she clapped her hands. "Thank you!"

"If you want to steal anything else of mine, you'd better ask first or there'll be painful consequences, understood?"

"Oh," she said, sounding nervous.

"Was that the only thing you've taken, Miss Korsgaard?"

"Well...yes."

"You don't sound sure."

"I didn't technically take it, but I should probably return your tie from Church's wedding."

"And why do you still have it?"

She winced. "Reasons."

"Reasons?"

"Nefarious reasons, Master. Can't we just pretend I gave it back?"

He shook his head and she sighed, but crawled to the headboard with a sexy grace that made him want to start the day off with sticking his stiff prick in her ass. From under her pillow she withdrew the tie, more creased than the last time he'd seen it.

"Have you been tying yourself up with my tie?"

She made a sound of scorn as she handed it to him, but didn't actually deny it and wouldn't meet his gaze. As soon as the silk touched his hand she headed for the shower, as though avoiding further questioning. At the door, she turned back, her face hopeful.

"Would you like to shower with me, Mister Leduc?"

"No. We have to be downtown in an hour to drop off a bike."

She sighed and gazed at him longingly, then strolled off into the attached bathroom, giving him one more enticing look over her shoulder before dropping the unbuttoned shirt to the floor and sauntering away.

The meeting was in an hour.

This wasn't the time.

His dick disowned him as he walked away from her invitation.

*

Watching Minnow throw one of her shapely, jeans-covered legs over the monster bike was an instant hard-on. The thing was too big for her, but she managed it fine, cruising along the highway at a dignified pace showing the confidence of a rider who didn't feel the need to grandstand to prove her skill.

By the time they reached Rodrigo's, he was ready to throw her down on the front lawn and screw her in front of the buyer.

Rodrigo and the buyer stepped out into the driveway just as they pulled up, and when Minnow pulled off her helmet, Ro grinned, looking impressed.

"That's a lot of bike for such a little girl," Rodrigo said, winking at her.

"I like them big," she shot back.

The innuendo made Severin roll his eyes, but Rodrigo smiled the dangerous grin he used to attract women – just for a moment before his gaze cut to Severin and the smile fell away. He liked her, but wouldn't betray Severin. At least, that's what Severin was starting to believe.

The buyer turned to face Severin, and there was a moment of unease. He never liked strangers, but this guy was...wrong. He smiled smoothly at Severin, ignoring Minnow completely as he strode toward him. Severin stood his ground and squared his shoulders, his hackles going up as the man moved to enter his personal space. His hands balled into fists, and he braced himself for the guy to take a swing. He'd deflect then pulverize the fucker's face.

Minnow stepped neatly in front of the man, halting his advance, and blocking Severin from launching his own attack.

"So you're Severin," he said, extending a hand trying to sidestep Minnow, who moved to stop him again.

"Mister Leduc doesn't shake hands," Minnow said icily, her body language implying she might maim the man if he wasn't careful. "Please step back."

"Please, honey, this is a business deal between men." He nudged her out of the way and she had to take a step to catch her balance.

Hot rage surged through Severin's brain, crackling and snapping just under his scalp. The fucker had touched her. Practically pushed her. Severin took the last two steps to the man and grabbed his throat. He backed the stumbling arse off the driveway and shoved him up against a tree, pinning him there by the neck.

"What's wrong with you?" The man gasped.

"You don't ignore my woman when she speaks to you, and you never fucking touch her – understand?" His knife had found its way to his free hand, and the adrenaline made him want to stab this fucker in the face.

The man's eyes were panicked, probably because Severin was tightening his grip. "Sorry, Leduc. I had no idea."

Severin sneered, but let his hand fall away from the buyer's throat.

"Mister Leduc," Minnow said quietly, "Rodrigo has offered to handle this transaction if you'd like to come inside."

Staring into the man's eyes, Severin cocked his head and let the man see just how unstable he was. He let Minnow take the knife out of his hand and lead him inside to the receiving room off the foyer. His body and mind were buzzing hard. Everything in him wanted to charge back outside and show the man exactly what happened when someone laid a hand on Minnow, but she was coaxing him into a chair, and jail seemed less interesting than watching her cleavage as she resheathed his knife in his boot.

"Mister Leduc!" she admonished. Red mottled her face and her chest heaved. Was she angry or afraid? He hadn't meant to scare her.

"What?"

"You can't go around choking people and threatening them with knives!" Her body shook.

"He almost knocked you down."

"You pulled a knife on him!"

"I did."

"If he presses charges, you could end up in jail!"

Severin smiled. "Don't worry, I'm too big and ugly to be someone's girlfriend."

"Jail, Mister Leduc. It's not a joke." She sidled up to him and leaned her leg on his, then moved back. He was sorry she did, because he'd liked it.

He grabbed her wrist and pulled her into his lap. Although she leaned away from him in protest, it was short lived. After a moment her stiff posture melted, and she let him pull her close.

"Did I scare you?"

She nodded. "I thought you might kill him."

"The thought crossed my mind. I won't tolerate you being treated with disrespect."

"Unless it's by you."

He kissed her forehead. "Yeah, but you get off on that."

Although she glared at him, she didn't deny it.

"Don't kill anyone because of me, okay?" She pressed her face against his chest. "I shouldn't have to tell you that, Mister Leduc. That should just be a given."

"Miss Korsgaard, when a man gifts you with the blood of your enemies, you're supposed to be flattered."

"You're just mad he touched your property."

"That too."

She thumped her forehead against his chest.

"Even if he didn't realize you were my woman, he should have showed you respect as my employee." He paused to see if she'd rise to his bait, but she didn't say a word. "That and the fact that you're a little fucking badass who could serve him his balls on toast."

"Screw that. If he wants toast with his balls, he can make it himself. I only cook for one man."

He brushed his knuckle over her bottom lip, loving her ferocity.

"So did you mean what you said?" she asked.

"All of it, but which part are you referring to?"

"That I'm your woman."

He grabbed her chin none too gently, and her eyes widened.

"Are you trying to say you're not?"

Her brows rose and before she could answer, he kissed the hell out of her. By the time they came up for air, Rodrigo was sitting in the chair across from them, watching with undisguised interest. He tossed Severin a thick envelope.

"He paid cash," Rodrigo said. "Usually that would get him a discount, but I made him pay extra for leaving footprints on my lawn."

Severin snorted and tossed the envelope back at him. "Keep it. Sorry about the scene."

"He had no business doing that to Min. I almost punched him myself, but you beat me to him." Rodrigo shook the envelope at him and slapped it down on the coffee table between them. "I'm not taking this, dumbass. I already took my cut."

"I don't want his money."

"Well I'm not taking more than my cut. Obviously I didn't do my job right if we're selling to someone like that."

"Fine." Severin picked up the envelope and dropped it onto Minnow's lap. "Buy yourself something pretty."

"What? No!"

"Mari is already here, by the way." Rodrigo leaned back in his chair and splayed his legs out in front of him."

"Good." He jounced Minnow on his lap. "Remember how you mocked me for not shopping like a rich man, Miss Korsgaard. We're making up for that today." He patted her ass.

"Where are we going?" she asked, eyes bright.

"Just upstairs," Rodrigo said, gesturing in that direction.

"Someone is here to sell things? Like what?" she asked.

"I'm having people over tonight, and your owner has decided you might like a social outing. One of my friends is here with options you may be interested in."

"I take it this isn't a Tupperware party?" she asked Severin.

He chuckled, enjoying her surprise. He wasn't the most interesting person to spend time with, and knew she got bored at the house. The idea of doing this for her had been exciting for him even though he was dreading it. "Not unless Tupperware has significantly broadened their product line."

"So you have a hard time with vanilla gatherings, but kink ones are fine?"

"No," Rodrigo said. "He's trying for your sake. He's never stayed more than five minutes at one of these, but with you here it may be easier. It's not a party, really. Just a few people. You can also bring him to hang out in his room if he needs a break."

He swallowed a growl. Could Ro make him sound more like an anxious child?

Minnow shifted on his lap, grinding her ass. It didn't seem like an accident. His little bitch liked playing with fire. "He has a room in your house?"

"Yes. I have a room in his house. It's only fair."

Severin shoved the girl up from his lap and swatted her ass. "Come on. Don't forget your money."

"Mister Leduc! I'm not taking this money. I didn't do a thing to earn it."

"Hazard pay."

"Hazard pay isn't the price of a custom bike. You don't just give away money like that. I wasn't wrestling piranhas or anything."

He pulled her to face him, not caring that Rodrigo was hearing this. "How many people could handle what I did to you last night? I know the money is awkward because of the employer/employee/sexual relationship thing, but just take it as an apology for what you have to put up with."

She reached out to put a hand on his chest, but didn't touch. He pulled her closer and when her hand connected with his chest, she ran her finger along the edge of his T-shirt's frayed neckline. The contact made him want to set her away, but he clenched his jaw and let it happen. It felt good, but it also made him tense.

"You don't need to pay me to put up with you. You're a complicated man to be in lo...volved with, but I'm with you because I...like you."

The way she'd paused in the middle of the word 'involved' made him wonder what she'd almost said. "Well, will you take it as a gift?"

"No. I'm more than willing to take gifts of orgasms, though."

The idea of apologizing to her until she begged him to stop was an interesting one. She dropped her hand away from the tentative exploration of his neckline, filling him with disappointment and relief.

"We'll talk later. For now let's go see what Mari brought with her." He picked up the envelope of money and tucked it into the inside pocket of her backpack.

"Hey!"

"I have nowhere to put it."

"So this is how it's going to go is it?" she teased. "You're pretending to like me so you can make me carry your shit? Typical millionaire."

"Billionaire," Rodrigo corrected quietly.

Severin shook his head at Minnow in mock disapproval. "You're so desperate to be punished you're resorting to bratting in front of our host?"

"Sorry," she said, narrowing her eyes in challenge, "I didn't realize we were still standing on ceremony with Mr. Solis after the other night."

Rodrigo winced and sauntered from the room, giving them privacy.

"Miss Korsgaard, is there a problem?" he asked, crowding her until she backed into the foyer, stopping when her ass hit the edge of the round table in the center.

Lust flared in her eyes, but she didn't answer.

He unzipped her jeans and tugged them down to her thighs, then turned her and bent her over the table, revealing a lacy purple thong that framed her bruised ass the way it deserved to be seen – bruises he'd left on her, that made him feel rabidly proprietary. Fuck, the woman made him crazy.

"Answer the question now, Miss Korsgaard."

"Yes!" she hissed. "There's a problem."

"And what's that?" He swatted her plump ass, watching it jiggle rather than leaning down to bite it the way he wanted to.

"You keep me on edge for ages, ask me to ride one of your big sexy bikes all the way here, which is like a fucking vibrator on steroids, then you go all caveman on a man who disrespects me. Then you sit me on your lap and pet me, and I know your dick is hard, and I'm about to lose my fucking mind." Although she'd started at a whisper, she was yelling by the end of it.

"So you're bratting because?"

"You're hot and you drive me crazy on purpose, yet no matter what I do you won't fuck me."

"I guess you've failed to give me the right incentive."

"I know you're hard. I was sitting on your lap."

That went without saying. The woman kept him perpetually hard. She was all he could think about.

"What the fuck do you want, Miss Korsgaard? You want me to breed you right here in Rodrigo's foyer, like some little bitch in heat?"

She gave a small whimper and thrust her ass back at him in blatant invitation. "Please," she whispered.

"You can wait."

"You have to let me come soon, Mister Leduc. I can't do this anymore."

He covered her body with his own, and he felt the heat of her pussy on his cock through his jeans. How could a man be desperate for something when he didn't even know how it felt? As much as he loved teasing her, he didn't think he'd be able to hold out much longer either. His balls felt perpetually bruised, and yet making her weep with frustration fed something inside him that was starving for her suffering. Maybe for his own, as well.

He bit her nape, tasting the fresh air from their ride on her skin while he rocked his cock against her ass. She arched her back, seeking more pressure on her pussy, so he pushed off the table away from her and patted her ass with as much condescension as he could fake.

As he tugged her jeans back up and buttoned them for her, she stayed unmoving on the table. She wept without tears, her back shaking with it. Brow furrowed and eyes wide, she looked lost.

How could he reconcile his need to torment her with his need to protect her? How was it even possible to feel both so strongly for the same person?

"Come pick out something to wear tonight," he said, hoping to distract her with shopping because he sure as hell wasn't fucking her for the first time in Rodrigo's foyer.

When she didn't move and didn't answer, he picked her up and carried her upstairs, not putting her down until he got to the main living room. Ro was looking through what Mari had brought. The wizened, stooped woman with the neat French braid was helping him sort through things, her knobby hands somehow graceful as she presented merchandise.

Minnow's face was buried against Severin's shoulder as he sat on one of the couches.

"I apologize. She's eager to see what you have, she's just having a hard day."

"Oh, did you just punish her?" Mari asked gleefully. "My Leon used to have such an evil mind before it went on him." She gave him a shockingly devilish grin. "I still have scars on my knees from when we were young and wild."

"You do?" Rodrigo asked, sounding as genuinely curious as Severin was.

"Oh yes. There weren't really rules back then, you understand. Just what happened between two people. He carved his name on my ass the night he married me. At the time I was so glad his name was short. Now the damn thing looks like it's in parentheses." She chortled. "When you're nineteen you never anticipate your future ass wrinkles."

Rodrigo choked on the bourbon he'd been sipping and Mari threw her own drink back as she snickered to herself.

Minnow sat up and looked around blearily, then rose when she saw the racks and piles of clothing and accessories.

"She's yours?" Mari asked Severin.

"Yes." He felt his chest inflate with undeserved pride. Yes, the lovely, intelligent woman was his, for now, but he'd done nothing to deserve her and soon she'd realize that.

"What do you want her in for this party?" When he looked at Mari blankly, she smiled – he wasn't sure she'd stopped smiling. "How do you like her dressed?"

"I –" He didn't know the answer to that. Not when it came to being in public. "We've never been to a party together before. I want to show her off, but I also don't want people looking at what's mine."

"I swear you all get your wiring installed at the same factory." Mari patted Minnow then eyed Rodrigo. "And what do you think, pretty boy?"

"I have no opinion on this one," he said, averting his gaze.

"Ah," Mari said, as though he'd revealed a lot. "Spoken like a man who's been given permission to play with her in the past, and doesn't want to fuck that up for the future."

Rodrigo's expression was so bland it was almost comical. Minnow appeared to be ignoring the conversation, but Severin knew better.

Minnow roused and slid off his lap, and immediately eyed a pair of high-heeled black boots that would look damn sexy on her, but she didn't pick them up. She knew he preferred her barefoot and wasn't even going to ask.

"Do you have those in a seven?" he asked Mari, pointing to the boots.

Minnow's gaze darted to them. "But I thought you preferred me barefoot."

"You won't be wearing them tonight, but I have no objection to you owning them for vanilla purposes."

A smile of pleasure graced her lips, and he noticed again how lovely she was. "But Master, I'm sure they're expensive."

"You just turned down the 80k in that envelope, Miss Korsgaard. I'm sure I can buy you some fucking boots."

Mari quoted him a price and he waved a hand to let her know Minnow was to have free rein.

*

The girl was, by far, the most beautiful woman in the room. Collared, leashed, kneeling at his feet, the piercings he'd had her marked with clearly outlined through the loose black silk of her dress, his bite marks on her neck – none of it was enough. Other couples tried to engage them in conversation, but for him there was only her, and she was so far into a trance-like subspace that her gaze never left him.

She rested her head on his knee, but although she hadn't asked, it felt right. He stroked her cheek and she latched onto his thumb when it grazed her lips, sucking as she looked up at him with her wide, sweet gaze. Although the suctioned tugging on his thumb made his balls ache, and the feel of her clever little tongue had him gritting his teeth, the underlying feelings she was giving him – of contentment and optimism, of not being alone, of having someone who was his who he belonged to as well – those feelings made him uneasy.

His first instinct was to ruin things before something else went drastically wrong – to ruin things on his own terms. This connection he had with Minnow was too good. The temptation to let go and enjoy it, even though it was temporary, was strong – but he didn't get to have this feeling without a price. It wouldn't be a price he could handle paying.

Rodrigo sat down in the chair next to Severin's and watched them for a few moments.

"See? You're fine at parties when you don't pay attention to anything except your girl's mouth."

Severin blinked and looked around. He'd been as entranced as she was. Rodrigo's little get together had turned into about twenty guests. Most people in the room were busy doing their own thing, either engaged in scenes or socializing, but a few watched them. It was hard to be self-conscious when only she mattered.

"You don't want to play with her here – show her off? You could just take her back to your room if you want to."

He wanted to take her back to his room, and yet he didn't. Attending this party was supposed to be for her, but she was too focused on him to enjoy the company of other people. Maybe he'd just use the other people watching them to edge her a bit more before he took her somewhere private.

"Up."

She rose, and her braless breasts swayed under the silk of her long gown, completely distracting him for a moment. He slid the straps off her shoulders and let the dress skim down her body and pool like a shadow at her feet. The black panties she wore were more tiny ribbons and bows than actual fabric, and he couldn't be sure if the groan he heard came from him or Rodrigo. Hell, Severin had dressed her – undressing her shouldn't be this exciting.

"Are you a good girl?" Severin asked her.

"I try to be, Mister Leduc."

"Then you'll let me do what I want, even if you don't like it?"

"Always, Mister Leduc."

There was another quiet groan, but this time Severin was pretty sure it had come from him.

Standing between him and Rodrigo, naked except for the panties, and his collar and leash, she was all softness and compliance.

He led her through the crowd until they were under a bar suspended from the ceiling. From his pocket, he withdrew the wide black sash he'd bought from Mari earlier and tied her wrists to the bar with a big, floppy bow.

Rodrigo had followed them, and surveyed his handiwork from behind her. "A gift?" he asked. "You shouldn't have."

"I could use an extra set of hands, actually."

Minnow let out a long, low whine. Severin and Rodrigo both shuddered.

"What are we doing to her this time?" Ro asked, his voice rough and his gaze hot on Severin.

"She was complaining about being frustrated earlier, so obviously we need to make sure she stays that way."

Rodrigo grinned cruelly. "Obviously."

Chapter Eleven

"Oh god," Minnow whispered. "Evil fucking bastards. I hate you both."

"Yeah." Rodrigo snorted. "I could see how much you hated Severin a few minutes ago."

She'd been so content and now Severin wanted to start this again?

They both leered at her and she stomped her foot impatiently, which made her round parts jiggle. Their interest only increased.

Severin gazed at her hungrily. "Touch her wherever you want, but no penetration."

"Hands only?" Rodrigo asked, eyeing her as though she was a sculpture she was working on.

"Not necessarily. Just keep your dick in your pants."

"Please, Mister Leduc – don't do this." Minnow protested, her tone sulky rather than adamant. She didn't want more teasing, but could she really bring herself to refuse this?

She could feel the hot gazes of strangers fixed on her, and it was hard to resist squirming the way her body was demanding.

Severin brushed his fingertips along the underside of her breasts, and her nipples tightened to excruciating peaks. She shivered and pouted at him prettily.

"Please – I've been so close all day. Two minutes of this and I'll be groveling so loud you'll be ashamed of me."

Rodrigo moved further behind her and his fingers grazed the sensitive flesh below her ass cheeks.

Both of them touching her? Teasing her? She was never going to survive this.

She gasped and frowned, her gaze flicking back toward Rodrigo even though she wouldn't be able to see him without craning her neck. Not being able to see him or anticipate what he'd do next freaked her out. Slowly, Severin trailed feather light touches up and down her skin, the feel of his rough, cruel hands being gentle and teasing was completely orgasmic. She quivered and tensed, muscles twitching and shifting. Rodrigo matched Severin's pace, their grazing touches exploring, meeting up, parting ways, never reaching her pussy even though her clit was already throbbing. Minnow mewled in protest, trying to shift away from their hands, but unable to go far.

"What's wrong?" Severin asked her, feigning confusion. "Women are supposed to like foreplay."

"A few minutes." She gasped. "Maybe an hour. Not weeks, you bloody sadist."

From nearby a woman said, "Weeks? I'd fucking kill you."

"Pardon me?" came the male response, the tone threatening.

There was the sound of a scuffle, but Minnow was too focused on what was happening to her to worry about some other submissive.

"Me fucking you wasn't enough?" Rodrigo whispered in her ear.

"You seemed to enjoy it at the time," Severin whispered in the other ear.

The heat from their bodies reached her naked skin, and she was forced to imagine them taking her that way – sharing, one in front and one behind.

Minnow cried out, her entire body shaking.

Maybe if the orgasm she'd had the other night hadn't been ruined on purpose it would have held her over, but now that entire evening was a blurred memory. That memory sometimes became a dream too, or a daydream, and sensations from it popped into her head at the worst possible times.

So many women thought they wanted two men at once, but what they didn't realize was it meant being helpless and picked on. Maybe it was different with vanilla men, but with dominant sadists who had an edging kink, she was overwhelmed and underfucked. Hell, she needed that written on a god damned T-shirt.

Severin trailed a series of small kisses down her neck to her collarbone, then along it. She jolted in surprise as Rodrigo's mouth brushed against her skin too.

Shit. Shit.

"Please, Mister Leduc, if you're not going to let me come today, just beat me unconscious. It would be kinder."

He chuckled, as if she was kidding, then kissed her, his mouth hot and demanding, his tongue seeking her own. She melted against him as his hand slipped into her panties to cup her sex. Rodrigo pressed against her from behind, his erection prodding her lower back as Severin's fingers explored her arousal, then slid up inside her. She fucked herself with Severin's fingers, kissing him more deeply.

People around them murmured, but the fact that they were watching her be tortured – were aroused by it, from their tone – just made it all burn hotter.

Rodrigo slid further down her body, grabbing her hips and rocking his erection against her ass. Severin sank to his knees and pusher her panties aside, then spread her labia and flicked his tongue between. He found her clit and angled his finger forward to rub against her g-spot. Her clit was sucked into his hot mouth, his tongue moving against her stroking, swirling.

Every muscle in her body tensed to come even as her mind knew this was a lie. Rodrigo ground against her ass, grunting in her ear, shoving her harder against Severin's mouth. Her body shivered on the knife's edge of orgasm. Severin's mouth was gone from her. Rodrigo's warm presence behind her disappeared.

She screamed. Swore. Wept.

Her wrists were suddenly untied and her knees buckled, but before she hit the floor someone tossed her over their shoulder. She had a raging tantrum as he carried her through the house, her eyes so blurred from angry tears she couldn't even identify the shirt two inches from her nose.

Severin or Rodrigo?

Shrieking, she fought his grip. She sailed through the air and landed, bouncing, on a mattress. Severin. She launched herself at him, hammering his chest with her fists. He pressed her back then wrestled off her underwear, ribbons popping and tearing as she fought him.

His mouth came down on hers hard, devouring her protests as she tried to scratch his face off. Big hands banded her wrists, pinning them over her head as he forced her legs apart with his knee. Bare skin against bare skin. Severin between her legs as he held her down.

"Do you want me to stop?" Severin rumbled, his voice hoarse and his body full of tension.

"If you want it you're going to have to take it," she snapped. "I'm not letting you torture me anymore."

He laughed, but the sound was sexy and dangerous.

"You're just lucky you're not ready for DP," Severin growled.

Horny, angry, she struggled, but it was like fighting a wall. DP with him and Rodrigo? Hell no.

"You're not going to call Rodrigo in here to do your dirty work for you again?" she growled back.

She wanted him so bad – just him – but he kept teasing her then withholding it. He was making her crazy. Maybe the feelings she had for him were unrequited. Maybe she was just a game to him.

The tip of his cock dragged along her pussy, and she struggled against the huge man's one-handed hold on her wrists, trying to twist her hips away or kick him as the broad head of his dick pushed against her entrance. Hot, like a brand. Maybe he wasn't messing with her this time. She sucked in a breath.

No condom. Fuck. She'd never done this before.

Chapter Twelve

Minnow gazed up at him, mouth open in surprise as he thrust forward. The fight drained out of her. He was tempted to stop and savor the moment, but the biological imperative to get inside her took over. What had Rodrigo done to make this work? He gripped his aching cock and coaxed the head slowly into her slick heat. She looked and felt too small to accommodate him, but the grip of her body was addictive. Her expression went from shocked to uncomfortable.

"Oh fuck – why do you have to be so big?" She squirmed under him, digging her heels into the mattress and forcing him deeper, pausing to gasp and adjust to his size, then taking another inch.

He tugged off his T-shirt and watched the process, finding it insanely erotic seeing his shaft slowly being worked into her small body. The fit was fucking tight for him, so he could only imagine how it felt to her.

Whoa. He was actually inside her. He'd assumed he'd die without knowing what sex with a woman was like, and yet inch by inch he was sinking into her exquisite heat.

He rubbed his thumb over her clit and she bucked under him, her pussy rippling around his cock and forcing him to grind his teeth and think about anything other than how hot and tight and wet she was, and how he was going get her off and then come inside her.

"Okay, stop," she gasped. "I need –" She whined and shook her head, squeezing her eyes shut.

"Hurts?" he asked breathlessly, trying to stay still while fighting the urge to drive the last inch into her even though he'd bottomed out.

"Yes," she hissed. "I've been too horny for too long and everything feels swollen, and if you touch my clit again I'm going to come and the squirming will hurt us both."

Her pussy was pulsing around him and the pleasure of it made him grit his teeth. His balls felt too tight and relief was so close, but he didn't want it to be over yet.

"God – your dick is too hot and you're not even wearing a condom." She whimpered.

They stared at each other nose to nose, both breathing carefully as if they were in danger of detonating. Her eyes were the deepest brown, warm, kind, patient with his ineptitude and awkwardness at the worst of times, but this astounded him. She wasn't even laughing at him.

She caused the best and most uncomfortable feelings in his chest. She raised her head and brushed her lips over his, but the way it tightened her inner muscles made them both groan so she relaxed against the bed again.

"Okay," she said, her voice still mildly hysterical, "do whatever you want. I can't hold off anymore."

He kissed her deeply, brushing the tip of his tongue over hers as he took his first experimental thrust. God – being inside her... Why and how the hell had he held off for so long?

"Oh fuck," she whispered, but then whined and tried to follow him with her hips as he pulled partway out. "No, no, no – give it back." She wrapped her legs around the back of his thighs and pulled him close.

He thrust into her harder and her eyes rolled back and she grunted low in her throat.

"Fuck," she said, sounding drunk. "Yesss."

"Are you trying to control what I'm doing, Miss Korsgaard?" he rumbled in warning.

She gave a hoarse cry with his next thrust, and not knowing whether he was giving her pleasure or hurting her was fucking with his head. Both thoughts turned him on. He fucked her hard and slow, and her sobs of helplessness, her soft body under him, taking him into her, clenching around him. She seemed almost mindless with it, but then, so was he. It was true – this was a primal thing. His body knew what it wanted, and he let it happen, guided by the tormented sounds the girl made. Raw. Nothing between them. He was going to fill her with come, and his only regret was she was on birth control. The idea of getting her pregnant – of making her that thoroughly his – was powerful.

For now he'd just make a mess of her.

He held her down and fucked her hard as she melted into the bed, her gaze glassy and yet rapt as she cried out for him. She went suddenly silent, and he wondered if he'd hurt her for all of a moment when she arched beneath him. She made a choking sound. In a panic he almost pulled out, but then she screamed and dug her nails into his arms.

Her pussy clenched on his cock, pulsing and rippling, until he lost all sense of what he was doing, other than to fuck her viciously into the mattress. She fell apart, shrieking and crying, completely beside herself as her body tried to crush his dick.

The pressure in his balls built until he thought he'd lose his fucking mind. He wrapped his hand around her jaw and forced her watery gaze to him as he came, pleasure exploding through him as his cock jerked again and again, filling her pussy with come.

She was so fucking his. He bit her shoulder over the marks Rodrigo had left, staking his claim again. A violent need to mark her more trembled through him, but he pushed it away, not wanting to ruin the moment with his fanatical bullshit. The adrenaline high was making his thoughts strange, and he had to work to subdue his sadistic impulses.

As the last of the aftershocks ebbed, he lowered himself until most of his weight was on her body. She twitched and shook beneath him, her tiny whimpers threatening to make his semi-hard cock stiffen again. He kissed her, trying to get her back to lucidity, but her brain seemed to be on a vacation.

"Too rough?" His voice sounded like sandpaper. He slid his arms under her and rolled onto his back, holding her to his chest. On top of him, she wriggled to get comfortable. His dick was still fully hard and he wondered when he was supposed to pull out. He didn't want to give her up yet.

"Yes, you were too rough," she complained, rubbing her cheek on his chest. For her, he made himself take it. Her hair, draped across his chest and shoulder, tickled every time she moved, and the sensuous feel of it made him want to groan. Despite her scowl of displeasure, she was gently rocking against him, apparently well aware he was hard.

"If you wanted me to stop, you shouldn't have pretended you liked it so much," he accused, amused.

"I didn't want to bruise your ego."

He grabbed her ass and thrust up into her, and she mewled so loudly it hurt his ears.

"Oh my god – I'm so sore!"

"Sorry," he said, not sorry and not letting go.

"I didn't say stop," she pointed out.

He dug his fingers harder into her ass cheeks and moved her on his cock. She bit her lip and tried valiantly to take more of him even though there was nowhere left to put him, then fell into the rhythm he'd set. Having her on top of him, capable of stopping and walking away, yet staying, was a boost to his ego. Grabbing the back of her hair and her jaw and dragged her down for a kiss.

"You like me," he said, hoping he wasn't wrong.

She frowned at him. "Mister Leduc, you're an idiot."

He meant to ask her why, but the way she moved her hips made him forget all about it.

*

The dread Severin had been feeling for days woke him again. He'd tried sleeping in her room, but couldn't fall asleep in the unfamiliar bed. He'd invited her into his bed, but couldn't sleep because he couldn't stop touching her. He couldn't rest if he didn't know she was safe, and kept wandering into whatever room she was asleep in to check on her.

For three nights he'd only dozed occasionally, his body cramped from the nights spent in one of the winged back chairs in front of his fireplace. He'd turned the chair so he could watch her, not even trying to hide what he was doing after the first night. She'd offered to sleep on the floor at the foot of his bed, but she was too far away there.

For now, he watched over her in the dark as he tried to sort through why he felt like she might disappear in the night. She wasn't a dream, even though it almost felt as though she was a shared dream with Rodrigo. There was an affection growing between the two of them, but he didn't mind it now, especially since it made it clear Severin was the one she deferred to first. He was the one she lived with. He was the one she looked to.

As light crept through the curtain into the room, his restlessness grew overwhelming. He rose and stretched, then prowled through the house looking for intruders he knew weren't present. When the sun rose, he checked on her, kissed her, and smiled as she burrowed into his pillow, looking so vulnerable and sweet as she slept.

He grabbed his coat and cell and went out into the yard, locking the door behind him, then completed a circuit of the property to make sure no one was sneaking around, waiting to harm her.

When he reached the forge he checked his phone. It was on silent, but the screen read TWELVE MISSED CALLS. And even as he watched, the message changed to: INCOMING CALL, BLOCKED NUMBER.

He sighed, hitting the green button. Better not be Church.

"What?" Hopefully it wasn't Sutton, because she fucking hated it when he answered the phone that way.

"Where the fuck have you been?"

"Church?" Severin tensed. His brother's voice was all wrong.

"Yeah." His voice broke on the word. "I've been trying to call the house all night."

"I turned the ringers off."

"Fuck." His brother sounded weird. Broken.

Severin held the phone away from his ear, letting his index finger hover over the END CALL button. Whatever Church had to say it was bad, and he didn't want to fucking hear it. This was what happened when you let yourself care about people.

He swore and put the phone back to his ear.

"Did you hear me?"

"No."

"I'm flying in to see you tonight."

"No."

"Sev – we need to talk."

"Just tell me who."

Church's silence said everything that needed to be said.

"When?"

"Last night. Late."

Of course. He'd probably been balls-deep in a woman while his mother lay dying.

"I don't want to see you." He punched the END CALL button.

The ground shifted strangely under his boots and he sat abruptly. He rose and walked a few feet. Sat again. His legs refused to obey him. Nerve endings all over his body prickled, numbing his legs, his face. His vision wavered. He got his legs under him again and staggered into the forge. He put his phone on one of his anvils and smashed it with a hammer, then stared at the pieces for so long his eyes hurt.

After all the promises she'd made, she'd left him.

Church's mom, Church, and now Sutton. Gone.

What was wrong with him?

Why did everyone leave?

He'd known he'd pay the price for what he had with Minnow, but he'd thought she'd be the one who would go.

Now he had her and Rodrigo. That was his whole world because he'd gotten greedy. Now he had no family left. Again. Gone.

One of the memories came of The Man with the big fingers and stinking breath fighting to pry open his mouth. Telling him to stop acting like a baby.

Suffocating.

Mother being angry. Telling him he was bad.

The tall servant and the black car.

The dream that came again and again, but hadn't begun as one.

He shoved those thoughts back behind the gate he never unlocked.

People went through worse and never complained.

He was walking in the woods, not sure how he'd ended up there. His legs shook, but if he stopped he'd never get up again. Deeper he went into the woods. Deeper. Cold permeated his flesh, got into his bones. They felt as hollow as the rest of him. People kept trying to convince him they could be trusted, but reality always intervened to make them liars, even if it had never been their intention.

Maybe if she'd come back when she was supposed to, she wouldn't have overtaxed herself. Maybe he would have noticed something was wrong and got her to the hospital on time. Although he didn't know the story – didn't want to know. It could have been an accident rather than illness.

Either way, she was gone.

She'd told him she loved him so many times, but if she'd really loved him she would have figured out how not to die. She'd let it happen because she was tired of living with his bullshit.

Thoughts flew through his mind, stupid, disjointed.

He'd trusted her more than anyone in the world, but in the end even her best intentions hadn't been worth much. Empty promises. He was alone, had always been alone, would die alone. Getting close to a woman who'd been old when he'd met her had been stupid, but she'd loved him like a son. She'd been his mother. The third mother who hadn't thought he was worth sticking around for. The third mother he'd exhausted.

He was too needy – too impossible – but he didn't know how to be different. It was too late now anyway.

How was he supposed to function without her?

Had she known she didn't have long left? Had she been hiding things?

Is that why she'd insisted on Minnow?

Frozen fingers gripping craggy rock, he climbed the cliff that overlooked the lake. Once on the precipice, the wind tore at his clothes and hair, but he needed to punish his body to keep himself from slipping into the weird numbness that wanted to shield him against the ugly emotions. When was denial supposed to happen? Shouldn't he have questioned whether this was real – how Church was sure?

No. He'd known this was coming from the day he'd met her.

Now, if Minnow left him, he might as well disappear.

The water beckoned, cold and unforgiving. It would punish his body more than walking or climbing. More than the tattoos and piercings. He could throw himself in. He might die if he hit wrong. He might die of hypothermia.

But then, that wasn't what Sutton wanted for him. She would smack him for thinking it – especially because of her. There had been enough of that thinking not long after she'd become his mother. He couldn't do that to her even if she wasn't around to have to deal with the aftermath.

And Minnow. He had to take care of Minnow.

He had to keep her close.

*

Church came, of course. He'd always been a man of his word, even as a boy. Like Sutton, he never left Severin alone no matter what he did or said. Until they both had, one after the other.

His brother's eyes were red, his dark skin blotchy from grieving, like Minnow's was. The two of them had found him in the woods and forced him to come back even though the whole house whispered with the spirits of dead mothers.

"Maybe tomorrow," Church said, his voice thick. "I can't even think about going through her things tonight, but I can't leave it for you, Sev, and I can only stay until the night of the cremation."

"You can leave it. It will stay like that until you have time to come and take what you want." Severin shrugged, ignoring the hot meal in front of him and nursing his beer instead.

"No. I know you. I'm not leaving it all for you to deal with, or the next time I come everything will be gone."

Severin inclined his head. True. Sentimental things made him uncomfortable and he rushed to get them over with. When Church's mother had died, Church had lingered over every little thing, reminiscing. It had made Severin profoundly uncomfortable, like picking and picking at a scab. Dwelling on unpleasant feelings only made them worse.

They cleared the dishes together then Severin went out to the forge, needing to get away from Church's storytelling and all of the emotion he and Minnow were emitting. It felt as if their emotions were beating at him. Controlling himself all evening and blocking their sorrow had been exhausting.

He had only enough time to kindle the fire in the forge before the outer door swung open. Church came in, stomping and blowing in his hands.

"You can hide out here if you want to, Sev, but sooner or later you're going to have to deal with this."

"I've dealt with it," he said coolly. "I'm not the one who keeps crying."

"The fact that you've shut yourself off means you're not dealing with it."

His brother sat on one of the stools and leaned his elbows on the work table where he often went down on Minnow when she dared to follow him out – which was pretty much daily. He was starting to think oral sex wasn't an effective threat.

"This is the third mother I've lost. I'm getting efficient."

"The fuck you are. You haven't dealt with any of them."

"People will always leave, Church. It only hurts when you let yourself believe they'll stay."

Church drummed his fingers on the table, his forehead creasing. "If I would have known she was going to visit her sister for so long I wouldn't have left when I did."

"Oh, please. I don't need a babysitter." Severin poked at the fire, stoking it higher and adding bigger logs. "I definitely didn't need a nanny anymore." He shrugged, watching the flames lick up a particularly dry log. "People die."

"Of course people die, but without loving people what the hell is the point of all this?" Church sighed. "You can't keep yourself detached from everyone like you do. It's not healthy."

"Oh, and crying like a baby over Sutton is healthy?" Her name came out as a growl, but he pushed away his mental image of her face, and the last words she'd said to him when she'd called the day before. "She was an old woman. We knew she was going to die sooner or later. Shocker. Old woman dies. Someone call CNN."

Church's gaze hardened. "Be a dick about Sutton. Be a dick to me, if you want. Just try to be nice to Minnow. Maybe we let you down, but she seems pretty set on sticking around."

"She should go too. Rodrigo likes her. Maybe he'll take her."

"Oh for fuck's sakes. You can't hand her off like a pet."

"She is a pet."

Church slammed his hand down in frustration. "You're going to do with her like you do with everyone. The closer she gets, the harder you'll test her. Eventually you're going to push everyone away, Severin, and you'll end up having a lonely fucking life. I'll always be around for you, but that only does so much good."

So Church didn't trust that she'd stay either. Had she been confiding in him? Was she already on the verge of leaving? Maybe she'd been planning to leave when Sutton came home and now felt obligated to stay.

Yes. That made sense.

Anxiety gnawed at him. He didn't want her to leave, but the feelings he had for her were one-sided, just as he'd suspected. Now Church would leave and Sutton was gone, and Minnow was as good as packing her bags. He'd be alone in his tomb of a house and he'd have to be okay with that.

He was a grown man. Grown men weren't supposed to need anyone. He'd gone out of his way to find ways to be alone in life, so why did the idea of being completely alone leave him with a vast, bleeding emptiness?

If there was no one to acknowledge his existence, would he disappear? He'd always been out of step with the world. Maybe he'd never been real.

A loud clapping sound drew him back out of his thoughts, and for a moment he was disoriented.

He was staring into flames. He was at the forge. Church was there.

"Severin, stop it!" Church said, his voice sharp. "You need to grieve. You can't let yourself disassociate after I go because Minnow won't know how to get you out of it. And so help me – I will call the fucking police to bring you to the hospital if you go too far down the rabbit hole this time."

"You have a life to get back to and enough people to take care of," he replied, remembering enough about normal human interactions to give his brother a reassuring half smile. "I'll be fine."

"My God, Sev. You've never *been* fine." Church rubbed a hand over his face. "You're the only family I have left in the world, and I need you to be okay. Maybe if you just talked to someone –"

The old argument and was still going nowhere.

"Some things become more real when you say them out loud. Poking a wound with a stick doesn't help it heal."

"Cleaning it out does. Talking can help with all that shit you carry around. If not me, and not a counselor, why not Minnow? Rodrigo? I don't know – maybe..."

"If you send me another fucking journal for Christmas we will have words."

Church chuckled, but it was a sad sound, then his expression sobered. "I can't believe she's gone, man. Christmas." He shook his head.

Sutton loved Christmas – she'd always decorated the hell out of the house and cooked for an army – bought them all the ridiculous things mothers bought their grown sons. New socks, the latest gadgets. She even knitted them ugly scarves.

A lump tried to form in Severin's throat, but he swallowed it down.

"We'll figure it out. Unless you're not coming?"

"Ilse and I both got a week off. If you don't let us stay here, we'll camp out on your doorstep."

Severin nodded, not really believing him. Something would come up. He'd probably never see his brother again. Maybe he'd die as soon as he left to go home. It hurt, but he shut off his feelings about that. If he'd learned anything in life, it was that there was nothing he could do to make people stay.

"No more Christmas scarves," Church murmured.

"You hated those."

"Well, we both did, but how many women would teach themselves to knit just so they could make hideous scarves for ungrateful teenagers who kept insisting they didn't need a mom?"

She'd made them new ones every year out of some sort of need to keep them warm and safe. The scarves had taken on a whole new level of jocularity when Ilse had started to come for Christmases. She called their scarf modeling antics Nordic skiing porn. They now had a whole shtick that went along with the scarves, including calling each other Sven and Bjorn, and throwing around skiing-inspired sexual innuendo. Sutton would always roll her eyes, but she laughed as much if not more than the rest of them.

As much as she'd arrived in their life as hired help, Sutton had made them a family again.

If there was one thing Severin could trust, though it was that all good things in his life came to a precipitous end.

Minnow had made him happy. Sutton had been taken in exchange. Some people would argue that those were coincidences, but he knew better.

He'd been stupid to think otherwise.

Chapter Thirteen

Severin stopped talking the day after Sutton's cremation – pretty much the moment Church left, as though holding things together for his brother had taxed him to the point of exhaustion. Although he hadn't shown much emotion, she'd thought maybe he was working through things in his own way.

Now, though, he'd sit alone by the hour, staring off into space, his expression grim. At first she'd given him time, taking care of the cooking and the house, fielding phone calls, and sitting quietly with him so he didn't feel alone. It was hard to know if she was helping, though. He ignored her, never making eye contact, and rarely seeming to notice anything that happened outside of his own head.

Church kept calling – he'd gotten home safe, and was struggling with his grief and the demands of the new job, but he had Ilse there to help him. It was weird how because he was one of the only people she spoke to in a day, he'd gone from stranger to friend, and now almost to family. She missed the daily calls from Sutton too. She always had nuggets of information and wisdom for Minnow to turn over in her head during the quietest times of her day, and now she'd lost that source of insight. Rodrigo had been with them for the ceremony when Sutton's ashes had been buried, but work was busy, and sometimes a few days would pass before he was able to call.

Two weeks in, she'd almost given up on getting Severin back. Emotionally, he'd walled himself off somewhere she couldn't get to. It hurt that he wouldn't even speak to her.

How long could she stand by a man who was this messed up without jeopardizing her own sanity? Living with him now was like solitary confinement. She'd gone into town a few times, just to get out, but every time she left, she felt like a traitor. She was worried about what he might do.

After taking a bath and finishing off a mystery novel, she went looking for Severin. He'd been sitting in his study most of the day, but when she went to check on him, he was gone.

Distant clattering led her downstairs. Clad in only her robe, she followed the sound, calling for Severin. He didn't answer.

A blast of cold air brought her to the double doors leading to the backyard.

Severin was there, doors propped open, dragging a familiar wooden dresser outside.

She clutched her robe more tightly around herself as the wind whipped at the hem.

"What are you doing?"

He ignored her, hefting one end of the heavy wood, and wrestling it out the door in an impressive display of muscle.

"You're moving the rest of her things out now? It's dark."

When he didn't respond, she closed the doors behind him and ran back upstairs to get dressed. In jeans, a sweater, her coat and boots, she left her room expecting to find him in the driveway, only to meet up with him where the servant's hallway met the main hallway. This time his arms were full of other things – pictures, books, and a few trailing pieces of clothing.

"Where are you going with that? Don't throw out pictures!" Horrified, she plucked a few from under his elbow, then an album from the crook of his arm.

He didn't deign to reply, striding down the stairs and out to the grounds as though he hadn't noticed her. In the distance she could see a bonfire glowing from the other side of the trees, where the fire pit was. Had he set Sutton's beautiful wooden dresser on fire?

She trotted after him, grabbing pictures and papers as they fluttered out of his overfull grip, not sure if he'd let her keep the things she thought she was saving from him.

Sure enough, the fire pit now had a lovely wooden dresser over it, fire licking up the sides as though the lacquer was a delicacy. He threw his armfuls onto the smoldering pile. A bottle of perfume smashed on the rock surrounding the pit, and the flames burst with new energy.

"Why?" she asked, grabbing yet another picture that had escaped the blaze. When she looked at it in the firelight two little boys covered in mud were grinning at her. Severin and Church. Her heart clenched.

"You're burning the pictures of your childhood?" she asked, aghast.

"You saved most of them, but that's enough now," he said, his voice rough. The fact that he'd said anything was a relief after the days upon days of strictly observed silence. He stalked past her, back toward the house. She followed him, stashing the pictures under her bed in her room while he was distracted with his mission. It felt strange standing in Sutton's room, watching Severin go through her things. He wasn't sorting. He was just dumping random items on the bed and gathering them to take outside.

She looked quickly around the room, but wasn't sure what was important. No more pictures were visible, but there were other things – children's art projects Sutton must have saved from Church's mom's collection, the apron Sutton wore when she cooked, a handmade quilt.

"She doesn't have other family who might want some of this?"

"No. I'm not sending it to her packrat sister. Other than her, there's just Church and me. He already took what he wanted. We're not nostalgic about things like you are."

"If you weren't, you'd be donating this stuff, not burning it."

He bared his teeth at her. "I don't want strangers touching her things."

Her heart melted. For all of his rough ways, he had a tender heart, even if his actions were odd. Maybe he just didn't know what to do with his feelings.

"Do you want me to help?"

"No. I need to do this myself."

She nodded and followed him out again.

The dresser had caught fire well now, and for a moment he stood watching the blaze, his arms still full of Sutton's possessions. He nodded to himself then flung his armload onto the blaze. A picture caught on the breeze and skated to the ground. Minnow crouched and picked it up. A chubby, grinning baby with pale blue eyes looked back at her from the photo. A baby. A picture from before he'd been sent here. She tucked it into her jacket pocket.

"No." Severin's voice was stern.

"But it's a baby picture of you."

"Yes. It's the only one that I know of." He held his hand out for it.

"No." She put her hand protectively over her pocket.

"It's not yours."

"I want to keep it." She took a step back. He took a step forward.

"That's nice. Give it to me."

"No," she objected. "You were so adorable. Please, can I keep it?"

Growling, he lunged for her. Responding to instinct, she spun and ran from him, feeling as if they were reliving the last time they'd been at the fire pit.

"Get back here, you little shit."

Little shit? If she had any breath to spare, she would have laughed. Affectionate name-calling was a good sign.

She ran, not knowing where she was going, but glad to distract him from the grief that had kept him dour and silent for so long.

He was swearing under his breath.

"You're going to be so fucking sorry when I catch you."

The threat made Minnow's long-dormant arousal flicker to life.

She ran for it, fleeing him and yet wanting to be caught – but not until she'd shaken him out of the withdrawn grief he'd retreated into. If he didn't talk to her, there was no way for her to help. Even irritating him like this was better than the lack of response he'd shown to everything else over the past days.

With the moonlight filtering through the trees, the path into the woods seemed creepier than usual, but she hurtled into it without pausing. What kind of animals might be awake and hunting at this time of night? Pushing herself to run faster, her every breath burned in her chest – heart beating faster than a run should have merited. Behind her she could hear Severin's footfalls. He was almost close enough to reach out and grab her. What would he do? Something unpleasant, but how unpleasant? Possibilities flicked through her mind. Maybe she should stop running before she pissed him off worse? That was probably a sound idea, but it was impossible to make herself stop with adrenaline coursing hot through her.

After a few minutes, she realized he had to be toying with her. She slowed, stopped. She was alone in a natural clearing, and Severin was nowhere in sight. But he'd been right behind her...

She held her breath, trying to listen for him over the loud thudding of her heart, but she could only hear the wind in the trees and the call of birds to each other in the darkness. Where had he disappeared to? Turning full circle, she felt her eyes going round with the effort to see through the gloom. Deeper shadows loomed near every tree. Was he watching her, or had he given up and gone back?

A nervous giggle escaped her. She blew out her held breath then tried to quiet herself. Playing games like this with him when he was in a strange state of mind was probably a mistake.

Pain exploded in her scalp. He spun her around and pressed her against the trunk of a tree, the bark digging into her cheek.

"Why are you still living in my house, Miss Korsgaard?"

His words stabbed into her heart, more painful than she would have expected.

"Do you want me to move out?" she asked, emotion thickening her throat. Tears pricked her eyes, but she blinked them back. Was he that angry about her saving the pictures?

"I haven't spoken to you in two weeks – barely acknowledged your existence – and still you're hanging around like a stray hoping for a meal."

"You just lost your mother. You're grieving."

"I didn't lose her. She's not missing. I know where her ashes are buried."

His body was pressed against her back, pinning her there – his words angry and harsh in her ear.

"Do you really want me to leave?"

"I don't want you staying out of fucking pity."

"I wasn't here out of pity in the first place, Mister Leduc. Why would our relationship suddenly be about pity?"

"You should leave while you can."

"Why?"

"For fuck's sakes, Minnow – I'm not right in the head! Why stay here when you could be with someone normal?"

"Is it that hard to believe that someone could love you?"

His body jerked as though she'd struck him.

"Fine. You don't want to listen? You want to fucking stay with me? You get what you get. Last chance."

She shook, waiting to see what he'd do.

"You little fucking idiot." He fumbled with the button of her jeans then shoved the stretch denim down to her knees. She felt him fiddling with his own pants, and tried to push him away, but he only shoved her harder against the tree, scraping her belly.

"You had your chance. I fucking warned you." His hand groped roughly between her thighs. "I've always been on my best behavior with you. That's over."

She gasped as his cold fingers parted her folds. Without any preamble, he slid one of his frigid fingers into her hot and swollen sex. It hurt, scraping a bit, but her body adjusted to the invasion and coated his callused finger with her arousal.

"Wet?"

She pressed her forehead against the rough bark, thrusting her ass back to meet him. Her breaths roughened as though she'd started to run again.

"You like being treated like a little whore, don't you, Miss Korsgaard."

By him? Fuck yes.

"No," she gasped. "I –"

He slipped his finger out of her even though she clenched her internal muscles in an attempt to keep it. She opened her mouth to protest, but the tip of his cock prodded at her, and before she could do more than tip her hips, he forced his huge dick into her inch by burning inch.

"Oh fuck – it hurts." She grunted, digging her nails into the tree.

He groaned in her ear then wrapped a huge arm around her waist, bracing himself against the tree with his other hand. He withdrew a few inches then slammed back into her hard enough her feet left the ground. The denim of his jeans scraped her ass cheeks, and his belt buckle was a cold brand on her thigh, but it was being skewered on his huge fucking dick that made her cry out against the sleeve of her jacket. It felt as if he was fucking her with a baseball bat. Her arousal dripped from her, but the lubrication wasn't helping. He felt so huge in this position.

There was no lust in his fucking, only a terrifying aggression. She clenched her teeth so they'd stop rattling together, but every thrust forced a squeal from her. His hot grunts in her ear, and his harsh use, made her delirious with discomfort and arousal. When he let go and reached between her legs, rather than rubbing her clit, he slapped her there. She cringed away from his hand, taking the next stroke of his cock too deep, and she could swear his cock piercing hit the back of her throat. A series of slaps landed on her clit, and she rocked back against his cock, only to be driven forward by his thrusts. Now they were both grunting, their breaths pluming in the chill night air.

His thrusts grew erratic, and she knew he had no intention of letting her orgasm. He swore quietly in her ear as his cock swelled alarmingly inside her, then began to pulse. Hard hands closed over her hips and he held her still as he got off, his come scalding and so copious it immediately began to slip past his thrusts to trickle down her thighs. Her clit throbbed, and she whined in distressed as he pulled out. A rush of his spendings followed his withdrawal, and as he rebuttoned his jeans, it left her feeling used, dirty, and exposed.

When she didn't move to cover herself, he yanked her panties and jeans back up, patting between her legs and making his mess seep into the fabric. He clamped a possessive, directive hand on the back of her neck, and led her back through the forest to the grounds.

"Sit," he grumbled, using his grip on her nape to push her down on the bench by the fire. "Stay."

He walked into the darkness, and she couldn't help but grind her pussy against the wood of the bench, trying to get relief. She gave up after a few minutes, shamed by her arousal as she again caught sight of Sutton's belongings burning. When would he insist she return the picture in her pocket so he could burn it?

"Good girl." He stroked her hair and she squeaked in surprise. "Are you sure you're not leaving?"

Shit. What was he going to do if she said no again?

She'd find out soon enough.

"No, Mister Leduc," she said, going for firm rather than meek.

"From now on, I do what I want to you when I want. You obey my orders immediately and without question."

Didn't she already do all that anyway?

"Yes, Master."

From behind, he lowered something over her and put it around her neck. It was cold. Metal? It felt solid. "If you want this off, you'll have to ask me to cut it off." There was a click. A thrill of panic shot through her. Too tight – she was suffocating! She lurched to her feet clawing at it.

"Get it off," she begged, hooking her fingers under it and tugging. It didn't budge.

"You're fine. Quit being a baby."

She realized her fingers fit under it easily, and tried to slow her heart rate. When she was calmer, she explored the thing with her fingers, finding the lock that was surprisingly solid for its size.

"Where's the key?"

"I melted it down."

Panic welled again.

"But what if I need it off?"

"I'll use bolt cutters," he said, sitting down beside her. "If you're staying, it will be on my terms."

"But why does anything have to change?"

"Because if I'm going to bother getting attached to you, I have to be sure you can't walk away."

"But that's not how life works!"

"It's how our life works from now on. If you want to go somewhere, I go with you. You don't leave the property without me."

"That's pretty much how things are already."

He glanced at her from the corner of his eye. "Well, now I've said it out loud."

"So I'm your captive?"

"Yes."

"But...I have a safeword and can leave whenever I want?"

He glared into the fire. "You stay with me."

Should she be afraid? He couldn't mean it the way it sounded, right?

"Go to bed."

She edged closer to him. "But...now?"

"Goodnight, Miss Korsgaard. Remember that you don't have permission to touch yourself." He turned his attention to the fire, dismissing her without another word or any sign of affection.

She crept away, thumbing the collar around her neck. It was only after she showered off the come and streaks of blood that she looked in the mirror and realized he must have made the thing. It was smooth steel with deliberate scorch marks – ugly and matching the look of his bikes. If anyone who knew his work saw the collar, they'd know whom she belonged to.

A shiver trembled through her lower belly.

The collar was bad enough, but the words stamped into them – even reading them backward in the mirror made her guts knot with fear and lust.

Property of Severin Leduc.

*

"Let me know if you need me to get you out."

Even over the phone, she could tell Rodrigo wasn't okay with her decision to stay. She leaned back in Severin's comfy leather desk chair, twirling the old-fashioned phone's cord around her finger and watching the rain come down outside. This whole room smelled clean and manly, and it made her want to stay there for hours and daydream about sex.

"Oh, like you're going to fly back from Italy and stage a prison break?" She laughed lightly, trying to pretend she wasn't nervous about staying. Severin making her nervous was part of the excitement of being with him, but she had to admit things with him were getting a bit scary. "Stop worrying about us and have fun. If we've gotten through things okay so far, we'll be fine."

He grumbled something in Spanish that she didn't understand then sighed.

"I love that idiot to death – you know that even if he doesn't get it – but if he wrecks things with you irreparably he'll never forgive himself." His voice lowered, as though Severin might overhear his half of the conversation. "And then there's you, *preciosa*. Just because he dominates you doesn't mean he gets to do anything he wants. Don't let him bully you." He mumbled something else she didn't catch.

She laughed. "Ro, this isn't my first rodeo. You don't have to tell me how to handle a bull. If things get too crazy, I'll just leave the ring."

"See? That's the problem. I'm afraid you'll end up so brainwashed out there alone with him that you won't realize things have gone too far. Hell, I don't know many women who wouldn't have left already." He cleared his throat. "He's not even the easiest person to be friends with – I can't imagine being his submissive."

"I'm fine. He's suffering right now, and I get that. He just needs some time, and someone to be here to help him through it."

"Right now you're not just his employee and his girlfriend, you're his slave, and his therapist, and his...everything. He's obsessed with you, even though he's trying to pretend he doesn't care."

"He'll settle down again. He just doesn't know how to process everything he's feeling. He's afraid I'll leave but sometimes he also wants me to hurry up and go before he gets too emotionally invested."

"You're young, Minnow, and maybe too optimistic for your own good. I can't make this decision for you, but just remember that you can't save him. He's a grown man and set in his ways."

"He doesn't need to change. He just needs someone to teach him how to trust."

"I think that part of him is broken. His stupid birth family broke it. He's hinted to me that something bad happened before they threw him out, but no matter what it was, I think the worst part for him has been feeling like he was disposable – like he wasn't worth having and wasn't worth entrusting to someone else."

Minnow's throat thickened. She pulled the baby picture of Severin she carried in her hoody pocket and looked at the trusting little face with the big silly grin. What the hell had happened? In the picture, he had pulled himself up to stand in a beautiful crib in a beautiful room. He was wearing an expensive-looking summer shorts and button-down shirt set. Like the royal baby pictures posted in Time magazine. There was nothing in the picture that suggested he'd been unwanted.

No child should have to go through what his family had put him through. Sure, she'd had her own issues with her parents, but nothing like what he'd survived. Really, it was no wonder he was a little messed up.

Rodrigo was still talking, but she'd missed some of it. "You're content there for now, but if you ever change your mind, or need to get out of there, just remember I'm an escape clause. You can stay with me until you decide what you want to do and get back on your feet. Hell, you can just stay – I'm rarely home anyway. You'd have free run of the house, and you don't have to worry that it would be awkward or that I'd expect anything."

"If I ever went there to stay with you, even temporarily, he'd think something was going on between us and he'd never forgive you. I won't be a wedge in your friendship. If things get bad I can always go to a shelter."

"Fuck that. I'd set you up at a hotel first."

They both sighed.

"I have to go get some work done. I'm serious though, Min, if something happens and you don't call me for help, I'll be pissed."

"I'm not your responsibility, Mr. Solis."

"Don't be ridiculous. Of course you are, *preciosa*," he said, his tone warm with passion and affection. "You both are."

She blushed. It was hard not to have a slight crush on him, considering how often they talked, and what she and Severin usually ended up doing with him when he came over.

They said their goodbyes, and Minnow hung up, rubbing her ear. She'd been on the phone with Church for almost an hour before Rodrigo had called.

"Who was that?"

Minnow screamed, then fell back in the chair clutching her chest. Severin stood in the doorway, shaggy and wild, anger in his pale gaze.

Why was he angry?

"That was Mr. Solis. He's on his way to Italy for a week, and wanted you to know. Before that I was on the phone with Church, who was looking for you. The girls are getting up to mischief, as usual, and he was calling to blame you for being a bad influence."

Only then did she notice he was carrying a large plastic container. Muddy and battered as it was, he still set it down on the clean floor. She wasn't about to complain about the mess it would make.

Would she be in trouble for sitting in his chair? She jumped up.

Without pausing, he walked to her, stopping only when he was standing practically on top of her. His proximity, paired with his incredible height, forced her back down into the seat. She had to look way up to see his expression.

His eyes were narrowed, menacing, and in response her heartbeat kicked up a notch. So close to his zipper, she fantasized about him drawing it down, and about him grabbing her hair and forcing her mouth down on his cock. With the kind of anger he'd been harboring, she could only imagine the ferocity of the facefucking he'd give her.

She shuddered, gazing up at him, fluttery feelings in her stomach that she seemed to have no control over. Lust – love? How was she supposed to interpret her visceral responses to him? Her feelings for him were far too complicated to sort out without a specialist developing some sort of graph or flow chart to explain it.

One of his big hands came up and traced the collar he'd locked around her neck with a slow, mesmerizing sensuality that made her pussy twitch. She angled her hips, trying to rub herself against the firm leather seat to take the edge off the ache.

"Am I in trouble?" she whispered.

The interest in his gaze flared into desire. "Maybe later. I found that bin on the side of the road when I was on my way back from the metal supplier. Take care of it." Without another word he walked out.

Take care of it? He couldn't have put the old bin out in the shed with the other garbage? And since when did start picking up garbage on the side of the highway?

Confused, she moved to pick up the dirty container and move it outside where it would stop dripping on her clean floor. Inside was a matted old fur coat.

She squealed in surprise when it moved.

A dog?

A little nose poked up, then another. Caterwauling began. Four sets of bright eyes. Four little beasts roly-poly tumbling over each other. They were wet and mud-splattered and shivering, and their legs were wobbly and seemed too short for their big round bellies.

"Mister Leduc!" she called. Puppies? Where on earth did he get puppies? Where was their mother?

He appeared in the doorway, frowning. "Is there a problem, Miss Korsgaard?"

"What am I supposed to do with them?"

He shrugged. "Someone dumped them on the side of the road in that bin. I didn't think you'd want me to leave them for the coyotes."

"Don't they need their mother?"

"Well, she didn't leave a note, so I guess they're shit out of luck. Should I put them back where I found them?"

She glared. "We need to bring them to a vet!"

"There's one coming. She'll hand them off to animal control."

"No!" she cried, trying not to look at their little faces, but failing miserably. "If they go to the pound they might get put down!"

She picked up the bin and carried it up toward the family wing, surprised at how heavy they were. Severin took the bin out of her hands when she got to the first landing.

"What are you doing with them?" he asked suspiciously.

"They need a warm bath. They're cold and filthy. And what are they going to eat?"

"I asked the vet to bring food for several ages of pups. I don't know how old they are. I think they may be weaned, or close to it."

"How could someone be so fucking cruel?" she snapped, following him to the bathroom.

"The world is an ugly place, Miss Korsgaard."

"Maybe Church will want one. And Rodrigo? Oh, maybe he's gone too much."

"They're mutts. No one is going to want them."

"That's not true." She peered into the bin as Severin put a bit of warm water in the bathtub. "Dogs don't have to be purebred for people to want them."

"I wouldn't know."

"You've never had a pet?"

"No. The closest I've come to having a pet is you." He tapped her collar.

Knowing he was just trying to goad her, she ignored that. "Look at their little faces. Oh my god, they're so cute!"

"Miss Korsgaard," he said, his tone mocking, "get your maternal instincts under control."

She rolled her eyes. "Mister Leduc, I can guarantee you I'm not the kind of woman who gets attached to small animals and talks to them in silly voices." The puppies were all looking up at her, threatening to turn her into a liar.

"There's no room in this house for a dog."

"No, no. Of course not." Not even one?

He was gone by the time she looked up from putting them in the tub, leaving her with puppy bathing and the visit from the vet. She blocked off her room and baby proofed it then gave the boys a blanket in a box, and put down puppy pads the vet had brought.

"I thought the vet was going to take them," Severin said when he stopped in front of her room later.

"They didn't tolerate the dewormer very well, so it's better if they stay here for now."

"What did you call them?"

She looked up from the one she was petting. "This one is Gilbert, then there's Montague, Harvey, and Theodore."

"Do the world a favor and let your future husband name your children."

She stuck her tongue out at him without thinking, and he quirked a brow.

"How long are they staying?" he asked coldly.

"A couple of weeks? I just need time to find them good homes. I'll post online first thing tomorrow."

"For their sakes, I hope their new owners have better taste in names."

Asshat.

He glared at them, then at her, and walked away. However, she could have sworn he looked at the pile of fluffy black-and-brown puppies longer than was strictly necessary.

Chapter Fourteen

For a few days the girl tiptoed around the house. Afraid to attract his attention? Possibly. A few people came by the house to look at her mutts, but left empty handed. They were up whining at all hours of the night, and Severin found the commotion and yipping irritating.

He stormed in and out, but spent most of his time working on the ugliest bike he'd ever made, forging and welding and attaching gruesome flourishes that probably weren't street legal, but it was hard to care. It would end up in his personal collection if no one would buy it.

The girl came to the forge at mealtimes, bringing trays of food he usually forgot to eat, then stole off again before he could punish her for annoying him. A cough – a soft word – anything could set him off. She hadn't run from him again, just submitted to his moody but controlled discipline and thanked him for it when he was done. He knew what she was doing, and maybe somewhere deep down he appreciated it, but it was hard to think past what he'd lost to think about how his behavior was affecting her.

Eventually, though, his self-imposed solitary confinement got lonely. He found himself looking forward to her visits, even though he was angry at her because there was no one else around to be angry at. There was a time where he'd been able to fake normalcy, but he couldn't remember how to do it. He couldn't even remember how to talk to someone he shared a house with. Barking at one of the only people who acknowledged his existence was stupid, and he needed to try to stop.

Having no one left to lose would be easier, but he was dependent on Minnow to make his life not suck. And even though he kept testing her, she kept not leaving. It went against everything in his head to trust that she wouldn't betray him and leave too, but there she was again, at the door. The prettiest zookeeper in the history of zoo keeping.

Most pathetic zoo ever. Him. Mutts. At least the mutts were cute.

Lunch came on a tray carried by a sexy little slave who wore a frilly, thigh-length dress and wooly white over-the-knee socks with pink ribbons laced through the tops. The cold had turned her normally pale skin pink. She set down her tray, turned to close the door then arranged the steaming bowl, sandwich, crackers, and utensils in an attractive display on a table.

"Mister Leduc, would you prefer coffee or beer? Or I could go back to the house for something else?" Her voice was low, neutral, but held a hint of fearful anticipation. He'd been unpredictable for days, even to himself, but wasn't sure how to apologize for that when it would probably keep happening. Maybe he did need help, other than the pretty girl who'd only been hired to teach him social skills. Instead, he'd taught her to endure his lack of social skills.

"Just leave everything there."

She nodded, hesitating by the table, either wanting to say something or wanting him to. He hadn't fucked her since the night in the woods. Was that what she wanted, coming into his space dressed like a naughty little girl who wanted attention?

"Is there anything I can help with?" she asked, her voice timid.

"Come here." He waved her over and she came to him immediately. He didn't need help, but his inner pervert wanted to get a better look at what she was wearing. "Straddle the seat and hang onto this piece."

Without hesitation, she put one of her sexy legs over the seat of the bike, flashing her little panties at him. The bike seat rucked up the hem of her dress, and the fluffy white eyelet made for an interesting contrast with the ugly Frankenbike.

She held the piece he'd indicated, and kept it still while he welded it in place. Over the past few months she'd helped often enough that she didn't even flinch anymore. He surveyed the piece longer than he needed to after it was firmly attached, but only as a cover for his perusal of her bared thighs. The over-the-knee socks with the dress. Hair in pigtails. Completely distracting.

Finally, he stepped back, knowing she'd caught onto the fact that it was her he was looking at, not the bike.

"Is that all, Mister Leduc?" she asked, getting off the bike while doing her mock best to maintain her modesty with a hand holding down the bottom of her skirt. She looked up at him coquettishly from under her lashes. Afraid of his moods but too horny to stay away?

"Did you come in here dressed like that because you need spanking?"

Her cheeks glowed pink, matching the ribbon around her waist, and the ones at the tops of her socks.

"I bought this online the other day. I thought I'd try it on and see what you thought." She put the end of one pigtail in her mouth and sucked on it. "Do you like these sorts of games, Mister Leduc?"

He wasn't sure how he felt about her pretending to be younger than she already was, but his dick was damned sure he was enjoying the view.

"I'm not sure how I feel about it," he admitted. "It's you, so it's hot, but it reminds me of how young you actually are."

He moved closer, and she tipped her head shyly to one side. Slowly, he reached out and touched one of her pigtails, then wrapped it around his hand and gave it a tug. The girl gasped in outrage but her eyes flared with lust. He led her to the table where she'd set out his lunch and pushed her belly down over an empty section, admiring the way the ruffled crinoline barely brushed the bottom of her ass. Minnow was made for him to fuck.

"Do you think of me as a daddy, Miss Korsgaard?"

"No." She wrinkled her nose adorably. "You're too mean to be a daddy. You're more like the monster under my bed."

"Yes. That would be more accurate."

"What are you doing?" she gasped as he lifted the back of her dress and draped it over her lower back. Her white panties had silly ruffles on the bum, but they left the sweet curve of her ass cheeks bare.

The taboo of it weirded him out but aroused him anyway.

"Monsters tend to do what they want," he pointed out.

"True." She laid her head on the table, watching him, trembling and pressing her thighs together.

Rather than touch her, he sat in front of his lunch and began to eat. He tore a small piece off his sandwich and pushed it into her mouth. She blinked slowly at him as she chewed, her eyes going soft and dreamy with every bit of food he gave her. When the sandwiches were gone, he pulled her into his lap. He ate the soup, savoring it and her subtle squirms, still impressed with how good a cook she was.

"This is good. Would you like some?"

She nodded, even though he could feel her pussy burning a hole in his thigh. Carefully, he spooned some into her mouth. That went well enough, but a bit of the next spoonful dribbled down her chin. He caught it with his tongue, and then they were suddenly kissing and he wasn't quite sure how it happened.

When he pulled back, he swatted her bare thigh. "Bad. I'm supposed to be working." Despite his words, he turned her back to his chest and found himself exploring the top of one sock with curious fingers.

"You're the boss in this place. You don't have to work at all, if you don't want to."

"Oh?" He followed the pink ribbon threaded through the top of the sock to the inside of her thigh, and tickled her there, but then dropped his arms back to his sides.

She squirmed in his lap, her giggle breathy.

"And am I supposed to make using your pretty cunt my job instead?"

She whimpered and spread her legs, draping them over either side of his and hooking the toes of her ballet flats behind his calves.

"Such a bad little girl, acting slutty for the monster when he's trying to have a conversation with you."

"It's not my fault. The monster has been ignoring me when he's not growling and it's making me crazy." Tentatively, she took his wrists and pulled her arms around her, then slid one of his hands between her legs, and the other into the bodice of her dress. He left his hands where she'd put them, but didn't take things any further.

She whined, but let her head fall back against his chest. Holding her facing away from him was easier than a real hug. "What do you want to talk about?"

"Dogs."

She sighed. "The people answering my ad don't seem very nice. I watch them with the boys, but they're either too rough, or too soft. I can't send them off with people who can't handle them." She grimaced. "And I was kind of hoping they'd go somewhere together."

"No one is going to take four mannerless puppies. They get into everything."

She nodded sadly.

Forget the silly dogs. He had questions he needed answers to.

"You let me do anything I want," he observed.

"What? Is this about the dogs?"

"No."

"Well you should let a girl know when you change the subject."

He swatted her thigh and she smiled shyly. Brat.

"This is about you. You never safeword. You let me toy with you, beat you, humiliate you. You obey my orders and don't ask for anything. Why?"

She tipped her hips toward his palm, rubbing herself against it. Wetness seeped through her panties, dampening his hand.

"I don't know. I just like it."

"Even if you don't get what you want?"

"I want whatever you give me. Whatever you choose not to give me. All of it turns me on. If it hurts too much in the moment, it just turns me on later when I'm remembering it."

"Pervert."

"You say that like it's a bad thing." She smiled impishly.

She was too fun. Too good. There was a catch somewhere, and he was impatient to find out what it was.

"What's your deal, Miss Korsgaard? You show up here for work and weeks later you have Sutton eating out of your hand," he heard his voice stumble over Sutton's name and the reality that she was gone forever washed over him again. "You're too fucking perfect. You follow me around and let me treat you like shit. You blow me and let me fuck you. Let me hit you. I locked a collar around your neck, claim you as my property, and you don't even question me or object." He blew out a breath. "Why?"

"Because I'm a submissive masochist and you have my fucking number, Mister Leduc." She groaned. "Can we finish discussing this after you give me an orgasm or two? I answer questions much better after sex."

"Nice try." He lifted her off his lap and sat her on the table. It would be easier to talk without the distraction of her squirming on his cock. "Why are you still here, Miss Korsgaard? What do you get out of this?"

"I like it here. I like you. Why does it have to be more complicated than that?" She propped the toe of one of her little ballet flats on his stool, between his legs, letting her dress slide up her thigh until he could almost see those distracting panties of hers. "You've decided you own me. I could try to fight and run away, but it would be pretty pointless seeing as how I was already here of my own free will. I also know part of the reason you collared me like this was to freak me out and scare me away. You'll just have to deal with me hanging around liking you." She leaned in, looking into his eyes, her own beseeching. When she looked at him that way it made him sorry he wasn't a decent guy. "Someday, if you're mean enough, I might leave, but I don't think that's what you really want."

He wrapped a hand around her calf. Compared to him she was so finely built that she felt disturbingly breakable. And yet she seemed to trust him more than he trusted himself.

"Why wouldn't you leave? Eventually you're going to want a normal life again. Unless you're in the witness protection program or something, why would you stay here?"

"My grandfather died about a year ago," she said, shrugging like it hadn't been unexpected. "My parents have basically disowned me, and my perfect sister doesn't speak to me. I don't know what you keep thinking I have to go back to. You're it. You and your family and your friends. I was alone before I came here."

"What about your own friends?"

"I lost most of them when I moved to Michigan. I spent so much time trying to finish school and make rent that I didn't have time to keep up with them. People grow apart. Maybe it makes me a bad friend, but we have nothing in common anymore. I talk to them online once in a while, but Jenna is married and has two kids, and all she wants to talk about is her husband's bitchy mistress, and Marisol is getting her master's in public health and I can't follow half of what she's saying. I don't have much to contribute."

"But your family?"

She shrugged. "My final transgression was apparently unforgivable."

"Were you a stripper or something? Call girl?"

Her laugh was incredulous. "I hate to have to break this to you, Mister Leduc, but I'm not exactly a hot commodity. I'm short. Silly. Quirky."

"You're perfect."

She blushed and rolled her eyes. "You're delusional."

"Antisocial and delusional are two different things. I'm not the only one who thinks you're perfect – Rodrigo would steal you from me in a heartbeat."

"Anyway," she continued, looking uncomfortable, "I didn't get disowned for anything as exciting as being a sex trade worker. I think my mom would have preferred that."

"Why did they disown you, if not for that? You said they thought you liked sex too much?" He felt himself relaxing. This was a much easier discussion than he'd thought it would be. He'd avoided asking her much about herself because he didn't want to think about other people who'd have a claim on her time – people she'd eventually go back to when she got bored of being at the house with him. As much as it made him an ass, he liked hearing she had no one too.

"When I came up here for school we did a segment on gerontology. It was a weird topic for me, because I never knew my grandparents, really. My dad's parents still live in Denmark, and my mom's mom died when she was twenty-two." She tapped her toe where it rested between his legs. "My mom's father has been in and out of jail since she was a little girl. He was a thief. She barely knew him. My parents pretended he didn't exist then got mad when I decided to look for him to interview him for a school assignment. I got to know him and started helping him out. He couldn't work anymore by the last time he'd been released from jail, and he was too sick to work anyway. He was stick thin when I found him."

In her agitation, she was tapping her foot on the stool he was sitting on, making it vibrate. He moved his grip to her ankle, then marveled at how his thumb and forefinger overlapped when he had his hand wrapped around it. She drew a sharp breath and her shudder shot through his palm.

"So what happened?" he asked quietly.

Her gaze settled on his, and she worried at her lower lip with her even white teeth. "I moved him in with me, and when my parents found out they were livid. We had a huge fight. I know Ben wasn't there for my mom when she was growing up. He was rough around the edges but he regretted a lot of the decisions he'd made in life by the time I'd met him. He'd tried to patch things up with my mom, but she didn't believe he'd changed, and was holding a grudge." She shrugged. "I guess that bridge was burned too far to repair. His emphysema was so bad he couldn't do much, and he had no one else."

"So you took care of him until he died?"

"Yeah," she mused, sounding sad. "He only lived a year, but it was nice to get to know him. It's funny how my mother couldn't stand him, but she has a lot of his mannerisms. He and I even have the same laugh. Genetics." She shrugged. "I never would have known that was a thing. Who'd have thought you could have the same laugh as someone you'd never met, just because of genes?"

He frowned. "So he died a year ago, but you're still not forgiven?"

"No. I may never be, but I'm okay with that."

"You'd think they'd be more forgiving, considering they're missionaries."

"I think this was just one of those soul-deep things for my mom. She couldn't get past it.

"Don't you miss them?"

She grimaced and shrugged. "It wasn't like we were close in the first place. I was never what they wanted me to be. I'm too dirty. I have a big mouth. I'm too opinionated. Anyway, they're far away, and they've disowned me, so whatever. I'm tired of pretending to be being a pale imitation of myself to please them. I think they're happier with me gone. They don't even send a card on my birthday."

Idiots.

"Do you feel like they've forgotten about you?"

She rolled her eyes. "I'm sure they won't even mention my name if they get together at Christmas."

He nodded slowly. "I know what you mean. I often imagine my family at these perfect family dinners, laughing together. I'm not sure why I do that to myself. I'm sure my sisters didn't have a great life either."

She laid her hand over the one that still held her ankle, then snatched it away again and gave him an apologetic smile. Not only had she forgotten he didn't like being touched, she'd almost made him forget that too.

"My sister, Pearl, got married about six months ago. I found out on Facebook – and only because someone posted pics. Of course I torturing myself by looking at them every few days. My family looks so perfect and happy without me."

Fuck. He didn't know how to comfort people. She wasn't crying, but her being sad about something he couldn't control made him antsy.

How did people navigate this?

He grunted. "Do you want me to...slash their tires or something?"

She burst out laughing then seemed to realize he was serious and her eyes went round.

"No!" She covered her mouth with one of her small hands, her eyes sparkling. "You can't slash people's tires just because they hurt my feelings!"

"Well – I – It's not fair that they did that to you. You took care of an old man. It's not like you tried to bring him over to their place. Why can't they just get over it?"

"I think they see it as a betrayal. Like I chose his side over my mom's. But when you see people suffering like that in real life, it's hard to walk away. Your heart goes out to them. Ben wasn't perfect, but he didn't deserve to die alone."

"Is that why you stay with me?"

She blew out a sigh of annoyance. "Oh my god, get it through that thick head of yours! I'm not here out of pity. This isn't about a job anymore, or do-gooding. What your family did to you – leaving you here – wasn't fair. It makes me protective, but I'm here because I care about you. I feel like we're connected somehow." She blushed hard, but went on so fast her words tripped over each other. "Maybe that feeling is one-sided and my imagination is just running away with me. Whatever. What it comes down to is that I'm here because I...like you. You're a good man." She opened his beer and took a sip, her gaze daring him to punish her for taking it without asking.

He arched a brow. "After everything I do to you, you think I'm a good man?"

She shifted to the very edge of the table, closer to him. "You know I like it. You wouldn't do it if I didn't."

He grabbed the backs of her thighs, just below her ass, and lifted her back into his lap to straddle him.

"So does that mean you'll be here for Christmas, Miss Korsgaard?"

"Unless you want me to go away. I have nowhere else to go, but I could get a hotel room. Although, I thought I wasn't allowed to leave the property without you."

"You're not. You're stuck on The Island of Misfit Toys, my poor little twisted doll." He kissed her and put his hand up her dress, finding the edge of her panties and tracing the leg band. "Rodrigo visits our island, but he can hide what he is. Church escaped, but he didn't belong here like we do."

He took the beer from her hand and turned her over his lap. A weird coil of lust shivered through him as he tugging down her frilly panties and bared her ass. He rubbed his palm over her quivering flesh, back and forth, lulling her until he couldn't hold off any longer. His first smack landed and she gave a plaintive moan, the sound perfect and needy.

It was hard to believe she fucking loved this the way he did. Using the belt on her was fucking hot, but having her vulnerable and half naked and over his lap did interesting things to his brain. It made him feel more connected to her. Anyone could hurt her, but this link between them went further than the administration of pain. He spanked her slowly, making her wait for each slap, waiting until she was whining and wriggling in invitation. This was exactly what she'd come in here hoping for, and he knew it without needing to be told. Finally being able to read what someone wanted from him was strange – wanting to give it was stranger.

Smack.

Smack.

Pause.

He let his hand hang in the air, threatening, and was rewarded with the girl looking over her shoulder at it impatiently. Her muscles strained as she angled herself more conveniently for him to hit.

She whined and arched back.

"Tease," she grumbled.

"You think so?"

He spanked the living fuck out of her ass, enjoying her attempt to stay quiet as the tension in her built. Her breaths grew louder, but then, so did his, the excitement of beating her spiking adrenalized blood straight to his dick. Her first cry of distress was met with his rumble of satisfaction. After a few minutes she squirmed to get away, but he held her still, raining sharp, hard smacks until his palm stung even past his calluses.

Her skin was bright, mottled darker in spots, bruising, with the obvious outline of his hand repeating over and over along the edges, reminding him how big his hands were compared to her luscious ass. He could nearly span both globes with one hand. He trailed tickling fingers over the handprints as her hectic breathing started to slow, and he worked on calming the drumming in his chest.

Between her whimpers and the scent of her arousal, he was ready to take her. Instead, he pulled her panties back up, then sat her on his lap and stroked her hair. She nestled against his chest, pouting up at him.

"What?"

"Just – a spanking and then nothing?" she asked sulkily.

"You shouldn't use your submission as a tool to get cock," he admonished, doing his best to seem serious. It was hard to object to her ulterior motives, but it was fun to tease her. "Not everything needs to be about sex, Miss Korsgaard."

Gently, she butted his chest with her forehead. "I just meant to talk."

"Of course. I could tell by how you were dressed."

She flushed, shifting in discomfort. "Maybe I was just trying to make sure I got your attention. We need to talk about Christmas. Church said he and Ilse are coming for the holidays with the kids, so I need to know what to get. What do you guys usually do to celebrate?"

"I don't know. Sutton – used to make dinner with Church. I watched TV. Ilse took care of the kids."

She shifted from one ass cheek to the other. She had to be sore.

"But this year..."

"What?"

"You're going to help with dinner and help with the kids?"

He grunted, sliding his finger under her panties to trace the smooth, damp seam of her slit. "Why would I do that?" he asked, distracted.

She whined impatiently, but he only kept teasing. "Because you have a family and you love them."

"Church left me."

"Your brother deserves to make his own way in life, if that what makes him happy."

Severin frowned at her. "I don't want to talk about them right now."

"No?" Their mouths were almost touching, and the caress of her breath on his lips was almost too erotic to bear. They breathed each other's air for several moments, while he coaxed a finger into her. She wriggled on it, trying to get him deeper, but he didn't allow it.

"What do you want for Christmas, Miss Korsgaard?"

"You're too evil to be Santa. I'm guessing you're Krampus."

"You know what Krampus does to bad girls."

"Gives them a birching?" Her pussy clenched around his finger and his cock twitched.

"Some bad girls like that too much. He has to find other ways to punish them."

"Oh?" Her eyelids fluttered, and her head fell back to his shoulder as he finger fucked her but only up until the first knuckle.

"Have you looked in the beer fridge today?"

"No, Master." She squeaked in dismay as he pulled his finger out of her pussy.

"Go get me the buttplug and lube I put in there this morning. You and I are going to have a serious discussion, young lady."

"About what, Mister Leduc?" she asked breathlessly.

"About what bad girls get for Christmas."

*

"Dress warm."

Without asking why, she left the screening room to comply, trailed by a parade of puppies falling over their humongous paws to follow their mistress. She came back in jeans and a sweater, holding the new winter coat he'd bought for her, and the two tandem dog leashes. The pups frisked around her legs, yipping with excitement.

"Why are there still four dogs living in my house?" he asked no one in particular, knowing what she'd say. He led the way down to the back of the house and the door.

"No one wants to take a puppy that still chews so close to Christmas, and they still piddle sometimes – right boys? Tell him you're just babies. You can't help it!" She patted two of them before slipping on her coat. "Oh – are we going into town, Mister Leduc, or are we staying on the property?"

"Leash the little jerks. We're going into the woods."

She frowned, looking thoughtful. "I wonder if they'll get into mischief out there."

"How? By chewing a tree? They've had their shots."

"What if they eat a mushroom and get sick? Or chase a porcupine?"

"If they're stupid they'll never survive in the city."

"Oh," she grimaced adorably, "I don't think they'd be happy living in the city, Mister Leduc."

They were already huge even though they were supposedly babies. They looked more like bear cubs than puppies.

"You have so many stipulations about where they can't live that I'm starting to wonder if you're hoping I forget you were supposed to get rid of them, Miss Korsgaard."

Her cheeks turned bright pink and she busied herself with attaching their leashes to their collars.

"So are we just going for a hike?"

"We're going to get a tree." He grabbed the axe from the umbrella stand, and opened the door. All four pups started to chase him, and the girl staggered after them because of how hard they pulled on the leashes.

"A tree?" she asked in confusion.

"A Christmas tree? I believe you're familiar with the concept."

"Oh!" She grinned at him, her dark eyes glittering with unrepressed excitement. "I've never done this before. My parents always bought one at the grocery store."

"They sell trees at the store?" He frowned, thinking. "You know, I don't think I've been to a grocery store. We've always had food delivered."

"Weirdo."

"Yes, yes. You're very bratty. I don't have time to spank you right now."

She sighed tragically.

"Come on. It's almost Christmas, Miss Korsgaard. Let's go murder a tree."

They set off through the grounds, and by the time they reached the forest, he had claimed one of the tandem leashes so that the four pups didn't drag Minnow off in their eager curiosity.

"You know, last year I didn't even have a tree," she said, a note of humor in her voice. "I assumed this year would be the same."

The thought of Minnow spending the previous Christmas by herself bothered him. "I thought you were taking care of a woman last year."

"I was. Her family came to visit for Christmas though, so I had the week off."

"And your grandfather had just died."

"Yes."

"So what did you do?"

The corner of her mouth twitched. "Watched porn and baked cookies. Well, I made cookie dough and ate it. The nice part was I had food poisoning after that, so I was busy."

He rounded on her and pulled her against his body, pressing her to him while trying not to knock her with the axe haft or yank the dogs around. Mauling her was getting more complicated lately.

"That is the saddest fucking Christmas I've ever heard of."

She laughed up into his face, her cheeks flushed with cold. Fuck, she was beautiful. So cheerful and full of life. It made him afraid for her. It felt like something bad would happen to her because he liked her.

"That's not even the worst part. I bought myself a few things from the dollar store and wrapped them, just so I'd have something to open."

"The dollar store. Wow. Krampus came early?"

"I got a chocolate bar and a lighter. I don't even smoke!" She started to shake with laughter.

He closed his eyes, not sure how to deal with all of the conflicting feelings she inspired. "How did I end up saddled with such a ridiculous woman?"

"You like me ridiculous." She stood on her toes and brushed his jaw with her lips, still chuckling. The fact that she took such a liberty shocked him, and he was frozen into inaction. He kind of liked it.

"How did you get something you didn't want for Christmas...from yourself?"

"I don't know!" She burst out laughing again. "It was supposed to be a chocolate bar and a pack of gum, but the cashier must have mixed up my order with someone else's. There wasn't time to go back and complain, so I just wrapped it anyway. Lighter fluid isn't very minty, just so you know."

He laughed out loud, surprising them both. "How were you ever single?"

"I don't know!" She leaned against his chest, giggling so hard she was falling over. "I'm fucking enchanting!"

"Like a fairy fucking princess."

They were staring at each other, grinning, and the anxiety that came with being unexpectedly happy made him pull away. Being too happy was a problem.

For a moment her brows drew together, as if she was vaguely embarrassed.

He slapped her awkwardly on the shoulder. "Well, you're my fairy fucking princess now, so you'll be getting something better than a lighter for Christmas."

"Is it anal? I bet I'm getting anal."

"It could be, brat."

She bit her bottom lip, blinking up at him shyly.

At that point he walked away, following Gilbert and Montague farther into the woods.

He could hear her tromping after him through the dead grass. "Do we have many ornaments? Knowing Sutton, I bet they're classy."

"Nothing I want on the tree this year. We'll have to get new ones."

"Where are the old ones?"

He'd almost thrown them in the fire, but hadn't been able to do that without talking to Church first. "In the attic. They're not classy, though. Just stupid ones we made when we were kids."

"Awww! I want to see them! Those need to go on the tree!"

"No." He snorted. "We kept trying to talk Sutton out of using those, but she insisted every year. When Ilse started coming around I thought Church was going to die – Sutton showed her every one and told her when we'd made them. So ridiculous. Just old art projects from when we were little. They belong in the garbage."

The pups were still frisking around their feet, showing no signs of playing themselves out. Silly things. Cute, but completely impractical.

"I bet Ilse thought your ornaments were adorable. The way Sutton felt about you two, I'm not surprised that's what she chose to decorate the tree with."

He grimaced.

"Guys are weirdly unsentimental," she said gravely, as if not wanting to hang on to ugly pinecone men with popsicle stick skis was a sign of gender-based inferiority.

At that point they arrived at the clearing he'd had in mind, and he stopped. "Here. I was thinking of using one of these ones," he said, pointing out five trees of various heights. They'd be easy to cut down and drag out because they were in the open. How big do you want it?"

She winked. "You know exactly how big I want it."

"I don't, actually," he pointed out. "Every time I fuck you, you start whining – Mister Leduc! It hurts! It's too big!"

She glared at him. "You should quit lifting weights with that thing. I swear it's bigger every time. It definitely didn't need the hardware, although it's really freakin' hot."

"The tree, woman. Focus. Why are you talking about my dick again?" Her obsession with his piercings and the attention she gave them amused him. When he'd had them done, he hadn't thought anyone would actually see them except Rodrigo. Well, at least his dick was a novelty – maybe more like a freak show – even if he wasn't the most skilled lover she'd ever had.

Her gaze traveled downward, to his zipper. He could force her to her knees and make her suck him. She never objected when he did.

"The tree."

"The tree?" She raised her gaze to his again then flushed. "Oh." Struggling with unruly puppies, she made her way closer to the trees. She walked back and forth, looking them over, then finally turned back to him and shrugged. "You're to one who has to chop it down and drag it back. You pick."

He trailed the ax down her arm, and she shuddered even though there were two layers of clothing between her and the blade.

"Miss Korsgaard, I told you to pick one. I don't think you want me to punish you out here in the cold, with your pups watching."

She sucked in a breath. "Tattoo."

"What?" he looked at her, baffled then remembered it was her safeword.

"Axe play – hard limit. I just thought I should let you know right away, in case you were having...thoughts."

Menacing her with an axe hadn't crossed his mind, but she didn't need to know that.

"Shit. There goes my festive kink idea. Would you prefer the chainsaw?"

"Mister Leduc!"

He was still smirking when he went to size up the tree.

*

The girl swept up the mess his empty coffee cup made after it had hit the flagstone floor. He'd pushed it off the edge of his desk when she wasn't looking, but only Rodrigo had seen it happen.

On her knees, she used the small brush and dustpan to get the sharp shards out of the grout between the stones, her every motion jiggling her perfect breasts. Not that Severin was watching. He was reading, and very pointedly not watching.

Just like he hadn't watched her in fascination as she made more decorations for their Christmas tree – although that had brought on completely different feelings.

"May I go to the kitchen to throw this out, Mister Leduc?"

"You may," he said with false distraction.

She rose and padded barefoot out of the room, her naked body small and lush compared to the cold grandeur and elegance of the house. In the distance he could hear the pups howling. All four of them. The hooligans were stuck in their bedroom behind a gate while Rodrigo visited, because they couldn't leave them unsupervised in most rooms of the house.

Rodrigo watched her go while Severin studied his appreciative gaze.

"I need to get one of those," his friend murmured, leaning sideways in his chair to keep her in view a moment longer.

"It's not like you'd have trouble finding one."

"It would be hard to find one like her." Rodrigo tapped his coffee cup thoughtfully. "You're keeping her naked all the time now?"

"Not all the time. Just when the mood strikes me and the dogs are gated in their room – otherwise that might get awkward. By the time Church, Ilse and the kids get here I'll have dressed her, but for you there's no point."

He'd also have to stop using her sexy little body anytime the mood struck him. After he'd fucked her on the dining room table the night before she'd complained she'd have to clean it again, but she'd been breathless and flushed. After he took her, her eyes got that sexy satisfied look, and she burrowed against him whether he liked it or not. At first he'd tolerated it, knowing he was supposed to allow it, but now he fucking lived for it.

Rodrigo shifted in his seat, as though pained. "Oh, there's a point to keeping her dressed around me. Being able to hang out here without having a perpetual boner would be nice."

Funny, her being naked gave Severin the same problem. "You've already had her. You're still interested?"

Rodrigo raised a brow. "In little Miss Korsgaard? Always. You're a lucky bastard."

Severin put his book down and stared at him hard. "If you ever try to take her from me, I'll fucking kill you."

For a long moment, Rodrigo just watched him in half-lidded indulgence, like a drunk guy patiently watching his drunk friend being an ass.

"The best part is I'm aware you mean that literally. Why would you think I'd do that to you? You're my best friend." Rodrigo shook his head. "You have no idea what to do with your feelings for her, so you're getting all grunty and territorial. You've already marked her as yours – between the bracelet and the nipple piercings and that monstrous collar I'd say you've made your claim pretty clear." Rodrigo sipped his coffee. "What else can you do? I won't tattoo your name on her face or anything like that, so forget about it."

"I'm planning to brand her today," Severin said as evenly as he could.

Rodrigo's mouth opened, then closed again. "I should talk you out of this, but honestly, I really need to watch."

"Will you hold her down for me?"

"Hell fucking yes."

"This is the worst idea I've ever had."

"Agreed."

They both turned to watch the door.

"Does she know?" Rodrigo asked.

"No." His mouth quirked. "I already made the brand, though."

Rodrigo gave a short laugh. "Knowing Minnow, she'll let you. If I ever find her equal, I'll marry the hell out of her."

Marriage?

Oh.

A ring might have been a better idea than a brand, but that wasn't how Severin's mind worked.

"Do you think I should marry her?"

Rodrigo hiked a shoulder. "You'd be an idiot not to."

"But she barely knows me. I have nothing to offer her."

The expression on Rodrigo's face said Severin had lost his mind.

"Money isn't everything, Ro. It's a solitary life out here. With Church gone and Sutton dead I have no family. She'd be better off marrying you. You have just as much money and you're way less fucked up."

"She doesn't seem to mind how fucked up you are – and you're far richer than I am, my friend, not that I'd have trouble providing for a family." He pushed his hair back. "Church moving doesn't mean he's not your brother anymore. That's not how it works. He hasn't abandoned you. He calls every damned day – you just won't talk to him."

The girl walked back into the room then hesitated after taking stock of their expressions.

"Ah, Miss Korsgaard. Just the girl we wanted to see," Severin said mildly.

Her face went ashen.

"Krampus has decided what you're getting for Christmas."

Her gaze fastened on him, as if she was afraid to look at Rodrigo. "Yes, Master?"

"A brand."

"A brand?"

"My brand."

She put her hand to the doorframe, as though she needed help staying upright. Her breath came in short gasps, drawing his attention to the hard buds of her pierced nipples.

"Isn't that going to hurt a lot?"

"Yes."

She shuddered hard, staring at Severin, her expression distressed. "O-okay."

Rodrigo groaned, and leaned his head back against his chair, as he palmed his crotch. "You two are going to be the death of me."

"Rodrigo is going to hold you down for me."

She nodded, probably expecting that from them by now.

"Am I branding your ass, or the front of your thigh?"

A slim shoulder went up in a shrug. "The real Krampus wouldn't give me a choice."

"She wants a beating before the branding?" Rodrigo asked.

"She gets brattier the longer she wears my collar. I must be doing something wrong."

"Too many orgasms. Put her on orgasm restriction and she'll get respectful fast."

"No! I'm sorry, Master. It's just the nerves talking." She swallowed hard and went to Severin, hovering as if she wanted comfort but didn't want to impose by touching him.

He gestured and she knelt at his feet then pulled her closer to put her head on leg. Automatically, his hand went to her hair, petting her. She sighed and pressed her forehead to his knee.

"Do you have questions, Miss Korsgaard?"

She turned her face up to look at him, her brown eyes wide and eager to please. "When will you do it? What will it look like? Can I be drunk? Will you dress like cowboys?"

Tightening his fist in her hair so she didn't bolt, he answered. "I'll do it in a few minutes, as soon as the brand I made is hot. It's the logo I put on my bikes. You can't get drunk fast enough for it to help. I don't think we own any cowboy costumes – I apologize for the oversight."

"You're doing it now? Today?" she squeaked and tried to squirm away, but his hold on her hair was too firm for her to go anywhere.

"Yes. You brought your bag, Ro?"

"Always. I'll get it from the car." He rose and went to fetch it, looking even more eager than Severin had anticipated.

"No! Let me go!" The girl tugged at his hands in a bid to get free. She couldn't have been very serious about escaping, though, if she wasn't using her safeword. "You could have given me some warning so I could brace myself."

"I decided it would be better to surprise you so you didn't have time to worry."

She seemed to give that some thought. "This isn't like piercing my nipples." Her grimace was almost funny enough to force a smile from him. "This is completely permanent."

"Yes."

"What if you get tired of me? What if you decide to send me away and I spend the rest of my life with your mark on me?"

He sighed and let go of her hair in favor of pulling her up by the arms and sitting her in his lap. She seemed to be there a lot lately, but she fit there so nicely, and she was warm, and soft, and smelled good even when she was sweaty and exhausted and full of come. Right then she was still clean and feisty. It was his job to fix that.

"Do you really think I'm going to mark you then abandon you?" He kissed her hair, and she melted against him with only a small shift of his arms.

"I don't know. We do this dance. We get closer to each other then you back off and treat me like I'm going to betray you. It's hard for me to deal with sometimes. You keep claiming me in different ways – like you want us to be permanent, but then sometimes you act like you wish I'd go away."

"I – want this to be permanent, but I have trouble believing you'd want to stay. Wondering when you'll leave eats at me. I want to mark you so that even when you go, you'll remember what we had."

With a pensive expression she nodded. "Okay. I want that too. To have something of yours to keep after you're finished with me." She lifted her face to his, offering her lips. He kissed her slow and deep, until she was clinging to his shirt and sighing into his mouth.

Finished with her? Never. Maybe she'd be better off without him, but it wouldn't be because he was finished with her.

Rodrigo came back and set out his supplies.

Severin coaxed Minnow to her feet.

"Where do you want it?" Rodrigo asked Severin, not Minnow.

"The front of her thigh so she can see it easily. It will help to remind her who she belongs to."

"Has she had a tetanus shot in the last few years?"

Minnow nodded.

"Do you want to hold her down or do the branding?" Rodrigo asked.

"You hold her down. I've been practicing and I'm feeling cocky."

A long, high-pitched whimper came from the girl. "Oh my god," she murmured. "Why did I say yes?"

"You like it when things hurt, Minnow," Rodrigo reminded her, his voice dripping with sadistic arousal. "You also like being a good girl for Mister Leduc."

"Am I a good girl, Master?" she asked Severin.

"Very," he replied. "I can't imagine another girl letting me do this." He draped her across the padded coffee table.

God, she was perfect, trembling, with her hand pressed to her mouth in fear. He leered down at her, drinking in her quiet terror, just as he knew he would enjoy her pain in a moment. Self-disgust rose, but he pushed the feeling away. It was so difficult to accept the way this made him feel without letting himself become appalled by his own reactions. What kind of man became aroused by the sight of his woman afraid and in pain?

Him.

Rodrigo.

Maybe it wasn't normal, but it was how they were wired, just like Minnow was wired to receive it from them. He had to force himself to remember there were two sides to the same page. Consenting adults, and all that.

"So are we doing this now, or do you think she needs to be in a more receptive mood first?" Severin asked.

Rodrigo laughed under his breath, more vibration in the air than sound. "Oh, I think she could use a distraction."

"Are you kidding me?" Minnow glared at Severin. He considered swatting her on the ass a few times to teach her not to glare at him like that. "Nothing you could do will distract me from this!"

"I'm betting DP would distract her."

"I haven't even fucked her ass yet," Severin admitted, "So yeah, I'd imagine that would go straight past distracting to distressing."

"How have you resisted her ass?" Rodrigo asked, incredulous. "Because man, if you want to see how it's done first, let me volunteer my services."

"No, I'm saving that honor for myself. No need to rush into anything when I can terrorize her with her imminent buggery week after week."

His partner in crime slapped him on the back, but rather than making him grit his teeth, he barely minded. "You are one sadistic fuck. You're like the fucking poster child for self-denial. The perfect dominant sadist."

"Don't encourage him!" the girl grumbled. Just as she was about to sit up again, Severin planted a firm hand on her chest and pushed her back down.

"Did I tell you to get up?" he asked quietly.

She blew out a quiet breath. "No. Sorry, Master."

He gave her a quelling look. "Remember to behave or I'll have to punish you. Don't cross me when I'm in this kind of mood, little girl."

"Punish me? How?" she asked, as if she couldn't think of anything worse than getting branded.

"Fucking her ass while I watch would be an excellent punishment – especially if you're rough." Rodrigo's jesting tone did nothing to hide that he was obviously hoping Severin would do just that. "Your sore little hole will make you forget all about having white hot metal pressed into your skin."

She whimpered, looking at Severin as though he'd save her. He wasn't at all interested in saving her right then. He was more interested in making her cry.

"If you behave, you won't have to find out what your punishment would be." He wasn't about to tell her he had no actual punishment planned. One of these days he'd have to sit down at the computer, or pick Rodrigo's brain, and come up with a list of sensible consequences. Coming up with punishments on the spot when his brain had migrated to his dick was too much to ask.

"Should we tie her down?" he asked Rodrigo. "I wouldn't want her to squirm at the last minute and get hurt."

Rodrigo sucked his teeth. "It would have to be tight bondage. Have you ever done that with her?"

"Not really. Usually I just hold her down. She's not very big"

Her gaze flashed with heat. She liked being held down, and he'd recently realized she also loved that he was so much bigger and stronger than she was. For so long he'd tried to avoid unintentionally scaring people with his size, and now with this slip of a girl it had become a desirable attribute.

"Does she get claustrophobic easily?"

"Not that I've noticed. We can always keep a sharp knife close by."

"Yeah," Rodrigo was leering at her now.

"I think Mister Leduc meant you could keep a sharp knife close by to cut the ropes in case I panic, Mr. Solis."

"Oh...right. I knew that."

Severin opened his bottom drawer, taking out several lengths of rope. "We're branding her tonight. I think we can probably hold off on the knife play for now."

They worked quickly, tying, touching, sliding their hands over her bare skin, until she was whimpering with need and tied spread-eagle on the padded coffee table.

"Fuck, she's so hot," Rodrigo said, standing back to gaze down at Minnow's completely immobilized body. Their vulnerable prey was trapped in their web of rough hemp. They were ready to devour her.

With her pierced nipples jutting up past the rope, her legs wide for them, and soft folds of her pussy slightly spread, her beauty was incomparable. Rodrigo moved to her head and freed her hair from where it was crushed beneath her, spreading the silken waves out to drape over the end of the table.

One of her hands opened in a futile attempt to reach for Severin. He squeezed it.

"What are we going to do with her? Skip right to the good part?"

"Which part do you consider the good part?" Severin smirked at him, loving the way the girl's attention was going back and forth between them, doubtlessly wanting to know what they were planning for her, and yet knowing better than to voice her preferences in the midst of a conversation between dominants.

"True. They're all good parts." Rodrigo smirked back then pointedly let his gaze caress her trembling body.

Severin let go of her hand to stroke his fingers over her. "Oh, little Miss Korsgaard. You are in the worst possible situation. What are we going to do to you?"

In response to his quiet observation, she struggled. It was obvious she was completely at their mercy, but he supposed she'd be remiss in her submissive duties if she didn't even check the rope work.

"It's so abrasive!" she complained, going very still. In several places her skin was already abraded from her attempts to free herself. "What on earth did you tie me down with?"

"His personality, obviously," Rodrigo replied.

"Fuck off, dickwad."

"See? Case in point." Rodrigo smiled mockingly at Severin before turning back to her. "Oh wait – he actually used rope. My bad. I think he chose this type just to be a bastard. Can't say I'm surprised. He's a bit of a bastard."

"Of course." Severin said, distracted by the way the rope held her breasts up and out for them. "When are her nipples safe to play with yet?"

"Gently? Now is fine. Nothing too rough."

Fascinated, Severin brushed a finger over the already tightening nipple closest to him. Rodrigo focused on the other one. Slowly, they tortured her, pinching gently before toying between and over them. After only a few minutes she was gasping, her hips thrusting at the air as much as she could move in her bindings.

"Look what you did," Severin accused.

"How is that my fault instead of yours? Besides, there's no proof it's turning her on. You might be imagining things."

"One of us should check."

"You check and I'll keep her quiet. I wouldn't want the neighbors to think anything weird was going on in here."

Considering how far away the neighbors were, they were completely safe even if they gave the girl a megaphone to scream into.

Severin slipped his hand between her thighs, finding out how soaked she was before he even got to her pussy. As he slipped a finger into her slick heat, she clenched around it, as though she was already on the verge of orgasm. She shuddered, but her choked cry was muffled. When he looked up, Rodrigo had a hand clamped over her mouth.

"Shh, pretty girl. Let him find out just how ready you are," Rodrigo murmured to her. She was looking up at Ro, gaze frantic, her hips straining to pump against Severin's hand even though she couldn't move enough to help get herself off.

Slowly, he stroked her hot core, feeling the telltale slip of the mess he'd left inside her earlier. He circled his thumb around her tiny clit, the bud of it hard and eager under his coarse touch. She screamed into Rodrigo's hand then babbled something Severin couldn't understand as he tormented the nub with gentle taps.

Her pleading sounds got louder, and her body stilled and tensed under Severin's attentions, loving how well he'd gotten to know her body and what it responded to. Right before she could come, he stopped, withdrawing his fingers.

"Is she wet?" Rodrigo asked him, his voice thick with sarcasm. "She doesn't seem very turned on."

Severin held up his fingers as evidence of her arousal. "So messy." He tsked. "She must be really into the idea of us using and marking her."

Rodrigo lifted his hand off her mouth and she gasped in air, even though he hadn't blocked her nose. Her skin flushed a dusky pink, and her nipples peaked, distended and stiff.

"That's not all me!" she cried. "You had sex with me before Mr. Solis got here."

"Did you almost come just now?" Severin asked quietly.

"I –"

He arched a brow.

"Yes. When you tied me down too."

Severin shrugged, the rest of her argument invalidated by her admission. "We should probably use her before we brand her. I don't think we should be distracted."

A slow, wicked smile spread across Rodrigo's face. "I get to use her too?"

"Pussy or mouth?" Severin offered. He wouldn't have it be said he was a bad host. He enjoyed having an extra cock to use on her, and Rodrigo always seemed to be game. Lord knew he was always complaining about not being able to find the right girl, and he wasn't one for casual sex, so it was probably Minnow or his hand.

"But Master!" she cried, but didn't follow that up with any actual objection.

"Hmm," Rodrigo said as though weighing his options. He ignored her unspecified complaint as bullshit just like Severin did. "Not to be contrary, but don't you think we'll both be more desperate for her *after* we brand her?"

"We can always use her again afterward. I'm not willing to wait anymore, and it's not like there's anything she can do to stop us. We'll just have to be careful not to infect her brand after I mark her."

"I like how you think." Rodrigo stripped off his shirt and unbuttoned his jeans. "You know you have a weird relationship with your best friend and his woman when you always bring your piercing and tattoo equipment when you visit, even if they don't ask. Oh, and condoms."

Severin stripped his shirt off too. He could feel Rodrigo's gaze slide over his chest, as it sometimes did, but he knew better than to make it too obvious.

"Would you rather visit couples that offer you canapés and polite conversation?"

"I'd rather make your pretty bitch gag on my cock."

"No," the girl whined.

Severin moved up so he could see her face better. "No what, Miss Korsgaard? You want DP instead? That can be arranged."

"No, Master, but you can't just *use* me," she begged, looking only at Severin.

Rodrigo smiled indulgently. "Actually, I can't see how you'll stop us, beautiful."

"Did you hear a safeword? I didn't hear a safeword," Severin pointed out. "She knows damned well telling two sadists 'no, please don't' is the worst possible fail when it comes to safewording."

Rodrigo plucked an antique bell from one of the bookcases then pressed it into Minnow's hand. "Your safeword, since your mouth will be full."

Oh, right. That was something Severin hadn't thought of.

Without preamble, Severin spat into his hand and coated his shaft with saliva, then knelt between her bound thighs and shoved into her. Fuck. She was tight, but so wet he slid in to the hilt. The girl cried out, her eyes rolling back. He felt her trying to edge away, but she was completely trapped.

"Did that hurt, beautiful?" Severin asked.

Her eyes focused on his face, and she nodded. He gave her three more ferocious strokes that left her gasping.

"Please, no," she sobbed.

Severin's dick spasmed, and he gritted his teeth as Minnow's pussy clenched around him like a fist.

"Yeah," Rodrigo crooned cruelly to her. "You fucking loved that."

Severin rocked into her a few more times, then stopped to get himself back under control.

"Condom?" Rodrigo asked.

"Have you been tested?" Severin asked.

"Yes. A month ago, and I haven't slept with anyone in over a year." He cast Severin a meaningful look, which he chose to ignore. "Minnow, are you okay with this?"

"Sure, but I won't blow you anyway, jerk."

Severin and Rodrigo both chuckled. Without hesitation, Rodrigo freed his cock from his pants and propped a knee by her shoulder. He traced her parted lips with the head of his cock. She pressed her lips together and turned away her face, as though they'd let her get away with refusing.

"Ah, ah," Rodrigo warned. "Do you really want to annoy the men who are about to brand you?"

"Grab her hair and stick your fingers in her mouth. Show her who's boss." Severin thrust into her hard enough to make her mouth open on a gasp. "She's submissive, all right, but you have to show her who's in charge every damn time."

Minnow shuddered beneath him, so close to coming he could feel her tight little pussy fluttering round him. It was hard to tell whether she trembled from arousal or fear.

Rodrigo grabbed her hair, and forced two fingers into her mouth. "Suck," he growled. "If you bite me you're going to be one sorry little girl."

Torturing his toy with Rodrigo was far too much fun. She struggled to jerk away, but although the bell in her hand teetered at the end of her fingertips with every thrust of his hips, he got the impression she was fucking with them. Rodrigo pried her mouth open and worked hard to shove his cock into it, but she fought the intrusion, trying to close her teeth and turn away.

When Rodrigo growled in frustration, backing off the table to reposition himself, Severin grabbed her face, holding her still, staring her down. After a moment, her gaze went soft, and the fight went out of her muscles.

"Open your fucking mouth, Miss Korsgaard."

Her mouth opened obediently, as though she couldn't help herself, and he spat in it, reminding her who owned it. A submissive haze had settled over her expression. She could deny him nothing when she got like this, and it was so fucking hot.

He held her still while Rodrigo angled himself above her again then slid his cock between her lips.

"Fuck," Rodrigo muttered. "I've been fantasizing about this."

"Now you're going to suck him like a good girl, aren't you?"

She whimpered in response and Rodrigo grunted in pleasure, then started to use her mouth in slow, deliberate thrusts, his stomach muscles rippling with tight control. Severin matched his pace – Rodrigo pulling out as he pushed in – and he imagined having to time things this way if he was in her ass and Ro was in her pussy. God, they'd never fit. She would cry and beg them to stop, but the little masochist would probably come anyway.

Pressure built in his balls and behind his eyes. Fuck. He was going to brand her. In five minutes his mark would be seared into her delicate flesh forever, even if she left him. The idea of sealing her to him with pain, of her taking that for him, made each of his thrusts harder.

The girl gagged on Rodrigo, struggling to breathe, and her pussy clamped down on Severin's cock in violent protest. He gasped, gritted his teeth, lost all control, coming hard into her grasping pussy just as Rodrigo swore, hips bucking, his grasp on her hair and throat completely immobilizing. There was a metallic crash and the sound of a bells clapper making one desperate plea for their attention.

"Fuck!"

Severin wasn't sure if it was he or Rodrigo who swore, but they both pulled out immediately. A last burst of come sprayed up her belly to her chin, and Rodrigo's come caught her across the cheek and into her hair.

Tears streamed from Minnow's eyes, and she gagged and choked for breath, coughing and gasping.

"You okay?" Rodrigo asked her hoarsely, as Severin gave her thigh what he hoped was a comforting squeeze.

"It was an accident," she complained, giggling to herself, her expression still dazed. "I didn't mean to drop it. Totally ruined my last orgasm."

Severin and Rodrigo were standing over her panting, and they both gave short, humorless laughs, then glanced at each other and away.

A tense, anxious excitement filled Severin as he pulled his jeans up and buttoned them. Rodrigo did the same. They weren't meeting each other's gazes.

They worked around her in silence, prepping things.

"Don't mind me – I'll just be here, still covered in the gift of your glorious seed," Minnow called sarcastically. "Cold, sticky come...everywhere"

Severin winced, appreciating that she wasn't too buzzed or too shy to call him on it. He liked that she understood he was a little screwed up and thoughtless even on the best of days, and would just tell him what she needed, usually making a joke of it, because it was just her way.

He grimaced. "I should have made sure you were okay. Sorry. I'm a little distracted."

Minnow laughed as he wiped her off with his discarded T-shirt. He pressed his forehead to hers and stroked her arms, realizing that despite all of her bravado, she was shaking.

"Do you still want to do this?" he asked.

"Didn't you tell me you owned me when you locked this collar around my neck?"

"Yes."

"I'm yours, Mister Leduc."

Fuck. The sight of her gazing up at him in that complete and utter submission, and yet with that spark of a dare lurking behind her eyes. She was daring him to dominate her, challenging him to do what he wanted and stop feeling guilty about it. Bound to his altar, covered in come and sweat, her eyeliner smeared, she was the most sensual thing he'd ever seen. The woman was a fucking drug. He was ready to fuck the hell out of her again.

Without direction from Rodrigo, Severin shaved her already smooth thigh and disinfected the area. The urge to do this quickly, before she realized this was a mistake – that he was a mistake – clawed at him.

He took the brand he'd made off the mantle and set it to heat over the fire. They waited, talking quietly about nothing, as though this was any other visit. Severin watched surreptitiously as Minnow shifted, becoming increasingly anxious until the palm-sized brand was glowing hot. He and Rodrigo put on surgical masks and Rodrigo put on gloves.

"Ready?"

They turned back to the girl, and she whimpered in a series of desperate, ragged sounds that made Severin's cock painfully stiff.

"Maybe I should have worn earplugs so I wouldn't get distracted." Rodrigo laughed. "I don't think I've ever been this hard before in my life."

"Me neither, but you've done this before."

"It's different when it's someone you've fucked. It must be even worse when you own her and it's your mark." He turned a hungry gaze on Minnow, and Severin found himself doing the same. She looked from one of them to the other, then away as though she couldn't bear the weight of their desire. That or she thought they were disgusting perverts.

She looked more excited and afraid by what was about to happen rather than disgusted by their excitement.

"Hold her down," Severin commanded, going to pull the brand from where it was suspended over the fire. The wooden handle was warm, but not hot to the touch.

"Shh," Rodrigo crooned to Minnow. "This will only hurt a little."

"Really?" she asked, gasping for air.

"Well, some people flinch a little, and some scream their heads off."

"If I scream, will you make fun of me?" she asked. "I'm so scared I might scream."

"You do what you need to do. We would never mock you for screaming," Severin managed to make himself say, approaching her with the angry orange brand glowing brightly in his grip.

Rodrigo pinned her down with one hand on her hip and one on her knee, immobilizing her even more thoroughly than the rope. He was panting, and the bulge in his jeans had to be as uncomfortable as Severin's own.

Minnow's terrified mewling was fucking with his head, making his breaths come hard and fast behind the mask. At least it wasn't just him. Rodrigo's mask was moving erratically over his own staccato breathing.

The girl's gaze locked on his, terrified. Hell, he loved scaring her. Loved hurting her.

"Your safeword is 'tattoo,' Miss Korsgaard."

"I know." She quieted under his gaze, going still, her eyes wide and clear. "I love you, Severin."

Euphoria flared through him, lightning through parts of him he'd thought long dead.

"You're mine, Minnow." With shaking hands he positioned the brand over her thigh, then pressed it firmly against her skin. Her body bowed in his bonds, back arching and mouth stretching wide.

Her bloodcurdling scream pierced the silence of the house. Fear and pain echoed through the room, ricocheting through his head. His cock bucked then spilled into his jeans, but it was inconsequential compared to pulling the branding iron away to see his symbol raised and red, marking her as his forever. He wanted to kiss her there – to lick it even if she burned his tongue. He wanted to brand her again – somewhere obvious where every man who wanted her could see it. Her arm. Her hand. Maybe that's what a ring was. A polite brand of ownership.

Rodrigo took the branding iron out of his hand, but he barely noticed in his haste to untie her. The girl – his girl – was panting, trembling, probably with the same burst of adrenaline he'd felt. His body felt like it would explode in a million directions, unable to cope with the magnitude of his emotions.

"That hurt less than I thought," she mused. "I was just so scared."

"It's done now. You're mine." The knots weren't coming undone fast enough.

"I already was."

Fear followed his elation. What if the brand got infected? What if she died and it was his fault? He needed to hire a live-in doctor. What if she fell down and hit her head, or choked or something one day? The house was so far from town. Paramedics might never get to her on time.

What if she went into shock and died right this minute?

He checked her pupils as he picked her up, walked to the couch with her then sat. She laid her head on his chest, and gazed up at him, her face full of an emotion he couldn't identify. When he glanced up to look for Rodrigo, he wasn't in the room.

"Are you okay, Mister Leduc?" she asked, her breath cooling the sheen of sweat on his chest.

He exhaled a long, shuddering breath. "You're the one who just got branded."

"I'm okay – just so sleepy. I don't want to stop staring at you, so just know that if my eyelids close, I'm still staring at you through them, okay?"

He shifted her even closer, holding her to his bare chest and enjoying the contact. This was his woman. She was like an extension of him. With their skin bare, chest to chest, and Minnow looking up into his eyes, he felt strange. Calm. As if breathing air that had already been inside her undid the knots of tension that held him together. His eyes prickled like a sneeze was coming, and he frowned.

"What's wrong?" she asked, her words slightly slurred the way they got when she was in subspace sometimes, or coming down afterward. "Buyer's remorse? Too late, sucker."

He laughed, but the feeling didn't pass. "No. Never that. If anything, you're the one who's going to regret this, not me."

Rodrigo came back into the room, still shirtless, and now wearing a pair of track pants he kept in his room upstairs. Severin liked him like this – relaxed, his civilized veneer gone. He pulled his gaze away before Ro noticed his perusal.

"When I decided to start leaving clothes here a few years ago, it was so I'd have something to wear the day after drinking. The possibility of coming in my jeans had never occurred to me. This shit isn't supposed to happen to grown men, Minnow."

Minnow shifted on Severin's lap but only to settle in closer. "I'd say sorry, but instead I'm just going to silently mock you."

"I have to change too," Severin admitted.

"Shh. You were supposed to let Rodrigo think you were able to hold out."

Severin squeezed her. "You knew?"

"Mister Leduc, I'm lying in it."

He probably should have been embarrassed, but he was too content to feel ashamed. Besides, it was all her fault. "We should have taped that scream. Sadists everywhere would pay to hear that."

"We'd be rich men," Rodrigo agreed.

"Like either of you need more money?"

Rodrigo moved around the room, cleaning things up, casting amused, affectionate looks at them that Severin was far too mellow to object to. It would be odd if Ro didn't feel anything for her at all.

Too bad for him. He'd have to go looking for some second-best girl. This one was his. Forever.

Chapter Fifteen

"They'll be fine." Severin looked down at her and squeezed her hand, amusement glinting in his pale blue eyes.

The mellow lighting of the church lit his face the same way firelight did at home, making him all hard, chiseled lines. This place was different from her parents' church, and with Severin and his family surrounding her, she felt happy rather than damned.

"It's a long time for them to be alone." She bit her lip, hoping the puppy gate would keep them in their room. There'd never been an issue before, but they'd always been nearby in case of emergency.

"It's only two hours, and there's nothing for them to get into." His gravelly voice was reassuring.

She tried to focus on the predicament at hand. Entering a crowded church for a Christmas service had to be freaking Severin out, but he was hiding his apprehension well, other than the customary public glower. People gave him wide berth even without the glare.

Church punched Severin's shoulder. "Quit scaring the villagers or they'll show up with torches and pitchforks."

Severin scowled then scowled harder when his brother hugged him.

"I missed you, you gigantic asshole."

Ilse hissed at her husband to watch his language.

"Asshole!" four-year-old Scarlet repeated loud enough for an older man in line ahead of them to snort in amusement.

"Scarlet, that's a bad word," Ilse told their younger daughter. "If you talk like that we're going to get kicked out of playgroup again."

Minnow bit her lip to keep herself from laughing, but Ilse only made it more difficult by giving her a helpless grimace. It couldn't be easy to keep the little ones from swearing, considering how much of it their father and uncle did in front of them.

"Daddy always calls you 'the asshole,' Uncle Sev," six-year-old Sage confided, from where she clung to Severin's other hand. "Then Mommy makes him put money in the swear jar and sometimes Daddy even gets a time out."

"A time out?" Severin asked.

"Yup. He's real bad sometimes."

Ilse nodded solemnly, her red curls bobbing impishly around her face. "Sometimes he's so bad I have to supervise his time outs."

"Supervise, huh? How about I watch the girls while you two go to confession?" Minnow teased.

Church waggled his brows.

Ilse laughed. "Confession? None of us are Catholic."

Minnow glanced around. "Then...why are we here?"

"Sutton loved the choir here, so we always attend their Christmas mass," Severin muttered, his voice low.

She looked from one to the other, frowning. "Sutton was Catholic though, right?"

Church shook his head. "Only if you count her watching *Sister Act* every few months."

"Oh my God, we're imposters!" Minnow whispered.

"Shh!" Ilse held a finger up to her lips. "Don't blaspheme, and don't panic! All we have to do is follow the crowd while they do the Catholic workout."

"Don't worry. When it comes to stand, sit, kneel, she's well trained." Severin growled, smirking at Minnow in the cocky way that made her toes curl.

"Mister Leduc!" Minnow swatted him.

"Why do you call Uncle Sev 'mister?'" Sage asked her.

"Um...he's my boss. It's polite."

The little girl frowned, her bright blue eyes startling against her dark skin. Church and Ilse's kids were so adorable. The family Christmas gathering was a lot more magical with little ones to share it with. It had been ages since she'd been around kids, and they were starting to make her wonder what it would be like to have her own, and not in a vague future context, either. Did Severin even want kids? He was good with them. He tried to be standoffish, but the girls wouldn't stand for it, and he'd been on the floor playing Lego with Sage for a good part of the morning.

"Uncle Sev is your boss? I don't think mommy kisses *her* boss."

She could feel Severin's gaze on her, and she flushed.

"Your uncle is too handsome. I can't stop myself from kissing him."

Sage laughed into her hand.

The service began, and Minnow listened with interest as the elderly priest gave a sermon on thankfulness. Afterward, the choir sang, and it was more beautiful than Minnow could have imagined.

The group was small, but gifted, their voices strong and harmonious, filling the candlelit stone building. The sound reverberated through her, keying something deep. Her emotion welled as she thought of Sutton missing this, and regretting the relationship she'd started with her that would never have a chance to grow.

The next piece was lighter, reflecting the joy of the season and the fun of winter. The sadness and regret sloughed off. She found herself smiling at Church's children, watching as their feet swung in time with the song, and enjoying their singing when that song moved into a few secular Christmas ones.

The priest picked up his sermon again, and she found herself contemplating the man who sat beside her, muscular thigh pressed tightly to hers. She was so small compared to him, and even sitting did nothing to disguise it.

The congregation knelt for silent contemplation, and Severin's gaze caught hers as she sank to her knees on the comfy kneeling bench. He remained sitting on the pew as she knelt at his feet. The weight of his gaze warmed the metal of her collar, which she'd disguised under yet another infinity scarf. She settled her palm over his brand and squeezed it reverently, as though a deity had marked her as his own. Every time she looked at his brand it made her feel special. Valued.

"Maybe I should get you one of those for home," he whispered in her ear. The murmur felt loud in the silence of the room. Had anyone heard that? She glanced around, but no one was staring. The sexual tension between them raised the small hairs on her arms, and her pierced nipples tightened against the soft cashmere of her sweater. Who went to Church wearing a collar and no bra? Thank goodness her coat was only slightly too warm.

"You want me to be more pious?" she whispered back, keeping her gaze focused on the hymnal in the rack in front of her.

"You're already perfect."

Her face heated at the undeserved praise, and she worked hard to pull her mind away from dirty thoughts of him.

Slowly, the hush of the church swept over her. The dignified spirituality of the old structure sank deep into her bones, reminding her of the forest behind the house. How many times had he taken her there now, to walk in silence, feeling the wind caress her face and tug at her hair, his hand warm around her own?

Through her own peace she felt his, attuned to him the way she'd never felt with anyone else – as though she could hear his energy and interpret it. He was calm. Happy. Possibly the calmest he'd ever been since they'd met. Having Church and his family home agreed with him.

Over the past few months she'd felt herself getting assimilated into this circle, accepted as she was...good enough in her own right. Maybe for some people their first family wasn't the right fit. Maybe the family that came to them later meant more.

She was far too aware of Severin's attention, focused entirely on her. He'd never said he loved her, but even so, she felt it to be true. It had only been a matter of months, but being alone together in the house day after day, night after night, had accelerated their relationship. She'd spent more time with Severin than she had with anyone else she'd ever dated – more than with any other friend or even family member as an adult. The more she got to know him, the more her protectiveness and adoration grew. In her heart she whispered to God, thanking him for unleashing this man in her life.

Severin touched her shoulder and the pulse of electricity between them followed his hand as it trailed down her arm to wrap possessively around her wrist. He pulled it back toward him and slid something heavy and hot onto her finger.

She twisted to look up at him. Around them people were sliding back onto their seats, but she knelt frozen at Severin's feet, staring up into his challenging gaze. She glanced down as he laced their fingers together. The smooth stainless ring on her finger that looked more like a wedding band than an engagement ring. A collar for her finger? It matched perfectly with the one around her neck.

Severin's cold, unyielding gaze said he wasn't fucking asking, either.

Heat bloomed in her cheeks and crept down her neck.

Church cleared his throat. Minnow looked around and realized she was the only person still on her knees.

Mouth twisted in a mocking smile, Severin pulled her up into his lap. He let her shift back onto the seat beside him, but pulled her possessively into the crook of his arm and leaned down to inhale her scent.

She stared down at the ring, her heart tripping over itself, not sure what she was supposed to do or say. Or how she was supposed to feel. Could a girl safeword a marriage...proposal? A marriage command? Did she even want to?

Did she want to marry Severin?

Hell yes.

He was rough and rude and unpredictable, but she couldn't seem to find that important anymore. He was the opposite of beautiful, all brutishness and sexual masculinity, but underneath that was a complicated man who'd been hurt. He was good in all of the ways that were important, despite all of the suffering he'd endured. His secrets and standoffishness when it came to personal things only made her want to be the one who was there for him and the one he trusted with .

The service ended not long afterward, and Church and Ilse converged on them.

"Did he just propose to you in church?" Ilse asked, grabbing Minnow's hand and scrutinizing the ring. "Where's the rock?" Minnow's sister-in-law-to-be glared over at Severin, who seemed unperturbed by her teasing.

"What woman wouldn't prefer a homemade ring?" Minnow asked.

Ilse laughed and rolled her eyes. "Oh my God, Sev, you found your perfect match. She's just as much of a weirdo as you are. Did he even ask you or did he just shove it on there?"

"If he asked she could have said no," Church pointed out, side-hugging Severin, then grabbing Minnow in a fierce bear hug that made her feet come off the floor. "He couldn't have risked that."

The priest had rounded back to them after chatting with a few of the lingering parishioners. "Glad to see you boys." He nodded at Severin then shook hands with Church, Ilse and Minnow, and then with the children. "I was so sorry to hear about your mother. I was shocked when I saw her obituary."

"It was sudden, Father James," Church replied solemnly.

Minnow moved in front of Severin to shield him just in case, but he dropped a reassuring hand onto her shoulder. He was okay with this man. He hadn't tried to shake Severin's hand, and she relaxed because the priest actually knew him. Apparently they weren't interlopers at all.

"We were so grateful for the donation you made here on her behalf. It will pay for the new roof and furnace, with some left over for the parish food bank. I know none of you are Catholic, but we count you as part of our congregation anyway."

"Thank you for welcoming us the way you do," Church replied.

The priest offered a blessing to the children, and they all headed for the door.

"You never gave me an answer," Severin said when they reached the privacy of his truck.

"Was it a question?"

"No." His expression was troubled, hooded.

"I won't safeword marrying you, if that's what you're wondering."

He relaxed back against the seat. The ring still felt warm. She wondered how long he'd waited with it in his hand before putting it on her. Had he been carrying it around since before today? Or had tonight been the plan all along?

"Do you want a better ring?"

"I love this ring." She hugged her hand protectively against her chest. She'd never been one much for jewelry, and the simplicity of the band meant it wouldn't get in the way when she worked. "Why tonight? Why there?"

"I was waiting for the right time," he said, dropping a possessive hand onto the back of her neck as he followed Church's car down the highway toward home.

"So tonight, while I was kneeling at your feet during a Christmas service at church it was the right time?" she asked innocently.

"Yes." He flashed her a brief smile that made her toes curl. "It was either that or in the woods behind the house, but tonight seemed more fitting."

"Why?"

"That Church was Sutton's favorite place. It was as close to having her there as I was going to get."

Minnow's throat thickened with emotion. "You think she would have approved of this? Of us? It's pretty fast."

"She knew, and I could tell she was already starting to love you. She would have told me if she'd had objections." He squeezed the back of her neck, and she melted under his hand. "Besides, even if she hated you, I'd marry you anyway."

*

After an entire day of board games and baking and a hike, Church and Ilse had said their farewells, climbing into the limo that would take them back to the airport. Severin had gone off to the forge for a few hours, wanting to be alone.

Minnow tinkered for a while, tidying, playing with the dogs then returning Rodrigo's call, before crawling into bed with a book.

On a whim, she grabbed her laptop and checked Facebook, scrolling through happy family Christmas and Hanukkah pics posted by her various friends.

Now she'd have pictures of her own to post, if she wanted to.

All too soon, pictures of her sister and parents posing in front of the tree at her sister's house popped up, along with pics of her and her husband.

Joyous news. They were expecting.

It was like a kick in the balls – well, the way she assumed a kick in the balls would feel if she had the requisite equipment.

Happy. They were all so...happy without her. Normal. Picture perfect.

She examined her mother and father, their tans accentuating the laugh lines around their eyes. Her sister was already glowing even though it was early yet.

So fucking awkward – should she send something? Flowers? Maybe Ilse would know what she should send. She found herself wallowing for a good half hour before she gave her head a shake. If they didn't want her there, why was she so upset?

She thought about last Christmas, then how different this one had been. She was damn lucky. Christmas with her new family had been relaxed and fun even. Loud, messy teamwork. They'd had a blast together. Her only regret was that they hadn't seen Rodrigo over the holidays.

No more wallowing.

Instead, she posted her own pictures – of the tree they'd decorated and the turkey they'd made and the pile of gifts. None of the people just yet. Not this year.

A few minutes later, Ilse posted pics of the girls opening presents. She also posted pictures of Minnow and Severin, announcing their engagement and tagging Minnow in them. Ilse gave no fucks. Minnow burst out laughing at the picture of Severin and Church grimacing at each other, wearing the matching sweaters Ilse had ordered for them for Christmas. Ilse sent her a private message saying she'd hoped it was all right. They chatted back and forth for a while before they went to catch their flight.

About one in the morning Minnow finally heard Severin in his shower, and he came to her room dressed in jeans and a T-shirt, his hair still damp and his feet bare.

"You're still awake." His voice was slightly slurred, and even lower and sexier than usual.

She wrinkled her nose at him, smelling the alcohol before he even got to the bed. "I was waiting for you."

He gazed at her intently, most likely wanting something but stopping himself either because of the booze.

"The boys behaved tonight?"

"They whined at the door for you a few times, but they were more interested in finding the Goldfish crackers the girls dropped everywhere."

He snorted. "Well, I'm in now. Go to sleep." He added wood to the fire in the fireplace then slouched into one of the chairs before it.

She slipped out of bed and padded over to him, her bare feet soundless on the bitingly cold flagstone. She knelt on the rug at his feet and pressed her cheek against his knee. His hand stroked her hair, then threaded through it, tightening until it hurt deliciously.

"I have a hard time sleeping when you're not with me."

He traced his fingers over her cheekbones and along her jaw, his expression rapt.

"I don't even sleep in your bed."

"So?"

He ran a thumb under one of her eyes. "Why were you crying?"

She shrugged. "Facebook."

"They came back to the States and no one told you?"

She nodded. "My sister, Pearl, is pregnant." She smiled tremulously. "I guess I'll ask Ilse what's appropriate in terms of gift giving."

"They didn't tell you themselves. You don't owe them a fucking thing. Not even a second fucking thought."

"I thought I'd take the high road."

"They blew up both fucking roads. You just forget those people. They don't deserve you."

His vehemence was adorable.

"You're good with kids," he said, rubbing her scalp the way she liked.

"Your nieces are great." She grinned, thinking about how much fun it was to play silly games with them and teach them how to handle the dogs.

"You want kids?"

She shrugged. Talking to him about this when he was half in the bag was probably a bad idea.

He released her and rose, walking to her dresser. As he opened her top drawer, she frowned, getting the feeling she knew what he was after. Sure enough, he turned back to her with her latest pack of birth control. Checking up on her?

Rather than looking at what day she was on, he stalked to her bathroom door and threw the pack. She heard it hit the garbage.

"Done." He fell back into his chair.

"But Mister Leduc –"

She'd be fishing those out of the garbage can as soon as he took his drunk ass out of her room.

"You want kids, so those have to go."

"Uh...I didn't say I was ready *now*. There's plenty of time. I'm not that old."

He pressed two fingers over her lips. "Shh. Don't remind me." His expression was comical, pained, as though she was a step away from jailbait.

"I'm just saying that we can wait. I wasn't even sure if you wanted kids."

"With you? I don't think I could resist." His smile turned soft and he rubbed a thumb over her bottom lip. "I'll probably be a shitty father, but I can hire someone to help you with baby things." He laughed and tipped back his head. "Money? That I can do. The parenting and affection not so much."

"But Master, we're not even married yet."

"No one cares what we do here, other than you and me, Miss Korsgaard." A low noise, like a growl, vibrated the air. "What you want, you get."

"Except if I've been a bad girl and need a spanking and some orgasm denial?"

"Precisely."

"Why do you think you'll be a bad father?" she asked, seeing the opportunity to question a drunk Severin when he was in a peculiar mood.

He sighed. "I don't know how to be a father. You know my history."

"Some of it. Church didn't really have a father since he died with Church was so young, but he figured it out. You'll have him as a role model, if nothing else."

He shrugged. "At least Church used to have a father. I don't remember my father. At all."

"Not everyone has a stellar childhood. I'm sure you'll figure it out if we have kids." She examined his strong face. His jaw was slightly clenched, but he was still mostly relaxed. Time to try again. "Do you remember much about your first mother?"

His lips went tight. "Some."

"What was she like?"

"Distant, mostly. Exacting otherwise. She was always on the phone or...hosting."

"Business stuff? Charity?"

His hands tightened on the arm of the chair and she waited for him to storm out, but he stayed.

"I think it was business. There's a lot I've had to piece together."

There was something there – she was so close to the thorn in his paw, but one wrong move and the lion would eat the mouse.

"So you were alone a lot? With servants, or..."

He relaxed. "Yes. I liked them. I remember one woman crying when the tall man took me away in the car. I thought he was going to take me home with him. The servants always left us after supper, but he took me to the airport. He cried too."

"Your father, maybe?"

"No, I don't think so. He wore a servant's uniform."

"He sounds like a nice guy."

Severin shrugged.

So when you did spend time with your mother, what did you do?"

He shrugged, shifting in his chair. "She had me in lessons – I guess the way rich kids are? I don't know. People taught me what forks to use, how to walk nicely, and singing, I think. I don't remember everything – I was so young. I remember getting punished when I wasn't polite. She took care of the harsher punishments herself."

"Harsh punishments? What could you have done that was so awful when you were so little?"

His gaze snapped to the crackling fire.

"Being a bad host." His jaw set in what looked like a painful clench, and he stared into the fire in silence for so long, she wondered if she'd lost him entirely.

"Severin?"

Nothing.

She pushed herself to her feet and went to the drink cart, and poured him a tumbler of whiskey. When she pressed it into his hand, he drank it in one long swallow.

Push or back off? She was so close, but did he need her to know, or did she just want to know? It was so hard to know what to do. Whatever had happened still ate at him twenty-five years later. She took back the glass and set it aside, then knelt at his feet. His hand wound into her hair again, as if it comforted him.

"Monsieur Charles was the one who visited the most, but there were three or four. I didn't like Monsieur Charles, but he liked me. Mother would leave us alone to play in my room." There was no whispering and no anger. Just fact.

Minnow's bones felt cold and hollow, and she suddenly wanted to beg him to stop telling her, but she'd wanted to know – had guessed maybe something like this had happened, but now that he was saying the words she didn't know if she was strong enough to hear them.

"He liked to play...games. His hands were clammy. His breath stank and he had big yellow teeth." Severin shuddered. "I told Maman I didn't like him. I told her about the games, and she told me to quit being a baby and be a good host – to do what Monsieur Charles wanted. The next time he visited, she stayed in my room with us, and I remember thinking this time she would see and stop him. He forced too far in my mouth. I choked and fought. I couldn't breathe. She kept yelling at me to be polite. I wasn't trying to be rude, I thought he was trying to suffocate me and she didn't care."

"Oh, God."

"I bit him. There was blood in my mouth. I had a big fit. I couldn't stop screaming. I scratched Maman's face and called her all the bad words I knew. I screamed and broke things for hours – all night I think – until the tall man came to our house and put me in the car. I begged him not to let Monsieur Charles do the same thing to the babies. My sisters were so small."

Minnow sobbed quietly, not wanting to interrupt him, but clinging to his leg as tightly as he was hanging onto her hair.

"Then I was here and there were strangers everywhere, jabbering at me. They didn't speak French. No Maman, no sisters. No servants I knew. But I also didn't have to be a host here. I stayed outside a lot. I didn't talk to the servants. I think the nanny was afraid of me. I used to growl and snap like the dogs outside our house in Marseilles. I ate out of a bowl with my hands or with my face and threw cutlery at people if they tried to tell me to use my manners." He shrugged. "I think that's why she never sent for me again. She knew I was too fucked up to use anymore."

"Then Church and his mother came?"

He nodded, smiling crookedly. "The first time Church tried to get me to play with him, I bit him. I remember plain as day thinking I had to get rid of these people fast. They were too nice. Church called me a bad dog and hit me with a newspaper. It became a game, and the next thing I knew he was my brother."

"It didn't matter that he missed the beginning of your life."

"I'm so glad he wasn't there. He doesn't feel like he's suffocating sometimes for no reason. He doesn't feel like people are touching him even when he's alone. There are no sisters he failed to save." He ran his tongue over his teeth, as though he felt like he needed a toothbrush. "If the girls had been crazy enough to bite, they would have ended up here with me, I guess. Or maybe it was just me that drew the men. Maybe because I was a boy. Or maybe there was something about me that encouraged that sort of thing."

"Severin, no."

"If I'd been a good boy and let it happen – did my best even though I didn't like it – then I would have been raised there with my family. Like a normal kid. Maybe I wouldn't be so fucked up."

"I can't imagine how staying would have been better." She squeezed his knee and he drew her up into his lap. "It would have been worse."

"I didn't want to tell you," he admitted. "I must disgust you. Knowing I was used as a whore."

She kissed the tick in his jaw, smoothing it away.

"Nothing about you disgusts me. I'm only disgusted that the person who was supposed to protect you let people abuse you."

He paused for a long time, and she could tell he was working up the nerve to tell her something. His mouth opened, closed. Opened again.

"Sometimes I cooperated." His expression was guarded, and she could feel him trying to shield himself from her judgment.

Fuck. She could tell he hadn't admitted that to anyone before.

"You'd been taught to cooperate. Groomed for it. You were so young." Such a strange way of thinking, for him to assume any of what had happened was his fault – to persist in thinking that even though he was an adult and he knew better. "If that had happened to me. Would you think it was my fault?"

He fell silent, then finally admitted, "No."

"Then why do you keep trying to take responsibility for what happened to you?"

He shrugged.

She raised her face for a kiss, and he took her mouth gently, but possessively. He drew back and blew out a breath.

"I didn't know if you'd still want me."

"Why on earth would I reject you after you trusted me with that?"

"Submissive women don't like weak men."

"Anyone who acts like they're not vulnerable – that they've never been hurt – is lying. I don't want there to be lies between us."

He twirled her hair around his finger then watched it unravel again. "So you really don't care?"

"Don't care?" she echoed, her tone cold. "Oh, I fucking care. I want to take a trip over to that bitch's house and beat the ever-loving crap out of her." She felt her fists curling but was helpless to stop her reaction.

He smiled then smoothed her hair back affectionately. "Sutton wanted to go after I told her, but I refused. My mother is a calculating woman with enough money and influence to make her own child disappear. I can't find anything much about my family online – not even my sisters. I assume the money comes from criminal activity. Sending Sutton there... What was she going to do? Knit my mother an angry sweater?"

"I'll go over there myself and eviscerate her with Sutton's knitting needles."

He chuckled, but the humor didn't reach his eyes. "Someday maybe I'll go speak to her – but not now. Someday when you and I are settled, and my head is on straight. I have to find my sisters and make sure they're okay. I tried to do it from here, but every effort I've made through investigators gets stonewalled."

"I'll go with you. We'll figure it out."

"There's nothing much to figure out. Just a person to tell off and two others to check on." He closed his eyes. "It's not like I can go back in time and fix things."

Chapter Sixteen

The letter arrived in a plain white envelope, hand addressed to S Leduc. Tucked in the midst of several letters of business, Minnow hadn't noticed it when she left them on his desk, but it probably wouldn't have drawn her eye the way it did to Severin.

The sender's handwriting was too similar to his own.

He held the letter at arm's length, his guts churning, then turned in his chair to suspend the thing over the fire. Burn it? Open it?

Gilbert and Montague roused from their nap in front of the hearth to look up at him then wagged their tails uncertainly. Together, the two of them were already big enough to pass as an overly alert bear rug.

"What would you do?" he asked them.

Both dogs cocked their heads to the side as though they were contemplating his dilemma, but diplomatically chose not to answer.

Minnow paused in the doorway, trailed by Harvey and Theodore. The dogs already came to her knee and they weren't yet full grown. Husky, German Shepherd, and probably a few other things. He'd taken to calling them the hellhounds.

"Mister Leduc?"

"Come here." He put the envelope on the desk, then wiped his hand on his jeans, as though holding it had left a taint.

The girl stopped at his knees, just short of touching him, and folded into a graceful kneel. Her canine attendants flopped on the floor behind her in front of the fire with their brothers.

"What's wrong, Master?"

"A letter. From someone in my original family."

She gazed over at his desk, brows lowered in distaste. "You can tell from the postmark?"

He hadn't even thought to check it. "Read or burn?"

"Can you tell who it's from? Maybe it's from one of your sisters?" she asked hopefully.

Grimacing, he held it out to her. He was pleased his hand didn't shake.

"You want me to decide?"

"It doesn't affect only my life."

"You need answers, for closure if nothing else." She accepted the envelope, but still paused before ripping it open. Her hands were shaking, and she didn't bother trying to hide that from him.

When she tried to hand it back, he shook his head. "Read it aloud for me."

She drew it out as though it might explode. "Dear Seb," she paused. It says here Seb instead of Sev. Is that you?"

Shock made his mouth drop open. His heart raced and heat flooded his cheeks. "They usually call me Severin in correspondence. That's what they told people my name was, but it used to be Sebastien."

Minnow bit her lip. "Are you sure you want me to read this?" Her eyes remained on his face, as though she didn't want to be rude by scanning ahead.

"Do it."

She drew a deep breath, bracing herself, then continued. "Dear Seb, I felt it important to inform you that after an extended and mysterious illness, our mother is dead. One quarter of her assets will be sent to you via your man of accounts, Rodrigo Solis. It was not a bequest. All of her monies were left to me, but I thought it fitting to liquidate and divide her wealth between her primary victims – her children. May she rot in hell." She paused and looked up, face white. "It's signed 'ton frère, Loïc.'"

That mother was dead too? Three for three. At least this one wasn't a fucking loss. It didn't even sound like she was a loss to a child she'd kept close.

Loïc. He had a fucking brother, and no one had ever told him. He'd signed the sale of this house to Severin, and he'd wondered who he was at the time.

He pushed back his chair and stood, taking the letter from her hand and reading it himself.

"He'd be younger than our sisters, unless he'd already been hidden away somewhere." Was he older, younger? Were their sisters upset about their mother's death? He read the line again 'her primary victims.' The girls had been abused too. A dim haze settled over him.

"Master, stop." Her voice came from far away. "Severin! Stop!"

The girl was at the door. He wasn't sure when she'd moved, but the dogs were gone, she was almost in the hallway, and his study was fucking trashed. He looked around at the destruction, bewildered.

A blackout? He hadn't had a blackout since he was a little boy.

His chest was heaving, and he had the strong urge to leave the house – to get away from Minnow and the dogs before he hurt someone by accident.

"Miss Korsgaard, the number for my psychiatrist is next to the kitchen phone. Dr. Jindal. Call her and tell her I need her to make a house call."

She stepped into the room instead, and Severin held up a staying hand. "No. Stay away from me until I'm sedated. I can't trust myself."

"Okay, Master, but I trust you." Her voice was thin. Needy. But he couldn't be there for her right now, and that pissed him off and shamed him.

"You shouldn't trust me. Did you get the boys somewhere safe?"

"They ran for their room."

"I didn't hurt them, did I? I didn't hurt you?" His hands tightened on the crumpled letter he still held in one hand, willing her to say no while he forced himself not to hug her and check her over.

"They're fine. I'm fine."

"It's not fine. I'm so sorry – I haven't had a blackout like that since I was young."

She swallowed hard and nodded. "That letter was a huge shock. I'm not surprised this happened."

His throat felt like it was on too tight. Like his emotions were strangling him.

"It could happen again. You should go to Rodrigo's. Take the dogs."

"No. I'm not leaving."

His chest ached. "Damn it, Minnow, this isn't the time to defy me!"

"I'm not leaving you alone when you need me here. If you start doing it again, I'll lock myself in the boys' room. Someone else should be here when the doctor comes, just in case you can't answer the door."

He gave a sharp nod.

"I love you, Severin. I need to be here."

His eyes burned, and he swallowed past the pain in his throat. She loved him? It wasn't a surprise so much as hearing her say it aloud was, especially now. He wanted to say it back, but couldn't even though everything in him ached to.

She knew, right? She had to know it.

"Shh. I know. Just sit."

How could she always read his mind?

He sank onto the padded coffee table where he'd branded her, looking around the room in despair. His moods were one thing, but expecting her to want to stay if the blackouts were back – that wasn't safe. And children were out of the question. The chance he might hurt her or the dogs was bad enough. But a baby? He thought of a little girl who looked just like Minnow – thought of waking from a blackout to her beaten or dead – and panic trembled through him.

"You have to go back on the pill. I have to start using condoms too." How fucked up would his kids be with his genetics? What the hell had he been thinking?

"Stop," she commanded. "I'm going to make that phone call, but I can't go to the kitchen if you're freaking yourself out."

"I'm okay. Call Rodrigo and tell him to come, if you won't leave. I don't want you alone with me, and I can't hire you a bodyguard tonight."

"Shut up and sit there, Severin Leduc. You're talking crazy." She walked away, her boots clicking on the floor as she made her way to the kitchen.

Back to the shrinks. Back to the meds. Why couldn't he function better? He'd been safe for twenty-five years.

He hated therapy – didn't want to start again – but for Minnow he'd do anything.

*

Severin watched the girl, wondering why the hell she stayed after all of his determination to drive her away. The warmth of the screening room was almost uncomfortable, but she was finely built and the price of dressing her to amuse himself was that he had to keep the house warmer than he normally choose to.

She knelt at his feet, her head leaned against his knee as he stroked her hair. They were watching one of his favorite alien movies with excellent special effects and gore, but very little plot.

Minnow hadn't seen it before – hell, she hadn't seen much of anything. It reminded him of their age disparity.

The movie's violence soothed him, and kept him from taking out all of the ugliness inside him on the girl. He'd been too afraid to use a belt on her or even to spank her since his blackout. Even though Rodrigo had basically moved in for the time being. At least until he was more settled.

After taking Dr. Jindal's advice, they were waiting for a response from Loïc. Severin had requested a meeting through Rodrigo a week ago, but his family had remained silent.

Waiting was difficult, especially since there was no guarantee his brother would ever answer, let alone agree to meet.

A jump scare made the girl clutch his leg, moving closer to him as though he could protect her from the CGI monster on the screen if it happened to come to life. His finger was still wet from her sucking it, and he traced the seam of her lips with the damp tip, and she took it into her mouth again, almost absently. She relaxed, melting against him, and the feel of her little tongue playing with his fingertip made his dick ache.

Rodrigo laughed and threw popcorn at the screen. "This is so stupid. Why does this guy think his knife blade won't dissolve when he stabs one of the aliens? The crew has seen their blood melting the metal floor grates."

"Shh. This is the good part," Severin admonished. The hotheaded member of the team unexpectedly exploded in a rage and attacked, killing one of the aliens through sheer berserk force. He was decapitated by the creature's blade-like tail whipping around and catching him in the neck just after he'd dispatched it, but saving the rest of his team.

"You *would* like that part." Rodrigo grimaced, pushing his dark hair back from his face. "Sure he died a hero, but now he's going to miss out on the wenching and drinking. He really didn't think that one through."

"Wenching? You've been watching too much *Game of Thrones*." Minnow laughed and threw popcorn at him.

Rodrigo caught some of what she'd thrown and popped it in his mouth, then chewed it thoughtfully. "Wenching is awesome. Maybe I'll open a whorehouse. I keep saying I should diversify my assets."

"A whorehouse?" Minnow laughed. Rodrigo always made her laugh. Severin couldn't recall more than a handful of times he'd even made her smile. "With a saloon and everything? We'll have to get you a ten-gallon hat for your birthday. Just remember, though, you're pretty. You'd be popular in jail."

"Maybe that would be good for my ego, since you picked Frankenstein's monster over me." He winked. They grinned at each other. "Not that I blame you."

Severin tried to figure out why she never looked at him that way. Probably because she and Rodrigo were friends, while he was her...owner. She and Rodrigo were so much better together, and yet she wanted Severin. She even said she loved him. Why wouldn't she want the life Rodrigo could give her – with the parties and people and fun? He even had a close-knit family she could get invited into. They'd love her. Hell – who wouldn't choose Ro?

Well...he hadn't. Couldn't. But that was different.

For Minnow, the choice made no sense, so he couldn't trust she'd stick to it. He wanted better for her.

The problem was, as much as she was locked into his collar, she was free to make her own mistakes, even if he was one of them.

Rodrigo caught his eye and grinned, trying to include him in their joking. The five o'clock shadow suited him. It wasn't often the man let himself relax, and sometimes Severin wondered if that was why he hung out with him out here.

The movie credits started to roll, and Rodrigo got to his feet and started to gather up the popcorn he'd thrown around.

"Tell me I can stay here and don't have to go to my sister's art exhibit," Rodrigo begged.

"You love Mayte's work!" Minnow admonished, throwing more popcorn at him. He arched a brow at her in the typical dominant fashion, but picked her mess up too.

"I can't stand stuffy parties. I have to go to my place and shave and put on dress clothes and make myself presentable."

Minnow smiled, but maybe it looked sad. Did she wish she could go too? She could meet Rodrigo's crazy family. As much as he complained the party would be stuffy, nothing was ever stuffy if Rodrigo's family was around. They were wild and fun, and Severin loved when their paths crossed, even though he'd heard Mayte call him *la bestia* behind his back. The beast. At least she said it quasi-affectionately.

"You should go as his date," Severin said to the girl.

Rodrigo and Minnow looked at each other then back at Severin.

"What?" Minnow asked, frowning up at him.

"Wouldn't you like to go to a party?"

She opened her mouth then closed it. "Not without you, Master, and I have nothing to wear to something like that – I wouldn't even know what to wear."

"Rodrigo could tell you. It wouldn't take long to pick something out. You could have fun instead of being stuck here."

She glared at him. "You said I wasn't allowed to leave the property without you. Were you lying?"

"I trust Rodrigo to take care of my slave."

"Maybe we'll go sometime, but that means you too. Not just me with Mr. Solis."

"As much as you like to share her with me, the two of us are just friends with benefits, Sev. You're not going to trick us into getting involved with each other and leaving you to rot in peace."

They both glared at him.

"Quit trying to get rid of me," Minnow grumbled.

"I just thought you might like to go," he said.

"He wants you to hurry up and fall in love with me so it will hurt less when it inevitably happens."

Severin felt his bottom jaw stick out more, and he clenched his teeth. "Go to your party, Sigmund. Maybe the crowd there will enjoy your psychoanalysis more than I do."

Rodrigo stood and bowed his head formally, as though he was a servant. "Should I tell Mayte you send your regards?"

"I sent flowers from him," Minnow said. "Severin told me to have them sign the card *la bestia* but wouldn't say why."

Rodrigo turned back to Severin, his dark eyes twinkling. "Always listening, hey, Sev? We should get you business cards that say that. Severin Leduc, *la bestia*. Appropriate. Succinct." Rodrigo gave him a hungry look. The man was in incorrigible flirt.

Severin raised a brow. "A bit melodramatic."

"That makes you Beauty, Minnow. All you need is a huge yellow ball gown and you're all set."

"The beast would just muss it up – although that could be fun." Her white teeth caught at her plump bottom lip, and the subtle violence of it aroused him.

They walked Rodrigo out, delaying him with conversation until he had to rush to get home on time to dress for the gallery. He'd become a fixture in the house. Things would be very different when he started dating someone seriously again. His previous girlfriend hadn't liked Severin much. It had made it difficult to hang out. Eventually Ro had ended things with her because of it.

When they were alone, Minnow turned her back to the door, and knelt in the foyer like a good little girl.

"You look like you want to ask me something."

"I do, Mister Leduc, but I doubt you'll approve."

Did she want to go with Rodrigo after all? "Why?"

"I want to do something to you, but you're going to say no." To him? "Like what?"

"You still don't let me touch you."

"Yes I do. A bit."

"Don't you like being touched?

"No."

"But what if I like touching you?" She crawled to him, slinking like a cat, sexy and self-possessed – a woman who'd crawled to a man before and knew the power it held. The sensual movement of her body offset the demeaning nature of her position, making her seem more femme fatale than demure submissive. Not for the first time, he wondered which of them was truly in charge. Using her sensual beauty against him was completely unfair. She could get him to agree to almost anything, if she played her cards right.

"What if I black out?"

"Dr. Jindal is on speed dial on my cell. So is 911, just like you wanted. You can't avoid being intimate with me forever. I won't allow it."

Brat. He chuckled, even though he was uncomfortable with the idea. It was true, though. If he wasn't going to send her away, he was going to have to trust himself a little sooner or later.

"What do you have in mind?" He reached down to grip her arm and dragged her to her feet, ruining the effect of what she'd been doing and taking back the power in their dynamic. "You're making it sound like I won't approve."

She gazed up at him, looking less certain. "I thought – I just thought..."

He waited while she muddled through her sentence.

"Would you let me give you a massage?"

"A massage," he repeated. It was a common enough thing even in vanilla relationships, from what he could understand, but the idea of having someone running their hands over him made him shudder with apprehension.

Minnow looked so hopeful, though, and he knew that his hang-up about touching bothered her. She deserved affection, considering everything he put her through, but it was difficult for him to allow it. Over time, she'd gotten him used to the feel of her mouth and hands on his cock when she gave him a blowjob, and her touch on his back and shoulders when he was deep inside her. She cuddled him sometimes, but maybe she noticed how uncomfortable it made him even though he'd thought he was doing a good job faking it. Sometimes he wasn't faking, though. Sometimes he loved it.

"Does it trigger you, or is it because you're not used to being touched?" she asked cautiously.

He blew out a long breath and gazed at the ceiling. Letting her into his head was always a chore.

His first inclination was to deny there was anything wrong with him other than typical male standoffishness, but Minnow was one of the select few who knew better.

"It's both."

"Can we try?"

His stomach churned, but he didn't let himself walk away. There was a flash of irritation that she was pushing this, but he had to admit that if anyone could help him work through this it was Minnow.

"Yes."

She nodded, but didn't gloat or give him pity. She was a no-nonsense girl, and she knew him well enough to keep condescending sentiments like pity to herself.

"If you ever want to talk about it more, I'll listen."

He had no intentions of spilling his guts to her regularly. She didn't need more gory details. She already knew more than anyone else ever had – at least, anyone who hadn't been there. When he didn't answer, she reached for him, letting her hand hover over his chest before she laid it there. His skin crawled, and he ground his teeth together against the unpleasant sensation.

"Shh... It's okay. Come on." She held out her hand, he took it then let her lead him up to her room. "Sit in the chair. I'll start with your shoulders and you can leave your shirt on, okay?"

"Exposure therapy?"

"Exactly."

He sank into the chair, anxiety making his chest tight. This felt like being led to the gallows. Minnow regarded him and pursed her lips.

"You need a distraction." She grabbed the hem of her T-shirt and peeled it off over her head. Her bra came off next, putting him more or less eye level with her pert breasts and their rosy, upturned nipples with the sexy piercings he'd helped put in. Blood surged to his cock, and his mind blanked.

"Better?" Her voice broke through his distraction.

He grabbed her ass under her short skirt and pulled her to stand between his knees, biting the fullness of the underside of her breast and watching her nipples pucker as her breath caught.

"Don't be rough," she reminded him. Her nipples were still incredibly sensitive, and Rodrigo had warned it could be a year before they were fully healed.

He snapped his teeth at her right nipple and she pouted and thrust her breasts closer to him, daring him to do it.

"If you stay around long enough for those to be healed, you are so fucking doomed."

She sighed in frustration. "You broke your toy the first day. Bad boy."

He smacked her ass and she chuckled. Cheeky little thing. She liked teasing him. Maybe she chummed around with Rodrigo, but around Severin she was like a bitch in heat. He fucking loved it.

"I'm going to massage your shoulders, okay? Can I sit on your lap?"

"Yes."

She put one knee by his hip then threw the other one over his lap, straddling him. A small squirm forward and her pussy pressed against him. He could feel her heat immediately, even through his jeans. Was she wearing panties?

"Why is your pussy so warm?"

She ground it against his shaft.

"I just spent an hour sucking your finger and fantasizing about sucking your cock. I'm a little turned on."

Her hands came up to his shoulders, and he flinched. She was in an awkward position to massage him, but having her to look at helped. She kneaded his muscles. Did she understand she was making him more tense, rather than less?

He kissed her, and her hands moved from his shoulders to the back of his neck. Instinctively, he pushed her hands away and brought his shoulders up.

"Too soon for the neck. Gotcha." She flicked his lips with her tongue, and he struggled with the urge to unzip and jam his dick into her. "Ah, ah. I can see what you're thinking, Master, and that's not the point of this exercise."

"Did I agree to doing an exercise?" he asked, clutching her hips and rocking against her.

She whimpered. "Um...I think so? I can't remember right now."

"Fine." He let her go, and enjoyed her groan of disappointment. "I haven't fucked you in days, but apparently you have other priorities."

She worried at her lip, as though weighing her options, but eventually grimaced. "This is important to me too. I like affection, and I want to be able to touch you sometimes without it needing to be related to sex."

"Get on with it," he grumbled. Maybe he should start getting Rodrigo to cuddle with her more when he was over, but the idea that he couldn't meet her needs himself rankled.

"May I take off your shirt?"

He sat forward and stripped it off for her. Eyes half-lidded, she checked him out.

"Master?"

"Yes?"

"Can I make a rule that you have to be naked in my presence?"

"My clothes are present for your safety."

"For my safety? I think we've established I can handle your dick," she said smugly.

"Good. It'll be in your ass later."

"Uh unh."

He'd put a bigger plug into her ass this morning, and she'd whined and whimpered so much he'd almost come in his jeans.

"The plug I used this morning is almost my size."

"No, it's not!"

"Well, you'd better think accommodating thoughts because as soon as this is done, it's my turn." She opened her mouth to complain, but when he grabbed her throat she fell silent. "Do I make myself clear?"

"Maybe you could try just the tip?" She laughed nervously. "Just – oh fuck. You have to go slow, okay?"

"So you're asking me to trust you, and yet you don't trust me?"

"I trust you!" She made a sound of frustration, then another of terror. "Okay. Just – don't hurt me there on purpose. Not the first time."

"Understood."

She got off his lap, one of her nipples grazing his cheek as she rose. Her intake of breath insinuated it was accidental.

Muscles in his shoulders bunched again as she walked behind him. He stared into the fire, willing himself not to overreact when her hands came back to him.

"I'm going to put my hands on you again. On your shoulders. Ready?"

He nodded tightly, holding his breath.

Her fingers came down gently, skimming along his skin and drawing goose bumps up in their wake. He fought panic.

Minnow. Her hands. Her scent.

She started to massage his shoulders with long, sensual strokes, and he focused on pretending he was normal for her. It usually worked, more or less. He could manage with this too.

Her thumbs found knots she'd created and warmed them, then worked at easing them away.

"So no one ever did this for you before?"

"No. Rodrigo has tried setting me up with friends of his a few times, but –" He broke off as she got too close to his neck. He gave an irritated jerk of his head, but she was already moving away from the spot. Minnow. It was Minnow, not some stranger. He owned her. She was his. She knew him better than anyone. He could ask her to stop, and she would stop. She knew he was fucked up, so there was no pressure to hide it.

Bit by bit he forced himself to relax back into the chair, and into her hands.

"I'm sorry you didn't feel like you could trust someone enough to do this for you before now. Touch is so important for a person's soul." She worked for a few more minutes, and every time he was about to tell her to stop, she somehow knew and would move away from whatever was making him uncomfortable. "It makes me wonder how you managed when you were small. There've been all sorts of studies showing that babies who don't get enough touch will fail to thrive. Someone must have taken care of you before you came here. You didn't give up and die. You've been through a lot, but you've come so far."

He thought of the smiling face he dreamed about sometimes. A servant, maybe? It was hard to say.

"There was a woman."

"Your mother, do you think?"

"No. I remember them both."

She made a sound of acknowledgement.

"Can I try your neck now?"

"Yes." He braced himself.

"Is it too much right now?"

"Just do it."

Her caressing thumbs skimmed lightly up the back of his neck, and he gasped, clutching the arms of the chair. A violent shudder wracked him, and his cock twitched. He couldn't figure out if he wanted to shove her away or fuck her.

"Whoa now. You okay?" Her hands stilled, and he was grateful for the moment to collect himself.

"It's...intense."

"Good or bad?"

"I don't know."

"Fair enough." She sounded amused, and that made him feel like it wasn't a big deal either way. She tried again.

He hissed out a breath and shivered, but tolerated it for a few minutes before he started to enjoy it.

"Can I run my fingers through your hair?"

He was used to the brush at least. "Yes," he said confidently.

"When was the last time you had a haircut?"

"I don't remember."

She petted his hair, smoothing it back from his face, as though she was going to put it in a ponytail. When that didn't faze him, she got bolder, running her fingers through it but careful not to tug at the tangles he'd picked up during the day. He hadn't braided it this morning, but they hadn't gone anywhere, so it was its usual shaggy mess. She didn't seem to mind it. Her nails gently running over his scalp made him groan.

"Should I cut my hair?"

"Maybe a trim, but if you cut it short, I'd be forced to kill you." Her tone suggested she wasn't joking. She sighed happily and buried both hands in his hair. "I've wanted to do this since the day I met you. Do you have any idea how fucking hot you are?"

Clearly, she was delusional.

"I'm not a handsome man, Miss Korsgaard," he said. "There's no need to stroke my ego by lying to me."

"I didn't say handsome – I said hot. You make the *la bestia* look work for you. Masculine. Brutish. Muscles and glares and that mean jaw." She sighed, and ran her nails over his scalp again, which was far more pleasurable than it should have been. "I was a little terrified you'd get me pregnant just from eye fucking me."

He snorted, but he wondered what that would be like – to join with her like that. To watch her growing round with his baby. It would have turned him on if it didn't come with the actual child to take care of. They could have children together, make a real family, but he didn't know anything about being a father at all, other than what he'd seen on television. He had vague shadows of memory of a man sitting with him and eating ice cream, but where had that kind face been when he'd been banished here? Why hadn't he ever come to visit, at least? Maybe the man had been a servant. Or maybe he'd been one of his abusers.

With parenting genes like Severin had, he had no business bringing children into the world. And again, the blackouts.

"It's a good thing that can't happen," he finally said. "I'm the last person in the world who should be a father."

"I don't think that's true. You're gentle when you want to be, and I have a hard time imagining you being cruel to a child."

True. He liked Church's kids, but couldn't imagine having to remember to feed someone, or keep an eye on them. And his genetics?

She leaned over his shoulder, brushing her mouth across his cheek to his lips. He kissed her even though she was upside down, and the slide of her mouth on his, her tongue in his mouth from this position was strangely erotic. He slid his hands into her hair, controlling the kiss, and didn't let her go again until she was moaning into his mouth.

"Quit distracting me," she accused.

"Quit letting yourself be distracted." He reached back and palmed her breasts, loving the feel of the mounds in his hands.

"Stop that!" she backed away and he lurched out of the chair, advancing on her as she shook her head and kept retreating, a gleam of mischief in her eyes.

"Don't run. You know what happens when you run."

Her breaths went shallow, and he could see her pulse fluttering in her neck. "I know what happens. You chase me. It scares me, but it gives me a major girl boner."

He charged and she squeaked, then turned and fled, her bare feet silent on the floor. The dogs lifted their heads as he blew past them, but they were too tired from their earlier walk to bother following.

This was more his element than gentleness and massages. Stalking the girl was his nature.

He chased her through the house, down the main floor corridor, up a side staircase, down an upper hall, then down the main staircase. Her breathing almost drowned out his. He wasn't winded, but the excitement of the chase flooded his body with adrenaline while her terrified shrieks had his cock throbbing. He let his booted footfalls sound heavily against the stone and wood flooring, and to toy with her he lunged and grunted, touching but not grabbing, but only because he wasn't ready for the game to end. When he caught her he was going to hurt her. Claim her. Fill every fucking hole with come.

"I'm going to catch you, Minnow."

She whimpered and dodged.

He caught at her arm and let her slip through his grip, tits bouncing as she bolted away.

"Fuck...I'm going to catch you and shove my dick in your ass," he reminded her, following her hasty retreat.

"No!"

He lunged and grabbed her hair, then pressed her against a wall, grinding against her ass. "Caught you, you little cunt, and here I was hoping you'd get away."

"Let me go!"

"I'm going to hurt you so bad."

"Oh fuck! Stop saying that!" She squealed, ducking out from under his arm to run again as soon as he let go of her hair.

"Are you going to cry for me?" he called after her. "You're so pretty when you cry."

As he rounded the corner downstairs, she disappeared. He skidded to a halt, his boots sliding in the silent hallway before he came to a full stop. Listening past the sound of his rapid heartbeat, he thought he heard something from the direction of the ballroom.

Quietly, he went to his study, which was almost directly across from the room she was hiding in. Out of his bottom drawer, he grabbed a few things and shoved them in the pockets of his jeans. He approached the double doors to the ballroom, grabbing one of the burnished brass handles and yanking the door wide. He strolled in, waiting for it to shut behind him. The room was darker than a blindfold.

"In the ballroom?" he whispered into the darkness. "Rodrigo never should have filled your head with romantic nonsense." He could hear her hectic breathing, but it echoed, and he wasn't completely sure what direction she was in. "Did you lure me in here hoping I'd transform into a prince, Miss Korsgaard?"

"If you did, it would ruin my fairytale, Mister Leduc," she admitted, voice shaking. Off to his left? He moved that way, hoping she would say something else. "It was the beast I fell in love with. The prince would bore the fuck out of me."

He could swear he was very close to where her voice had come from, but when he reached out, he touched nothing.

"You won't get romantic moments in ballrooms with me. You'll get taken down and fucked in the ass like a little whore."

"Only if you can catch me, Leduc," she mocked quietly.

Her words drew a snarl of aggression from his lips. She knew what challenging him made him do, and yet she persisted in doing it.

"You like baiting me."

"Smart boy".

So brave, in the dark. So stupid to think it would stop him from finding her.

"You're bratty for a girl who can't see her dominant's expression."

"It's easier to be bratty when I can't see you."

"So my face scares you?"

"Your face scares everybody. Are you glaring at me really ferociously right now?" Her voice hitched on the word ferocious.

He narrowed his eyes, scanning the unrelenting blackness. She was moving.

"You think this is funny, but when I catch you, you're going to be a very...very sorry little girl."

He could hear her unsteady breaths nearer now, even though he'd stopped moving to listen. She could hear where he was and was approaching anyway.

"How sorry?" she asked from right behind him.

He whirled and grabbed for her, but she fled to what sounded like the far side of the hall again, giggling quietly.

"I'm going to catch you sooner or later, my little bitch, so why don't you come kiss my boots and ask for leniency?"

"Why don't you make me?"

Aroused aggression spiked harder through him and he strode across the room, feeling where she was even in the dark.

Her whispered, "Oh my god, oh my god," was beautiful in his ears.

"For that," he growled, "you'd better hope there's still lube in your ass from when I plugged you this morning, because that's all you're going to get."

"Dry? My first time?" she blurted. "You can't!"

"Are you going to cry when I shove my cock in your tight little virgin hole? Are you going to beg me to stop?"

"Cry? What kind of monster would enjoy making his poor submissive cry?" she said, her voice faint, but she was close. She just couldn't stop running her mouth.

"The monster you chose." He lunged, capturing a handful of her silken hair. She gasped and lashed out. Blows landed harmlessly on his shoulders and chest, but he used his grip on lovely hair to force her slowly to the floor.

"No, no. I'm sorry! Please, Master. I shouldn't have said what I did. It was the adrenaline talking."

When he had her down, he forced her head to the floor then stepped on her hair to keep her where he wanted her before pulling her ass up. The sound of his belt coming off made her whine.

"But you can't see!"

"No, but I can feel. I'd suggest you stay very still."

Roughly, he groped her ass, then choked up on his belt and started to lay into her. After each yelp of pain, he'd landmark with his free hand, seeking out the hot welt, then give her another.

When she was writhing and sweating, he shifted his foot off her hair and grabbed the bondage tape from his pocket while keeping a hand on her back. She tried to rise to scramble away, but he caught her around the waist and pulled her over his lap, spanking her already burning-to-the-touch ass.

"Are you done?" he growled.

"Never!" She fought like a little hell cat, scratching and biting, and basically just going out of her way to wriggle all over his throbbing dick and make him eager to master her yet again. She loved to fight him, and he loved to force her to submit to his control.

He shoved her off his lap to the floor. As she struggled to break his hold, he jerked the bondage tape out of his pocket and secured her wrist to ankle on each side, leaving her ass exposed and vulnerable.

"You're going to fight while I fuck your ass? Good. It'll hurt more."

"No please, Mister Leduc! Don't!"

"I told you what was going to happen."

"You said you'd be gentle because it was my first time."

He positioned her twice more as she tried to roll to the side, but he managed to get his jeans unzipped. His cock was so relieved to be out it was almost as good as sex. Not really, but close.

"I said I'd be gentle when you were being a good girl and cooperating. Bad girls don't get treated like pretty dolls – they get treated like the spoils of war."

"You're going to take me by force?"

"Force?" He laughed cruelly. "Yes, but you like that."

"Let me go!"

"Never."

Chapter Seventeen

"No, no – please don't hurt me!" he mocked, his voice chilling her. "But you like to be hurt, Miss Korsgaard. So much so that you've never used your safeword with me. I bet you could take a lot more than I dish out. I bet I'm nowhere near as frightening as some of the other men you've been with."

Fear and adrenaline throbbed through her body. She was so scared she felt as if she had to pee. She'd seen him lose control the other day, but he was okay now. Wasn't he? He was talking. Playing. Kind of.

In the dark she couldn't see his expression. She could only strain to hear his intonation and to feel the tension in his body.

"No, Mister Leduc. I've never submitted to a man as thoroughly as I have to you. I played at clubs a few times and had bedroom only kink relationships, but never like this. Never like you. You scare me more than any of them ever did."

He went still. "Because you don't trust me?"

Did she trust him? Mostly. She hadn't doubted him – much – until he'd blacked out. And Rodrigo wasn't here as back-up. She shouldn't have pushed him so hard tonight without Ro nearby.

"I trust you to hurt me, but only the way I like it."

He exhaled. "Maybe you shouldn't trust me, because sometimes I get urges to do things you wouldn't like."

"I'm open to negotiation."

His wordless snarl echoed through the cavernous room.

There was a click, and she felt the tips of his fingers slide up and down the divide of her ass, far too slick for a man who'd just threatened her with lubeless anal. He really did like her. She had to force herself not to laugh in relief, but as he worked first one finger, and then two into her ass she realized her relief would be short lived. Two fingers – Severin-sized fingers – was the most she'd ever taken. It was bigger than the biggest plug he'd used and his dick was far bigger.

"Please, Mister Leduc!" she begged.

"Please what?" His voice was thick with lust.

She shuddered. "Please don't."

"You're so fucking tight."

He withdrew his fingers and although she'd thought it would be a relief, she was uncomfortable and empty.

"Maybe we could wait?" she begged, hopeful for a reprieve, but also really wanting him to ignore her pleading.

"We could."

"We could?"

"No." The tip of his cock brushed her anus, and she shivered.

"You're going to take my ass for the first time in the dark, on the floor, while you have me bound?"

"Were you expecting roses? Wooing?"

He lowered himself over her, surrounding her with his muscular body. The position made her feel diminutive and fragile.

"Don't move."

He pressed the tip of his cock against her ass and started to push, coaxing her body to open to him, slowly, slowly, until she felt stretched mind-bogglingly wide.

"Please tell me that's all of it," she gasped.

"All of the tip." He grunted.

Fuck.

Despite the fear and discomfort – or maybe because of it – her arousal dripped down her thigh, making her feel even dirtier. She wriggled, helping him slowly impale her on his iron-hard shaft, until both of them were panting. Goose bumps spread, sending prickling chills coursing over her overheated skin. She was keening beneath him, so quietly it sounded like a rogue mosquito had invaded the far side of the room.

He made a strange guttural noise that made her shudder with need.

"Fuck. Shh. Don't move, beautiful." His words were laced with euphoria and pain. That was only fair, because he'd spitted her like a pig.

"I'm too scared to move." She whimpered. Grit dug into her cheek, and she listened to his tortured breathing, the sound alone almost enough to make her orgasm.

His cock throbbed deep in her ass, and she was pretty sure her heart had synced to it, but double time.

When she couldn't stand the fullness anymore, she tried to draw away, but he seized her hips and viscously yanked her back onto his dick.

A cry burst from her lips as his testicles slapped her aching clit. Fuck, her ass ached, her clit throbbed and empty pussy was begging to be filled.

"Fuck!" The word was a shout in the empty room, and his hips bucked against her, his cock withdrawing slightly before plunging deeper, prying her open so wide she clenched her eyes shut.

Severin railed into her tender ass, his animalistic grunts filling the silence, the slap of skin against skin, her arousal spiraled out of control, slicking her thighs, the smack of his balls against her clit bringing her ever closer to the brink. It hurt. She was too full.

She needed to touch her clit – one tiny bit of stimulation and she'd come so fucking hard. She panted through clenched teeth as he thrust again and again, too shaken to tell him that she needed him to touch her.

As though he could read her mind, he groped her breasts, pinching one nipple then the other, hard enough to make her scream and struggle. After so long without rough nipple play, it hurt, making her eyes brim with tears.

"You'd better stop fighting, Minnow. You're going to hurt yourself."

"You're making me!" she wailed.

"Stop fighting. Submit," he gritted through clenched teeth. His hand slid from her breasts and down her belly, delving between her thighs, discovering how soaked she was. He groaned. "You fucking love this."

"No." She sniffled. "It hurts."

His finger circled her clit hood and she stiffened, spreading her legs and making the most pathetic begging noises she could ever remember making. He mashed the heel of his hand against her clit, wiggling two fingers into her pussy.

"Fuck! Fuck! Fuck!" The words tore from her mouth as she first went rigid, then bucked back into his thrust.

Her asshole pulsed around the burning brand of his cock as her pussy milked at his fingers. The demanding clench of her body undid him. Pricks of light burst behind her eyes, and she felt his balls tighten. His cock stiffened and swelled to the point of agony. He emptied, spurt after spurt, huge and demanding into the heat of her ass, and she cried out as each jet of come scalded her insides.

She crumpled beneath him, going boneless as her orgasm ebbed, and he followed her down to wrap his body protectively around hers.

Her breathing took a long while to slow, and even when it finally did, it was ragged, shuddering. He'd need light to untape her, but she was loath for him to even leave her for a moment.

Chapter Eighteen

He held her to him, wanting to get to the door, yet not wanting to leave her.

The thought of her tiny, crumpled form defenseless on the dusty floor made all of his new, protective urges surge to the forefront of his mind. Easier to stay. More pleasant to turn them both to their sides and continue to feel her soft nakedness pressed against his chest and thighs – to feel the silk of her hair pressed under his chin and tickling his chest. She lay in his arms, trembling. His erection had started to ebb, but the aftershocks of her orgasm tightened his balls yet again. This woman – he could never get enough of her.

He brushed his lips over the tip of her ear, and a breathy mewl escaped her.

The high of dominant euphoria made him feel as if he could bench press the damn house. The need to master her warred with his tenderness. She'd completely submitted – there was no need to prove anything more, but the urge to take things one step further was hard to resist. What else could he do to her to prove she was his? Cut her? Taste her blood again? Piercing her and branding her wasn't enough? What about the collar she couldn't remove?

Why did he always feel like she'd eventually discard him no matter how he claimed her?

He loved her and hated that he did.

There were no guarantees.

He needed to chain her again. The feeling of her impending escape was driving him mad.

"You're mine, Minnow. Every inch of you is fucking mine. Understand me?"

Full of desperate energy, he pulled out, then rose and hauled her limp form into his arms. She was so still that panic made him check her breathing. Deep. Steady. Her warm breaths curled over his bare shoulder.

Too many feelings.

Protect her. Comfort her. Hurt her. Get rid of her.

He tried to shut them off as he strode down the hall, her unresponsive body cradled delicately against his chest. Her eyes were wide and unseeing, and he wasn't sure she'd blinked since they got into the comparatively bright hallway.

The pups frolicked around his legs, shortening his strides as he made his way to her room.

"Shh, boys. She's okay." He hoped.

He brought her into her bedroom and went straight through to the bathroom to run her a bath. He sat on the toilet lid with her in his lap, and started the water and peeled the bondage tape off. Her wrists and ankles were the wrong color, and he massaged them. Come and lube dripped out of her, slicking his leg.

The pups had stopped at the bathroom doorway, having been trained to stay out. They whined and grumbled, and he shushed them.

"Miss Korsgaard."

She didn't respond, just kept staring off into nothing.

"Minnow?"

Again, nothing. Had he hurt her? Fuck. He'd been too rough.

He turned her ass up in his lap and inspected her. Even though he kept his touch on her anus gentle she whimpered, edging away from his fingers. Thankfully there were no signs of damage even though he'd taken her too hard for her first time.

"You're okay, he told her after he'd reassured himself, then flipped her back over and held her close. Her skin felt too cool against his own. Sweat was drying on them both. When the tub was full, he placed her carefully in the steaming water, wincing when she yelped and hissed, clutching at the stripes on her ass. He stripped and got in behind her and she shifted to her side and leaned against his chest.

He stroked her hair, draping it up over his shoulder and onto the ledge behind him to keep it dry. She was looking at him now, seeming more lucid, but she still wasn't speaking. Such intelligence and patience in those eyes. He'd never done anything in his life to deserve this kind of unwavering devotion. He wanted to deserve her, but wasn't sure how to go about doing that.

One of the pups whined for them, and the sound was the perfect match to how he was feeling. Desperate. Vulnerable.

"I love you," he said, staring down into her lovely face.

Her gaze flickered with some emotion – shock? – then her eyes filled with tears. The words had come without his permission, but even so, they were completely true. He'd never said the words to anyone – not Sutton, not Church, not even Rodrigo when they'd been drinking, even though Ro had said it to him often enough. Even if he'd loved anyone as a child, he would have said the words in French.

The strange part was he didn't even need to hear her say it back again. The words were a fact, not a ploy to get a response. Not part of a game.

She was so small and sweet. She just...let him. She let him do everything he wanted, and somehow that was changing him. He was the dominant. Her relationship with him should have been changing her, not the other way around. She been hired to fix him, and slowly she was accomplishing that, just not in any way Sutton could have anticipated.

It hurt that Sutton would never get to know her well. They'd liked each other, but in time he was sure his last mother would have loved her too.

"You do?" she finally asked, her brow wrinkling. "Because I let you..." She grimaced slightly to fill in the words she'd avoided saying aloud.

He barked a laugh. "No. You know I've felt like this for a long time."

"We haven't known each other a long time," she objected, her bath-warmed fingers grazing shyly over his chest hair. He forced himself not to pin her hand to make her stop.

"It feels like we have. Sometimes I feel like I was put in this house to wait for you."

She smiled up at him even though a tear leaked from the corner of her eye. She stroked a hand more boldly down his side, and it actually felt good.

"When did you realize you loved me?" she asked.

"I knew I was in trouble the day we went skinny dipping."

"Mister Leduc, lust and love aren't the same thing."

He chuckled. "No. They aren't. I felt lust for you that day – of course I did. Fuck – the way you looked in your bra and panties, jutting your chin at me like you weren't scared even though you were shaking –"

"I was cold!"

"You felt the connection between us just like I did. I tried to act like I didn't care, but I don't think I fooled you at all."

"No. You were a bossy jerk with everyone, but there was something special about me that made you especially boorish."

He snorted. "You like me boorish."

"Maybe," she said, biting her lip.

She lifted her finger to his mouth, and he flinched, but allowed her to brush the pad of it over his bottom lip.

See? He could do this. She was even starting to make him like it. Maybe someday he'd be able to fake normal so well some of it would stick.

He caught her fingertip between his lips and sucked, enjoying her whimpered response and the haze of desire that crept into her gaze.

"Severin?" she said, planting a kiss on his chest, over his heart. "I love you too."

When he'd washed her and dried her, he settled her into bed, already asleep. He kissed her forehead, liking the strange feeling in his chest. It filled him with an eagerness for the future he'd never felt before. He wanted to keep her, but more importantly he wanted her to want to stay.

He padded down the hall to his room, throwing on some clothes that weren't covered in come and lube, so he could take the pups out for a pee. He returned to Minnow's bedroom afterward and settled into his customary chair, grinning as the dogs flopped all over each other on the carpet in front of the fire, falling asleep before they'd even gotten comfortable. Ridiculous beasts. Minnow treated them like babies, and they'd decided to extend their overwhelming affection to him despite his initial distaste. Minnow said it was because they somehow knew he'd saved them from starving or freezing to death.

"Mister Leduc?" Minnow asked groggily, pushing herself up on one arm and looking around the room.

"Yes, Miss Korsgaard?" he asked in amusement.

"Do you think I'm a whore?"

"Of course not." He rose from his chair and went to her. Acting on impulse, he crawled into bed behind her and pulled her into the curve of his body. She was warm against his chest, and he loved the way she felt there. "You let me do what I wanted tonight, just like I always do. It's not your place to tell me no, woman."

She laughed mirthlessly. "So I'm not a whore, I'm just a doormat."

"You're not a doormat. Far from it."

"I know. I just..." She shrugged. "I let you do things to me and sometimes, later, I feel dirty."

"Shh." He squeezed her closer. "You're the most important person in my life. I'll respect you enough for both of us until you catch up, okay?"

There was a long pause, and he wondered if she'd fallen asleep.

"Okay."

"If you never want to do that again, we don't have to."

"Well..." She squirmed a bit, her naked bottom pressing against his groin, which immediately started to respond to her. "It wasn't so bad by the end."

"No?"

"I might have gotten off on it. A little."

"A little?"

Her back shook, and he was relieved when he established she was laughing rather than crying.

"What's so funny?"

"You fucked my ass on the floor in the dark, then told me the most beautiful things. I think I have emotional whiplash."

"Kinky."

She giggled, sobbed, then started to laugh again.

He let her process her feelings in silence as he held her close, trying to let her know with his body all the words and feelings that gathered chaotically in his head. Eventually she drifted off into sleep, sweet and tiny in his arms.

Even though it broke all of his rules, he stayed.

Chapter Nineteen

The dogs were barking.

Minnow forced her eyes open, staring at the wall long enough to realize she was in her room, and bright sun was shining in. A weight lifted off her hip, and with it went a significant amount of warmth. She sat up. The sheet pooled around her waist, leaving her breasts bare to the cool air. At some point during the night the fire had died down to nothing. Her ass cheeks and asshole ached, and she leaned gingerly off to one side.

She was greeted by the sight of Severin's glorious bare ass as he slid on a pair of jeans. God – he'd slept in bed with her? All night! Warmth trickled through her body like a shot of tequila. Sleeping in the same bed? Such a mundane thing, and yet her cheeks heated and she felt a bit giddy.

"What's wrong with the dogs?" she asked, blinking in confusion.

"I think someone's at the door."

"Maybe it's a delivery?" She glanced at the clock. At seven in the morning? She slid out of bed and carefully pulled on a long cashmere sweater and some leggings before following him down the hall to the door. Every muscle in her body complained as if she'd run a marathon. She kind of had.

Rodrigo came from the kitchen, dressed like he'd come in from his sister's party not long ago, his dress shirt half unbuttoned, looking dashingly mussed.

She half laughed. Only in a hermit's secluded house would the doorbell ringing be the reason for so much curiosity.

"Who's here at this hour?" Rodrigo asked her.

She shrugged. "Church?"

"Why would he ring the doorbell?" Severin strode to the door and swung it open.

A young man stood surveying the manicured front lawn, turning to grin at Severin. It was a sly grin, full of secret amusement.

"Can I help you?" Severin asked in irritation.

Minnow gasped, her hand rising to cover her mouth to stifle her shock.

Rodrigo blew out a shocked breath. "Holy shit."

Only Severin didn't seem to see it.

The man gave him a long, sweeping look. "You really are a big bastard, aren't you? The rumors pale, of course." His English was thickly accented with French. He sketched a mocking bow.

Severin's shoulders tensed, and Minnow had to stop herself from stepping between them to spare him this. She'd pick up the pieces if things went south, but it wasn't her place to intervene. Not this time.

"Do I know you?" Severin asked.

Minnow could feel the shift in his thoughts as the pennies dropped into place.

The young man cocked his head to the side. "No, I've never had the pleasure of making your acquaintance." There was a hint of madness in his pale blue eyes that was all too familiar. "Mr. Solis, your man of affairs, sent me a letter. I thought it would be more polite to visit, rather than trying to introduce myself in writing." He cleared his throat. "Forgive my intrusion, Sebastien...*pardon*...Severin. My name is Loïc Leduc. I'm your little brother."

To be continued in Tragic King, September 2017

Acknowledgements

Once upon a time, Rodrigo appeared and ordered us to write him into this book. He was supposed to be a side character, but quickly became an integral part of the story. The only problem? Rodrigo didn't realize that neither Sorcha nor Leia spoke Spanish, and apparently online translation tools leave a lot to be desired! Thanks to **Heimy Roa** for being Rodrigo's last minute Spanish checker – especially since we had it wrong!

Once again, thanks to **Nerine Dorman**, Vampire Queen of the South, for her quick and thorough editing work. We'd say Reliable was Nerine's middle name, but we're pretty sure her middle name would be a much cooler, more intriguing word…possibly a thesaurus full of them.

Thank to **Rebel Book Design** (www.rebelbookdesign.com) for designing our gorgeous covers and doing Severin justice. We'd like to do Severin in other ways too, but licking the cover will have to suffice.

And, as always, thanks to our hilarious, wild, bratty street teams, **The Badass Brats**, and **Sparrow's Circus**! We love you all!!!!!!!!! <3

Also by Sparrow Beckett…

Masters Unleashed Series

Finding Master Right

Playing Hard to Master

To Have and to Master

Masters of Adrenaline Series

Stealing His Thunder

Fueling His Hunger

Pushing Her Limits

Printed in Great Britain
by Amazon

64742993R00215